To Mr. ~~████████~~

MANY

THE UNION CLUB

A Subversive Thriller

—⁓—

Don Winston

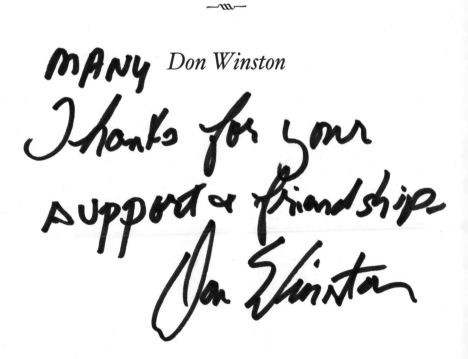

MANY
Thanks for your
support & friendship
Don Winston

Copyright © 2014 Don Winston

Cover design: Chad Zimmerman

Author photograph: Owen Moogan

The Gristmill Playhouse Teaser Illustrations: Steven Stines
All rights reserved.

ISBN: 0615955398
ISBN 13: 9780615955391
Library of Congress Control Number: 2014901149
Tigerfish, Los Angeles, CA

The Union Club

A Subversive Thriller by

DON WINSTON

TIGERFISH

For Mr. Robert Evans

Author's Note

For those familiar with San Francisco, and Nob Hill in particular, you have likely seen, at the very top and directly across from the Fairmont Hotel, a grand manor. It is brown and stately and humorless and is one of the town's oldest and most prestigious private clubs. I've met a few of their members and am longtime friends with one, and I'm sure it's a harmless place. But it doesn't feel harmless.

The club in the following story is, clearly, inspired by that building. But this club and story are fictional and merely modeled on its architecture and location and prominence within the city's history. All other similarities are entirely coincidental. And cause for real alarm.

"Remain true to yourself, but move ever upward toward greater consciousness and greater love! At the summit you will find yourselves united with all those who, from every direction, have made the same ascent. For everything that rises must converge."

—Pierre Teilhard de Chardin, *The Future of Man*

November 2

Congressman-elect Dean Willing was dead before he reached the podium.

It felt different than he'd expected. The whole night had. He'd had plenty of time to prepare, since San Francisco was a one-party town, and his election was assured after the primary, which was also assured.

But it was difficult to prepare adequately for the moment of one's death.

Up in the presidential suite, where they awaited his opponent's concession, his mother had quibbled with his wife over the tie. It would be reddish, of course, but while his wife preferred the Ferragamo, his mother insisted on the less pretentious Brooks Brothers she'd bought the day before. His mother usually—and with acquired restraint—deferred to his wife, but tonight was different, because it was his *big day* and *last night*, and his mother would have the final say.

His wife came into the master bedroom where he dressed and flung the Brooks Brothers at him. "It's not even Golden Fleece."

In the living room, his father worked the phone wired to the wall. He wasn't checking returns, which were irrelevant, but the timing. His opponent would concede at 8:43 p.m. in the Governor's Ballroom of the four-star St. Francis on the rim of Union Square. At 9:06, he would walk onstage in the Grand Ballroom at the Fairmont on top of Nob Hill. Both rooms would be full, but the actual numbers would not be comparable.

His father hung up. "We're on the move!"

His mother, in simple navy, straightened his straight tie and smoothed his smooth hair. She held his face but didn't look him in the eye and said, "My handsome boy," and the local reporter on TV recapped his military service and business résumé for the viewers. The camera held steady on the ballroom podium, and to vamp, the reporter ran an interview she had done earlier in the day with his wife.

"Let's do this." His wife breezed past in her pink Chanel suit, and they followed his father into the hallway, where two aides in suits and earpieces stood ready.

They rode down the service elevator in silence.

The ballroom was loud and festive, and backstage was still and quiet, and at 8:58, his parents walked onstage to cheers. His father spoke and then signaled to his mother, who resisted and then relented, and the crowd cheered louder as she stepped up. She strained to reach the mike and growled at her husband, and the crowd laughed at her sassy pique, which they knew and loved.

Backstage, he felt a sudden jolt of stage fright. He took his wife's hand at the end of her pink sleeve, and she yanked it away reflexively before collecting herself and cupping his with both of hers. She patted it in apology.

His father was back at the podium, winding the crowd up tighter, and as the teleprompter scrolled its final line, the room erupted, and it was time. An aide tapped him on the shoulder. His wife led him into the light.

Unlike in the movies, you would never mistake the sound for the popping of a balloon. He went down immediately, and after a confused hush, heard the panic swell and spread. He felt his wife kneel next to him and then collapse on top of him, and the ballroom got louder and more bothered.

The networks, which weren't covering this nonevent on such a busy night, would break in to cover it now. There would be live updates, and soon a hastily put together memorial package, and possibly even an official investigation, although, from the sounds of returning gunfire, his assassin was unlikely to be of much intel use soon. Police and ambulances were most certainly already screaming up Nob Hill.

But now it was quieter, and it really didn't hurt much at all, and his wife was still but breathing. He listened to the music from the speakers and watched the white moldings darken around the ceiling. It felt too soon. He was not yet thirty.

PHASE I

Chapter One

"Bring the left corner down an inch," Claire Willing directed her husband, Clay, both twenty-six. "A little more. That's better. I think."

"Best is out back in the Dumpster," Clay, in paint-marked overalls, said as he surveyed the enormous, maybe-straight canvas.

"Nonsense," Claire said. "Never." It was a perfectly proficient sunset, and it fit just right over their rawhide sofa. Even cockeyed.

"It makes the room," she insisted, tilting up at the twenty-foot-high loft ceiling. Plus she'd spent hours packing and unpacking it for the move, along with the rest of his landscapes. There was plenty of wall here for all of them. Even the orangish adobe, which was not her favorite, being a bit too on the nose, although she'd never admit that, because it was one of Clay's firsts. Fortunately, it was small and would fit best in their bedroom. "Between the windows!"

Claire and Clay had arrived earlier in the day in his 1983 purple Mustang. Amazingly, it had survived the trip from Santa Fe, thanks in part to her insistence on a last-minute full tune-up, as the heretofore undiagnosed leaky radiator would have stranded them in the desert. Claire had quickly unloaded her hybrid Accord on a fellow teacher, but Clay had refused to leave his shiny toy behind, in spite of California's out-of-state car penalties. It was wholly unsuitable for their new city life, and he promised to park it at his parents' once they settled in. In her mind, Claire had already circled a blue-gray Ford Escape that would fit in the single parking space that came with their lease. "No minivans!" Clay had decreed to Claire's taunting giggles.

A Grand Canyon detour had added a day to their journey— neither had seen it before—and Clay insisted on a "soul-cleansing" pit stop at Joshua Tree, another half day's out-of-the-way adventure. He seemed in little hurry to get to San Francisco, and Claire didn't mind their leisurely pace after the rather frantic rush of their packing. Clay's relocation allowance afforded full-service pros, although she'd spent an exhausting week editing—three and a half years' worth!—before they arrived. Nonetheless, her visit to the Hearst Castle would have to wait, since the movers were right on schedule, and the still-under-renovation Townsend Lofts lacked the proper staff to let them in.

"Where do you want your Hitler Youth?" Clay held up Claire's homeroom class photos—rows of seated children, mostly brown, in white polos and navy pants or skirts, Claire proudly to the left. Clay's stale joke aside, Hitler would have approved the uniforms—the wearers, not so much. She herself had long been conflicted about public school uniform policy, especially at that young age. San Francisco, she'd learned, had the same policy. They'd probably invented it.

Claire took another look at little detached Marisa on the front row and felt a prick of concern, then pushed it away. She'd make it to fourth grade on her own. Hopefully.

"Probably the upstairs hall," she said. "Just lean them against the wall for now."

The three-bedroom duplex apartment was freshly painted white, gallery like, although they'd thankfully kept the exposed brick on the outward walls. She'd found it online and signed up from the slide show alone, with Clay's bemused approval. In addition to the airy spaciousness, she liked the hardwood floors for their Navajo rugs, the Neutra-esque slat staircase, and the Miele/Viking/Silestone kitchen. The stainless Sub-Zero still had its protective plastic film.

Most important, the SOMA Warehouse District—technically Mission Bay, if you looked closely at the map—was far removed from the Pacific Heights/Presidio Heights/Sea cliffs of Clay's youth. It didn't feel so obviously like coming home.

The master bedroom looked out over the China Basin toward the Bay, cinematic in the early February gloom. The guest bedroom would double as Clay's studio, although it fronted Townsend and would provide less inspiration. The third bedroom sat empty, for now.

The whole place was offensively expensive—part of Claire's San Francisco acclimation. She considered downsizing to a cramped two-bedroom in the same building, or even the less-offensive Castro, but Clay vetoed both. "Stop pinching," he encouraged her.

They repositioned their Aztec cane chairs with green serape cushions three times before giving up. They didn't work anywhere. Neither did the pine and cowhide. At least the rugs fit, Claire tried to convince herself.

"Stop scowling!" Clay laughed, pulling her onto the cowhide, and Claire mock pouted. "They look so *podunk* here," she said. Clay said, "My parents are renovating. We'll get their castoffs."

"Oh, goody," Claire mocked on, and Clay retaliated with an octopus tickle. "Stop! Stop!" Claire shrieked, fighting back. "*Careful!*" She resisted when his hands stopped tickling and got serious. "Not now. She'll be here any minute."

"For good luck," Clay pressed quietly in her ear. "In our new home…"

The doorbell rang.

"She hasn't lost her sixth sense," Clay growled, and Claire giggled, pushing him off.

—⚏—

"My God, you could dock the Space Shuttle in here," Martha announced instantly, before hugs—quick to Clay, tight to Claire. She put the chilled Veuve on the kitchen counter and paced, inspector like. She wore blue scrubs and had dark circles and needed a root touchup. She'd put on weight. Medical residency was a shock to the system, and Martha was still adjusting. She smelled and sounded like she'd just had a cigarette.

"Lotta room for *two people*," she declared, making a point of peering upward and side to side. "You keeping the wigwam furniture?"

"It's Southwestern," Claire said, relishing Martha's digs. Thank God she hadn't changed.

Martha sized up Claire's chambray shirt and turquoise necklace and said, "Well, Tigerlily, you could've sent up smoke signals. I cannot believe I had to read about Clay's new job in the *Chronicle*. Is that our new normal?"

Claire made hurried excuses/explanations—"It happened so quickly"; "I was going to call earlier"—while Clay's hospitality morphed into familiar tolerance. His and Martha's uneasy copresence had held static since freshman year at Yale. She'd never quite excused him for snapping up her roommate so quickly.

Martha nodded—"Uh-huh"; "Yeah, yeah, okay"; "Glad you got here safely"—and commented on the neighborhood and then pivoted the conversation craftily. "You know, they tow on Townsend at four."

4

"Hurry!" Claire said, and Clay, *released*, said, "Gotta do a drugstore run anyway. Where's your list?" He pushed into his clogs and raced out.

"Pull that main door behind you!" Martha ordered. "I waltzed right in off the street." She turned back, unsmiling. "What the hell is going on here?"

—w—

Claire was cornered. Hoisted on her own petards.

Yes, she'd shrugged off corporate America even before it was fashionable, or necessary. *Guilty*—after the latest financial collapse, when Goldman Morgan Citi Bank of America descended on Yale to skim the best and brightest—of championing, quietly at first, then louder, a bolder, more socially responsible path. Not for profits, Peace Corps, volunteerism, even startups were preferable to being a tool—*gear*, really—in the Wall Street Brain-Drain Machine. She was hardly alone.

Teach for America had sent her to Lansing for two years—"*Where?*" Clay had griped—after which they'd settled in Clay's choice (she'd preferred Jackson Hole but didn't push it). She taught, he painted; they made friends and stayed thrifty.

That was then.

"Dean's death changed a lot," Claire explained. "Well, everything." Abruptly. Clay had talked to his parents in a flurry of calls, had even gone on a never-before-happened father-son getaway for a long, post-Christmas weekend, and came back to announce— and shock—that he was joining his father's firm.

Welcome to San Francisco.

"Welcome to the New World Order," Martha quipped.

And goodbye to her third graders—midyear: devilish Teresa, nosebleed Ernesto, and fingers-crossed-god speed to Marisa, whose mother never did come to a parent-teacher meeting.

5

Claire didn't get to say goodbye, so jerked was her departure.

"You hear me?" Martha said.

"Ignoring you," Claire said.

Martha's ribbing had started gently enough. Just e-mail links to the Forbes 400 after Claire and Clay first met in college. Then, as they became inseparable, news articles about Clay's father on White House economic councils, international corporate boards, sightings to and from the Council on Foreign Relations. ("Yep. Holding the door for Kissinger. Yep, yep.") By the time they were very much in love, Martha's obsession with Mr. Willing had turned almost stalker like: a Sun Valley retreat ("Gates, Buffett, *Oprah*."), the Bohemian Grove ("Camping with Cheney!"), and a super secret—i.e., "shadowy"—conference called the Bilderberg Group ("God *knows* who else is there") outside Bilbao, Spain. Martha had his annual itinerary down cold.

She crossed the line a bit, an ill-advised Hail Mary, as their marriage became inevitable. She'd discovered some crackpot New World Order conspiracy theorist—Claire forgot his no-name—on the Internet who accused the Willings and their *ilk* of ruinous financial crimes, gross human rights violations, and a wild parade of horribles that would have been funny at a distance. But Claire was no longer at a distance.

Not that she was close to Clay's parents. They'd met only a couple times, back at Yale—homecoming her sophomore year and then again at graduation, both over dinner at Mory's. They never spent holidays together, much less vacations or quick visits. They weren't at the wedding. Claire herself didn't go—wasn't invited—to Dean's memorial, although she did send flowers and received a thank-you note, signed by both.

Clay's father, once a lowly gear, *had* amassed an unconscionable fortune on his way up to running the Machine. Such wealth in one lifetime rarely came clean. That he came from nothing—in *Texas*, of all places—only fueled his critics more. Without taking sides, Claire hoped they had the decency for a time-out from their barbs after the tragedy last November.

But she wouldn't know, since she and Clay lived a removed, independent life. Until now.

"That's a tricky family you're getting sucked into," Martha had warned for years, but she didn't today, because she'd been proved right. She refilled her own glass and let Claire convince herself.

"Clay was ready for a change," Claire said. "And I...have to support him. We're a team, you know?"

Martha nodded.

"It *is* the first time his parents have paid much attention to him," Claire mused. "But that never bothered him before."

"At some point, we all grow up a little," Claire continued.

Martha shrug-nodded.

"And let's face it," Claire said. "It's not like his art career was really taking off."

Martha glanced about the walls without comment.

"Oh, shut up, Martha!"

Martha cackled. "Relax, bitch! I'm psyched you're here," she said. "Relieved, actually."

"And who am I to talk?" she added. "I wouldn't turn down Charles Manson at this point. You know, I joined the fucking DAR just for its singles night?"

"Don't transfer to Chicago," Claire begged. "I just got here. I *need* you."

"I've already dated the five straight men in this town," Martha said. "And I have doubts about two of them."

"Don't you have a blind date tonight?"

"If that were *literally* true, I might stand a chance." Martha inspected her bags in the microwave door. *Harrumph.*

"Hey!" she said, turning back. "You two should join us!"

"Tonight?"

"Double date," Martha insisted. "We're good like that."

"We have plans," Claire said.

"What? Where?"

"The Union Club," Claire said simply.

Martha collapsed to the floor, flailed with drama. "Oh my God," she said, her eyes frozen upward. "You've already joined the Union Club."

"No, no, no...," Claire protested.

Martha sprang up. "You don't understand. *Nobody* gets in the Union. Half its *members* can't get in!"

"We're not members," Claire said. "Clay's parents are taking us."

"I see." Martha sucked her front teeth once. "In-law night. Is *that* why you're not drinking?"

Claire looked at her full champagne. Back at Martha. She took a breath and held it.

"Well..." She exhaled.

Martha squealed first.

—ᴠᴠ—

"Let's wait, Clay. Please. It's too early."

"Relax. When did you get superstitious?"

"Can you slow down?" Claire said. "Or at least send a Sherpa to help me?"

The steep incline up Nob Hill was murder in her heels. Clay had offered to drop her off, but she didn't want to wait alone while he looked for a street spot. Apparently, his muscle car wasn't suitable for the club's private lot. God save their cranky parking brake on the hill.

"We're late," Clay said. It was normally a nonconcern. And normally Claire didn't change outfits three times, the root of their lateness. They were both a-wonk tonight.

"I just don't want a big deal until we're absolutely...Ack!" Claire stood on one foot, her broken heel clinging by one nail.

"Clay, we have to go back. I have to change."

"They're waiting," he said.

"How am I going to explain this?" She hobbled up and down in a circle.

"Polio?" he suggested.

"That's not funny," Claire said, and Clay said, "Yes, it is. And so are you."

The piggyback ride both embarrassed and relieved her. They'd been pecking at each other more the past couple of weeks—rushed, disorienting weeks with big changes on the other side. It had zapped their humor. Clay's gallumping carriage was playful and helpful, traits that typically came easy to him. Claire held on tight.

"Good evening." She nodded at an older couple heading into the Masonic Auditorium on the corner for a touring performance of *Henry IV.* They smiled and "Good evening"-ed back.

"You cool from here?" Clay asked at the summit, as the sidewalk leveled out.

Claire looked ahead.

"Good God," she said. "Is that it?" A pointless question.

The Union Club stood sentry at the top of the hill, a beaux arts dark mansion on the border of a grassy space. It hugged the edge, away from the public playground, separated by an ornate, round, alive fountain. It was lit from within by dozens of windows, each glowing through shrouding sheers.

"Yes'm," Clay said, Dickens-like. "Where I spent much of me youth."

"Well, that explains a lot," she replied in earnest, instantly wishing she'd made it a quip.

Ringing the square stood taller residential buildings, a massive church, the familiar and very grand Fairmont Hotel, its bank of international flags snapping in unison above the porte cochere.

The Union Club was the smallest building on Nob Hill, and it dwarfed the rest.

"Not yet," Claire said, still clinging. "Closer."

He waited for the cable car to clang past, tourists pressed against the far side, and carried her across California Street.

"You gonna sit on my lap during dinner, too?" he asked.

"Just to the front door." She giddy-upped him. They passed the surrounding low stone wall with swirling, bronze railing—fishes or dragons or sea monsters, hard to tell at night. The stone wall matched the manor walls, which matched the portico, the window moldings, the roof railing, the two flanking wings, the four streaming chimneys—all reddish brown, serious and stately. A lavish monolith.

Neoclassical, Claire recalled from her one architecture class in college. Palladian windows. The square columns either Doric or Ionic; she could never keep them straight. Definitely not the leafy Corinthian. There was neither sign, awning, nor welcome mat. Other than the light-shrouding windows, a burnished lantern above the portico cast the only glow, dim-watted at that. The mansion stood silent, hiding its life within. Or not.

"You sure it's open tonight?" she asked, as he mounted the reddish-brown stone stairs two at a time. She looked up at the dark, silent door. "Is Lurch gonna answer?"

Clay unshouldered her, and she scanned the hedge lining the stairs. "What are you looking for?" he said.

"Doesn't Cousin Itt hide in the bushes?" she asked.

"You're awfully breezy tonight," he joked. "Did Martha get you tipsy?" Claire *tee-hee*'d and opened the bronze mailbox, peering inside.

"Why, good *evening*, Thing! Thank you for your kind invitation." She shook the imaginary hand.

"You rang?" a man asked from the front door. Claire shut the mailbox and stood upright on one foot.

"Allen!" Clay said, handshaking and shoulder-clasping the smiling man with doorman hat and doorman coat. "Welcome back, Clay," Allen said. "Your parents asked me to keep a lookout."

"A pleasure, Claire," he said, taking her hand, tipping his hat at their introduction. "I was joking about the Lurch thing," Claire apologized. "Not at all," he said, smiling. "I *have* felt a bit ooky today."

Claire laughed and clarified quickly, "And Clay was joking about the tipsy." Allen nodded, blank, and Claire added, "I'm totally sober." Allen, still blank, said, "That's good!"

"I don't think he heard me," Clay said *sotto voce*, and Claire said, "Oh!", and Allen held open the glass-windowed wooden door into the vestibule. "Let's get you inside, why not?"

A low, beeping alarm sounded as they crossed the threshold.

"We check our...cell phone?" Claire asked when sent to the coatroom just inside. A powerful black man outfitted like Allen, but without hat, sat behind the counter and smiled warmly, expecting her.

"The club discourages business." He nodded in agreement, almost in apology, at her confusion. He wore a wedding ring and had the kind, knowing face of a father. Claire wondered how many, how young, and how unfortunate their father worked night hours. "We'll take good care of it."

He took her coat and phone, both of which Clay had left at home. She held out her hand for the claim ticket, and when none came, she pulled back and wrapped her pashmina around her shoulder, an involuntary correction. The man grinned and placed her phone in a cubbyhole along the wall. "Safe and sound," he assured her.

"Oh, I know," Claire said quickly. She nodded and turned to go, collapsing on her broken heel and catching herself on the counter.

"Sorry," she said, smiling, but freshly concerned. "That hill..." The man held out his hand. "May I?"

He reached into a drawer under the counter and pulled out an at-the-ready tube. He surgically superglued the heel, holding it tight to set. "You aren't the first lady to limp in here." He chuckled. She strapped her shoe back on, and he added, "Just go easy until after dinner. Then tear up the dance floor."

"Claire, honey," Clay called from the vestibule. "This evening?"

"Thank you," she said, checking her savior's name tag, "Jess." She slid a folded five-dollar tip across the counter.

"My pleasure, Claire," Jess replied, politely sliding it back.

She turned and laughed. "How...do you know my name?"

Jess laughed, too, and said, "Welcome to the Union."

Allen held open the door of solid oak. Claire and Clay walked through it.

Chapter Two

The manor indeed hid its life within.

Its fragrance reached her first: top notes of pinion toasting in the oversized fireplace—a comforting New Mexico aroma she'd never smelled anywhere else and thought she'd just imagined outside. A sweet explosion of Casablanca lilies and pink roses brimmed a chinoiserie vase on the round, marble-topped Grand Foyer table. Intermingled throughout, a mercurial symphony of drifting perfumes, as the women moved here, moved there.

They clustered in small groups, mostly apart from their husbands, who huddled separately, farther from the tuxedoed jazz trio in the corner. One middle-aged dandy with cornflower in his lapel bunched with the women, preferring their company. A vast, well-trod Heriz rug almost hid the Carrera floor, limestone-wall-to-limestone-wall. Majestic kentia palms potted in Imari porcelain anchored the four corners. Two women—*ladies*, really—descended the Grand Staircase, which centered the far reach, one gliding a hand down its glossed mahogany bannister. Purred conversations, an occasional flare of laughter, glasses ice-tinkling.

"Champagne?" A white-coated waiter offered his silver tray. "Or something from the bar?" "Club soda, please?" Claire asked, and Clay said, "Stella," before opting to take a flute, there and ready. They stood together on the edge.

The room felt candlelit—soft, gauzy, unfocused. The air seemed woven with cashmere. Claire wished there were a wall nearby to lean against, a chair to steady. Luckily, her heel was holding.

A glamorous eccentric across the way—silver mane, cat-eye glasses, scarlet lips that matched the wrap thrown around her black sheath, a neck dripping with what looked like, but couldn't have been, dozens of diamonds—poised her unlit cigarette in a long holder, Cruella-like, and eyed Clay, unabashed. *What comes after cougar?* Claire asked herself. *Grand*cougar?

"Do you...know these people?" Claire asked quietly.

"I will again soon." He nodded and reconsidered his drink before swallowing down a third of it.

But they knew him, one at a time, until most had glanced, nodded, pleasantly inspected. More unnerving than treading this stage for the first time was, perhaps, returning after an absence.

She took his free hand, which should have warmed by now, and said, "Let's mingle. Before they throw a net on us." She led him across the rug and gasped. "Oh my." Her eye grabbed upward to the vast, Tiffany glass dome that crowned the room, its million-color floral mosaic glow-lit from above. "Spectacular," she whispered.

The dandy had locked in on Clay and was approaching when three soft chimes sounded from the dining room. Rekindlings would have to wait.

The waiter returned trayless. "I've put your drink at your table, ma'am," he said. "Mr. Willing, your parents are seated."

—∿—

14

Slade Willing—"Not 'Mr.,'" he urged Claire. "We're family now"—disproved the axiom: You could, in fact, take the Texas out of the boy. Most of it, anyway.

He stood at their table, pinging his fork on a water glass. Claire's dinner had been serviceable, she thought. Normally she'd have had the salmon, but tonight she'd chosen prime rib, which she'd judged too pink, and with no other options, had picked at the rice pilaf and baked tomato. She wasn't particularly hungry anyway.

Her mother-in-law, Nora, disrupting the boy-girl protocol to sit next to her, patted her hand and leaned in. "Don't sweat it," she assured her. "The food's not very good here." She pushed her own dry salmon around in solidarity. "We've been working on that for *years*. But don't expect farm-to-table anytime soon."

The Grand Dining Room—they liked the word "grand"—was wedding like with white cloth–covered round tables that grew louder with each course and wine pairing. It was one of the flanking wings that Claire guessed, if her bearings were straight, faced out over the fountain/playground/park. The shrouding sheers disoriented both ways.

Most of the men wore business suits, having come straight from the office. Those in sport coats were either retired or confirmed *bon vivants*, Claire suspected. The women—coiffed, fresh, and controlled—never had an office, she sensed. The median age was old.

Dinner conversation at the Willing table, in the center of the room, had been surprisingly effortless—like a weekly get-together, rather than a four-year gap no one referenced. Slade and Nora tumbled over each other with practical, local advice: unsung-gem eateries (Slade, surprisingly a foodie), secret sample sales (Nora, unexpected spendthrift), and—"Oh yes, tell them, Slade. Tell them!"—traffic shortcuts (both impatient).

The setup was comfortably less formal than Claire had expected. The matching plates, heavy and old, were ringed in burgundy around the club's interlocking insignia in chipped gold. Glasses were restaurant issue. Silverware substantial and tarnished, napkins starchy. White-jacketed waiters efficient without hovering. Guests poured their own wine and passed bread baskets.

There was a fifth place setting, empty, and after the salad course, Nora ordered it cleared away. "She's obviously not coming," she said to Slade.

"That's too bad," he said with a shrug, signaling another cocktail. Nora nursed her chardonnay and monitored her husband's tally.

"Is it always this full during the week?" Claire asked, a couple squeezing past her seat. Nora shook her head. "They're here to see you."

"Oh," said Claire.

"Pass the butter, Claire?" Slade asked.

Slade shared Clay's height, his lean, athletic build, and vibrant green eyes. From the pocket of his chalk-striped navy suit with black and cream glen plaid tie peeked a white handkerchief, straight-edged. Nora had given Clay his sandy locks, but unlike his shag, hers was blown and set. Claire loved his curly, unruly mop, but Slade's initial once-over suggested a taming lay in its future. Nora wore a tweedy Chanel suit jacket, paired confidently, rebelliously, with slim loden pants and doughboy heels. "Your mother ignores the dress code," Slade apologized to them both.

"Your mother ignores the dress code," Nora affirmed.

They were warm, magnetic, bracing, just like she remembered from graduation. They looked the same as four years ago, without enhancements. Perhaps a little color in Nora's hair, but Claire classified that as simple maintenance—one she'd subscribe to at the first sign of gray. Slade's lines were happy ones; his full, slicked shock less salt-and-pepper than silver-streaked and badger-gray. Agewise, they hovered a little under the club's median.

"You're coming with us Saturday to the deYoung, aren't you?" Nora asked. "One of the rare events where the guests are actually *younger* than the art. Clay's friends, the sober ones, would love to meet you." Claire pivoted to Clay with a look: *You never mentioned this....* Clay: *We'll decide later; no pressure.* Claire: *Okay.*

"And we've got *Book of Mormon* on Sunday at the Orpheum," Nora added, turning to Slade. "We can get two extra seats, right?"

"I hear it o-ffends," he said.

"Nonsense," she scoffed. "You're not wildly religious, are you, Claire? No, you went to Yale. You're not *Mormon,* are you? *What,* Slade? It's an innocent question."

"Not Mormon. We'd love to go." Claire laughed. "As long as we finish painting the upstairs." Nora said, "I'm happy to send my people," and Claire said, "Thank you, Nora, but we can do it ourselves."

"*Paint?*" Slade reared up, back from his cocktail. "Paint *what?*" "The walls, Dad," Clay assured him. "Just the walls." "Okay," Slade said, pulling back.

"He'll keep painting pictures, too," Claire clarified. "He's too good to quit." She'd been itching to make this point since the move, and now she dialed it up so Slade understood.

"Oh. Kay," Slade said, in separate words. "Hobbies are healthy." At that moment, Claire glimpsed the Texan: the hidden edge she remembered from Lone Star college friends, whom she liked but never comfortably embraced.

"How's the neighborhood?" Nora asked, with skepticism. "For living, I mean." Before Claire could praise the views, Nora added, "I mean, it's very *pioneering,* but is it safe?"

"The pioneers are fine, Mom," Clay said, and Claire opted not to mention the newly discovered Hooverville that sprang up after dark. It saddened more than worried her, but she made a note to invite the Willings during the daytime.

"Well, do your mom a favor and get *unlisted* at least," Nora said. "It's just not wise....Claire?"

But Claire was suddenly transfixed by the tall, good-looking waiter clearing plates. "I'm so sorry," she said when she tipped her water glass. Nora thanked the waiter after he'd mopped the spill and left.

"You okay?" Clay asked, and Claire answered, "Yes," shaking it off. "It's just..."

"He looks like Dean, I know," Nora said, nodding. "Almost like a stand-in. It used to creep me out." Slade said, "I've told you we can get rid of him...," but Nora cut him off. "Oh, put down the sledgehammer, Slade. It's not his fault. He's just doing his job."

The long-married couple less finished each other's sentences than challenged them. It was a roundabout spar, everything and nothing, occasionally hostile, and at one point, Claire swiveled a peek at Clay, who swiveled back from his amused, jaw-jutting silence. Nora caught this and huffed out a laugh. "Oh, just shut up, Slade! No one gives a *damn* what you think."

Then she said abruptly, "Claire, you don't drink?"

"I do...well...," Claire stammered. "Excuse me?"

Slade and Nora leaned closer. Claire hesitated, feigned bewilderment, looked at Clay, looked back. Then, brimming, she leaned in to her family.

"Nora, you happy to have your boy back?" the glamorous grand-cougar interrupted from the next table, flashing a brilliant grin.

"No, Edie," Nora shot back, still leaning and listening, not looking. "I'm miserable."

"Why so serious?" Edie pestered, her grin frozen. Nora shooed her off like a gnat. Claire whispered two words, and the table unhuddled, leaning back.

"My, my," Nora said. "That's wonderful." "Just please—" Claire started, and Nora interrupted, "No, no, of course we won't," zipping her lip.

And then Slade stood and pinged his water glass. The room silenced quickly.

"*Slade!*" Nora teethed. "Dad, c'mon...," Clay urged. *What?* Claire thought, and then thought, *Oh no, no, no!*

"My friends," he began, as if host at his own home. "King Solomon got it right: To everything, there is indeed a season."

"Oh Jeezus," Nora murmured down at her napkin.

"A time to weep, to laugh, to mourn, to dance," he went on. "For the past three months, you've comforted and supported us in our mourning. For that we are deeply, eternally grateful."

Nora smiled, nodded, then turned to Claire and crossed-uncrossed her eyes.

"But the seasons have changed. And tonight, we dance."

Claire sat helpless. Under the table, Clay held and thumbed her hand.

"Not only has our prodigal son returned to join Pacific Trust," Slade crescendoed, "it is my proudest joy to announce his lovely wife, Claire, has seen fit to provide us our very first grandchild!"

The dining room answered and applauded. Claire smiled and sank into herself.

"Turn, turn, turn!" Slade raised his cocktail. The room followed and roared approval.

"I'm cutting off the Yellow Tails, you soak," Nora growled as he sat down, surgically removing his glass. "Like I said, Claire, we'll keep this between you, me, and a hundred and fifty total strangers."

"Payback for eloping," Slade said, smiling at Claire. "You owe us that." Claire smiled back falsely. *Hello, Texas!*

"Don't worry," Nora said, pointing at the air. "They don't talk."

"No. They don't," Slade agreed. Clay shot her a look of apology. Claire held his stare for a moment and then dropped it. *Whatever.*

The pilgrimage was immediate, and the Willing table stood-sat-stood to receive the good wishes. The nosy grandcougar was first in line—"Such bright, happy news!"—diamonds real, and more than dozens. A sommelier in a longer white coat hustled up and popped the cork from a bottle of Martinelli's sparkling cider and filled Claire's flute. She politely checked the label. "It's nonalcoholic," said the sommelier with a smile. Gluten and preservative-free as well, she read, smiling back. She raised, clinked her glass, took a sip.

Another waiter brought dessert—"floating islands," he called it— meringue clouds swimming in a custard sauce that made Claire somewhat queasy on sight, but since they'd stuck a lit candle in the middle, she felt obliged for a spoonful.

"You don't have to finish it," Nora said, breaking from a well-wisher to take the spoon away. "It's not their best dessert."

Claire hoped not. She washed it down with the sparkling cider and ignored the rest.

"Atta boy, Prodigal!" A round and rosy fellow their age shoulder-clapped Clay. "Always knew you'd circle back."

"Nice to meet you, Bing," Claire said when introduced, relieved to meet someone so far below the median.

"Still the town's most confirmed, confirmed bachelor?" Clay asked. "*Eligible*, my man," Bing stressed. "Very eligible." "I'll remember that," Claire said with raised eyebrow, charmed by his clumsy sweetness. Bing had just sold his startup video game company to one of the "Big Boys" and was now "in the chips," for which he credited "the Godfather" Slade. "Nonsense," Slade protested. "All you, kind sir." From Bing's easy pride, Claire deduced he'd made a killing.

"*Games*." Nora sniffed. "How refreshing. No thinking required."

Bing nodded, missing the barb, and then said, "Slade, the colonel asked for you. Something about the Children's Hospital dustup?"

"Well, that didn't take long," Slade grumbled, wiping his mouth.

"The *colonel* can wait till after coffee, I'm sure," Nora said, stopping him. "Honestly, Slade, if I'd known being president would ruin every meal, every *celebration*..."

Clay and Bing spoke in the code and shorthand of a shared childhood, which intrigued Claire. Bing asked if they could "camp" together at "the Grove" this year, which Claire didn't understand and Clay eagerly accepted. She gleaned they had gone their separate ways for boarding school—Clay, she knew, to St. Paul's; Bing apparently to Groton—and, to her surprise, had reunited at Yale. Bing, Claire surmised, must have been a year ahead or behind, or maybe just didn't get out much, as she'd never seen him before.

Bing invited Clay as his guest to the club's "Thursday Men's Night," where the secretary of defense was soon scheduled to speak. Surely a former one, Claire thought, hoping the current one had better things to do. Surprisingly, Clay accepted on the spot.

"I'll hit you up," Bing called back as he made his exit. "So much better than those boring Bones lectures, I promise you."

That was a code and shorthand she understood. Every Yalie did.

"Bones?" she asked and paused. "Skull and Bones?"

"Whoops," Nora said. Claire looked at Clay, who looked down at the table.

"Clay, were you in...?" but Slade's sudden burst of laughter roiled the question. Claire laughed once herself, then turned to Nora in disbelief and back to Clay, fighting his own laughter.

"Those Thursdays you said you were in *art lab*?" Claire built her case, with witnesses. "You were actually in a *secret society*?"

By now the whole family, including Claire, was laughing at the dupe. And yet...

"I mean, why didn't you tell me?" she asked.

"Because it's secret," Slade answered for him. "That's the point."

"Were you in it, too?" Claire asked Slade, who feigned deafness, which only made Nora laugh harder. She snorted.

"Whatever." Claire leaned back in her chair and tossed her napkin on the table. "I mean, it's just so *silly*."

"No, Claire." Slade unsheathed his edge a bit. "It's not."

"You'll get used to the all-male cabal around here," Nora said. "Men's nights, secret camping trips. I thought they were plotting all kinds of evil, but it's far more harmless."

"What are they doing?" Claire asked, and Nora said, "Screwing each other, of course."

"Nora!" Slade scolded in mock offense. "It's okay, honey," Nora said, patting his hand. "Just play safe."

There was a sudden peal of trumpet, and the doors were flung open, unveiling a transformed Grand Foyer. Gone were the furniture and rug, revealing the expanse of Carrera marble and a ten-piece big band orchestra on a platform stage. Instant ballroom.

Percussion and banjo joined the brass, and when a clarinet weaved in, center stage, the ready-lit crowd erupted in cheers. "Skokiaan!" a man yelled from the back, and others echoed with hoots and whistles. The party started.

"Right on cue," Nora said, checking her watch.

Slade stood up. "I'd better get upstairs," he said.

"Run, Slade, run!" Nora ribbed. "How high can you *jump?*"

A conga line had formed, snaking through the dining room, growing along the way. Grandcougar Edie brought up the rear and grabbed Clay as she passed. He turned to Claire. "You cool?" he asked. She shrugged and said, "Knock yourself out, *Bonesman.*"

Claire laughed as the conga made its way clumsily toward the music. "You wanna join?" she asked Nora.

"No fucking way," Nora said above the noise. "*Freaks.*"

—⁓—

Claire hoped no one could hear her vomit.

She successfully timed it to the flush of toilets, the running of the faucets, the pleasant prattle beyond. Fortunately, the Ladies' Lounge was large and acoustically complex.

She'd been lucky so far in her first trimester, dodging the typical symptoms: insomnia, mood swings, and, for the most part, morning sickness. Her ob-gyn in Santa Fe warned they could strike anytime.

The dessert was probably too rich. Fortunately, Nora, who'd no doubt had it before, had stopped her after one spoonful. Or was it two? And twirling with Clay on the dance floor, after he pried himself from Eccentric Edie, couldn't have helped either. Not to mention the move, the drive, the deceptive drain of a new life, all stacking on top of her. No wonder she'd suddenly gotten dizzy and nauseated.

At least she'd been giving her school kids good advice over the years: Emptying an upset stomach *did* make it better. Fast. Even so, it was time to call it a night. Claire dabbed her mouth and flushed again and listened for silence. Then she left the stall.

"Claire, was that you? Are you all right?"

It took an off-putting instant to identify the young woman at the sink, in the mirror.

"They sent me up to check on you," her sister-in-law, Madison, said with a Stepford smile.

"I'm fine, Madison. Thank you," Claire said, halting. "Just let me..."

"Yes, of course, go right ahead," Madison said quickly. The uniformed Latina washroom attendant turned the faucet and pumped mouthwash into a pleated paper cup.

Claire had met Madison only once, two years ago, when she and Dean had taken an anniversary trip to Taos. Clay and Claire had driven to join them for dinner near their rented Ski Valley cabin, and when an offer to stay the night was not forthcoming, they'd driven back the same evening. Perhaps Madison had a lot on her mind that night or just didn't appreciate visitors on her anniversary. Who could blame her? In any event, she was much warmer now—almost nurturing.

On her home turf, she was even more archly elegant than Claire remembered: straight flaxen hair pulled tight and braid-knotted, makeup restrained and seemingly professional—masking the freckles Claire remembered and liked—her knee-length dress a shimmer of silvery lace. "The Ice Empress," as Clay had coined her, fit visually but seemed unfair and cruel otherwise. Especially after what she'd been through.

"I'm sorry I missed dinner." Madison filled the silence as Claire washed and rinsed. "I was stuck on boring club business." Claire nodded and turned to her, presentable.

"Oh, congratulations." Madison embraced her with one arm, the other balanced on the sink. "Slade can simmer down now. He's getting an heir!"

"Yes," said Claire, unsure how to respond.

"He badgered Dean and me for years," Madison continued into the mirror. "In hindsight, of course, it's a blessing we didn't live our lives according to his timeline. Don't you agree?"

"Yes," Claire repeated, still unsure.

Madison shooed away the mood. "Claire, it needn't be awkward," she assured her in earnest. "If I didn't have total faith in some master plan, I'd be done by now. It's a joy that you're expecting. I really am happy for you."

"Thank you, Madison," Claire said, relieved. "I'm glad we're both happy."

"And if you have more of *this*"—Madison swirled her hand around her stomach—"my doctor can give you some pills. Homeopathic. Do you have a doctor yet?"

"I have leads," Claire said, hoping to pivot focus from her digestive tract. She held a folded five and looked for a tip jar. The washroom attendant smiled and shook her head. "We don't do that here," Madison said, turning to leave. Claire tucked the five into the attendant's uniform pocket and shushed her lips.

Madison grabbed the crutch leaning in the corner, clipped it around her upper arm, clutched the handle, and hobbled back through the salon. "I won't need this much longer," she said as she stalked across the Aubusson rug, anticipating Claire's unspoken shock at the extent of her injury. "I won't be running the San Francisco Marathon anytime soon, but I hadn't planned on it anyway.

"Oh." Madison stopped mid-Aubusson and changed the subject before Claire could calibrate a response. "You ran a charity in Santa Fe, right? For children? Didn't you tell me that?"

"It wasn't really a charity," Claire said. "I started an after-school tutoring program. Teaching English to immigrant children—"

"Can you help me?" Madison interrupted. "They just made me chair of the club's Outreach Committee. I'm sure Slade was behind it. I don't know where to begin. I know how to write a *check*, but..."

"It's not that difficult," Claire said. "You just find a need, and you fill it."

"You just found a need!" Madison said with a laugh. "Thank you!"

Claire laughed with her, realizing she'd just volunteered.

"And when you're ready, I know the best place for maternity clothes," Madison went on. "Pregnant, bloated, and bipolar never looked so good."

"Thank you," Claire said. "I'd love to go shopping sometime."

"Just bring the plastic," Madison called back as she maneuvered toward a group of friends in the pink-and-cream salon. "*His.*"

Claire nodded at the coven of young women, all perfectly Madison-esque, who had sized her up and, as far as she could tell, were fine with her. Shimmery metallics, apparently popular here, had yet to hit Santa Fe, and likely never would. Her own Kate Middleton long curls, which she'd just grown out and mastered, were seemingly passé. That didn't take long.

Claire considered, and then reconsidered, descending the Grand Staircase to rejoin the party below, having been promenaded in front of strangers enough for one evening.

"Excuse me," she asked a pair of female Asian employees strolling the hallway. "Is there an elevator?" They smiled and pointed, and Claire regretted having disturbed them, as they seemed on break, but they didn't mind and resumed gossiping in their native tongue. Housekeepers, Claire thought, or maybe kitchen staff, as their white jackets were much longer than the waiters', down to their knees. One carried a fat book, and they walked into a solid wood wall, which was a door, and disappeared into the fluorescence beyond. The door swung back and became a wall again, funhouse style.

She missed the first elevator, its doors closing just then. She pressed the button, and its twin dinged open. But a much larger twin, with double doors and a long, roomy cabin—almost institutional-like, were it not for the mahogany moldings and smoky mirrors that blended with the rest of the club, a seamless renovation.

The control panel gave it away: modern down to the Braille buttons. At the bottom, below the starred main floor, was the "Pool," ostensibly underground. Claire was intrigued, but there was a key lock next to it, and the button wouldn't light. Someday she'd have Clay show her, as he must have spent many hours there in his boyhood. But not tonight; she was ready to go, and Clay must be wondering where she was. She reached for the first floor.

The doors shut with efficient force. The elevator went up.

Trapped, Claire thought with a smile that inexplicably turned to giggles. "Help!" she cried out to herself, which made her laugh more as the elevator went higher. She pulled herself together as it stopped and the doors opened.

Another Asian stood facing her, this one male and tall and gaunt. He had thinning hair, wore a shorter white jacket that matched his pallor, and carried a tray with dirty dishes on one hand and a folding stand in the other. His name tag read "Ling," and he betrayed no reaction to Claire, who stepped back from the door so he could join her. He didn't.

After a moment, Claire said, "Sorry, am I on the wrong elevator?" Ling's steady silence was potentially her answer, and she apologized again and got off on the unknown floor. Ling got on and set the heavy tray on the folding stand in the large, efficient service elevator that first-time-guest Claire had commandeered as her own.

"Sorry," she said a third time as the doors closed on Ling's still, silent gaze.

Claire turned around.

Chapter Three

The floor Claire found herself marooned on was dim and silent, the ceilings lower.

It felt like a hotel hallway, which, with the matching doors evenly spaced and the humorless Ling's room service apparatus, was likely true. She waited a sufficient beat to avoid boomeranging his elevator back open—she could only imagine his nonexpression then—before pressing the button to summon the other car. It whirred to life below.

Behind her, a short, perpendicular hallway dead-ended at a window casting a glow inward. Keeping one eye on the elevator, she peered out into the interior light well—a central cavity, open to the sky, hidden from the outside. Floodlights shone down onto cream-painted brick walls ringed with windows, both sheered and not, looking out onto each other. Camouflaged with matching paint were fire escape ladders dropping down from wide cornice ledges that rounded each floor, although escaping into the center of a burning building seemed a questionable strategy.

Down below sprawled the massive Tiffany glass dome, equally splendid from above. Through its translucent, jewel-toned mosaic she saw the shadows of dancing figures in the Grand Foyer. Including, she knew, Clay, likely trapped again by Edie or some other matron and itching to give Claire *that look* when she resurfaced—if only she had her cell to text that she'd be right down to rescue him.

Motion to the right of the light well spun her attention: a row of windows on her floor, freshly re-sheered, ruffling from movement just beyond. One large room, she deduced, with several tall, male silhouettes circulating inside. Cigar smoke, to be sure. Gender segregation was alive and well at the Union.

Behind her, the elevator dinged its arrival. Claire turned to it, open and empty, and thought. Clay was having fun with old friends; Nora was proudly showing him off after his long absence. Claire would only be in their way. She stood still, and the elevator slowly withdrew its invitation. Claire pulled her pashmina tighter and wandered the camel carpet down the hallway. After all, she'd likely never be up here again.

Dotted along the walls upholstered in dark tartan fabric above mahogany wainscoting were eight architectural blueprints framed in burled maple. Front and side reliefs, floor plan cutaways, ornate and important buildings, each different and yet seemingly of a collection. They were signed, illegibly, by the same architect, labeled with name and location. The University Club (New York), the Monolith (Moscow), the Chang An (Beijing), the chain wrapped around the continents, with the Union last in the lineup.

The pops and dancing lights of a fireplace drew her toward the cracked door at the end. She listened for people, heard none, eased the door open. The club's library was round and two stories high, linked by a rolling ladder to access the thousands of books. Tufted leather, more Heriz, the fire—seemingly stoked moments earlier—very much alive behind its brass and padded fender bench. Carved into the marble mantel was a Latin phrase, of which the only word she could decipher was a dead-language version of "justify." A grave gentleman in oil peered down from above, from a different century, with big issues on his mind. The domed ceiling was midnight blue and twinkled with a vast painted galaxy of constellations.

Claire stepped through the empty room, past the small librarian desk with its orderly paperwork and relic Smith and Corona electric typewriter. She spun the massive, antique floor globe, caressed the tarnished silver of a trophy cup table lamp. *Mrs. Peacock, in the study, with the candlestick,* she thought, suppressing a fresh giggle.

"Oh my," she said softly, turning around. Across the library, by a window, was a built-in cabinet of three glass shelves, spotlighted from above. They sat fronting a faded, copper-toned atlas wraparound backdrop that reminded Claire of swank, boutique wrapping paper. Spaced out evenly were eight large, sparkling Fabergé eggs—crystal-clear, sharply cut, and bejeweled with precious stones, each with one more than the last, a numerical progression that set them apart.

Claire instinctively reached for her cell to take a photo, a futile gesture. She'd have to describe them to Martha instead. They were glorious.

Knowing better, but unable to resist, Claire picked up the first single-jeweled egg from its gilded perch. Floating deep inside was a gleaming yellow "yolk," that, when she turned it and squinted, seemed to be a canary diamond ring, clutching a tiny scroll in its finger bed. Claire pondered and inspected the latch and hinge across the egg's equator. She'd never seen such a priceless stone up close and likely wouldn't again. She carefully thumbed the latch upward.

A sudden fluttering and wisp of breeze spun her, still clutching the egg. Face-to-face she was with a large bird, wings partially spread. It was a hawk-looking creature, fat and beige with hundreds of brown spots that nearly merged into stripes. Its dark purple eyes, trained on Claire, were ringed in black, not white. It sat motionless on one leg, the other tucked into its belly, and Claire thought perhaps it was stuffed, that she'd imagined the fluttering and breeze in her heightened intruder state. But when she moved her head, the purple eyes followed. *Well, why not?* she thought.

The creature grasped a well-worn perch with sharp talons on its withered foot. Below the perch—an odd contraption—sat a red-upholstered pillow fringed in gold, atop a tall marble column. The bird looked ancient and earth-bound fat, but its beak was sharp, its wings held in pounce-ready stance. Claire backed away slowly, returned the egg to the shelf, and the bird tucked its wings back to its side.

"That better?" Claire asked the creature. It cocked its head to the side. Amused, Claire did the same. "Caw?" She laughed and then said again, "Caw?"

The bird unfurled its wings full span, tilted back its head, and released a piercing screech.

Claire nearly tripped in her retreat. She regrouped and challenged it. "Ssh!" she ordered.

The bird folded its wings and waited for her next move. Then the books behind Claire started talking.

She pivoted to the shelves, which she'd already guessed were a hidden door to a secret room, keeping one eye on the bird that was now done with her, having sounded its alarm. It rested its head on its breast and settled into stillness. In the room beyond—far beyond, it seemed—a heated discussion grew hotter. The all-male cabal, preferably plotting evil instead of screwing each other. With the old bird now asleep, its dark purples shut, Claire focused past the shelves and listened.

It was a disappointment. The men were arguing over a charitable donation to a local hospital—a good thing, Claire thought, but not particularly juicy. How, she wondered, could a donation "fall flat," as one of the men bemoaned? "Money talks," another man added. "But even they have limits." Yet another complained, with disdain, that they were the "weakest link" of the "seven sisters." Club code. Their own lingo.

One man accused the others of "failing to recruit the right members with the right skills."

That set another man off. This was getting good.

"Why not volunteer your own?" he fired back at the accuser. "You've got four already. Another on the way. Give till it hurts, as they say." A chorus of nays drowned him out. "Out of order!" and "Bad form!" Claire swore she heard one man shout, "Bully!"—a groovy, old-fashioned term she made a mental note of incorporating. The chorus grew louder, ganging up on the poor, set-off man.

And then Slade took over. Even his voice was that of a natural-born leader.

"Gentlemen!" He silenced them. "This fractious infighting is unmanly, unproductive, and has plagued the club for far too long." The new president—and Texan transplant—laid down the law. "I was elected to think outside the box. Methodically and with efficiency." Yellow Tails or not, Slade was impressive at the helm.

"A new approach is already underway," he continued. "We're all ears, Slade," another man challenged. Claire leaned in closer as the distant room grew quiet under his spell.

An arm blocked the door.

"I'm so sorry!" Claire jumped back without looking, and the bookshelf door swung shut. "I was just...," she started to explain.

"Be my guest, Claire," the voice of the arm said gently. "Only..." The hand connected to the arm indicated the tarnished plaque that read "Gentlemen's Lounge."

"You wouldn't want to find yourself in a compromising situation," the voice added, with humor.

The man was tall with silver hair, trim and parted to the side. He wore a beaded-stripe navy three-piece suit with a correct shirt and regimental tie. He had a manicured mustache and was above the club's median age.

"I'm Colonel Crowe," he said, extending his dry hand, and Claire shook it with her clammy one. "I'm so sorry," she repeated quietly. "And, yes, I was snooping."

The man smiled and waved it away. "They'll bicker all night," he said. "Silly club matters that once seemed so important to me. I'm rather enjoying my retirement."

"I would imagine." Claire had regained her composure in the gentleman's elegant presence. "It sounds testy in there."

"They push new ideas," the colonel said with a slight shrug. "I protect old traditions. Thus we maintain our delicate balance." He was the club's chairman emeritus, he clarified, and Claire silently wondered which branch of the military a colonel was part of and how he could afford such an expensive suit. Perhaps it was just a nickname.

She also wondered how he knew her name. It was likely, even probable, he'd been in the dining room when Slade blew her cover with his toast, but he hadn't mentioned her name, had he? Then again, she was a new face, and between Allen and Jess and the grandcougar, word probably got around. The Union Club, she decided, was a very small world.

"I got off on the wrong floor," Claire explained. "And was just admiring your beautiful library."

The colonel fit perfectly in the room and seemed proud to show it off. "Our oasis of knowledge and wisdom," he said, gliding toward the center. "Glad you appreciate it."

He peered up at the grumpy man above the fireplace. "Our founder, James Flick," he schooled her. "A true American hero. This was his favorite room, as well. So steeped in history. The UN hatched here, before moving to that monstrosity in New York."

Claire smiled and nodded, even though the timeline of founder/building/UN, if she remembered her history, didn't add up. Maybe the colonel was a few Yellow Tails in himself. She'd Wikipedia it later, if she cared enough.

"What does the inscription mean?" Claire asked, less curious than trying to appear politely interested. The colonel seemed to notice it for the first time. "I should know, shouldn't I?" he pondered. "Alas, my Latin's a bit rusty."

Claire moved toward him, and the old bird, now awake, elbowed its wings in a familiar, half-threatening stance. "Now, now, Sting," the colonel gently scolded, pulling a small Ziploc of goldfish crackers from his trousers. "Claire's a friend." He rewarded the calmed creature and pet its back like a cat.

"That's a lovely, big...bird," Claire said with a half laugh. The colonel nodded, not sharing her humor. "Sting was a gift from our sister club in London," he said. "She's a peregrine falcon." "A falcon, of course," Claire said. "I thought she was a hawk." "No, she's not a hawk," the colonel said and fed it another.

"A girl down the hall in college had a ferret," Claire said, instantly wondering why she had, and compounded the weirdness by adding, "She wore it around on her shoulder."

"A ferret?" The colonel looked at her. "Is that so?"

"On her shoulder," Claire said. "Is that so?" the colonel repeated. Claire stopped talking.

"A peregrine falcon has the fastest dive on the planet," the colonel continued, admiring the creature's past-its-prime wings. "The air force copied its breathing system for their fighter jets." Claire joined his admiration of the old bird and concluded that colonels must be part of the air force, although that didn't sound right. Army sounded right. Maybe both. None of this mattered.

"Territorial, too," the colonel went on, still smitten with Sting. "Only leaves her perch to hunt." "Hunt *what?*" Claire huffed, her last attempt at levity. The colonel finally gave in and smiled warmly at her. "You'll never find a rat in this club," he said. Then he pivoted the conversation.

"I hear congratulations are in order," he said, moving past the floor globe. Before Claire could thank him, he added, "You must be very proud of Clay." Maybe he hadn't heard about her own big news after all. It was hard to track his thinking.

Claire followed, not just to get away from Sting, but to talk without raising her voice. The colonel seemed to inspect the room for dust. Claire was glad she hadn't moved anything before he arrived. Then she remembered and glanced back at the priceless crystal egg, slightly tilted on the shelf.

"I *am* proud of him," she said, turning back quickly to the colonel, who had turned to her. "It's just an adjustment. A change from what we were—"

"Youth must have its day," he interrupted. "We understand that."

And then he pivoted again. "I hope your parents will come visit soon."

Claire nodded in gratitude and said simply, "My mother died. When I was very young." An effortless answer she'd given countless times.

"That must have been challenging," the colonel replied, as simply. "And your father?"

"I don't know," Claire said.

"You don't know where he's living now, or...?"

"I mean I don't know," Claire repeated, equally effortless.

The colonel didn't blink. "I see," he said. "Quite resourceful of you, then, to end up at Yale."

"They came to me, actually," she said, now getting the interview and unafraid of it, or him. "Recruited me. I mean, I worked—earned my way—in the art library."

"And is that where you met Clay?"

"At Yale, yes."

"No, I meant the art library."

Claire thought and then nodded. "Yes. We did meet there, yes."

The colonel smiled his biggest yet and nodded back. "Leave it to Yale." He chuckled, impressed. "The best and brightest." Claire met his laugh without understanding it.

"Well, it's a pleasure to have you, Claire," the colonel said, finishing the interview, and then looked over her shoulder. He walked to the glass shelves and righted the tilted egg.

"That was me," Claire confessed without apology. "I put it back wrong."

"Have you had dessert?" the colonel asked, cordially leading her from the library. "Let's take the back stairs, why not?"

"I look forward to learning more," he added, a gentle and firm hand against her back. "There's so much we don't know about you."

—⁂—

The rich *are* different from you and me, Claire agreed. They're *goofy*.

From her mezzanine perch, she looked down on the Grand Foyer/ Ballroom, where the evening wound down. Stompy Jones, the band leader—at least according to the drum marquee—looked like a skinny seventies Motown star but had covered the jazz gamut from Louis Armstrong to Sinatra to Tony Bennett with almost eerie mimicry; if you closed your eyes, you'd scarcely know the difference. She half expected him to break out in Peggy Lee.

Now he slowed the pace, and the crowd began their goodbyes. It was a school night, and there were few dance partners for the ladies anyway. Most men of a certain age were likely ensconced in the heated meeting upstairs, leaving only the very young, the very old, and the very dandy behind. But where was Clay? Probably hiding from Edie.

Claire herself was hiding from the colonel, who had led her downstairs and for whom she'd wearied of answering personal questions. She begged off for the unneeded Ladies' Lounge and now scoured the main floor for her husband. A surgical strike and beeline exit would finally end their evening, although she had to admit it had been more pleasant—even delightful—than she'd expected. Notwithstanding the colonel's needling, the perfectly dressed and groomed elites had been surprisingly embracing. Cordial, inviting and, yes, goofy.

"The Prom of the Living Dead," Nora had barbed earlier when the dancing began right after dinner, as Claire hugged the edge and tried to ignore the creeping nausea that ultimately forced her upstairs. Nora had mistaken her apparent discomfort for nervous inadequacy and tried to becalm her further.

"The first time I walked in here, boy, did I feel out of my league," she'd confessed to her daughter-in-law, arm around her shoulder. "But it's just a building. And they're just people, these silly socialites."

Nora continued. "As Dorothy Parker said, If all these broads were laid end to end, I wouldn't be a bit surprised." Claire laughed out loud and turned to Nora, who added, without smiling, "We're so happy to have you, Claire. You belong here now, as much as anyone." It had almost sounded like a plea, and Nora held her gaze before turning back to the dance floor. She patted Claire's shoulder in solidarity. Moments later, Claire had excused herself, just in time.

Now Nora was downstairs, cornered at the fireplace by a tipsy old coot who prattled on with happy, high energy. Nora nodded, indulging him. The coot leaned in and dribbled red wine from his glass down her Chanel top without noticing. Nora stepped back to staunch the flow and looked up at Claire as if she'd seen her there the whole time. Nora smiled falsely and rolled her eyes, pointed at the oblivious coot and then at the grandcougar and other assorted zombies and shrugged at the absurdities of her life. Claire laughed back from the railing and gave Nora a thumbs-up.

Edie straightened the dandy's bow tie, Madison hobbled with surprising grace to a waiting chair seemingly reserved for her, Jess hand-delivered coats, wraps, and hats by special request. While not exactly the Addams Family, it was an extended family of its own strange rhythm and charm.

The "important men" returned, released from their lounge squabble, and fanned across the room toward their significant others. Colonel Crowe emerged from the edge—had he been lying in wait for Claire all this time?—and intercepted Slade on his way to his wife. Fatherlike, he steered him by the elbow to an empty corner for a private chat. Nora, rescue-*interruptus*, gave up the pretense of civility and abandoned the still-prattling coot to go sit on the grand piano bench and wait it out. From Claire's aerial vantage, the ballet was priceless. *How high can you jump, Slade?* She could almost feel Nora stew.

Familiar arms wrapped around Claire's waist. "Welcome to the club," Clay teased in her ear.

"I thought I'd have to hitch a ride." Claire half turned to him. "Where have you been?"

"Looking for you," he said. "Hiding out up here?"

"I took a little tour," Claire answered. "Were you upstairs with the cabal?"

Clay spun her around as Stompy Jones began a slow Dean Martin, signaling the night's end. They danced on the mezzanine. "You enchanted everyone," he said. "I hope you didn't meet too many freaks."

"I can handle the freaks," Claire responded. "I have experience." Clay dipped her extra low and held her there until she cried uncle! "And I was thinking," she said, once righted, "for our child: no puppy or kitten. How 'bout a warm, fuzzy bird of prey?"

"Oh God." Clay laughed. "Is Sting still alive? How is that even possible?"

Claire crossed her wrists behind his neck. "Now, listen, Mr. Bonesman. No more secrets. No matter how silly. Deal?"

"That was just stupid college stuff. So long ago," he said, massaging her lower back as they swayed. "But if you're feeling silly, there is a secret room down the hall we can sneak into and..." Claire feigned offense and swatted him on the shoulder. She glanced back down at the ballroom.

Everyone stood still, watching them.

"Okay, don't look now," Claire dummied through a frozen smile. "But we seem to be making a spectacle of ourselves." Clay kept dancing. Stompy got to the final chorus.

"We still haven't christened our new home," Clay said. "Is that all you think about?" Claire asked, twirling out.

Clay wheeled her back close. "Let's go home," he whispered into her neck, and Claire giggled and said, "Let's go home."

Chapter Four

Everyone had suspected, when Claire and Clay got married so young and quietly, that she was pregnant. But since this wasn't the 1950s, that wasn't true. Claire married Clay because she was in love and chose to build a life with him. That was all the explanation anyone needed.

The marriage chagrined not only Martha, but also other female classmates—Rockefeller, Whitney, DuPont—who couldn't fathom how amiable Claire No-Name had graduated from fling to college sweetheart to life partner of their year's most eligible Eli. After all, the Willings were the Kennedys of San Francisco, even if Clay was the black sheep.

Children hadn't entered her mind—no timeline or ticking clock. There was no plan, which was unusual for Claire with her discipline and lists and type-A foresight that had steered her life. Clay typically coasted, waiting for inspiration or drop-dead deadlines and pulling all-nighters in college for term papers that Claire had finished days ahead of schedule. If Claire had put Clay in charge of their move to San Francisco, they'd still be in Santa Fe staring at the walls.

But she didn't plan a family, at least not consciously. Midthirties would have been fine, as seemed to be the goal of her school friends who'd launched power careers. No children at all, while remote, was also a possibility. A college pregnancy was out of the question, and she took precautions then, which she'd maintained after their marriage, with increasingly less rigor. Much less, apparently.

Her type-A instinctively kicked into Claire-drive once she got the news—earlier, in fact, since she *knew* before the first home test, the first doctor confirmation. She sampled, then eschewed, the thousands of pregnancy websites with their conflicting and sometimes bizarre new-age advice, and settled on the old-school basics. She immediately started prenatal vitamins—a bit late and concerned, as she had not been planning to conceive—cut out all the forbiddens (she wouldn't miss her occasional white wine, but caffeine had been an addiction since her teens), and kept far away from secondhand smoke—easier, she suspected, in smoke-phobic San Francisco. *"Everything You Need to Know...,"* she did.

Her doctor in Santa Fe had urged her to "take it easy," a formidable challenge she vowed to accept once all the "must-dos" of a new life in a new city were done. Her list was long.

After an oddly fitful night—she'd never had trouble sleeping in a strange place before—she slipped out of bed in predawn darkness, started to unpack a box but decided it was too noisy, straightened Clay's paintings and watched the morning rise over the Bay. At six thirty, she showered and dressed quietly. At least the morning brought no sickness.

The new car could wait—Clay had run into parental resistance at ditching his Mustang in their driveway—but groceries and home necessities could not. Claire tiptoed past the quiet Hooverville and carefully crossed in front of a slow-moving brown Chevelle with tinted windows looking for street parking. She bought a Clipper transit card at Walgreens and, location-enabled iPhone map in hand, attacked the town Muni-style. She shopped organic at Pathmark, signed a delivery voucher, texted Clay to be *awake* to receive.

"Deets!" Martha demanded from the hospital on a short break from her twenty-four-hour shift. Amid machine-gun questions, Claire filled her in on the members, their clothes, the food, the *bird*. "Where does the damn bird shit?" Martha demanded, which Claire hadn't considered but stumped her now.

"Ling? They have an Asian dude named *Ling*?" Martha said. "Do they have a Negro named Beulah?"

She peppered Claire with family questions.

"I like that Madison Willing these days," said Martha, a rare compliment. "Just from the magazines. With that *crutch*. Fearless. She gets my sympathy vote."

"She's a survivor," Claire agreed. She didn't realize Madison was a local celebrity, but it made sense. Wealth plus beauty, humbled by tragedy, equals the thawing of an ice empress.

"I'm sure it's stunning inside," Martha said, soaking up Claire's vivid descriptions. "Evil has its privileges." Later, she said, "You should have pocketed one of those eggs," and, "Of course that colonel dude knows everything about you. I'm sure they have a dossier." Martha's humor was drier and more cloaked than Claire remembered. It didn't sound like humor at all.

"I'm just glad you made it out alive," Martha finished with a hacking laugh. "I gotta jet. Someone appears to be dying." The irony of a medical resident who smoked seemed lost on her. "No, missy," Martha corrected before hanging up, "it is not lost on me at all."

Claire delighted on the historic streetcars on the F line down bustling Market Street. She marveled at the cable car turnaround and was tempted to hop on, but the tourist line was already long, and her to-do list was longer. She stuck to her schedule and tore through the Container Store and Bloomingdale's at the San Francisco Centre mall—a converted old factory turned shiny, elegant place with an enormous food court down below, which Claire suspected bustled with workers from nearby office towers on their lunch hour. Lucky for her, the Beard Papa's wasn't open yet. The mocha cream puffs on the poster screamed her name, sirenlike.

Martha couldn't break away for lunch but e-mailed the requested list of ob-gyns. From the Nordstrom lounge, Claire made three consultation appointments, with Martha's own doctor the only one willing to fit her in the following week. *She's good*, Martha texted. *Cancel the others.*

If you say so, Claire responded.

Of course I say so, Martha texted back, closing the subject. *Dinner soon?* And then she texted shortly after: *Have you Googled Anonymous yet?*

—✲—

It was ridiculously premature, Claire realized, but she couldn't help herself. The cluster of public school children on Fourth Street—yep, in uniform—set her thinking about her own child's education.

Chill, Claire scolded herself. *It's just an embryo. Right now, it's more like a clot.*

Claire would not, she'd pledged weeks ago, overpreen and fuss. She'd safeguard and raise a healthy, well-adjusted child but she refused to fall victim to the new mother's curse and make a fool of herself in the process. Her pregnancy would not be the subject of every dinner conversation, she'd never bore friends with a "brag book" of photos, and she'd made Clay promise to rescind her computer privileges at her first Facebook posting of maternal-hypochondriac panic. No helicopter parent she, nor Clay either.

Her child would be the center of hers and Clay's universe, as it should be, but no one else's. Maybe the grandparents. They had a stake, and that was normal. So did her doctor, whoever it turned out to be. She already liked Martha's; the others seemed too *busy*. If they didn't realize an expectant mother couldn't wait two weeks just for a consultation, then they weren't the right fit.

Claire sat on a Market Street bench to catch her breath. She needed to pace herself. She was walking for two now. Luckily, she'd taken Martha's advice to dress in layers, a necessary precaution against the city's infamous microclimates. She took off her coat to cool down.

She'd research the San Francisco public school system. The one in Tampa had served her well, and she had great faith—from the inside—in Santa Fe's. She'd test the waters here as a substitute teacher once she navigated the bureaucratic labyrinth of certifications. Slade would inevitably push for Town School for Boys if they had a son and Hamlin for a daughter. Claire didn't want her child cloistered with rich white kids. She'd set boundaries with the in-laws, and Clay would side with her. He'd better. A fight for another day.

Did San Francisco have a Montessori school?

Why were there so many homeless people in this city?

"You're welcome," she said, smiling, handing out another dollar. She got up from the bench—better a moving target than a sitting duck. Newly chilled, she donned her coat again. It was nearly noon, her wallet was light, and her list was only one-third complete. She found an ATM at a Wells Fargo clustered with picketers and signed their petition without looking. She texted Clay to open local accounts to avoid these fees. *Better yet*, she texted moments later, *a credit union.*

All roads led to Union Square, which pulled her. She crossed Powell to a perky shop called Sprout and window-shopped prams and peace sign onesies. It was a smart shop—the cribs were already bumperless, per the new AAP recommendations. One in particular would work nicely in her room, since the same guidelines said a baby should sleep near the parents for the first year.

A salesgirl inside smiled an invite, and Claire, embarrassed, politely declined.

And so it begins. She laughed at her reflection before turning in profile and touching her womb apologetically. *Not a clot,* she decided.

Union Square was boiling with a mob that chanted and marched with signs. Many wore smiling Guy Fawkes masks, and the hand-drawn signs read "99%" and "Revolution" and "Collapse." One wore a mask and business suit and held up "The Beginning Is Near." There was a chorus of war drums. Claire watched with tourists from the edge, and she agreed with the protesters in the swarm but couldn't join in their anger today.

She sat on the wall to catch her breath. She shouldn't push herself so hard. The rest of her list could wait.

It wasn't until she was safely on the streetcar heading home that the drums faded away.

—ₘ—

Protest and civil disobedience were old hat to Claire. As a freshman, she'd joined the Yale chapter of Students for Social Responsibility and participated in a two-day sit-in at Sheffield Library when the school with a world-famous endowment cut the benefits of underprivileged campus workers. But she quit the group senior year when they invited Louis Farrakhan, whose venom repelled her. She had tired of polarization and opted for nonconfrontational fun in her final year.

But the real world had spiraled steeply since. Unrest and rage were global and local. Everything was on fire "over there," and it was coming here. Indeed, it had arrived.

Gloom led to confusion, which bred anger and a growing whiff of violence. Claire had followed the progression and participated early, marching with the teachers in Lansing and Santa Fe. She knew things would get better, as they always had. And when they didn't—when they got much, much worse—the anger grew into rage, and the protests grew hotter, and the spiral began. She'd heard the words "simmering" and "powder keg" and "upheaval" so often, she finally stopped watching the news and took NPR off her iPod.

And why not? She was soon to bring a child into this world.

"This one?" Clay asked, tapping a block on the paint store's color display. "Claire?"

"Sorry, what?" She started and then scanned the rainbow of yellows. "No, brighter. Sunnier."

They had decided to keep their child's gender a secret, even from themselves. This would inevitably rankle Slade, who surely wanted a starter grandson. To his credit, Clay could still rankle when necessary and would back her up. Their child needn't be saddled with great expectations in utero.

Yellow was gender neutral and, according to a child psychology blog she favored, "emotionally stimulating." She found a VOC-free, milk paint specialist in the Castro and bought three pints in different shades for testing. She gently nudged Clay away from gunmetal gray for their bedroom—"The walls will close in on us, honey"—and saddled him up with brushes, rollers, and drop cloths. The salesperson thanked them many times.

The Castro, though grimy, was colorful and festively defiant. The young gay boys were fit and chatty. The older men, far fewer, shared a bittersweet gravity. They'd survived their own holocaust not so long ago. The mostly brown children of mostly white lesbians were quiet and well mannered, as if conditioned to tread softly in life.

Don't, Claire silently urged. *Tread loudly*.

They passed several vacant shops. A Charles Busch film festival at the Castro Theatre. A sidewalk pen of homeless pets for adoption. An elderly terrier mix blinked at Claire from a curled position. *Someday*, she blinked back. The mutt put its head back on its paws.

Clay stopped at the light by the billboard-sized rainbow flag. "Back home?" he asked.

On an abandoned storefront, three posters reminded Claire "The Beginning Is Near." Guy Fawkes smiled down, in triptych.

—⚡—

The cable guy arrived at 1:23 p.m. to set up their bundle—modem/cable card/tuning adapter for their TiVo. Clay wanted a landline, too, which they'd never had before. "Nice place," the crisply dressed technician said. "Thank you," Claire said, bringing him a lime seltzer with ice as he tested the local HD channels.

"Jesus," he said with an inhale.

Carnage at Oakland City Hall. Seven in critical condition. Police crackdown. Mob push back. Breakdown.

"It's getting ugly." The technician shook his head, tracking the breaking story channel to channel.

"Do we get Smithsonian HD?" Claire asked, avoiding the screen. "Is that part of our package?"

—⚡—

The doorbell rang. A delivery of eight custom suits from Wilkes Bashford, hanging separately in clear plastic bags with breathable mesh backs. Navies, grays, chalk stripe, windowpane. One chocolate brown and one tuxedo—all single-breast, notch lapel.

"When did you buy these?" Claire asked, marveling at Clay's name embroidered on the inside pocket. "I didn't," Clay answered.

"Mr. Willing?" The squat, bespectacled tailor grinned, summoning chalk from his apprentice. "Arms down to your sides?"

Shirts, ties, shoes came in waves, as the young Hispanic assistant scurried several trips.

"Mini-Slade." Claire giggled. Clay ignored her, stared ahead, as the kneeling tailor chalked his waist and legs quickly. "You look very handsome," she clarified.

And then she said to the tailor: "I'm sorry, how did you get inside? Was the downstairs door open?"

—⚹—

Claire hadn't been in the mood much lately, but she did her best, and after Clay fell asleep and she couldn't, she slipped downstairs and made chamomile tea with organic honey. She sat in the dark at the kitchen counter with her laptop and waited for her stomach to settle. Outside, at a distance, a siren sliced the silence and then faded. More sirens, more fading. The pros and cons of living near a hospital.

Carpet for the stairs, she mused at the bare wood slats. *Better traction.* She liked camel, but it would show too much dirt.

She Yelped for a prenatal yoga class and compared reviews—expectant mothers were opinionated and *wordy*—and circled one in the Mission. She saved the DMV driver's license application to her desktop; she'd have to take the damn written test. She was scanning the list of required documents for her teacher certification when her e-mail dinged.

Martha was up early, or late, or on a break. "Watch Me!" she ordered.

The link was long and random. Claire expected something funny. It wasn't.

A Guy Fawkes mask filled the screen, computer-animated.

"Greetings, friends. We are Anonymous," it purred in live voice over what vaguely sounded like seventies porn music. "We are the ninety-nine percent. We are legion." The accent was crisply British. There was no pause button. Claire lowered the volume.

The Mask's eyes followed hers. It blinked.

49

"Anonymous," she knew, was a disjointed online community of activism—a *notion*, really—a shared global brain of chaos and anarchy. Their laundry list of grievances, and demands, was long and ever-changing. Its tactics were often criminal. Each major city had its own, like Bozo.

Martha had been obsessed with it for years, especially after Claire's marriage into the Willing "dynasty." Devilish Martha, stirring up trouble again. "There's a revolution coming," she'd often warn, needling. Claire had yet to take the bait.

San Francisco Anonymous, with its clichéd mask, took aim at Oakland. It vowed revenge the following day.

Today, Claire realized.

The Mask gave the location. Claire mapped it.

"We do not forgive; we do not forget." The Mask smiled and nodded with British politeness. "Expect us."

The voice synched perfectly with the computer-animated lips. A high-tech job. The head tipped an invitation.

Wanna go? Martha e-mailed. *I'm off at noon.*

Busy, Claire responded. She scrolled down the website's sidebar. Dozens of video messages. Warnings all.

Y the fuck r u awake? Martha dinged back. It's *three a.m!*

Claire closed her laptop. Brown carpet for the stairs. Maybe gray, since Clay liked that.

A siren in the distance. It faded off without getting close.

—⚋⚋—

Madison called the landline at 8:07 the next morning.

"I hope I'm not waking you," she said, and Claire said, "I've been up a while," balancing the cordless against her neck while she alphabetized the fiction in the living room bookshelves by author. "I didn't realize anyone had this number."

"Everyone does," Madison reported. "It's listed." Claire remembered and said, "Yes. How are you?"

It was a friendly chat of newcomer advice and general nothingness.

"Awful about Oakland," Claire said, and Madison, after a pause, said, "Yes. Awful."

Claire, sleep-deprived and sloppy, kicked herself for broaching the topic, a scant three months after a madman had killed Madison's husband and crippled her, roughly in that order. She missed her coffee.

"Will we see you Saturday at the deYoung?" Madison asked, and Claire said, "I think so. I hope so."

"How are you feeling?"

"I'm fine. Still getting used to this little critter wreaking havoc on my system."

"Ha-ha," Madison said literally, without laughing. "Critter. I'm just checking because of your spell at the club. Anything since?"

"I haven't vomited since, no," Claire said, getting to the point. "But if I do again, no biggie."

"No biggie," Madison agreed, amused by the term. "No pain or bleeding or anything?"

"Neither, thank God," Claire said and laughed, and Madison laughed with her. "Well, that's good," she said. "Why don't you join me at the club for lunch? My treat."

"You're sweet." Claire thanked her, but her day was booked.

"If you change your mind, just drop in," Madison said. "You're always welcome."

"You're sweet," Claire said again. "Soon."

"Will we see you Saturday at the deYoung?" Madison repeated.

—⟶⟵—

51

Claire sat on the vintage F line, heading downtown on Market toward the high-end shopping district. Martha had convinced her Chico's and Bebe wouldn't cut it for the deYoung. Emporio Armani or Ralph Lauren or the comparables in the area. "Glam it up before you start showing," Martha ordered. "Get whatever you want," Clay encouraged in his handsome new suit, on his way out the door. He didn't start work until Monday but was meeting with someone in human resources to set up his 401K. "Back early," he promised.

Claire had never bought a designer dress and wouldn't now. But she'd steal ideas to cobble together from her existing wardrobe, which was entirely adequate. Then maybe on to Ghirardelli Square for an in-law gift. Who was she kidding? Ghirardelli for *her*.

In a pinch, she could borrow a dress from Madison, as they were roughly the same size. Maybe one of the metallics. She'd dry-clean it after.

The streetcar was crowded and quiet. At Yerba Linda, Claire gave her seat to an elderly woman with groceries. "Pardon me," Claire said to a young Goth teen, nearly stepping on his foot, but he couldn't hear through his earbuds. She smiled at an older black man glancing up from his paper. He nodded back, then returned her smile, an afterthought.

Madison's lunch offer was kind, and she'd return the favor soon. Someplace in SOMA or Pacific Heights. Not the Union Club. Claire didn't want to imply she was gunning for membership.

Unless Madison wasn't comfortable in public because of her crutch. Claire would be sensitive to that. But Martha had seen the crutch in the magazines, so clearly Madison didn't hide it. And why should she? Everyone already knew about the tragedy.

One day, thought Claire, we'll learn how to communicate. Eventually, they'd resolve the slight awkwardness between them. They were both trying.

The streetcar stopped abruptly. Claire clutched the ceiling strap to keep steady.

"What the hell?" the older black man said. The young Goth hit the pause button. The elderly woman squinted ahead. Claire ducked to see out the front window.

A mob swarmed toward them, not in panic, but in exodus. Angry hundreds turned the busy street into a pedestrian walkway, halting traffic in both directions. The conductor didn't ring his bell; no one honked. In the distance, police mounted on horses herded the masses away. Riot police with shields and helmets backed them up.

The crowd thronged on either side of the streetcar, moving past. Not hundreds, Claire realized. *Thousands*. The signs were homemade: "Revolution" and "Delete the Elite." Farther back, a sagging banner read "Eat the Rich," which, on a different day, different year, might have seemed comical. Several carried backpacks and sleeping bags and a mess of crumpled tents. Some had drums and masks. One dragged a dummy in top hat and banker's suit noosed to a stick. They were young and old, unwashed, tired, defiant.

Disintegration, thought Claire. *Unraveling.*

They weren't walking or running; they were marching. Inside, the streetcar was silent.

The black gentleman gave a thumbs-up through the window. "That's right," he said. The old woman nodded and clutched her grocery bag. The Goth suddenly bolted out the door, blending into the mob.

The conductor asked everyone to remain seated. The black gentleman got off, folded into the crowd.

Claire took his seat.

—ɯɯ—

"I'm surprised you didn't join in," Clay called down later, while changing upstairs. "How would I have gotten home?" Claire asked, remote in hand. The mayor had ordered the forced evacuation of the Federal

Reserve protest, fearing the Oakland violence would spread. Tear gas. Seventy-six arrests. Blood.

"They *do* have a point," she added, watching the news. "The protesters, I mean."

"What was that?" Clay called from the walk-in upstairs. Claire repeated it, and Clay, thinking, said, "Yes. They do."

"Why did you head straight into that mess in the first place?" He laughed, padding down the stairs, shirtless, on his way to the dryer. "You looking for trouble?"

"That mess," Claire said, muting the report, "is everywhere."

They begged off from Slade and Nora's dinner invitation—a new Peruvian spot near the Presidio—and curled up for the first time in their living room, streaming a *Frontline* documentary about the anthrax investigation from their just-set-up Netflix.

While Clay slept, Claire made her next day's to-do list and checked in with the Mask, whom she now also followed on Twitter and Facebook. He acknowledged the day's crackdown and announced, with calm, crisp diction, a new strategy targeting the one percent, at their homes.

Paint upstairs—9 a.m., Claire wrote. *DMV application—1 p.m. Yoga— 2 p.m.*

The Mask listed names on the scrolling sidebar. Slade's was prominent. The point-zero-one percent.

Cheese/crackers/wine—Claire scribbled, in case the in-laws came up before dinner (count on it).

"We know the enemy," Anonymous said. "We know where you live."

Slade/Nora—7 p.m. deYoung—8 p.m. Home—10:30.

"Expect us."

The Mask tipped his head politely. In the distance, a car alarm sounded.

Fix the downstairs door, Claire underlined.

Chapter Five

"They must have left it on the moving van." Claire paced the kitchen with her cell and chamomile. "A small tackle box. Marked 'Claire, Personal.'

"You can't miss it," she added. "It's bright red."

"It's very important I find it," she stressed. "Thank you."

"I thought you signed off on everything," Clay said after she hung up. She'd let him sleep while she searched downstairs. Unsuccessful, she'd attacked the bedroom, nursery, bathroom, upending everything. She'd run down to the garage and checked the Mustang's trunk. She'd called Mrs. Biddle, their dear old landlady in Santa Fe. No luck.

"It'll turn up." Clay yawned over coffee. "It's not like it's valuable."

"My birth certificate, medical records, *jewelry*," Claire snapped. "No, Clay, not valuable. Just my whole life."

How many workers had been in their apartment the past few days? How many deliveries? The cable guy had been well dressed and hadn't left her sight. The tailor had been with Clay, although his young apprentice had run in and out a few times, through the *broken, unlocked* outer door. The alarm technician had been all over, for hours, securing every window. Now she couldn't even remember the alarm code.

Gas hookup, grocery boy, flower delivery—a tastefully extravagant arrangement of pink and blue roses from Slade and Nora, for which she'd planned to write a thank-you note first thing this morning, if only her stationery weren't in the missing red box!

She had run upstairs to get the flower man a tip, she remembered, leaving him alone.

Stop it, Claire, she scolded herself.

"I thought you packed it with the rest of the boxes," Clay said.

"I don't know," Claire replied. "We were *rushed,* remember?" And *someone* wasn't very helpful. Had she seen it since they arrived? No. She would have put it someplace obvious.

She couldn't get her driver's license without her birth certificate. She couldn't teach without her documents and accreditations. All replaceable, with enough bureaucratic hassle and delay. The jewelry was costume and forgettable; she'd packed her good stuff in her suitcase.

The problem was the confusion, the mystery. Claire didn't like either. Especially the confusion.

"Did you get any sleep at all?" Clay asked, holding her face for a belated morning kiss.

Not much in the past four nights. That didn't help. But knowing that lack of sleep was part of her problem and the potential root of her anxiety made it worse. Which was causing which?

She worried about vaccines, air quality, Clay's new job, the clothes she would need as she got fatter—soon. *How fat?* she wondered and worried. Negotiations for a new car. The driving test on unfamiliar and busy, steep streets.

Where would she park the new car, with only one space? Was street parking safe in their neighborhood, with the nightly Hooverville and quasi-aggressive homeless who sometimes, when it rained, took shelter in the building's lobby? They seemed harmless and polite—almost apologetic—but might one of them be deranged, even dangerous? It took only one.

"They're fixing the door on Monday," Clay said. "They promised."

What if the new door angered one of them? By locking them out in the rain?

Clay mixed the milk paint in the splattering sink. Did he measure correctly? It had to be precise, or the color would be off. Permanently, on-the-wall off.

"Let me do it," she said. "Go tape the moldings. The *blue* tape."

"And the drop cloths," she added as he footed upstairs. "Spread them correctly." Then, in afterthought, she said, "Please."

She worried about the chemicals from the building's renovation. The gloss on the Neutra-esque wooden stairs. If they'd found—and properly removed—asbestos. Many old buildings had it, deadly when unsettled and airborne, like anthrax.

She worried about autism. How could she not? It had jumped seventy-eight percent in the last decade.

"Martha, I'll call you back in five," she said when her phone piggybacked calls as she measured paint powder. The movers were beeping in, still searching for her box. They would contact their other local deliveries for mix-ups but couldn't give out names, for privacy reasons. Claire thanked them and hung up.

They should have rented a U-Haul and moved themselves, but Clay's Mustang couldn't have pulled a trailer that far. *Irrelevant now*, she told herself, second-guessing the measuring cup.

How long had the movers' truck been sitting open on the street that day, for anyone to help themselves? It wasn't her job to think of that. But nothing else was missing, as far as she knew. She'd taped and labeled the contents of each box carefully: kitchen/bathroom/bedroom/odds and ends. She'd untaped and unpacked them all herself, albeit in a rush.

It started raining outside. It was always damp in this town. She worried about toxic mold. It caused asthma in children.

"I'll do the edges, honey," Clay offered. "You do the roller." He was better with a brush, especially with her trembling hands. "You were right about the color," he added.

Her iPhone under the dresser drop cloth kept buzzing new e-mails. Facebook/Twitter updates, she knew—new postings, names, addresses—from the anarchist with the clichéd, grinning mask. Giving orders to its vigilante followers to escalate the mayhem and destruction, fomenting—*inciting*—violence; keeping her city, and cities worldwide, on edge. The Mask had crossed the line.

Thanks for that introduction, Martha, she thought. Martha definitely needed a boyfriend.

She forgot to call Martha back. She didn't want to.

"My parents won't want snacks," Clay said as she dressed for a market run while the first coat dried. "They're just picking us up."

"I have to offer them *something*," Claire stressed, fishing her phone from under the cloth. "What would your mother think?" Men didn't understand these things. "Have you seen the umbrella?"

Anonymous, she'd Wiki-learned, had a disturbing history since it first materialized—from where, no one knew—on the Internet ten years ago, quickly spreading. It started with website hackings—criminal, but pranklike and essentially harmless—before escalating to full-blown protests worldwide. It claimed credit for the violent clashes of the last G8 Summit, the WTO conference in Zurich, the Arab Spring.

The brown Chevelle stopped to let her cross in the rain. She waved a thank-you.

In retaliation for various alleged offenses, it targeted Facebook, Bank of America, the Knesset in Israel. It targeted the San Francisco BART for shutting down cell service in their stations, which, ironically, had been a precaution against violent threats spread through social media. High-tech anarchists, they were. Terrorists, really.

Now it targeted individuals by name. And address.

It promised more retaliation.

Expect us.

At the K&L wine store she picked up a Cameron Hughes Meritage and a Riesling—good and reasonable. She darted through the rain to the high-quality, unfriendly Rainbow Grocery for artisanal cheeses.

At night, in the dark silence, when she couldn't sleep, she'd scrolled through previous video messages from San Francisco Anonymous. There were dozens, hundreds, in chronological order of threat, all with the same Noël Coward–esque British diction, and computer-animated mask. Last November, it had taken aim at Dean on the eve of his election. It had vowed to end the "Willing Dynasty." It promised "disruption," without specifics.

The morning after Dean's murder—*assassination*, it called it—Anonymous gloated without taking credit. It called the murder "not surprising" and "a warning shot." The Mask was clownish, knowing, *smug.*

"ID?" the surly Rainbow cashier boy demanded when she swiped her debit card. He studied her New Mexico license longer than necessary, she thought. "I haven't gotten my California one yet," she explained and heard apology in her voice.

"Willing," he said louder than necessary, and Claire shut her wallet and smiled back at the line and up to the baggers, avoiding their eyes.

"Oh, I need one of these." Claire took a reusable cloth bag from the rack and paid cash. She bagged her own and smiled a last time before giving up on the cashier.

Willing—a common last name that meant nothing in Santa Fe. It meant something here. Nora was right: They should get unlisted. Today.

Claire hurried home in the rain, hoping Clay had finished painting upstairs. His parents would want the full tour.

The Anonymous site had links to other websites—crazy, conspiracy sites—with kooky warnings from hotted-up freaks about the Federal Reserve, the collapsing dollar, police state surveillance, poisonous vaccines (called "government shots"), population control. They sounded the alarm about a "prison planet" and "shadow government" and the "New World Order"—Martha had clearly spent too much time on these sites—and the links led to more links, and if one were up at night, unable to sleep, one could spend hours falling deeper into the spiral, until morning was in the room and it was time to start the day.

"Thank you," she said to the homeless man she recognized when he held open her lobby door. The landing wasn't much cover. "Would you... like to come inside?" she asked. "Into the lobby?"

"No, thank you," he responded, smiling. His long overcoat was wool—warm but wet. Claire straddled the threshold, set down her bag inside, and shook out her umbrella, away from him.

"Here." She held it out. "You need this."

"No, thank you," he repeated.

"No, really. I have another one," she insisted.

"Thank you," he said, taking it. "I do need it."

He was still smiling at her as the elevator door closed.

Remove our name from the keypad, Claire noted to herself. *On Monday. When they fix the door.*

—⁊⁊—

That night, when Claire lost her child, would forever remain a blur.

Clay had finished the second coat by the time she returned. The gray-blue still seemed too dark, but it would lighten, she hoped, once dry and when the skies brightened, if they ever did.

There were more flowers and deliveries. Pink and blue hydrangeas from Madison, plus a shimmery gown in a hanging bag, a generous loaner for the night; lilies and eucalyptus from Edie; an elaborately wrapped housewarming care package of Agraria candles and bath salts from a Mrs. Rathbone. It looked and smelled expensive.

"Christmas in February." Clay laughed as Claire opened the cards of "baby" congratulations. She didn't recognize most of the names. "Club folks," Clay explained. "Overkill. Not surprising."

And bad luck, Claire thought, *in the first trimester. Thanks, Slade.*

On the kitchen counter—tucked among the flowers and candles and, weirdly, an ornate metal birdcage with two stuffed parakeets perched over a nest with a single egg ("Clancy." Clay pegged it to the club's dandy, who owned an estate antiques store as a hobby)—sat a reed basket with two chilled bottles of champagne.

One Veuve Cliquot, one Martinelli's sparkling cider.

Attached was an envelope, already opened, with a heavy-stock cream card embossed with the Union Club's interlocking insignia in burgundy. The message was preprinted.

The membership committee welcomed them without fanfare.

"Oh, Clay, what is this?" Claire tucked her card hand on her hip. Clay's returning laugh was infectious, and she joined him. But still. "What have you done?" she pressed.

"It's nothing," he said, reaching for the card, which she pulled back. "It's hardly nothing," she corrected. "Did you join?"

"*No*," Clay insisted. "It doesn't work that way."

He explained it was a "provisional" membership, lacking full privileges, common for adult children of members. They could come and go, for meals, select parties and events, or just a quiet refuge from the city. Or not.

"It's an audition," he said, shrugging.

"It's very presumptuous of them," said Claire. "And it's not like us. Private clubs, I mean." She thought and then said, "I mean, it's not like *me*."

"So forget about it," Clay said. "I'll probably only use it for business lunches...."

"And I think it's dangerous," she added. Clay laughed once and stopped. "Dangerous?" he asked.

"This segregation, this exclusive *caste* system. It's wrong, and it's making people...angry."

"Claire." He looked at her, inspecting her. "It's just a building. An old house."

"*They* don't see it that way," she said, pointing out the window, at the television.

"Who's 'they?'" Clay asked. "What are you talking about?"

"We're already saddled with this last name, you've joined your father's company, why put another target on our backs?" A poor choice of words she regretted but stuck to. Her pregnancy book said her heart rate shouldn't go above 135. She needed to get a monitor.

"Claire. Honey." Clay wrapped his arms around her. "You're trembling.

"Where did all this angst come from?" he asked. She told him.

"A cartoon mask?" He laughed.

"It's not funny, Clay," she scolded when he threatened to cut off her Internet privileges.

"No one's out to get us," he said. "No one's paying any attention to us.

"And the rest of this stuff," he added—the window, the TV—"will settle down, eventually.

"All this anxiety, it can't be good for the baby," he said. "Is that what you're worried about? Is there something wrong with the baby?"

"Why would you say that?" she asked.

"Just making sure it's not a symptom of something," he said. "Do you need to see a doctor?"

"I'm going next week," she said. "The baby is fine."

"Good," he said. "Then nothing else matters." He took the Union's card, folded and tore it in half. "Do *not* give this stupid thing any more thought."

"Let's cancel tonight," Clay said. "The weather sucks."

Claire shook her head. "No. Your mother wants to show you off. She'll blame me." Clay laughed and said, "We'll go to the next one. There's one every week. At least."

"I'm fine," Claire insisted. "And Madison lent me a gown. A nice one."

"I refuse," she added, "to succumb to the prepartum crazies."

"Are you sure?" he asked, unwrapping the Veuve foil. He popped the cork.

"That club is so funny," she said, picking up the familiar sparkling cider. "But thoughtful."

"Bring it upstairs," Clay said, stroking her face. "We've got a couple hours to kill."

She checked the label. Same as the one at the club. All-natural. Gluten-free.

Claire popped the cork.

—⁄⁄⁄—

Clay's touch was all she needed. It did the trick every time.

She slipped out of bed and bathed while he napped. The rain thrummed outside as she soaked in her new Agraria salts. Her pulse was calm and steady.

She looked forward to the party, the dinner, the deYoung. She looked forward to making new friends. "Younger than the art," Nora had promised. Madison would introduce her around.

Her mind recalibrated, her reason returned. The panic that had mounted over the past few days was false and chemical, detached from reality. She knew the symptoms well. They kicked in with each move—cities, apartments, foster homes—what her therapist at Yale called "a vital need to control the environment." Everybody had it; Claire had it worse. Her chaotic adolescence spawned a constant search for stability and order, for routine. Anything less, and her fertile imagination would paint in the darkest, most preposterous and unrelated doomsday scenarios. "Don't go looking for ghosts," her therapist, paraphrasing Ibsen, urged her. Claire thought she'd improved. This week, her latest transition, a temporary setback to bad habits. "Don't beat yourself up," her therapist would say. "Get back on the horse."

Clay was right: Nobody was out to get them. Or even paying attention. Why would they? They weren't celebrities, or royalty.

It's a big city, Claire thought with a smile. *Don't flatter yourself.*

New apartment fine. Husband fine. Baby fine. She rested her hand on her stomach.

Tasting suds, she woke with a start in the hot bath. She could soak for hours. Tonight she'd sleep well. And sleep in finally. She briefly considered Clay's offer to skip the party, but it was too late to cancel on Slade and Nora. She'd shake off her fatigue.

Wanding the Waterworks hand shower, she rinsed her hair. Brushed, blew it straight. Light makeup. Spritzed Tresor, Clay's favorite. Hers too.

Snap out of it, she ordered herself, yawning. She wrapped herself in her terry robe. Took another swig of cider from the bedside table while Clay snored on. She needed the sugar jolt.

"Wake up." She shook his shoulder. "Your parents will be here soon." She found and kissed his forehead, steadying herself on the mattress. He mumbled resistance. She pulled back the covers and smacked his bare behind. "*Ándele!*" she commanded.

"Okay!" He relented and rolled out, yawning. Claire unbagged Madison's gown—freshly cleaned, tissued, and perfect.

"You okay?" Clay laughed. "Hmm?" Claire asked. "You're swaying," he said.

"Just sleepy," she said. "I'm okay." "I said we don't have to—" Clay started, but Claire cut him off. "We. Do." Clay held her face and ran his finger under her bottom lip. "You painted outside the lines," he said, his finger pink with lipstick.

"I did?" Claire asked, touching her face. It was hot.

"Heavy on the mascara?" he asked. "Is that the new thing?" "What?" she puzzled, wondering why the bathroom mirror seemed so far away.

Downstairs, the phone rang.

"Clay, hurry!" She pushed him naked toward the shower. "They're probably on their way."

"Remind Mom to TiVo the Coyotes," he called back, turning on the shower. "Our HD's not working yet." "Yes," Claire said, opening the door to the ringing below.

The apartment was pitch-black. She fanned her hand along the wall, found no switch, peered down. The lights off the distant Bay were blurry and pulsing, and the phone was screaming, the in-laws calling.

Claire swooned on the stairs, clutched the banister, foot-felt her way down on the bare slats, one at a time. The cordless phone strobed red from its cradle, in sync with its ringing. Across the white Silestone counter sliced a sharp triangle of light—a bright, welcome target that oriented her in the darkness.

A light that spilled through the front door, ajar.

"Clay?" she called up to the running shower. "Did you leave the front door open?"

The door slowly creaked shut. The light gone. The phone rang. The wind whistled; the rain thrummed.

Claire felt cold, wet prints under her bare feet.

Expect us, she thought in the blackness.

Claire moved toward the strobing light on the screaming phone, past the inset microwave that blinked 6:13 in green. She banged her hip on the counter and flung out her hand, overreaching and knocking the phone off its cradle. It clattered across the floor, facedown, light lost.

Her legs slewed out from under her, an involuntary reaction. She made them work again, but the presence was closer in the room, the ringing phone hidden and useless. She turned too quickly, dizzying herself, toward the sound and light, across the room and upstairs, where her husband showered. The glossy slats—dozens, hundreds—bounced light from the window.

Her left leg now undependable, she hobbled and clutched toward the staircase. A chair upended and fell backward. The presence, in no hurry, followed. Her right leg joined her left and she collapsed on the stairs, one hand clawing up, the other shielding her womb.

Upstairs, the shower stopped. Her husband's voice echoed down. The phone kept ringing.

Her throat dry, brittle, unresponsive, she called out feebly and felt a sharp spasm in her neck that switched off her arms. She slid into the strong, protective hands of her attacker.

"Please," she mumbled, submitting to peaceful exhaustion. "I'm pregnant." Her attacker cradled her, buffered her head from the stairs, smoothed her hair. Clay's jaunty voice echoed from above, a casual question she could neither decipher nor answer. The powerful arms carried her down, laid her delicately on the floor, preparing her. Removed her limp, disobedient arm from her stomach and gently turned, exposed it. It swabbed the crook with a cotton ball, a glistening stamp over a vein. The hand drew back and returned gloved in rubber, aiming a syringe whose needle caught the light.

"No, no, no," Claire mumbled in the silence, her hand, barely enlivened, pushing back, flicking spastically. The phone had stopped ringing. Clay's voice echoed again. The gloved hands moved quickly, eased her head back. She looked into the darkness and felt nothing but warmth and security, and her dizziness settled when she submitted and closed her eyes.

"Tickets please!" the carny barked, but Claire had special privileges because she was pregnant. Not just front-of-the-line, but a private ride through the haunted house at the Florida State Fair. The car was jerky on the track, as it should be, but it was flat-backed for extra thrills, and Claire peered up through the blurry darkness at the tunnel's ceiling lanterns that trafficked by. The kind man who had carried her pushed from behind, steadied as they turned a corner. She rolled her head to the side toward a boarded-up tunnel door, expecting a ghoul to jump out, but it was a misdirect, and she knew the real scares lay ahead.

Clay—fearless snowboarder, skydiver, and extreme sports daredevil—got wiggy on indoor rides and waited on the other side. Above, in the distance, the children's train cling-clanged its happy bell as it whirred along the track. Claire wanted to ride that next, but first she had to make it through the twists and shocks that were coming. She hoped they wouldn't scare the baby inside her, and she moved to cover her stomach, but they had strapped her arms down for her own safety.

The track was rickety and jolting, for maximum insecurity, especially as she rattled up an incline, feetfirst. She was at the end of the ride now, disappointingly thrill-free, and the fair's workers in their white uniforms scurried around the exit bay, cavernous and ornate with an intricate Guastavino tiled, arched ceiling—an elaborate facade tedious to dismantle when they traveled to the next city. She turned her head to glittering murals of hills and trees and clouds, squinted to make out the elaborate mosaics that ringed the ride. Nora was a few cars ahead and cleared the floor when she got out, livid at another passenger who had tried to cut the line earlier. "That fucking bastard!" she railed. "Did he really think he was going to get away with this? How *dumb* does he think we are?"

Claire giggled, thankful not to be the target of Nora's fury. She lifted her head off the pillow to watch the showdown, but Slade in his tuxedo was already trying to calm his wife in her midnight-blue evening gown with simple pearls. Nora was understandably testy, having so overdressed for the fair, and was in no mood for soothing. "If you won't stand up to him, I will!" she raged, finger stabbing his chest with rhythmic punctuation. "Who makes the rules here now? *You* or *him*?" "Neither," Slade said, trying to lower the temperature. "You know that."

The kind man pushing Claire's car eased her head back on the pillow—thoughtful, as her neck was getting tired, like the rest of her. And anyway, she didn't want Nora to catch her looking at such a public meltdown she'd likely regret later. "I'm not backing down this time!" she roared louder. "I want a goddamned *appeal*. I want it *now*. I want no fucking *backtalk*!"

Claire's car came to a stop in a white room under blinding lights, and craving a corn dog, she was ready to unbuckle and go. The man undid her straps and unknotted the belt around her waist from the special robe they had given her. "No, thank you," she whispered, because she was naked underneath, but they needed it for the next rider and slipped it off her body anyway.

"Fine," Slade said in the corner of the room, "but we have to do this now. It'll only get worse if we wait." The ride workers rushed to her side and put a sheet over to keep her warm and placed her feet on special pedals to help her balance, and Slade said, "Make sure she doesn't remember any of this." "She won't, sir," one of the workers said, and because of a chemical spill, which made the room smell too-sharply clean, they wore masks over their noses and mouths and thoughtfully brought her one, too. She initially declined, because she could make it out on her own—and go find Clay, and get a corn dog, and take him on the little train with its happy bell—but they gently insisted, and she didn't want to make trouble, and it was the right decision for the baby, and her calm breathing echoed into the mask.

It was cruel of them to make her pass by her mother on the way out, especially in her withered, non-wigged, nonresponsive condition. They had raised her hospital bed too high, and Claire had to stand on her tip-toes and peer past a mechanical jungle of contraptions that beeped and ticked and breathed robotically. She reached up to touch her mother's gray hand, but the tall nurse kept her at a distance, lest she dislodge the plastic tubes that snaked into her in all places. She'd never liked these nurses, and today they were very disrespectful, mimicking Slade and Nora from the hospital room door. Nurse Nora said, "Where's Clay?" and Nurse Slade said, "He's waiting upstairs. We should explain it together." But they stayed and watched her because she was wearing her mother's favorite Sunday outfit and had curled her own hair and wiped down her patent-leather shoes to look her best, but her mother had already said goodbye just before she arrived, and the machine's slow beeping got slower and became a solid alarm.

The nurses rushed to comfort her as she collapsed with a stomach hurt, which she often got when scared, but this was worse and piercing, because her mother was now dead, and she was alone and terrified.

Chapter Six

Claire was warm and comfortable. She heard the high-pitched beeping and sporadic, muffled voices she recognized. She knew where she was, in the aftermath of a crisis that had passed, and now she was safe. She was too exhausted to open her eyes, and she slept.

"She's awake," Nora said from across the room in her midnight-blue evening gown, and Claire mumbled, "Not yet," and slept again.

A nurse checked her blood pressure, her temperature, and her pulse, but Claire wasn't ready to talk, to hear answers she already knew.

Clay was bedside when she came to. He wore a navy hooded sweatshirt and his carpenter jeans and Red Wings baseball cap. He smiled but looked stricken and gently smoothed her hair from her forehead. "Hey, princess," he said in his morning voice. "How you feeling?"

Her arm, heavy but working, went to her still-tender stomach. "The baby," she said. "Careful," he said, her arm linked to a plastic drip tube and beeping pulse monitor next to the bed. "The baby," Claire repeated. "You're fine," Clay soothed. "You're okay now." His eyes were red.

The baby was dead, of course. Claire slept while Clay tried to rub her hand warm.

She felt Nora's presence and woke again. "Hi, honey," Nora said softly, carrying a floral Neiman Marcus shopping bag. Now she wore a deep purple cable-knit turtleneck under an olive quilted vest with slim khaki jodhpurs that few women half her age could pull off. She held a Starbucks tall and wore more makeup than Claire remembered. She had on tortoiseshell glasses and said with apology, "Sorry I'm just getting here, but Neiman's opens late on Sundays, and...you know..." She pointed to Claire's thin hospital gown. "We'll get you changed in a little while," she added, raising the bag.

The hospital room resembled a deluxe hotel suite, but the bed was standard. Clay still held her hand, and Claire slept.

"Did they catch him?" Claire asked when she woke again. Nora stopped texting from the upholstered chair by the television. "Catch whom?" she asked sharply. Clay roused from dozing bedside and said, "What?" and Nora, alert and straight, repeated, "Catch *whom*, Claire?"

"There was a man," Claire said, ransacking her memory. "In the apartment."

"You blacked out," Clay explained. "At the bottom of the stairs. We're lucky you didn't break your neck."

"She says there was a man," Nora said, now closer, and Clay said, "There were *two*, once the ambulance arrived. EMTs." "Is that what you remember?" Nora asked.

"A man. With a needle," Claire said, searching. "They gave you a shot," Clay said, nodding, "to stabilize you. Your blood pressure was very low." He pointed to the tubed needle in the crook of her arm. "And now you're getting fluids. Now you're okay, Claire."

Clay had found her unconscious, right after his shower. The ringing phone had been Nora, to let her know they were on their way. Clay had called an ambulance and then his parents, who met them at the hospital, where she'd seen, hazily, Nora in her midnight-blue evening gown and Slade in his tux. In the ER, or recovery room.

"But you're okay now," Clay repeated, rubbing both hands again. "They were so cold when I found you. They're warmer now."

The attending doctor, slightly north of Claire's age and eagerly thorough, made his rounds and explained from her chart their diagnosis. All signs pointed to a "vasovagal attack," which he described as "transient" and typically brought on by "emotional stress and fear."

"Real or imagined," he said, "it doesn't matter." Accumulated anxiety, he said, could also trigger an attack. It was, he said, a "not uncommon" cause of miscarriage.

"I'm very sorry," he said, meaning it, and Claire said, "Thank you."

After he left, she said, "I'm so sorry," to Clay, who held her face and kissed her forehead and said, "No, princess. No." She felt his left-behind tear.

"Do you remember the EMTs?" Nora prodded. "Or do you think there was *another* man there? Beforehand?"

"I...I don't know," Claire said, and she didn't. "I would have seen him," Clay said. "If there's any question, any *doubt*," Nora said, "the chief of police is a friend of Slade. We'll go straight to him."

She remembered the gurney, being flat on her back and wheeled and gently lifted by strong arms that weren't Clay's. She remembered the front door ajar, spilling a triangle of light onto the kitchen counter before swinging shut. But she also knew her hands and mind had been full when she'd returned from her shopping trip earlier and couldn't recall, with certainty, if she'd closed it firmly. The outside wind, through a cracked door or window anywhere in the building, could have just as easily blown it both ways.

She only knew her baby was dead.

Slade, dressed Sunday-casual, tiptoed into the room, and before he could unpack the boxed brunch from orange Ella's bags, Nora said,

"Claire thinks she was attacked." Slade looked over from the suite's dining room table and said, "Attacked? By whom?"

Claire said, "I didn't say that. I'm not sure if—"

"Well, she *thinks* she was," Nora interrupted, still looking at Slade. "And if there's any suspicion of that, even a *suspicion*, I said you'd call Ernie and he'd put his best detectives on the case. I'm sure they'd come over right now and get to the bottom of it.

"Because we'd all like to know *exactly* what happened," she added. It seemed a challenge, bordering on taunt.

"Well, I don't want to bother the chief of police if there's no evidence," Slade said carefully, inspecting Claire. "Can you describe this person?"

"I'm not sure there was a person," Claire said, regretting she'd mentioned it, and Nora said to Slade, "It's not a bother. It's Ernie's *job*. I'm sure his best detectives would ask the right questions to trigger her memory. They're professionals.

"Because if someone attacked an *expectant mother*," she went on, punching words, "which resulted in the *loss of a child*..."

"Mom, please," Clay said. "Let her rest."

"...then that person should be behind bars..." Nora trailed off and sat in the chair by the television and murmured, "For a long time."

Claire dozed fitfully while Slade heated his chicken hash in the kitchenette's microwave and Nora picked grumpily at her Cobb salad ("I said dressing on the *side*, Slade; it's all soupy now"). They chatted in hushed tones with time-passing topics of his upcoming business trips, the dashboard light on her car, the neighbor's creeping hedge that blocked their view. Claire peered past the heavy drapes onto a vast park far off and down—"The Presidio," Clay pointed out—while the nurse took her vitals and announced her discharge for the following morning. "You're all good," she said, smiling and unhooking her drip, gauzing the wound. "Just a little more observation." Clay ran back to the apartment for her shampoo and a change of clothes.

"You don't need to stay," Claire assured her in-laws. "I'm fine. I'm doing much better." Her fog and anxiety were gone, and only the slight discomfort and tinge of violation that followed a gynecological exam remained. Slade checked his watch and said, "I do have a board meeting at the club," and Nora said, "I'm going with you." Slade hesitated, and Nora said, "*What?* I have a piece of *business* to introduce."

They waited for Clay to return and promised to come back later, and with the nurse's help, Claire showered and styled and felt Carole-Lombard glamorous in the ivory silk boyfriend pajamas and pale pink La Perla cashmere robe Nora had brought from Neiman's. Clay had, surprisingly, remembered her compact, and she was smoothing lipstick when a shocked Martha in blue scrubs stormed in.

"When a Willing is admitted to the Willing Wing," she said, "they put out an APB around here." Claire explained, and there were tears and hugs, and Martha balanced her humor, alternating hats between best friend and on-duty pro. "It's unfortunate and a bummer," Martha said, putting it in perspective with impressive bedside finesse, "but it's not tragic. It could be worse." "I know," Claire agreed. "I'll be fine."

"I'm very sorry," Martha said to Clay, who hovered and thanked her.

"My gyn is here on a delivery," she added. "I'll send her by before she leaves, to look over your charts. She's marvelous." Clay cautioned that Claire needed rest, and Martha said, "She's a physician, not a drill sergeant." Claire said, "Please send her by," and Martha's phone buzzed, and she kissed Claire on the forehead and told her she looked like a movie star, "a queen, really," and promised, with a hand squeeze, to check back the next morning.

Dr. Kerr was lovely—a blond Julianne Moore—with a lilting, peppy voice that belied a crackerjack mind. She sipped a pink smoothie from a Styrofoam cup. "The only meal I have time for these days," she said, laughing. After condolences to Claire and Clay, she noted "trace irregularities" in Claire's blood work—"just slight elevations in certain areas"—that she attributed to the stabilizing shots the EMTs administered at the scene. After ruling out alcohol and prescription meds— "None," Claire insisted. "None at all"—and asking more lifestyle questions, she rechecked her chart quizzically and then dismissed these "rapid tests" as often unreliable with false positives of "this and that."

"Come by my office next week for more thorough ones," Dr. Kerr invited, and Claire said, "I will. Thank you."

"Miscarriages are not uncommon in first pregnancies," she explained with tender professionalism. "Sometimes the body isn't ready, or the fetus has abnormalities your system corrects early on. It doesn't mean you can't conceive and carry successfully to term next time."

"Have you experienced unusual stress or anxiety lately?" Dr. Kerr asked simply, perched on the side of the bed. Claire glanced at Clay with a tinge of apology and confessed, "Yes. Yes, I have." "Starting when? Do you remember?" the doctor pressed.

"We just moved here," Clay said. "Rather suddenly." Dr. Kerr nodded without looking at him, her eyes still trained on Claire. "It started the day after," Claire said. "It just sorta of crept up. I don't know why." She was too embarrassed to mention her Anonymous obsession, which now seemed ignorantly paranoid and ridiculously based on nothing real. And eons ago. And over.

"Did you eat or drink anything unusual that day? Or the night before?" the doctor asked. Claire thought and said, "I was nauseous the night before. For the first time." She hadn't touched the too-rare prime rib at the club, but she'd had one bite of the custard dessert. "That wouldn't be a problem," Dr. Kerr dismissed. "We probably won't figure this out."

"The last thing before I fell that night, on the staircase, was a spasm. In my neck," Claire added, having just remembered. "Like someone had..." She stopped and thought and said, "Well, like a spasm."

Dr. Kerr nodded and said, "Muscle spasms are often manifestations of extreme levels of stress.

"And stress is a significant cause of miscarriage," Dr. Kerr explained. "We don't typically tell our patients that because it tends to cause more stress. We'll keep an eye on that when you're ready to try again." She stood up.

"I'm glad you're feeling better. You look great. Martha thinks the world of you." She left her card. "Come see me for those tests." She was gone.

"New age," Clay discounted, and Claire said, "She's wonderful."

Claire was hungry, and Clay called ahead to his parents, and after a dinner of hot-and-sour matzo ball soup and kung pao blinis from a new Asian/Jewish mash-up Slade had discovered and which confounded his wife, Nora announced abruptly, "We don't think you should return to that apartment. We think that well has been poisoned."

"We don't advocate living in fear," Slade added. "Just prudence."

"That neighborhood, that building," Nora said, shaking her head. "Plus you're listed and anybody can track you down. I say start fresh. Out of an abundance of caution." Clay seemed startled and said, "We can discuss it," and Claire startled herself by saying, "I agree with them."

"I don't feel comfortable there," she said. "It's not the right place for us."

"And Clay will be traveling quite a bit until the merger is done," Slade added, sealing the deal with his unspoken implications.

"The sad truth," Nora said, shrugging, "is that although we try to be a normal family, we're just not."

"Where would we move?" Clay asked, and Nora said, "Someplace else."

"I'll put my Realtor on it," Nora offered. "There's no rush. In the meantime, you're welcome to stay with us."

Clay's glance to Claire said, *No way*, and hers back to him said, *Ditto.* But she said, "That's very kind of you, Nora."

"But since I doubt that appeals to you," Nora continued, "we're happy to put you up at the club. Our treat."

"Oh," said Claire.

"The guest rooms are quite nice," Nora said. "Especially the Flick Suite." "That's reserved for visiting dignitaries," Slade reminded Nora, who replied, "Then *unreserve* it, *el Presidente.*"

"You'd be doing us a favor," Nora added, "since we never use up the club minimum and have to pay it anyway. Such a waste."

"Yes, I think the club is our best option," she went on. "Until we get everything sorted out."

"Stay as long as you need until you find the perfect place." Nora finished her pitch and made a face. "Good grief, are these *pastrami* egg rolls? Slade, no one's pregnant anymore."

"That's...very generous," Claire said, and Clay, squeezing her hand under the table, said, "We'll talk it over, Mom."

After his parents left, Clay said to Claire, "It's no different from a hotel. Except more private. And cheaper. Although we don't need to worry about that."

"Well, I *do* worry about that," Claire said, leery of racking up her in-laws' tab, but leerier of returning to the apartment building on a sketchy street with the broken doors, ongoing construction, and revolving Hooverville. With the listed address and phone number that would be futile to fix and reverse now. The apartment she'd taken sight unseen— off the Internet!—and where she'd yet to sleep soundly. With the ten-day "out" clause baked into the lease so they'd only forfeit their security deposit.

The poisoned well her mother-in-law, who knew the city much better than she, urged them leave "out of an abundance of caution." With which her father-in-law, who practically owned the town, agreed out of "prudence."

"Let's do it," Claire said. "Just temporarily. I'll find us a new place soon."

Clay showered in the hospital suite, and the nurse converted his chair into a twin-sized bed with sheets, pillow, and blanket. But he curled up next to Claire in her hospital bed at 8:47 p.m., and they slept, interlocked and breathing together, through sunrise, until breakfast came.

—ɯ—

"There's a turn-lock inside, for privacy," Allen said proudly, opening the door to the Flick Suite. "But no need to lock the door when you're gone."

The eager attending doctor had signed off on her discharge during his morning rounds and had added his praise of Dr. Kerr —"My wife swears by her. All her friends, too."—as he'd written out a course of antibiotics. Claire thanked the floor nurses as Clay wheeled her out, protesting that she was perfectly fine to walk, and Jess had been waiting in Nora's hunter-green Range Rover to load in and drive them to the club. "An exceptionally fine morning," he said, beaming, and Claire rode shotgun and said, "Thank you, Jess, but we really could have taken a cab."

"Clay, do you have my cell?" she asked. "I need to call Martha."

Martha had snuck into Claire's room predawn while they slept intertwined and left a bedside note in a hasty scrawl. *Too cute. And nauseating. Call later. xx M.*

"It's back at the apartment." Clay yawned from the backseat. "The movers will get it."

"Please run and get it today," she urged. "And my jewelry."

Jess dropped them off at the club's back entrance by the parking lot, and Allen took her bag and whisked them to the elevator, so as not to run into club members in the public areas. "I'm sure you'd like some privacy," he said, and Claire said, "Thank you, Allen."

"Oh my," she said, when he opened the unlocked door to the Flick Suite.

King-sized, hand-carved walnut four-poster bed, stacked with chocolate-brown banker-stripe and herringbone shams, warmed by an olive cashmere cable-knit blanket, softened by deep navy and burgundy paisley linens, canopied over circus-like with black watch tartan drapes lined in silk shirting stripes, tied back with gold braid tassels. Walls upholstered in light brown glen plaid wool tweed above burnished cherry mahogany wainscoting. Muted jewel-toned needlepoint rug over camel low-pile carpeting. Spacious and separate bathrooms: hers—pastel *trompe l'oeil*/polished nickel/marble lattice tile with claw-foot tub and potted orchids; his—darker, haberdashery, gentlemanly. Windsor-green lacquered fireplace crackling pinion during the day, flanked by bronze English firedogs. Pink roses, white lilies, magnolia greens. Regal, worldly, and slightly bohemian.

"Originally Mr. Flick's, when it was his private home," Allen explained with pride. "Mrs. Flick's, too, of course."

"Most of the pieces are original," he added. "From his world travels."

"Is there anything...*less*?" Claire asked of the suite, which took up a full third of the top floor. Allen smiled, crestfallen, and said, "Is this not sufficient, ma'am?" "It's overly sufficient," Claire clarified. "A standard room would be sufficient."

"It's fine," Clay interjected. "Mom requested this one. It's only temporary."

Claire looked from the horsey oil painting to the hand-loomed wall tapestry to the tufted leather tub chair draped with fringed navy windowpane throw to Allen's expectant face. "It's wonderful, Allen. Thank you." She smiled. "It's only temporary."

"The old forced heat system can get a bit stifling up here," he apologized. "The club prefers the outer windows kept shut for security reasons, but the bathroom window facing in can provide a refreshing cross-breeze, if needed." He showed her, and Claire nodded in gratitude. "Yes, that feels nice," she said, peering down into the club's light well.

"Stationery wardrobe for your written correspondence," Allen said, presenting the club's burgundy and ecru letterhead and envelopes organized on the polished secretary. "Just pop it in the slot"—he pointed to the glass mail chute by the door—"and we'll stamp and post for you downstairs." "That's very convenient," said Claire, unable to remember the last time she'd handwritten a letter.

"There's a mini-fridge hidden in the cabinet." Allen indicated toward it. "But I assume you'll be taking your meals downstairs. Or room service, if you prefer." "Thank you, Allen," Claire repeated. "Just think of us as a full-service hotel," Allen said, "for the duration of your visit." He showed her the button on the bedside phone to summon "anything you need."

"Our second honeymoon." Clay trampolined and sprawled across the bed after Allen left, catapulting a sham. Claire peered past the loden velvet drapes, fingered through the dimity sheers, to the club's mostly empty private parking lot below, over to the looming Fairmont, ahead to the views far down Mason Street, water distant off the horizon—the Pacific? the Bay?—and forced a sunny reply.

Clay showered and donned one of his new suits already in residence in his paneled dressing room. Claire dutifully straightened his tie, and he held her close. She assured him she'd be fine and here when he got back from work. "I can skip it," he said, and she shook her head. "It's your first day. And you're already late."

She soaked in the claw-footed tub under the elaborate English garden mural and found her clothes on satin-padded hangers in her floral dressing room and her delicates butterflied and organized in the ebony and gold-painted bombé chest. She considered/unconsidered the cold poached salmon with dill sauce from the room service menu and took an antibiotic and clicked on/off the dismal news with its screaming pundits on the flat screen and put another log from the sea-grass basket onto the fire.

She paced Mr. Flick's bedroom and turned on the bedside Bose preset to a public radio jazz station and flipped through a collection of Flannery O'Connor short stories from the bookshelf before placing it on the brown-striped zebra-skin ottoman in front of the fireplace. She itched to get out for a stroll around the neighborhood—"Gentle exercise only," the young doctor had prescribed for the first two weeks—but the fog was rolling in, and there were footfalls in the hallway outside her door, and the parking lot was fuller now, the club more dauntingly active as the afternoon stretched. She changed back into her white pajamas and pink robe and filed her nails in the lamplight.

Down the hall in the library, the grandfather clock struck something-thirty and gentlemen were warming to cocktails, populating the lounge, and Claire felt a dull pang of residual discomfort in her gut and sat on the upholstered window seat with her feet up and watched Town Cars and rentals unload at the Fairmont until it passed. She watched the light vanish over the Pacific and the gray dusk settle onto Nob Hill and heard her own abrupt, racking sob. Her hand shot to her mouth to muffle the heaving.

Claire wept for the child she had frightened away. Her firstborn she had scared to death.

PHASE II

Chapter One

"**G**ood morning, Ling," Claire said at 7:13 and, "Good afternoon, Ling," at 4:04. "You're here awfully late," she said after dinner, at 9:26. "Don't you ever go home?"

Ling never smiled or responded, but silently brought a continental breakfast and the morning papers—*Times/Journal/Chronicle*—and afternoon tea, and kept the fireplace roaring with relentless, robotic efficiency.

"He doesn't seem very happy, does he?" Claire fretted one night as Clay brushed his teeth. He rinsed and spat and said, "It's a cultural thing. The Chinese don't exactly whistle while they work."

Claire added the thawing of Ling, or at least détente, to her ever-growing Union Club to-do list. After four sequestered days and nights, absolving herself with Clay's steady encouragement—"It's not your fault, honey. We'll try again."—she deemed it self-indulgent and borderline ungracious, as a sudden, unexpected guest, to stay locked away in the club's choicest suite. She forced herself to multitask, mourning in silence.

Nora had kindly offered to find her a therapist, as part of her recovery. "You swing a dead cat in this town, and *each paw* will hit a shrink," she said, but Claire declined for now. She knew from experience and previous therapy that only time healed a painful loss, with forward action the most effective accelerant.

She'd worked through, on her own, the lingering and silly suspicion that she'd been attacked. Several days' rest had cleared and freed her mind. Even Nora had dropped the subject. But her initial fears had been justified, she comforted herself, by the family's recent history. She'd lain awake worrying about Dean's assassination, even though she knew, from the nonstop press coverage at the time, that the gunman was a lone wolf—a Chinese immigrant, unemployed, undocumented, and unhinged. No radical affiliations, no friends or family, just a deranged psychopath who'd snapped. A shamed Chinese government resisted his body's return after security shot him dead in the ballroom.

The story died with him, because there was nothing more to report. No evidence of a conspiracy or wider plot. No specific threat. That existed only in Claire's imagination. Yet her in-laws took any potential threat seriously, which is why she was here, safe and surrounded at their club, out of an "abundance of caution."

A different life this, she told herself, falling asleep more easily with each passing night, tucked in her husband's arms, awaking one morning restless and surefooted. And curious.

After Clay left for the office, more casual since it was Saturday, Claire washed and curled her hair, smoothed pale lipstick, and slipped on a knee-length floral tea dress and sandy cardigan and, breakfast tray in hand, took the elevator to the main floor.

"Good *morning*, Ms. Willing," Allen said brightly, spiriting away her tray. "The brunch buffet is up till noon." "Thank you, Allen," Claire replied. "But we had breakfast in the room."

Clancy came quickly from the dining room, fork in hand, white napkin tucked into his collar. "Won't you join me for a Bellini?" he asked. "Or a biscuit?"

"Everyone drank too much last night," he explained of the semi-full dining room's murmured hush, while Claire picked at a chocolate croissant, "biscuit" being the dandy's generic term for all things carb. Claire smiled at his welcoming effort and asked, "Was there a party last night?"

"There was *drinking*," he answered. "But Stompy didn't play. We didn't want to disturb you." Claire, taken aback, swallowed quickly. "Please," she urged. "You mustn't worry about that. Ever." "Stompy will play again," he assured her, dabbing his corners as a waiter cleared the table. "Stompy always plays again."

A cashmere-wrapped Edie approached Claire at the magazine rack in the "Silence Please" Reading Room after brunch and kissed her on each cheek, European-style, planting traces of luxury perfume. She wagged her finger and touched it to Claire's lips when she started to respond, added a "no explanations needed" look and a final peck on the forehead before whisking away *Foreign Affairs* and *Harper's Bazaar.*

"Oh, hi, dear." Madison embraced her with one arm in the fire-blazing Grand Foyer later. "Allen told me you'd emerged. I'm very sorry about all that stuff." She twirled her hand around her stomach. "Thank you, Madison," Claire replied, briefly flummoxed by the cavalier tone until she realized that compared to what Madison had been through, "all that stuff" certainly seemed minor.

"I hope you don't mind; we went ahead and told everyone," Madison added, signaling the club. "So you don't have to explain it over and over." "I see," Claire said, hiding a wince before agreeing with the wisdom of it. "Well, thank you."

"It is what it is." Madison closed the subject. "I'm just sorry it happened to you."

"How's your room?" Madison asked, laughing. "Did they fix that bipolar shower yet?" "I guess so," Claire answered. "It works fine." And then she said, "Have you stayed there, too?"

Madison nodded. "The week before the election," she said. "Those final days were so intense, and it was just easier to burrow here. Especially since Dean was learning the..." Madison trailed off, lost, and her face tightened before snapping back. "It was just easier," she finished.

"Come to think of it," Madison mused, "we spent our last night in that room. Funny how one blocks things out."

"The room's fine," Claire said. "It's only temporary." Madison smiled thinly.

"If you ever want to talk about...any of that," Claire added, "I'm always happy to—"

"I'm booked up with silly errands today," Madison interrupted, hiking her Birkin higher on her brace-arm shoulder, "which would bore you, but now that you're up and about, I intend to keep you busy." "Thanks, Madison," Claire said, "but I don't want to be a bother." "If you were a bother, I wouldn't offer," Madison replied, starting her journey across the foyer. "Plus I still need your help with that charity stuff."

Madison stopped halfway to the door and turned back. "Did you just call yourself a 'bother'?" she asked rhetorically, shooting a "don't be silly" look before carrying on.

Warmer, thought Claire. *We're getting warmer.*

Claire roamed at will, as the club largely cleared out after brunch. The remaining old coots migrated to the outer wings to read and play backgammon as rain thrummed hypnotically on the Tiffany dome. Claire inspected the club's bulletin board with the schedule of upcoming movie nights (*Frost/Nixon*, *Hoosiers*, *March of the Penguins*), Thursday men's-night speakers ("TBD"), an events calendar for the Masonic Auditorium across the square—Claire doubted there'd be many takers from the club for the Tom Jones concert in March—an ornate, calligraphy reminder about something called the Justice Ball far off in April, lost-and-found alerts (a tortoiseshell Montblanc fountain pen, one faux pearl clip-on earring, a rose porcelain box with half a blue pill), and, most embarrassing, a surprisingly long list of members "in arrears," with names and totals of their running debt. Mr. Randall Nevins topped the deadbeats with a whopping $1,263, and Claire was tempted to pay off Mrs. Amanda Fowler's $6.32 just to get her off the list. Fortunately, the list was Willing-free.

Either Sting had slipped into a coma on its perch, or was already bored with Claire. The fat, speckled creature sat fast asleep on one leg, warmed by the library's fire, as Claire picked through shelves and braved the rolling ladder up to the narrow upper level. There she found nonclassics from famous authors whose better work lived down below. Grouped separately were travel guides—Fodor's, Lonely Planet, Eyewitness—covering an impressive swath of countries and a notably large collection of medical textbooks: Guyton and Hall, Brunner and Suddarth's, the obligatory *Gray's Anatomy*, all current editions. Slightly segregated from the rest, hemmed in by Asian foo dog bookends, was a medical reference shelf in Mandarin Chinese just below eye level, where several gaps suggested more were in circulation.

Claire inched around to a forgotten section, isolated on the bottom shelf. She pulled out an ancient, loosely bound folder of photos and architectural sketches of the Flick Mansion's construction, a timeline of its history. Built in 1889, one of several Nob Hill manors, the lone survivor of the apocalyptic earthquake and fire of 1906. The elder statesman of the neighborhood as it gradually rebuilt over the decades: the Fairmont, Grace Cathedral, the Masonic Temple, all linked, in one elevation sketch, back to the Union Club with dotted lines that, if Claire let her imagination run wild, suggested underground passageways.

Tethered to the Mother Ship, she tittered to herself, knowing the dots were either gradient marks on the steep hill, or possibly plumbing lines, if she remembered anything from her urban planning course junior year. The folder's dry, leather binding flaked off in her hand, and she slid it back onto the shelf, where it bumped against a book behind, hidden from view. Claire reached in.

The faded red clothbound book had a Dewey decimal label on its spine and "San Francisco Public Library" stamped on the inside. It was tiny and slim, pamphletlike. It seemed authorless and titleless, except for the gold-embossed "IX" on the cover. Claire flipped the pages of homemade, typewritten print.

"Do be careful, please," a spinsterish woman with cat-eye glasses on a chain called from below. "I'm sorry," Claire said, quickly returning the orphan book to its home. "Am I not allowed up here?" "We prefer to send staff to fetch books on that level," the librarian-looking woman said, grimacing as Claire descended the rolling ladder, "ever since Mr. Cooper fell looking for *Billy Bud*." She smiled again once Claire was safely on the floor.

"I think there's a book from the public library up there," Claire said, and the club librarian looked upward with a weary sigh and said, "That wouldn't surprise me."

She offered a large album of labeled black-and-white photos from club social events over the years—"If you're interested," she said, and Claire said, "I am, thank you." Page after page of smiling splendidness: Mardi Gras Masquerade, "Prom" Night, Easter Sunday with costumed bunny and makeshift petting zoo in the hay-floored Grand Foyer, a suspiciously Allen-looking Santa Claus with two adorable, matching velvet-clad toddlers on his lap. Even without the name and date labels, Claire could have picked out Clay's mischievous twinkle as he pulled on the white beard, while the mannered Dean, unsmiling and face-forward, already seemed burdened with his father's expectations.

Poor kid, thought Claire. *Sad kid.*

"These photos are a fascinating chronicle," Claire said. "They should publish this book." The club librarian said, "I don't expect that to happen," as she pulled a ziplocked sandwich and baby carrots from her purse.

"What's that mean?" Claire asked, pointing to the Latin mantel engraving. "*Eventus Modos Justificant.* Do you know?"

The librarian nodded. "'The Ends Justify the Means.' I believe it was a common phrase among the robber barons of Mr. Flick's era. I've never much liked the sound of it." She stood with a fresh sigh.

"Feel free to sign out books," she said, indicating the pad on her desk. "Certain rare ones can't leave the library, but the rest can be enjoyed anywhere." She took her little bag lunch and left.

Most of the usual suspects featured prominently in the album. Man-eater Edie, chronically dressed in versions of expensive black, apparently cycled through a husband per decade, and the dandy had his own share of younger male "guests." Colonel Crowe must be perennially camera shy, or eschewed parties altogether, as he didn't show up at all.

Slade's dash and charisma launched off each photo; Nora's smiles were brittle and false, never fully submitting to the festivities, although she gamely channeled Dorothy—Toto and all—to her husband's Tin Man one midnineties Halloween. Dean loosened up some as the years went on, ironically thawed with the addition of Madison; Clay morphed from boyishly cute to rakishly hot, where he held today.

The egalitarian album included staff photos, too. *Caught you!* Claire thought, as a white-coated Ling beamed for the camera, his arm around a petite Asian woman in kitchen uniform. Claire squinted to make out her wedding ring and was relieved that Ling at least had this joy in his life. Hopefully children, too, now or soon.

"The Three Musketeers!" headlined a New Year's Eve buddy pic of Allen, Jess, and a much younger staff member named Ethan, whom she'd yet to run across. They were uniformed and confetti-dusted and,

Claire suspected from Jess's sloppy eyes, a few swigs into their own stash of bubbly. Ethan looked roughly her age, slightly older, with a rangy, artistic, mad scientist air that sparked through his regimented attire. *Survival job*, she thought. *Not his career.*

He showed up again the following July 4, in a star-spangled staff photo. Off to the side, thinner, raccoon-eyed. Nonsmiling. Noticeably aged. Claire squinted to make sure it was he.

"Ethan," she mused aloud, flipping ahead for more photos and finding none. "Ethan, Ethan..."

Claire felt eyes and glanced up to Sting staring at her.

"Hello, bird," she said, and Sting stared, unblinking. Claire stood up, and Sting elbowed out its spotted wings once, a subtle warning, before tucking them back to its side.

"Do *not* start that again," she scolded, closing the album on the ottoman. She'd table this friendship for later; it was difficult to warm up to a peregrine falcon.

Chapter Two

"Claire, won't you join us for bridge?" an old coot in tweeds asked later that afternoon as she peered out at the sad weather, still trapping her inside. "I don't know how," Claire apologized. "Spades?" he pressed, twinkling. "Go Fish?"

Claire laughed. "I think I remember Spades," she said. "Well, now...," he said with a grin, shuffle-leading her back toward the Card Room.

"I am shocked, *shocked* to find gambling going on here!" Nora interrupted an hour later, with Claire $3.75 in the hole. She playfully swatted one of the coots and said, "I'm rescuing my daughter-in-law before you sharks rob her blind!"

Nora entwined her arm with Claire's, leading her through the foyer. "Is everyone making you welcome?" she asked as they reached the staircase. "Any attitude? Just tell me, and I'll set them straight."

"Everyone's been very friendly." Claire laughed. "But honestly, we can move to a smaller room...."

"Why would you do that?" Nora asked before dismissing the notion.

"We'll be out of everyone's hair soon," Claire added, and when Nora shrugged her response, Claire said, "I really appreciate what you've done for us, for me."

"Claire, you're family, and we love you," Nora said in earnest. "It's taken us too long to come together and that's partially my fault and I have no good excuse for it. But I've got your back from now on. You're very special to me." Nora fought a spike of emotion and censored herself by embracing Claire, clinging briefly.

"And that's as sappy as I get," Nora said, releasing and locking up again. Claire smiled and said, "I love you too, Nora," and Nora said, "Blah, blah, blah..." before dabbing an eye with her little finger and snorting once. Ling passed, and Claire quickly changed the tone and subject.

"Oh, Ling," she called out. "I've already brought down my tray. I can clean up after myself. You needn't bother. But thank you." He paused only slightly in his trajectory and disappeared down the hall.

"I haven't managed to win him over." Claire chose her words carefully. "Does he ever smile? Or talk?"

"Ling's a special case." Nora hemmed, choosing her words with equal care. "A sad one. He's never been Mr. Sunshine, but we cut him more slack these days. His wife died two weeks ago."

"That's terrible," Claire said, feeling villainous for singling him out. "I think I saw her picture in the album upstairs." Nora nodded and said, "Yes, she worked in the kitchen."

"It was fast," she added. "Stage four something, and of course there's no stage five. The club covered the costs, including the funeral. We offered him a paid bereavement, but"—she shrugged—"we each handle grief in our own way, I suppose."

"Do they have children?" Claire asked.

"I don't think so," Nora said. "You needn't say anything to him, but that's where his head is."

"Yes, of course," Claire said.

"You two joining us for dinner?" Nora asked. "It's Lobster Night."

The club livened up as cocktail hour drew closer, and Clay sent word through Jess that he'd be late. Claire hadn't missed her cell phone—which she knew sat lifeless in its coatroom cubbyhole—as she hadn't been in the mood for chitchat over the past week anyway. She'd maintained sporadic e-mail correspondence with Martha from her room laptop via Ethernet plugged into the wall—the Union Club had yet to go wireless and likely never would. But in a positive sign, at least to her, she felt ready to reconnect with the outside world again.

"Jess," she asked, "can I use my cell in my room? I won't do any business deals, I promise. I don't have a business." Jess chuckled and said, "I'd have to ask for permission."

"Please don't bother," Claire said, not wanting to cause trouble as an interloping guest. "I'll just use it in the coatroom." "I'm happy to ask," Jess repeated. "I think Colonel Crowe makes those decisions."

"*Don't* bother Colonel Crowe," Claire said quickly, and Jess laughed again.

Claire, less brazen than Nora, ruled out slacks and, after showering, changed into a simple navy wrap dress—freshly steamed, on satin-padded hangers, like the rest of her wardrobe. Her clothes and personal belongings had been expertly transferred to her temporary home, except for her red box, now officially lost and a headache for another day. She added her pearl strand and slipped down the back stairs—a faster, less conspicuous route than the elevators—and plugged her beyond-dead cell into her charger in the coatroom as more members arrived, shaking wet umbrellas.

"Is this a Santa Fe designer?" a glittering Madison asked of Claire's dress. "I find offbeat designers so fascinating."

The politics, alliances, cliques, and divides of the club came into sharper focus during cocktail hour. The young bucks—Bing, Ford,

Quinn, others—were the most conservative and well mannered, watching and learning. The titans, late thirties to retirement age, were a boorish group at the height of their powers and exuded a brash confidence. A welcome subset were the red merries: heroic drinkers who'd fallen short of their career pinnacle and the first to polish the bar at five thirty. The old coots—all ages north, some twinkly, some crotchety—were fewer and unbound and the most sartorial with giddy ties and happy whale corduroys.

Edie—overdressed in a military-inspired jacket with gold epaulets over a gray sequined floor skirt—was an equal-opportunity flirt whom the wives eyed warily. Slade was the undisputed emcee, effortless in all company. Nora, in a cream satin blouse and trim tux pants, warmed most to the coots, was cordial to wives, tolerant of Madison, dismissive of Edie, coldly hostile to Colonel Crowe, who had, it seemed, long given up on winning her over. At least he had Madison in his camp, one on one, by the fireplace.

"My, my, who is *that* handsome fellow?" Edie cooed, and dandy Clancy said, "Very smart!" and Claire turned and covered a gasp.

Clay held a self-conscious grin, his unruly locks shorn, a trim, glossy *Mad Men* cut in its place. "They got me," he whispered to Claire. "They got me good.

"Hi, I'm Clay," he said, off her speechless stare. "I'm your husband."

"I...like it," Claire stammered. "It's just different." Clay wasn't buying it, so Claire added, "It brings out your greens," which it did.

"Is that Brylcreem?" she ribbed, lightly patting. "Do they still make that?" Clay retaliated with a concealed goosing before moving off to handclasp one of the titans.

"You two are so beautiful together," Edie told Claire. "Such magic charisma. I do hope it works out." Claire laughed and said, "Well, thank you, Edie. Me too."

Nora and Madison took turns debriefing her on the notables in the crowd. The mayor of San Francisco—surprisingly young and movie-star handsome—once a rising political star, turned "crashing meteor" (Nora's verdict) after a "skanky" affair (with his chief of staff's wife, no less) had quashed his national ambitions. "Our locals are more tolerant of that sort of thing than the flyovers," Madison conceded. "*I'm* not!" Nora growled. Claire thought her own husband's wattage eclipsed his anyway, and said so.

"I agree," Nora said. "No contest."

The publisher of the *San Francisco Chronicle* was chatting with Slade near the Reading Room, the Google CEO tipped heads with Colonel Crowe by the stairs, and a mouthy female justice from the Ninth Circuit Court of Appeals switched out her third glass of champagne. "She's not a member." Madison sniffed. "Just Mr. Baumgartner's guest."

"Do you remember when he brought that jester Robin Williams?" Madison asked a nodding Nora before pivoting back to Claire. "*That* won't happen again."

The dinner chimes sounded.

Clancy joined the Willings at their table and regaled them, apparently for the umpteenth time, with the "Night of the Zombie Lobster Boil."

"Not tonight," Nora begged, already starting to giggle.

"There was a new cook downstairs," he explained to Claire, "and he hadn't boiled them sufficiently." Claire said, "Oh no!" and Nora covered her ears and shook with laughter and said, "I can't listen!"

"And old Mrs. Hardcastle, God rest her soul, was yammering on in her Ethel Barrymore voice and with her ample bosom sagging on the table...."

"Stop! Stop!" Nora pleaded, now snorting, tears rolling down her cheeks, more fascinating to Claire than the story.

"And her lobster woke up and slowly *clack-clacked* its way off the plate...."

"No!" Claire said, and Nora shrieked, "*No!*"

"And *latched* on with both claws, full *beep-beep*, and Mrs. Hardcastle shot up, and it held on, clacking and dangling!" At this, Nora nearly hyperventilated.

"Allen had to fetch a bottle opener," Clancy finished, "to pry the beast off!"

The table roiled as the not-Dean waiter brought dinner—thankfully deshelled tails—and Edie at the next table said, "Clancy's telling the teats story again."

"Now I've lost my appetite, you old queer," Nora said, and the table burst into laughter anew. Claire was hesitant, until she realized this must be fair game. Nora instantly snapped back to normal.

"That goddamned story kills me," she said, blotting her nose with her napkin. "Every time."

"The judge eats like a badger," said Madison, back from her scour.

Claire and Clay joined the post-dinner fox-trot, and Clay said, "These people are crazy," and Claire said, "They're sweet." She tousled his hair and said, "I think it's very sexy." "It is *not* sexy," he said, and she said, "It is to me. My own personal Ken doll."

Stompy switched from Bobby Darin to Talking Heads as the night heated up. Slade and Nora left the floor, and Edie seemed to do a solo rain dance to "Wild Wild Life" in the middle of the Grand Foyer. Claire took advantage of the spectacle to slip off to the coatroom.

—◆—

Dr. Kerr had left three messages.

The first, a courtesy call from her office to set up an appointment. The next from Dr. Kerr herself, asking Claire to come see her that week.

The third, a few hours ago, detailed "highly irregular" findings in her blood work. She left her personal cell number and urged Claire to call back "as soon as possible."

"Ms. Willing, is anything wrong?" Jess asked from behind the counter.

—◊—

"Highly irregular?" Clay asked when Claire returned to her family. "What the hell does that mean?"

"She called them 'inducing chemicals' in her message," Claire said, focusing to get the terms straight. "She said the miscarriage was not a... an 'organic occurrence.'"

"Did you call her back?" Nora asked. "Her service said she's at the hospital on a delivery," Claire said.

"'Inducing chemical'?" Madison said. "Does she mean a *drug*?"

"I don't know what she means," Claire said.

"Slade's on the board of the hospital," Nora said, turning to her husband. "Tell them to pull the doctor out." "No, don't do that," Claire insisted. "Not during a delivery."

"How do you feel?" Clay asked. "Do you feel okay?" "I feel fine," Claire said. "I feel perfectly normal."

"Send Jess to get that doctor," Nora ordered her husband. "Or we can all go to the hospital right now."

"If she feels fine," Slade said, "then it can wait until Monday. I don't like pulling rank unless it's an emergency." Nora threw up her hands and looked away.

"Is it an emergency, Claire?" Slade probed. "Would you like me to call?"

"It's not an emergency," Claire said. "It can wait till Monday."

"Dr. *Kerr*?" Madison said. "I've never heard of her. She's your doctor?"

"She's a little new age," Clay said, and Claire said, "She's wonderful. She's Martha's doctor, too." "Who's *Martha*?" Madison asked.

Stompy started his next set with "Disco Inferno," and Claire's family made her sit to the side and brought her apple juice. She wasn't in a dancing mood, so Edie dragged Clay to the floor while Nora upbraided a stoic Slade in the dining room. Up on the mezzanine, Madison chatted with Colonel Crowe—*Not about my personal stuff*, Claire hoped—and Bing pulled up a chair to prattle on, a thoughtful gesture made annoying by the blaring music. Claire smiled and nodded and nodded.

Members and guests retrieved their own coats and umbrellas, as Jess had abandoned his post, and Edie waved "Ta-ta!" to Claire checking her cell and finding no new messages. She was tempted to call Dr. Kerr's personal cell, but it was after midnight, and she felt perfectly normal, and it could wait until Sunday—not Monday—right after breakfast.

—⚋—

"First of all, he didn't even pick me up. We met at the restaurant, like an Internet hookup," Martha complained when Claire called the next morning, from the club's front steps.

"And he was seventeen minutes late, and they wouldn't seat me," she went on, "so I stood there like a barfly, a very attractive pose on a Saturday night, and then he already had plans to meet *his* friends after dinner! And what sucks is he's hot.

"I ironed my hair for this!" she railed.

"Martha, have you seen Dr. Kerr?" Claire asked. "Is she at the hospital today? Now?"

"Oh God, you haven't heard?" Martha said. "I can't believe I forgot to tell you."

"Heard what?" Claire asked. "Tell me what?"

"Dr. Kerr had a stroke last night," Martha said. "Isn't that *awful*?"

Chapter Three

*D*on't get used to this, Claire told herself, of the daily fresh sheets and towels and even duvet covers, the newspaper deliveries, the ever-sparkling bathrooms, the French laundry service, the all-inclusive meals and nightly live entertainment. *This cruise can't last forever.*

"My Realtor's got her eye on a few potentials," Nora told her one night over dinner at the club. "We'll look when she's back in town. No rush."

Claire worked out daily at the Fairmont's Club One—the Union's own basement gym was "Precambrian" and "reeked of old men," according to Madison—and ran the Nob Hill stairs with occasional wind sprints on the edge of Huntington Park next to the surprising James Flick Fountain that fronted the club. It was three-tiered and elegant and ringed by intricately carved bronze children with linked hands who laughed and danced around it Maypole-style. It was gleeful and un-Flick-like, and Claire was heartened that the grim, stoic tycoon whose room she lived in might have been a secret softie for children after all.

On rare sunny days, she read Cheever and Franzen on the benches near the playground with the other neighbors. She kicked the soccer ball with the red-shirted kids who spilled out every afternoon from Grace Cathedral and befriended the weary clergyman who tended his young, mostly ethnic flock. He invited her to the church's yoga class on Thursday nights—"Right inside on the labyrinth"—as well as weekly forums with their rotating "Artist in Residence."

"I love Anna Deavere Smith," Claire said, impressed. "Thank you."

The clergyman excused himself to break up a swing-set spat. He seemed overwhelmed by his scrappy flock.

"Congratulations," she said, delighting at a young mother who rocked her newborn in its pram. "He's really beautiful." "Thank you," the mother said, beaming "This is Martin."

She checked in several times daily with Clay, on his first training trip to New York, usually leaving messages, which he'd return at night from his room at the University Club.

"We might as well throw away our cells," she joked from her bed, twirling the phone cord. "We're like 1950s teenagers."

She circumvented the club's dress code by slipping down the back stairs, through the servants' halls and industrial kitchen, and out the service entrance by the parking lot. Staff faces were easy to remember; the names, especially the exotic ones, not so much.

"Miss Claire, if you got special music requests, you let me know," Stompy, in a bathrobe, said over his morning coffee and cigarette from the back stoop as she dashed out in running shorts.

"Florence and the Machine?" Claire tested. "*Who*?" Stompy said to her laughter.

"You need to quit smoking, Stompy," she said, and he said, "Yep, yep."

She helped the little maids clean her room each morning, marveling how they ironed the sheets right on the bed, and flatly refused Jess's kind offer to chauffeur her around in the club's Lincoln. "I'm sure you have better things to do," she said. "I've got my Clipper card." The touristy cable cars were the only mass transit up and down Nob Hill, which Martha mock sniffed was "To keep out the riffraff." Indeed, unlike the streets below, Nob Hill was notably vagrant free.

Claire was relieved to get the "all clear" on her latest blood work from her new doctor, who'd inherited Dr. Kerr's patients. "I can't find the results Dr. Kerr was referencing," the new doctor said, "and, of course, I can't ask her." Dr. Kerr had suffered an aneurism, not a stroke, and still lay in a vegetative state, perhaps permanently.

"It's senseless," the new doctor said. "Senseless and tragic."

"She's only forty-three," Martha said when Claire tracked her down at the hospital after her appointment. "But an aneurism can strike anytime. I hear she just collapsed in the delivery room around two a.m. OBs have such crazy, spastic hours.

"She never even had time to *eat*," Martha lamented. "Always running around with those damn pink smoothies." "I still can't believe it," Claire said. "It's just so terrible."

"So how long you gonna be locked up in Hell House?" Martha asked. "Is that like a permanent thing?"

"I'm not *locked up*, and it's only for a couple weeks," Claire said. "Everyone at the club has been very welcoming. Wacky, but welcoming."

"Do I have to go through a pat down to see you from now on, Your Highness?" Martha asked, and Claire said, "Shut it."

"You *do* have to be careful," Martha added in earnest. "There's lots of crazies out there. Now more than ever." "I'm not worried," Claire said. "No one's out to get me." Then she laughed and said, "Really, I'm just not that special."

Martha was summoned to the ICU, and Claire promised they'd all get together once Clay returned from training in New York.

"'Training'?" Martha jabbed. "Is that what the New World Order calls it these days? How crafty..."

"I'm over your conspiracy theories," Claire said. "And I'm done with Anonymous."

"Nobody listens to that crank anymore," Martha called back from down the hall. "Now it's all about *Stu!*"

———

The human resources woman at the San Francisco Unified School District was professional but had no use for Claire, even as a substitute teacher.

"It's too late in the academic year," the woman explained, directing her to the website with forms, certifications, and hoop-jumping regulations. "You can apply for next year."

Claire's offer of volunteer work was shot down, too. "The screening and application process is past," the woman said.

"I mean an after-school program," Claire pressed. "Tutoring, mentoring. I'm bilingual, have years of experience. I can get references, dozens of them...."

"That's outside the parameter of our responsibilities," the woman said.

"Your minority dropout rate is nearly forty percent," Claire said, and the woman said, "You think I don't know that?"

Claire remembered well the red tape when she'd started her own program in Santa Fe. Background checks, fingerprinting, layers of bureaucrats who seemingly prided their role as obstacles. The human resources woman made clear the process would be even more roadblocked in "red tape capital" San Francisco. "It's out of my hands," she apologized.

"Meanwhile," Claire unloaded, "our kids can't read or write, let alone add and subtract. Forget art and music, but they know guns and drugs and screwing. Wash, rinse, repeat. The cycle seems almost intentional." She went to the door and mock shrugged in frustration. "Out of our hands..."

"Ms. Willing," the woman called after her. "With all due respect, it's not like you need a job."

"Actually," Claire replied, "I do."

—ɷ—

Claire picked up a brochure at ACT for their upcoming Mainstage season—a rarely produced Brecht play caught her eye—and bought red velvet cupcakes from the luscious-smelling Lotta's, which she'd leave in the kitchen for the club staff, minus the ones she gave to homeless men clustered around the bakery door. She was relieved the usual Union Square protest crowd had been replaced by a twenty-four-hour public reading of *Finnegan's Wake*. She waved "thank you" to the brown Chevelle with tinted windows that let her cross Post Street and clanged up Powell on the cable car, now sea-legged enough to perch off the side, hanging on the bar.

She rode the elevator to the Top of the Mark hotel restaurant and, over a decaf cappuccino at a window table, looked out across her new city, down at Huntington Park, where the red-shirt platoon lay siege to the retired cable car parked on the playground's edge, the clergyman's weariness palpable from nineteen floors up. She peered at the Union Club, into its cream-painted light well, and singled out her inward bathroom window. Her outer bedroom sheers rustled, doubtless from Ling, who refreshed and plumped and restocked flowers and firewood on an unerring timetable.

She ruled out an afternoon movie—she couldn't sit still in a theater with the rest of the world being productive—and skimmed back issues of the *Economist* and listened to the hushed nothingspeak of staff setting tables for dinner. She roamed the endless, silent hallways and admired the Versailles parquet floors and bronze sculptures and the artistry of the wedding cake plasterwork in the arches.

She envied Clay for his busy work schedule, his new adventure, which accentuated her own idleness. *Uselessness*, she amplified to herself.

"How was it today?" she'd ask, and "What did you do today?" and "What is your job exactly?"

"If I told you, I'd have to kill you," Clay parried that first week, playful with the newness of it.

"I learn," Clay answered the same questions a couple of weeks later, typically bushed and non-talkative when he got back to their suite late at night. "I watch and listen and learn. That's my job, I guess." The pressures, it seemed, had started to kick in.

"Is it interesting, at least?" she needled, and he said, "I'd rather be painting."

"I know, honey," she said, stroking his back. *Youth must have its day*, Colonel Crowe had correctly pegged it, however patronizing. It seemed to weigh on Clay that youth's day, for him, was over. Claire was equal parts sympathetic and pragmatic. From Clay's first paycheck alone, she had paid off the seventeen-hundred-and-change balance on their credit card, which had gnawed at her for months.

She learned and mastered "bar dice" with the red merries in the Tap Room. "Dice, be nice!" Mr. McCrady called out as he rattled and tossed, and Claire shook her leather cup and said, "Dice, be nice!" "Here, let me bring you up to speed," Stanwick, the bartender, regularly joked, refilling her Diet Coke from the gun and plunking in a stemmed cherry. On Mondays and Wednesdays during cocktail hour, she delighted in the surprisingly harmonic barbershop chorus that rehearsed in the upstairs Music Room. The songs were strange and charmingly old-school, laced with archaic jokes and code words. "Sing 'The Whiffenpoof Song' again!" Claire would ask, the only one she knew, and with a *"Baa! Baa! Baa!"* they would cheerily comply.

"What the hell are you doing?" Nora demanded one night when Claire started to clear plates from the table, post-dinner. "Good grief, stop that!"

"Just trying to earn my keep, Nora," Claire said, acquiescing.

"Shut up and sit down." Nora chortled. "Trust me; you'll earn it."

But Claire wasn't earning anything, or doing anything, and knew she'd reached the nadir of inertia when she found herself addicted to Stu.

—✵—

"We're on the march, and the Order is on the run!"

So began Claire's giddy "indoctrination" into the rabid cult of Stu Savage.

She'd ignored Martha's repeated sales pitch, still kicking herself for her pitiable Anonymous obsession, but caught the bug one morning after her shower, when she opened her bathroom window to clear the steam. From a window across the well, one floor below, echoed the radio warnings of the imminent collapse of civilization over Darth Vader marching music. Cigarette smoke streamed from the window, a club no-no, as a fellow guest's anxiety, or fascination, trumped the house rules.

The fascination was contagious. By the time Claire had finished drying and primping, in between desperate commercials for gold and "food insurance," she had to hear more.

She e-mailed Martha. *What station is Stu Savage on?*

His own, Martha responded with a winky face, before coughing up the dial number and streaming website, whose logo read "Prison Planet" over a grinning death mask globe.

Stu Savage, on a tinny, local public access station, was frothing and blustery—a Glenn Beck on acid, warning of the New World Order and coming totalitarian state. He breathed fire with a slightly Southern twang and pounded his desk, hypnotically, for emphasis. His alarmist populism mirrored the radical anarchism of Anonymous, proof positive the current climate of paranoia was bipartisan.

In a backwoods town, Claire suspected, Stu's screeds might have been a call to arms; in San Francisco, it was rollicking, train-wreck entertainment. And, like a hot new restaurant, the city's latest obsession.

He claimed a "demonic network of global elites" was nearing the "endgame of worldwide domination" and the "willing enslavement" of the masses. He ranted about "wireless mind control" and "sodium fluoride–poisoned water" and "genocidal population control." He knew *"for a fact!"* the government was hoarding hybrid "Franken-seeds" in secret storage facilities at the Arctic Circle.

He did on-air interviews with survivalist preppers in doomsday enclaves coast-to-coast, stockpiling food and guns, ahead of the "inevitable martial-law crackdown." He did live commercials for colloidal silver.

She quickly muted the radio when Ling knocked on the door. "Thank you, Ling, but I'm all stocked with firewood."

Claire huddled closer to her bedside Bose.

"There is a war on for your mind!" Stu bellowed.

"War and poverty, disease and misery, these aren't accidents, folks," he told her. "It's all controlled chaos puppeteered by the unseen hand of the New World Order from their Satanic shadows of power, with only one purpose: to break you down and force you to submit to their long-planned colossal world monarchy!"

Stu railed on. "They are the chess masters, the world is their board, and make no mistake: You've been numbered for slavery."

Oh goody, thought Claire.

Stu peppered his rants with "occult," "pagan," "Satanic," "despots," "dictators," "merchants of death." He railed against the "globalist, eugenicist control freaks."

"Don't take my word for anything!" he ordered repeatedly in his gravelly smoker's voice. "Look it up for yourself!"

"I think I'll have lunch in my room today," she phoned down to the kitchen. "A tuna melt, please. With fruit."

His daily two-hour show, which he called a "transmission," repeated on autoloop, and Claire quickly learned when his diatribe was fresh and new. His website had streaming archives stretching back months for endless Stu.

From the JFK assassination—not even a CIA hit, but a "false flag, phony, staged" event—to the invention of "population-thinning" AIDS and "vaccine-caused" autism, with ever-more disastrous "superbugs" in the pipeline, to the domestic paramilitary force training at a secret Texas compound just waiting for the go-ahead, Stu left no conspiracy unturned.

"What the hell is this?" Clay yawned the next morning, when the radio alarm woke to Stu's bombastic warning of the imminent destruction of the world's power grid by electromagnetic pulse.

"Nothing, honey," Claire said, quickly hitting snooze. While he showered, she reprogrammed the alarm to keep her private oddity and guilty passion to herself.

He condemned the global "corptocracy," whose dehumanizing criminal atrocities were gleefully ignored by the "presstitute media." He pulled back the curtain on "race-specific bioweapons," and insisted Claire was merely "fuel" being slowly conditioned to accept her own imprisonment and "soft kill."

Stu Savage became the ambient noise and background music of her day. She loaded his podcasts and did cardio to the coming cataclysm.

Stu was delightfully, un-turn-offably insane.

But only a nut would take him seriously, Claire thought, slightly chilled that plenty of listeners out there likely did.

Claire checked herself when, a few days later, her mental grocery list for her eventual new kitchen included several of the thirty-seven "must-have" foodstuffs for surviving the apocalypse, a critical portion of which would fit into her go-bag for the inevitable "bug-out" when it all "hit the fan." When she circled potential new homes in the real estate section, she looked for even the tiniest spot of land in which to plant her crisis garden. On her room service tray sat the still-unopened Diet Coke, made with the chemical weapon aspartame, which was, after all, as studies had proven, genetically modified bacteria feces engineered by big pharma to cause blindness.

"Oh Lord." Claire laughed at herself, switching off Stu and inspecting her outfit in the mirror, relieved, for once, that her sister-in-law was on the way.

Chapter Four

Madison was late, per usual, and an emboldened Claire waited in the Reading Room, which she typically avoided because of its hushed, all-eyes-turn atmosphere. Today, a lone coot with a whiny hearing aid read a pinkish newspaper by the window, taking no notice of her.

She perused the club membership roster tucked discreetly along the back wall. Below the "active members" whose names were increasingly familiar (Gettys, Pritzkers, Crockers), the "nonresident" list included even more famous—or infamous—ones such as Rockefeller, Rothschild, Bass, Kissinger, and Soros, alongside a number of unpronounceables from Denmark and South Africa. "In Memoriam" honored luminaries like William Randolph Hearst, Secretary Caspar Weinberger, Secretary Robert McNamara, and Ambassador Jean Kirkpatrick. It also honored the late Congressman-elect Dean Willing.

There was a stand-alone oil portrait of Margaret Sanger, a birth control pioneer and civil rights trailblazer, who was the club's first female member, admitted in 1922, according to the burnished plaque. Claire remembered her from a women's studies class at Yale. The portrait, the room, the club itself felt more stately and substantial with her presence.

"Sorry." Madison clacked up behind her. "My trainer was brutal today. Have you tried Extreme Tabata? I'd prefer bulimia."

Madison sized up Claire's chambray blouse, wool serape skirt, and concha belt and said, "Your style is so refreshingly rebellious." She squinted at Claire's necklace. "Turquoise, too? One can almost hear the tom-toms."

"All these names." Claire indicated the roster. "It's like a who's who of modern history."

"Oh, that's just a partial list," Madison said, rounding a corner and pointing at an oversized black-and-white photograph of the club. At first Claire didn't understand.

"Look closer," Madison said, monitoring her reaction.

"Oh God," said Claire.

The "photograph" was a quasi-pointillist ink sketch by an expert hand—an intricate matrix of circles, linked by lines and dashes to others, family-tree-like. Each circle contained a name in tiny lettering in a tangled, connect-the-dot constellation outlining the building.

"It's like a giant game of Where's Waldo?" Madison said, twinkling. "I'll give you a hint: Our family's under the front chimney."

On the roof, Slade and Nora began the Willing line, begetting Dean and Clay. Madison's circle sprang off Dean's; Clay's sat alone and bachelorlike, as the artist, like the rest of the club at the time, was unaware of Claire's existence.

"It's stunning," Claire said, drawing closer. The canvas itself was a patchwork of Union mementos—old menus from special events, meeting minutes, membership invitations. The modern artwork, in a club full of cracked oil portraits and landscapes, was signed "ES."

"It's multimedia," Madison explained, pointing out the "Jackson Pollock touches."

"He misspelled Brzezinski." She *ts*ked, pointing at an upstairs window. "But that's a common error. In this country, at least."

"Who's 'he'?" Claire asked. "Who did this?"

"Ethan," Madison said, and then added sadly: "The one who got away."

"I saw his photo in an album upstairs," said Claire, and Madison said, "You've been snooping through the library? That's encouraging."

"Ethan worked here for a number of years, a part of the family," Madison continued. "A gifted, unsung genius. So much potential. Such a shame..."

"Drugs, of course," Madison explained, when Claire asked what happened. "He went off the beam, soon after finishing this. Spying on members, stealing things, a true paranoid." She sighed. "We can't save them all."

The hearing-aid coot stood next to Madison with a hand-scrawled "Quiet!" on his newspaper.

"What do you want, Mr. Beasley?" Madison asked. He emphatically gestured at the "Silence Please" sign.

She smiled and hugged him. "So sorry," she said. "You're right: rules are rules.

"Now go change your diapers, you dead fuck," she added, patting his head.

The near-deaf coot smiled and shuffled away, and Madison shot a did-I-just-say-that "whoops!" to Claire, who stifled a snicker. Madison tapped her crutch on the floor.

"Ever since the incident, I've developed such an arch sense of humor," she explained. "My therapist calls it a coping mechanism."

So is the word 'incident,' thought Claire.

"Ling," Madison called out. "We'll take our tea up in the Music Room."

—⟩⟨⟨—

As chairman of the Outreach Committee, Madison seemed dissatisfied with their brainstorming laundry list.

Indeed, livestock donations to Third World villages (Oxfam), global warming groups (Earthwatch Institute), even rare disease charities (each with a different bracelet)—all honorable and worthy—seemed impersonal, distant, and unimaginative to Claire.

"We need something fresh and flashy for the Justice Ball," Madison said, stump-pacing the Music Room. "We need the 'wow' factor."

Claire found Madison's obsession with the Justice Ball unseemly. An annual rotating gathering of their sister clubs, to be hosted this year by the Union, it reminded Claire of the "red-carpet activism" in glossy social pages she'd always thought distasteful. It shouldn't, she felt, take a lavish party to coax charity from the rich, as if good deeds were an afterthought. From Madison's description, the Justice Ball, with its long weekend gala and presentations of charitable one-upsmanship, sounded like another phony do-gooder smackdown.

"Our motive shouldn't be to impress the other clubs." She weighed her words carefully. "It should be to help those in need."

"Yes, of course," Madison said, chastened, parting the sheers to peer out toward Huntington Park. "I knew I was the wrong person for this job."

"You have this great facility," Claire said, gesturing, "right in the middle of town. Think of all the local people you could help. Soup kitchens, reading classes, even a free clinic. I'm talking hands-on, improving lives directly."

"It's such a pity," Madison said, still lost out the window.

Claire asked what she meant.

"Same time every day," Madison continued. "It breaks my heart."

Down below, in the playground, the red-shirt brigade ran helter-skelter, while the clergyman sat on a bench, listening to his iPod.

"Who are they?" Claire asked. "The kids, I mean."

"Orphans," Madison said. "Wards of the state." Claire winced at the word "orphan," having thought it long replaced with the more sensitive "displaced youth." At least Madison hadn't used the word "coloreds."

"The church fosters them, in a manner of speaking," Madison continued. "I hear they stack them in dorms. Of course, no one's going to adopt them. They're past their expiration date." Claire winced again.

"Concrete sidewalks, a few trees, that one man." Madison sighed. "Their whole world, until they're eighteen. And then God knows what."

"That's exactly what I'm talking about," Claire said. "That's a real need, right on the block."

"We've offered many times over the years," Madison said. "Our building, our talent and resources." She turned to Claire. "Don't you know that man? The preacher man?"

"I don't exactly *know* him," Claire said, and Madison said, "I thought I'd seen you talking from time to time. Aren't you friends by now?"

Claire grinned and said, "Madison, do you want me to ask him?"

"Given your...personal background, not to mention your experience with children, perhaps he'd be more amenable to your overture."

"Should you clear it with someone first?" Claire asked. "Does Colonel Crowe have to sign off?"

Madison scoffed and said, "I've got the colonel in my back pocket.

"After all, some young blood is exactly what this club needs," she added. "Don't you agree?"

—⚍—

The clergyman was surprised and appreciative, but a tough sell.

"It's always very kind of the club, indeed," he said, before listing the obstacles of the state's "guardian laws" that tied their hands. "We only foster them," he explained, "and other than school, they aren't supposed to leave the vicinity or our supervision."

"They wouldn't," Claire said. "They'd just be inside the club, right there, and you're welcome to join us." The clergyman eyed the dark mansion, and Claire laughed. "It's not as scary as it looks, believe me," she said. The clergyman joined her laugh and nodded.

Claire described her after-school program for "underserved students" and "at-risk youth" in Santa Fe, with its emphasis on arts, music, and tutoring. "Stuff you know they're not getting in school," she said. She listed outcome statistics of similar Safe Harbor programs around the country with lower dropout rates, fewer pregnancies and arrests, better grades, fewer drugs, less drinking and smoking. She proposed a three o'clock to five o'clock weekday-afternoon schedule. "Saturdays, too, if you want," she added.

"I'm happy to talk to your church bosses," she said. "We can work out the curriculum together."

The clergyman softened. "It is such a generous offer. We could certainly use the help. And it would be nice to reestablish a kinship with our neighbors on the square," he added. "I've often wondered why we lost it along the way. Nobody seems to remember."

"That would be an added bonus," Claire said, smiling.

"May I ask what prompted this?" the clergyman said. "This unexpected kindness?"

"It's partially selfish," Claire admitted. "I miss my kids. I miss helping them grow. And I've got nothing but time right now.

"And, quite frankly," she added, "you seem way over your head."

"Alas, alack," he agreed. "I'll ask my superiors. This evening."

The red-shirts occupied themselves somewhat orderly on the playground, on the grassy field, at the dancing-child fountain. The sun was setting.

Inside the defunct cable car past the monkey bars sat a young Hispanic red-shirt boy, alone.

"Is he one of yours?" Claire asked. "I've never seen him."

The clergyman nodded. "Edgar is brand-new to us. His mother was killed last fall. By her boyfriend. Edgar was there."

"My God."

"He has no other family here," the clergyman continued. "And those in Honduras aren't clamoring to have him back.

"Child Services advised us to give him space," he added. "And time. To come out of his shell. They still give him counseling once a week."

"That's not nearly enough," Claire said, and the clergyman said, "I agree."

Edgar didn't look up from his lap when Claire poked her head in.

"Permission to board, Captain?" she asked. "Just for a couple stops?" She climbed the running board and sat across the aisle. "*Se llamo* Claire," she said, looking at the top of Edgar's brown, shiny head. "What's yours?

"How old are you?" she asked, to silence. "Are you four? Five? Are you forty?" Edgar, startled, glanced up and then back down. "Yes, apparently that's a scary age," Claire said. The boy peered not at his lap, but at his Smurf toy watch, whose blue arms were stuck at the wrong time.

"I think he needs a new battery," Claire said. "May I look?" Negative.

"Mr. Conductor," she called toward the front. "Can you please take us to town? We need to get our watch fixed." Edgar looked ahead, back at Claire, fought a smile, looked back down. "Can you please hurry?" she called out, and then said to Edgar, "Grab on to the strap. This car goes fast.

"Hold on!" she urged at the imaginary plunge they were about to take. Edgar grabbed his strap and looked out the front window. They plummeted down Nob Hill, around the AT&T ball park, then lifted into the air, over the Bay, and high above the Golden Gate Bridge. It was getting dark, so Claire clanged the bell at the front to bring them back again. Edgar stopped laughing and looked down, smiling.

"Thanks for the ride," Claire said, hopping off the side. "We'll fix your watch next time, okay?"

Halfway to the club, Claire turned back and caught Edgar looking through his window. He quickly turned away, and the clergyman called, "C'mon, Edgar. Time for dinner," before waving a thanks to Claire. She waved back, strolled past the joyous child fountain.

Upstairs, in the Music Room window, Madison looked down and smiled and nodded. Claire gave a discreet thumbs-up as she neared.

Madison smiled and nodded.

Chapter Five

N ow Claire had a purpose, and her mental to-do lists morphed into a practical road map and classroom plan, using the teacher's software on her laptop.

She plotted out a daily schedule, subject to the clergyman's approval, that combined study time, physical exercise, and the occasional field trip to local sights with educational value. Madison secured the almost-never-used Music Room as home base for their new Safe Harbor program. "We can spruce it up any way you want," she said.

"How the hell did you get the church to agree?" a surprised Nora asked. "We've been offering for years!"

Nora *ping*ed her glass and proudly announced the program at Friday's dinner. She credited her "resourceful daughters-in-law" and, from her glower, practically dared any member to object. "We're opening our doors again to those less fortunate," Nora lectured her fellow members. "It's the right thing to do, and long overdue."

Nora explained to Claire later, "That was a preemptive strike. The old coots will howl at noisy brown kids tearing through the club." Then she shrugged and said, "Fuck 'em."

"Terrific! Very cool, honey," Clay said from the corporate jet on his way from New York to London, the next leg of a two-week globe-trotting business trip to meet "the principals," whoever they were. Claire had started to tell him about her new project the night before he left, but he'd seemed so preoccupied and saddled with pressure that she'd tabled her excitement and helped him pick out the right ties instead. She thought his newfound desire to make a good impression surprisingly sexy.

He listed the cities he'd be visiting and where he'd be staying in each. "That's funny," Claire said. "Those are the clubs hanging in the hall."

"You want anything from Zurich?" he asked before getting pulled into an in-flight meeting. "Miss you! Love you!" they said, over static.

Claire marveled at how the women of the club, particularly the empty nesters, rose to the occasion. Mrs. Newhall teamed with Mrs. Rathbone to buy desks and chairs. Mrs. Kingsbury paid for new game board carpeting in bold, stain-forgiving colors. Even Edie wrote a blank check—"And I do mean blank!"—to cover crayons, easels, and "anything else you need."

"Bully," said Claire, laughing. "And thank you."

"Can I get a list of the children's names and sizes?" Madison asked one morning. "I'm making something special for them." Then she corrected herself: "I mean, I'm having it made."

Nora went above and beyond. She ponied up for five computers loaded with scholastic software and oversaw the refurbishment of the cots, which had been stacked in the basement since her own "Room at the Inn" program for the homeless had ended a few years earlier. She brought in all-new pillows and "Peanuts" cartoon sheets and commandeered an adjoining room for nap time. "I almost forgot about that,"

Claire said, and Nora said, "It's the most important damn twenty minutes of the day!"

Claire insisted on an upgraded Internet for educational purposes, which triggered Madison's only pushback. "Is that really necessary?" she asked. "What about online predators?"

"We'll keep an eye on them," Claire assured her. "The web is a crucial learning tool."

"I'm not sure the board will approve," Madison said, and Claire said, "Well, that's ridiculous." Then she said, "I'll pay for it myself, but I won't run the program without it." She suggested a wireless network for the club, which Madison shot down as a "nonstarter."

"The board will never agree to that," she insisted, ultimately getting reluctant approval for hard-wired installation in the upstairs room, coupled with faster speeds. Nevertheless, Madison taped over the camera holes on each iMac. "One can never be too careful," she said.

Claire inspected the room's two windows, which abutted the roof of the dining room wing, almost like a deck overlooking the park. Much too risky and tempting for curious kids. She asked Jess to install window guards, to block them at six inches.

"I would never have thought of that," said Madison. "You would have," said Claire, "after the first day."

The drab and wainscoted Music Room needed additional brightening, and Madison envisioned a sunny "Small World"-esque wall mural since "these kids are rather international." That reasoning stumped Claire, who liked the idea anyway. Their initial sketches were hopeless. Claire considered recruiting Clay to help, but decided against it; he was always exhausted and often punchy after work and might take offense at an art project so trivial.

"I wish we still had Ethan around," Claire said.

"We all do," said Madison.

Claire decided the kids would paint it themselves, their first art project when they arrived the next week. She sourced out the best place for supplies, and Edie's grant in hand, set out on foot for yet another shopping mission.

And that's when she finally accepted what she'd suspected for weeks but could no longer ignore: The brown Chevelle with tinted windows was following her. Everywhere.

—∿—

She'd made note of it the third time it stopped to let her cross in front of her old apartment that first week. She'd seen it parked on the street—mostly days, occasionally nights—and assumed it was a neighbor's. At the time, her inexplicable panic about everything in her new life excluded something as mundane as a neighborhood car.

But now, clearheaded and calmer, her panic a distant memory, she realized the Chevelle had followed her to her new location. She noted when it idled outside the bakery where she bought her cupcakes, when it pulled over in front of the doctor's office, when it circled the block as she waited for an ATM on Market Street. Its omnipresence was less frightening than galling: How clueless did it think she was?

It left her alone atop Nob Hill, and she never saw it when she dashed to the Fairmont to exercise, or when she read on the benches of Huntington Park. She didn't see it from the front or back door of the club, or from her bedroom window. It seemed to lurk on streets just below, waiting for her to step off the cable car at Powell or California. It would stop-start trail her on her daily errands in the crowded heart of town, then vanish on her return ascent. Google told her "surveillance techniques" often included partners in vehicles and on foot, passing off the target back and forth, assembly-line style. Claire eyed the Huntington Park suspects—the elderly man in tweeds and bow tie, the young mother with her pram-bound newborn, the now-a-friend clergyman—and felt chagrined at her own intricate delusions.

And yet she wasn't deluded. The brown Chevelle shadowed her off her home turf. Daily.

She should have alerted someone. Nora, Madison, certainly Clay. She almost mentioned it to Martha when it waited across from their lunch spot near the hospital, but she didn't want to fuel any more conspiracy theories from her alarmist, I-told-you-so best friend. She pushed from her mind, as best she could, the possibility that the trailing car—and its phantom driver—was linked to the events leading up to her miscarriage, which she had convinced herself was just a natural occurrence. She refused to sink back into the paranoia that had plagued her before and kept her awake at night, skyrocketed her blood pressure, and potentially cost her her pregnancy. No longer with a baby to overprotect, Claire was less fearful for herself and more emboldened, bordering on itchy.

She'd had a stalker before, at Yale—an off-center grad student she'd ultimately scared away without the need for a restraining order. She'd successfully navigated the sketchy, crime-ridden New Haven streets for four years. Her foster-home-to-orphanage-merry-go-round upbringing was hardly delicate. And the pesky brown Chevelle was getting on her nerves.

"Thank you, Allen," she said walking through the opened door on the morning she set out with her classroom supplies shopping list. She wore a bright red scarf and strolled down California past the Tonga Room and boarded the cable car at Powell. She got off a stop later, one steep block down the hill, at Pine. She walked the block crosswise to Mason, and by the time she backtracked her steps, baitlike, the Chevelle had appeared amid the sparse traffic.

Had she continued down the hill on the street's sidewalk, the pursuit would have been easier, but Claire upped the challenge by a sudden dart down the stone staircase midblock. She waited on Bush Street, through two traffic light cycles, until the Chevelle crept along, having rounded the block. Claire flung her red scarf around her neck so it wouldn't miss her and crossed at the light, heading farther downhill.

Claire had chosen her obstacle course carefully. She walked over to the Stockton tunnel overpass, a geographical impossibility for cars. She glanced back at her impotent follower as she pivoted down the pedestrian stairs and emerged on the busier street far below, the gateway to Union Square. A city bus blew past her, its side ad screaming "Get Savage!" in frantic neon with Stu's AM dial numbers right below. She stopped to check her e-mail in front of a dry cleaner on Sutton. She checked her Facebook and the *Huffington Post*. The Chevelle never found her.

She was almost disappointed in her stalker, meandering past the bigger stores, eyeing the choked traffic. She crossed Post Street onto the grassy knolls of Union Square Park. She gave a dollar to a homeless man next to an open suitcase with tabby kittens. She bought a half-caff mocha and read the monument plaque on the Corinthian column in the middle of the square. She considered the rows of street art and pottery under the white market umbrellas and scanned the circling border streets.

She saw the Chevelle idling under the portico of the St. Francis Hotel on the plaza's edge.

Claire walked toward it.

"I'm so sorry!" she said, leaping off the elaborate sidewalk chalk art she'd trod across. "I really am very sorry." She made adequate, sincere eye contact with the offended artist and looked back at the Chevelle. Heavy bursts of soot sputtered from its rattly tailpipe. A uniformed doorman with a mustache held open the hotel door for a guest and then dropped his smile, approached the car, and waved it away. It sat still.

Claire got closer. The doorman knocked on the driver's window and leaned down when it unrolled. From the sidewalk across the street, she strained to see in, but the uniformed man with his big hat blocked her view. The driver must have said something amusing, for the doorman grinned and nodded and stood upright again as the window rolled back up. The Chevelle pulled out of the hotel driveway, and the doorman slapped the trunk godspeed.

It rounded the square as Claire hurried along the Post Street sidewalk. Midway across the park, opposite Tiffany's, the Chevelle made a sudden turn at the Union Square parking entrance and disappeared down into the underground lot. Claire bisected the park, toward Macy's on the far side. By the time she'd descended the stairs at the park's southern rim, the Chevelle had resurfaced at the Geary Street exit and was waiting for her.

Claire considered heading east to the Neiman Marcus, where taxicabs sat in line, but opted to move back toward Powell, where she could hop on a crowded cable car, if necessary, in either direction. The Chevelle, seemingly as fed up as Claire and equally stubborn, crept right behind her, to the red light. Emboldened by the hoards buffering her on all sides, Claire stared down the driver's side of the tinted windshield and pulled her phone from her purse. She threaded to the curb's edge and took a series of photos at close range, thwarted by the throngs at a clean shot of the license plate. She started to join the pedestrians in the crosswalk directly in front of the Chevelle but thought the better of it. Instead, she looked the other way across the Powell intersection.

On the corner sat a traffic cop astride his parked bike. When the light changed, Claire stood still, while crowds flooded around her across the street. The Chevelle stood still, too. A horn complained from the delivery truck right behind it, and then a harmonica of horns further behind protested louder. Claire watched the signal countdown. When it got to "1," she dashed into the crosswalk. The Chevelle followed through the intersection, as the green light ticked yellow.

Claire stopped mid-crosswalk. The Chevelle, trapped in the snarl, the traffic cop right ahead, accepted defeat and flowed through the box. Claire smiled and raised her phone and focused on the rear license plate, waiting for the clearest shot. The delivery truck rode its tail, blocking her view, and the Chevelle disappeared.

That's when she heard, off her shoulder and seemingly simultaneous, the clanging of bells, roar of rubber, symphony of horns. The scream chorus and crunch of metal came together an instant later, followed by silence.

—⁂—

Claire waited until everyone who wanted medical attention got it.

Fortunately, the injuries were negligible, mostly jolted nerves, since the packed cable car had barely rolled into the intersection when the conductor noticed the clueless tourist in the crosswalk, taking pictures of Geary Street with her phone. The FedEx driver right behind had slower reflexes. The low-impact collision would have been a mere pullover had mass transit not been involved.

Claire kept apologizing—to the passengers, the conductor, the furious drivers held hostage in the traffic lockdown—although it was impossible to win them over, having collectively ruined their day. She stayed for over an hour, while the paramedics signed off on everyone, until the commercial-sized tow machines had removed both vehicles, until she'd given all her information to the traffic cop, who handed her a jaywalking ticket.

She nodded and thanked him, walked to Neiman's, flagged a cab. Riding back up Nob Hill, she sat on her hands, to calm their trembling.

—⁂—

From her room, Claire called the police station to report her stalker. The female desk sergeant empathized but couldn't help.

"Driving on public streets isn't a crime," she explained. "Has he made any overt threats?" Claire couldn't confirm it was a "he" at all, further weakening her case.

She paced with the phone, the cord at full stretch, as the desk sergeant rattled off the standardized list of safety precautions for women. Down below, the Chevelle slowly rolled past her window and idled outside the club's parking lot.

"Thank you very much," Claire said, interrupting the sergeant, and hung up.

She grabbed a mop as she stormed through the kitchen and out the back. The Chevelle waited on the street. "What do you want?" she shouted as she got closer. She knocked on the driver's window. "What do you want?" she repeated.

The door was locked, so she tried the back. She walked around the front and struck the mop on the windshield, glancing off. She shook the passenger-door knob and beat her fist against the window and shouted, "What the hell do you want?" She choked tighter on the mop and hammered its metal end against the glass until it cracked and spread. She hammered until the window exploded inward, and the driver cross-shielded his face from the shards and cried, "Miss Claire! Stop!"

Claire stepped back from the Chevelle.

"*Jess?*" she said.

—⚌—

"Where is she?" Nora demanded from the club's back door, barreling toward the front parlor, where Jess had seated Claire. The staff had brought her tea and unasked-for strawberry ice cream with sprinkles in a crystal bowl.

"Don't look at my hair!" Nora ordered, one side coiffed, the other damp and tangly. "Fredo hasn't finished yet." She wore her quilted jacket over faded denim jeans, too harried to care about the flagrant dress code violation.

"You haven't told her anything, have you?" she challenged Jess, who shook his head.

Nora turned to Claire with her tea and untouched ice cream and took a breath.

"This is all my fault," she said. "I pay Jess to follow you. To keep tabs on you.

"With Clay traveling so much," Nora continued, "and you don't know your way around town, and you just saunter off on your own, and I get nervous. Jess moonlights for various members, doing odd jobs and this and that, so I tripled his fee to get him exclusively for us, for our family." She turned to Jess and emphasized, "And he will *not* work for anyone else in this club—that's our deal—and so I pay him to follow you during the day. Just so you don't get lost.

"And to keep you safe," she added, when her "lost" explanation fell flat.

"I was in Special Forces, a long time ago," Jess explained to Claire's silence. "I have skills."

"God, I hope you were more competent back then," Nora said. "Or else this country is in worse shape than I thought." Jess absorbed the good-natured dig and nodded.

"Keep me safe?" Claire probed, ignoring the banter. "Safe from what?"

"What do you think? Safe from *aliens*?" Nora snapped and quickly recovered. "Safe from bad people who might mean you harm.

"When you're here, in the club, or on the square," she stammered, "you're in a secure, controlled environment. With certain...rules. Rules of civility.

"But out there," she went on, jabbing her finger past the window, "there are no rules. All bets are off!"

Jess sat next to Claire and said, "Basically, she wants you to have a bodyguard when you leave the club."

"Just a minder, a watcher," Nora corrected. "A chaperone, really." She palmed back the unruly tangle of hair from her left side, the right side obediently bobbed.

"Why do I need a bodyguard?" Claire asked her mother-in-law. "You don't have one."

"I don't roam the streets and sidewalks," Nora explained. "I don't hang off cable cars like Doris Day."

"Nora, is there something you're not telling me?" Claire asked after a pause. "Am I in danger?"

"Frankly, I don't know!" Nora shrugged with force and slapped her thighs. "Were you attacked? Were you *not* attacked? Do you even know? Do you think I like worrying about these things?"

Nora looked skyward and collected her thoughts.

"I don't know where danger comes from or when it's coming next," she said with precision. "But after last November, after Dean, I don't take any chances." She seemed to deliberate for a moment and said, "Because you and Clay are all I have left in this world." She drummed her fingers on the table, to distract from her quivering lip.

Claire struck a deal. As long as she was a guest of her in-laws at their club, she'd do what they asked. "But once Clay finishes training and we find a home of our own," she said, her hand on top of Nora's, "we'll have to make these decisions for ourselves."

"Yes, of course," Nora said.

"I understand being careful," Claire added, "but we can't live our lives in fear." Nora shook her head and said, "No, we don't want that. That's no way to go through life."

"And one more condition," Claire said, turning to Jess. "You let me buy you a new window." Jess guffawed and said, "Fine by me!" Nora said, "Hell, we'll buy you a new car."

"I'm glad that's all settled," Nora said. "I'm glad it's all out in the open." She kissed the top of Claire's head and buddy-slapped Jess and said, "Fredo's waiting."

"Don't look at my hair!" she ordered everyone as she hurried out the back door.

Claire pulled a piece of paper from her pocket and smiled. "My shopping list is still full," she said. Jess bowed and extended his hand. "Madame, your chariot awaits," he announced.

"How very kind." She curtsied, taking his hand. "I don't mind if I do."

Jess chauffeured her in the club's Town Car. "Just call me Jeeves," he joked, although Claire insisted on riding shotgun. New allies, they relived the morning's wild-goose chase, minus the crosswalk collision, which Jess hadn't seen and Claire didn't volunteer.

Claire finished her shopping errands quickly.

"Thanks again, Jeeves," she said in the club parking lot, unloading bags from the trunk. "I could get used to this."

Chapter Six

C lay sounded hoarse and exhausted over the phone. Granted, it was three a.m. in Moscow.

"Are you getting any sleep?" Claire asked from her room. From Bonn to Beijing to Johannesburg, it was hard to keep track of his time zone. Apparently, he'd been making a good enough impression that Slade had extended the world tour to meet all the "principals."

"I can't wait to be back in our bed," Clay told her, and Claire said, "It's not even our bed!"

She was more excited about her upcoming project than he seemed of his.

"Clay? You there, honey?" she asked to silence, after prattling on about her Safe Harbor plans. "Mm?" he mumbled. "I'm here. I'm listening."

"Hit the hay," she told him. "I miss you." "I'm back next week," he said. "I love you."

Claire Googled the Monolith Club of Moscow, just to see where he was staying. There wasn't much.

—⁊⁊—

At the risk of alienating Nora, Claire had warmed up to Colonel Crowe.

She'd never understood the cause of their rift, and Nora hadn't elaborated. It was a lopsided animosity, as the colonel maintained his charm and grace even while Nora scarcely cloaked her snarls.

After their chilly introduction that first night in the library, Claire had kept her distance and observed him from afar. The thaw began her second week at the club. With almost clairvoyant timing, he'd waited until she'd recovered from her initial trauma and was comfortable in her temporary new home to reach out. He was simultaneously embracing and distant, welcoming her in while giving her space. Colonel Crowe, while too reserved and self-aware for politics, would have made an impressive diplomat, she felt.

Claire found herself eavesdropping on his lively table when they sat nearby at dinner. His guests rotated nightly with a broad cross section of members and sparred over a startling array of topics, minus the classic taboos of sex, politics, and religion, which didn't appear to interest them anyway. None of the members seemed devout in any religion or remotely exercised about even the hottest partisan issues. Sex, mercifully, was miles off the radar. Dinner talk at the Union avoided pettiness while tackling enormous global issues at a high-minded, theoretical level. At times, Claire thought she was back in a Yale classroom.

From the Willing table, between beet salad and Dover sole with vegetable terrine, Claire overheard a rare dabbling into politics when the colonel's table dissected a recent *Chronicle* editorial, but even that seemed more like club politics than the policy kind. "You've really turned against Senator Engle," one of the titans said to the paper's publisher, seated two places over. "That's just runoff from our last board meeting," the colonel interjected. "Don't worry. He'll curl up in the senator's lap again soon." He turned to the publisher and smiled. "Isn't that right?"

Another night, an old coot bemoaned the lack of "towering families of national importance," which he called his generation's "role models." A fellow coot agreed: "Look how sloppy the Kennedys have become." Another: "You'd be hard-pressed to find a Rockefeller worth his salt these days. Ditto the Gettys." And: "The Vanderbilts have vanished completely." One of the young bucks called the concept of such role models "antiquated, like royalty."

The colonel was more optimistic. "There's always a new dynasty on the rise, clawing toward the top," he said, declining dessert. "I suspect royalty will gain favor again, when the world needs it."

Once, a guest speaker for the Thursday men's night joined them at dinner—a visiting dean from a Tennessee university Claire hadn't heard of. Tweedy and soothing with twinkling blue eyes, he hypnotized the diners with descriptions of "breakthrough experiments" that sounded unnervingly sci-fi. Edie latched on and said, "Would you care to join me outside for a cigarette?"

"Very tempting," the dean said, twinkling brighter, "but I gave it up not so long ago."

Claire perked up one Sunday brunch when a red merry at the colonel's table brought up "that crackpot" Stu Savage. Surprisingly, the others had strong opinions. The consensus was that Stu had "jumped the shark," according to a buck who explained the term to the coots, although Claire doubted a pre-shark-jumping Stu was even possible. She was further surprised that the colonel came to Stu's defense.

"The true believer," he insisted, "cannot be over-the-top."

She wondered if one of Stu's fans was her downstairs chain-smoking neighbor who played him around the clock. Mostly she was heartened not to be the only Stu addict.

"Did you hear we're conspiring to impose a Satanic totalitarian regime on the unsuspecting masses?" a member asked to table laughter. "Totalitarian sounds fun enough," said another. "Satanic is just icing on the cake." "When do we start?" someone asked. "The sooner the better," another answered. More laughter.

"Methinks Stu doth protest too much," a skeptical older woman complained. "I wish we had a fraction of the power he claims we do," one of the titans said. "Can we at least get advance notice before the collapse?" a wife asked. "I'd like to plan a final garden party."

"He used to be somewhat thought-provoking, but he's pushing the end-of-days stuff so hard, he sounds berserk," someone said. "Perhaps that's the point," the colonel posited. "In the current climate, berserk is ratings gold."

"But it also risks apocalypse-fatigue," said another, and the colonel considered this and said, "Perhaps that's the point, as well." At the foyer piano, Stompy crooned "Some Fine Day" in his best Bobby Short.

"I've often wondered why 'apocalypse' has such a negative connotation," the colonel mused. "It simply means 'change.' Perhaps a change for the better, why not?" This launched a spirited discussion that spread to the neighboring tables, most of which Claire missed, as Nora was holding forth on the new Ann Patchett novel she was midway through. "I heard her on the *Diane Rehm Show*," Nora was telling her table. "I was hoping she'd have a new one out soon."

"Y2K, 2012, the so-called Rapture, these have all been shams, of course," the colonel went on next door. "Where's our resident biblical expert?" He looked around to a neighboring table. "Horace," he called out to a soon-to-be-coot nearby, "what does the good book say about the end of days?"

Horace, honored to answer, wiped his mouth and quoted loudly: "'No one knows about that day or hour, not even the angels in heaven.'" Colonel Crowe smiled and pivoted back to his table. "I don't see the point in arguing with that," he said.

"It seems there's a perverse pleasure to be had in the contemplation of apocalypse," the colonel posited. "The apocalypse is never boring."

"But History shows that catastrophes are actually a blessing," the colonel continued. "From the biblical flood, to the Great Chicago Fire, to our own city's earthquake and subsequent devastation more than a century ago, the worst holocausts often lead to a more dynamic, more just, much improved civilization."

"The apocalypse," he added, cheek-tongued, "is a terrible thing to waste." Titters spread from table to table, including Claire's.

"I've been following Patchett since *Run*," Nora said, pointedly ignoring the room's rippling conversation. "Although I was a bit let down by *The Magician's Assistant*."

"This age-old terror that Mr. Savage is cashing in on is simply a fear of change, of the future," the colonel decreed calmly, as the quieted room seemed to lean toward him. "Such fear is both irrational and faulty.

"The future will not be appalling," he concluded. "It will not be so-so. It will be a glory."

Claire neither flinched nor looked away when the colonel gazed beyond his table and caught her staring.

"*Have* you?" asked Nora sharply. Claire turned back and said, "Have I what?" "Read *Bel Canto*?" Nora said, and before a flustered Claire could answer, added, "Oh, forget it!"

"Good God, the freaks are discussing doomsday again. On a Sunday," Nora huffed to an amused Bing, the table's stand-in for the traveling Slade and Clay. "I've never understood this club's sick obsession with the end of the world. Even Claire's starting to catch it."

"It's fascinating," Claire admitted brightly, adding, "And ridiculous, of course."

The following evening, Colonel Crowe invited Claire to join his table.

Nora was elsewhere, which Claire had encouraged. "You needn't come to the club every night just for me," she'd assured her. "I'm remarkably self-sufficient."

As Claire entered the Grand Dining Room, she stood briefly and scanned and was moving toward the Hammonds' table when she felt a gentle hand on the curve of her back.

"Won't you?" the colonel offered and held her chair. Over the next few nights, he introduced her to more members, folded her into conversations and, professorlike, thoughtfully considered her occasionally unorthodox points of view without condescension.

"Claire's our resident public education expert," the colonel boasted to his table one night, amid an erudite discussion of its current challenges. He turned and asked for her prescription.

"Simple," she answered, grounding their loftiness with specifics. "Smaller classes. More funding." When a young titan countered that greater spending had led to much worse outcomes, calling the public schools "drug-infested war zones," Claire reared up.

"Not everyone is born into private schools, summer camps, and custom-made suits," she schooled, reining in before she could add *silver spoon.*

"That money never gets to the kids," she added. "It doesn't go to the tools we need to educate our exploding number of students. So many of these kids come from broken homes, or ones that don't speak English, or from parents slaving several jobs just to keep a roof over their heads...." Claire herself seemed overwhelmed by the enormity of it. "Frankly, I don't know where all the money goes."

"What we need, I think," she concluded, "is an overhaul of the whole system."

"Hear, hear," the colonel said, perking. "Shall we put you in charge?"

Claire tipped her head in mock flattery and then demurred. "I don't want that much control," she said. "I'm not qualified anyway."

"The teacher appears when the student is ready," the colonel said, lifting his burgundy-ringed coffee cup.

"Control can be very liberating," he added. "Don't you see? Don't you agree?"

On another night, over lamb with mint jelly, the colonel volleyed global warming. "That's the biggest crisis of our lifetime," Edie declared. "That should terrify everyone on the planet!" Bing disagreed, calling the worldwide debt crisis the "imminent catastrophe" that would "bring it all down."

Others chimed in with the usual suspects: terrorism, the Middle East, political upheaval and cultural disintegration. Claire had to bite her tongue when a sable-collared youngish wife lamented about "hunger and poverty" while a white-coated waiter cleared her nibbled dinner and refilled her Tattinger.

Colonel Crowe brought up the recent news that the world population had ballooned to seven billion and growing. Everyone agreed this was "unsustainable," although Claire was less full-throated.

"That's the root of all our problems," Edie insisted, wanding her unlit cigarette holder. "Mother Earth isn't designed to take care of that many. Can't you hear her groaning under the pressure? I can."

The colonel turned to Claire. "What do you think is the world's biggest crisis?" he asked. "Its cancer, if you will."

Claire, who'd had two glasses of wine when she usually kept to one, looked around the table, around the Grand Dining Room, and said, "Honestly, I think it's us. And people like us." "Yes, I suspected that." The colonel smiled and nodded. "Won't you elaborate? I'm afraid you've shocked our friends."

Clancy said, "I think I know what she means," and the Colonel said, "Let her elaborate anyway."

"Look where we are," Claire said, indicating the club. "And how much we have, cloistered away up here. All the money and power concentrated in this building. And right outside those doors, so much of the world is in despair, in panic."

She went on, emboldened. "I think the collapse, the 'apocalypse' as you call it, has already started. It's here. If we were serious, we'd channel our energy and brain power and resources to figure out a way, any way, to turn it around. Because right now, we're living high above it all and doing nothing. We're just hypocrites. And phonies."

There was brief silence, then offended protests from the table, but Colonel Crowe cut them off.

"Claire is merely paraphrasing the good book of Luke," he defended her. "'From whom much is given, much is expected.' Isn't that right?"

Claire simmered down and said, "Now more than ever."

"Wouldn't it be nice to have a 'reset' button, Noah-style?" the colonel asked, to lighten the mood. "And just start the world anew?" The tabled laughed and nodded, and so did Claire. Waiters brought profiteroles.

"I hope I didn't overstep my bounds, especially as a guest," she told the colonel later by the staircase. "But since you asked..."

He shook his head. "It was just the jolt they needed," he said. "You're a breath of fresh air in this club, Claire. And all the attendant clichés." Heading upstairs, he added, "We've more in common than I first thought."

Nora, who'd been watching from her bridge table in the card room, came to Claire at once.

"How can you sit at that man's table?" she steamed. "How can you break bread with him?"

"He invited me." Claire shrugged. "He's much friendlier than I first thought."

"You don't know him." Nora shook her head, walking back toward her bridge game, and then turned back, wagged her finger, and repeated, too loudly, "You don't know him at all."

Madison, who walked the same tightrope, later warned Claire against drilling down to the source of their conflict. "That's the club's Rube Goldberg machine," she said, startled by her own analogy. "Don't get caught in its gears."

Chapter Seven

O n Monday afternoon at 3:05, the Union Club learned the term "youthquake."

Ilza and Anthony, the oldest at eleven, led the buddy-charge past Allen into the Grand Foyer. "Slow," the clergyman reminded them, gazing up to the Tiffany dome. "Careful."

"Welcome!" Claire embraced him while counting heads. "Is there an extra one?" The clergyman nodded and said, "He joined us last week. I hope you don't mind. This is Caesar." Claire shook the small boy's hand and said, "Welcome, Caesar! The more the merrier!"

"We call him Little Caesar," Ilza announced. "I don't think that's very nice," Claire said, and the clergyman said, "Actually, he seems to like it." "Well then, welcome Little Caesar!" Claire cheered. She smiled and waved at the cluster of curious coots in the Reading Room doorway. "Good afternoon, Mr. Beasley," she called out in vain.

"Aren't they adorable!" Madison said, introducing herself to the children. "I have a surprise for you later!" Anthony looked at her arm crutch and said, "I broke my leg once." "Isn't it an encumbrance?" Madison said.

The clergyman said Madison was "even prettier in person than in the newspaper." Madison turned to Claire and said, "This one may stay."

Edgar resisted his buddies' pull into the center of things, preferring the security of a corner kentia palm. Claire had her eye on him from the start and squatted down to his level from across the foyer and made a face until he grinned and looked away.

The clergyman was overwhelmed by the transformed Safe Harbor room upstairs. "I didn't expect anything like this," he said of the computers and easels and reading tables and fresh game board carpeting. "I'm blown away." Claire offered to show him her teacher's plan, but he shook his head. "Totally unnecessary," he said. "I trust you completely."

Nora weaved in past the noisy children overtaking their new playroom and invited the clergyman for a club tour and "adult beverage." "It's so nice to finally meet our neighbor," she said, leading him out by the arm. "We've been strangers far too long."

"Who wants to play dress up?" Madison called from the room closet, where she'd hidden her surprise box of personalized baseball jerseys for "Team Claire." "Madison, you shouldn't have gone to all that trouble," said an embarrassed Claire, her name embroidered in elaborate cursive on each. Madison said, "Why not? It's organic cotton." Coachlike, Madison matched the named and numbered overshirts to each clamoring child in a roll call and marked notes in her leather binder with color-coded dividers.

"Please wear the jersey assigned to you," she gently chided Rodney and CJ midswap and then whispered to Claire, "I'll never keep them straight otherwise."

They sat in a "new friend circle," and Miss Claire led off the introductions. Ilza and Little Caesar eagerly volunteered their favorite books, sports, and school subjects, but others were more reticent and "passed" on their turn. Edgar sat outside the circle and resisted Ilza's orders to join.

"Let's mind our own business, please," Claire told the precocious girl. "Edgar's fine where he is."

Claire knew there'd be no teaching or learning this first day, but she established the schedule they'd follow from here on: a mix of education, culture, and exercise, plus the all-important short nap. Angel and Condi played "Reader Rabbit" and "Clifford's Thinking Adventures" on the iMacs, while Little Caesar and CJ took turns with "Socks in Space" on PBS Online. Rodney bemoaned the lack of TV, but Claire had ruled out idle entertainment and paired him up with Anthony on a *Cars*-themed Scrabble game, which they took to surprisingly quickly.

"May I?" Claire asked of Edgar, who stood by the window that looked out toward Grace Cathedral. She pointed at his non-ticking Smurf watch and held out her hand. "I think we can wake him up," she said. Edgar didn't hesitate, and Claire carefully opened the back with a paper clip and tried the different batteries she'd bought, until the right one set the second hand moving. "Let's put his arms in place," Claire said, adjusting the time before handing the watch back over. Edgar held it to his ear and listened, then smiled at the sweeping hand. "I told you we'd fix it," Claire said. At recess on the playground, Edgar followed the other kids down the slide, shielding his watch protectively.

"Take a breather, won't you?" Madison said after Claire herded the troops back upstairs for refreshments. "I can handle snack time." Three Asian women from the kitchen brought a rolling tray of cookies and flavored milk in individual cartons, and Madison made the children sit in assigned seats at the crafts table. She oversaw the serving of the cartons like a proper tea, assuring the kids the milk was 2 percent and came from "hormone-free" cows. "Mr. Stimson owns the dairy," she told them. "These are some of his new flavors." Claire was bemused by

Madison's airy awkwardness around children, as seemed the children themselves.

"Drink your milk, Edgar," Madison urged, scanning down a list in her leather binder. "I gave you white chocolate, right? Don't you like it?"

"Are you keeping notes?" Claire asked, further bemused. Madison nodded and said, "I told Mr. Stimson I'd report back on the kids' reactions to the new products, since he's kind enough to donate." Then she playfully shooed Claire away and said, "Go take a break! You've done everything so far."

As Claire closed the door behind her, Madison was explaining the cookies to a perplexed Ilza. "They're *macarons,*" she said. "The Parisian style. Not to be confused with the coconut variety common in the Jewish culture. Who's been to France?"

Nora had perhaps served the clergyman one too many adult beverages, for he was unusually breezy and clearly charmed as Claire helped him corral the kids back across the square at the end of their successful first day.

"Your mother-in-law is a hoot," he said. "And so gracious. She insists I'm not needed and should take the afternoons off."

"She's right," Claire said. "The three of us can handle this gang. If there's any trouble, you're right across the way."

Claire stood by the swing set and watched the buddied-up troop cross Taylor Street and disappear into the church. Edgar turned back at the door and looked at her. He waved first, and she smiled and waved back. Bashful, he beamed and ducked inside.

Madison had a chardonnay waiting for her back at the club.

"Congratulations, Claire," she said, clinking glasses. "I think we're off to such a promising start."

"Cheers, Madison." Claire smiled, swirling the wine. "I agree."

—⁓—

Clay and Claire spent two days and nights in their bedroom suite when he returned. It had been their longest separation in years.

He'd brought her an intricately embroidered cheongsam dress from China and a hand-carved stone elephant from South Africa. "Are those tusks real ivory?" Claire asked, grimacing. She put it on a side table. "Poor elephant," she said.

They made love and slept and ordered room service, and Clay took the rest of the week off. Claire left him for only a few hours each day to take care of her kids. Jet lag took its toll on Clay's sleep and moods, and Claire tried to boost his spirits, but he wasn't up for dinner out at a restaurant or a movie or even Dane Cook at the Masonic Auditorium right across the square.

He feigned interest in Angel's conjugation of irregular verbs and CJ's nascent appreciation of Mozart, but he wasn't fooling Claire, and she stopped boring him with her daily updates. He didn't talk about his own work, so they mostly watched PBS and Discovery on TV, his head in her lap while she stroked his hair.

Twice she woke to an empty bed with Clay sitting on the window seat staring into the night.

"Honey, can't you sleep?" she asked. "Jet lag," he reminded her.

Stress, she knew. Even after a five-day break from his job, he couldn't get it out of his mind.

—⟋⟍—

After a particularly active afternoon with the kids, Claire went from her shower to her walk-in closet and found it full of dazzling clothes.

From the bars hung dozens of dresses in clear, breathable bags. There were florals and solids and retro prints, silks and satins and woolens, day and tea and a few evening lengths. They were from top-shelf designers—Prada, Céline, Proenza Schouler—and several still dangled their jaw-dropping price tags.

Stacked in the armoire were tissue-folded cashmere sweaters in spring pastels and rich fall tones, cable-knits and cardigans and matching sets of both in various weights. There were slacks of gray flannel and gabardines and crepes and charmeuse.

Claire only glanced at the Burberry trench coats and Dior fitted jackets and alligator belts and shoes.

"Ling, where did these come from?" she asked when he brought up Clay's dry-cleaned tuxedo, although she already suspected the answer.

She found Madison downstairs.

"I finally got around to my spring cleaning and thought you'd have use for them, since we're the same size," Madison explained. "I have to make room for next season anyway. Apparently oxblood is *the* color for fall. I still can't wrap my brain around that."

"That's very kind," Claire said, "but they're just too valuable."

"They have no value at all," said Madison, "since I'm giving them away."

"Honestly, I don't need you to dress me," Claire said, and Madison said, "Oh relax, Claire. We're family." And then she said, "But yes, frankly, it wouldn't hurt to up your game a bit. You're a Willing, you know. Give yourself permission to live a little grander. It's expected."

Madison closed the subject. "Wear them or don't. If you decide to expand your palette, now you'll have lots to play with!"

Claire dressed for dinner in her own clothes. But midway down the hall, she returned and threw a primrose-pink Jil Sander cashmere cardigan over her shoulders, since the dining room was often drafty.

—⟁—

As burdened and weighed down as Clay seemed by his job, Claire was equally liberated and airborne with her new daily rhythm. Her joy was infectious.

Jess and Ling carried a long, sturdy table into the Safe Harbor room. One night after dinner, Claire covered it with a drop cloth, climbed on top, and painted the drab walls above the wainscoting with chalkboard paint in sky blue and rolling hills green. Her glued cotton ball cloud formations impressed even Clay. "Cool mixed media," he said, before leaving her to finish.

The smocked children added their own chalk self-portraits. Ilza became a magical princess with a freakishly large head, and CJ zoomed across the hills on a motorcycle. Claire held Little Caesar up so he could draw himself captaining an airplane high above it all.

"I didn't dress for crafts," Madison said, so Claire drew both their stick figures, in triangle skirts, framing the others. "Does my hair really look that severe?" Madison complained. Claire erased Madison's head and started all over.

Edgar watched and fidgeted and eventually held his arms up to be lifted onto the table. He stood by Claire's self-portrait and pointed his instructions. She drew a big purple monster, and he shook his head. "You're not a purple people eater?" she double-checked before erasing it.

He wasn't a flower or a rabbit either, or a mix of both, although each made him laugh. Finally, he approved a simple stick figure boy, standing next to Claire on the green hills. He pointed again, and Claire drew his hand reaching up and redrew her own until they touched.

Stompy at the piano taught the kids "On the Sunny Side of the Street," and they taught him "Kumbaya." He thrilled them with his spot-on Donald Duck impression, including a slobbery temper tantrum. "Stompy, you smell like smoke," Ilza scolded.

Ballroom dancing enthusiast Nora paired up with Angel to demonstrate the box step and fox-trot. "What?" she snapped at the taunting boys. "Girls can dance with girls!"

In the classroom and on the playground, Claire stressed "active" over "passive."

"You may *read The Lorax*," she told the kids. "You may not *watch The Lorax*."

She taught the kids "active listening" with hand signals and got them hooked on the daily mantra she'd used for years. She'd start the call randomly with, "Education is my future," and they'd answer back in unison, "And my future is now!"

"What are we gonna do tomorrow?" she'd ask at the end of each day.

"Make it better!" the kids would yell, loving the game.

"That's precious," Madison said.

"CJ, no!" Claire warned as he dropped his toy FedEx truck down the room's mail chute. "Bye-bye, truck," she said, ignoring his pleas to fetch it back.

Future doctor Ilza found a pink squeeze flashlight and demanded the others open wide for her inspection. "Edgar's tonsils are red," she announced. "His tonsils are fine," Claire said, sticking out her tongue while Ilza peered in before moving on to her next patient.

One afternoon, they Skyped with Claire's old class in Santa Fe, albeit via one-way cam since Madison wouldn't let them untape their own. Teresa was still causing mischief, but Marisa looked better groomed and cared for than Claire remembered. Perhaps her mother had cleaned up her act. The third graders introduced themselves in roll call and sang "I Don't Want to Live on the Moon" for the rapt Safe Harbor kids.

"Miss you! Love you!" a proud Claire said, signing off and promising to visit "someday."

Jess came dressed as a leprechaun on St. Patrick's Day and tossed handfuls of coin chocolates from his pot o' gold to the jumping children. "He's what you call 'black Irish,'" Madison said, self-amused, as she oversaw the passing out of the day's green-colored milk. "No, Rodney," she corrected. "That's Condi's. Stick to your own, please."

They rented a van and took field trips to the Exploratorium, the Golden Gate Park, the Academy of Sciences planetarium and simulated rain forest. They rode the newly restored vintage carousel in the Children's Playground and roamed the Conservatory of Flowers.

They gaped at the African lions and rhinos and grizzlies at the San Francisco Zoo. They squealed at the showoff penguins whose dim underwater viewing "iceberg" stank like a public bathroom. "Emmy Fleishhackers' grandfather created this zoo in the 1930s," Madison lectured over their daily snacks, which club staff had brought and served on a picnic table outside the Leaping Lemur Cafe. "The Union has long been involved in wildlife preservation." Then she thought and added, "Like Noah."

Slade arranged an afternoon at the police headquarters with the chief and a veteran detective. "They have guns," said a wide-eyed Rodney. "Guns are very bad," Madison told him. "Except for police. Because they protect us."

The handsome, glad-handing young mayor set up a private tour of City Hall and huddled them around his desk for a photo op. "The city's future," he called them through his high-wattage smile. "Cheater," Madison murmured in Claire's ear by his wall-of-fame photos. "*Quel* pig."

They crossed over to the public library for Puppet Storybook Hour and checked out dozens of books on Madison's card. "I don't like all these dystopian novels," Claire said, thumbing through the "Most Popular" shelves by the check-out desk. "They're all about doom and death and slavery. Much too dark for children."

Madison agreed. "Yes, the future won't be quite as oppressive as these books make it out to be," she said. Claire laughed and said, "I certainly hope not!"

"And all this nuclear holocaust stuff is just silly," Madison went on, flipping through. "I mean, it won't be nuclear." She closed the book and declared, "That doesn't make sense at all."

"No," Claire said, rounding up the children. "It doesn't."

"Miss Madison, what's wrong with you?" Ilza asked on another field trip, pointing to her crutch as she limped through the Japanese Tea Garden.

"A crazy man shot me," Madison said. "He shot and killed my husband first, and then he shot at me, and the bullet grazed my spine."

"Madison, please," Claire said.

"What?" Madison asked. "What is the point in shielding our youth from the horrors of our world? Besides, it was on live television."

"You were on TV?" CJ marveled, and Madison nodded and said, "And on the Internet. We can YouTube it later."

"No, we can't," Claire said. "We won't."

"I'm sorry he shot you in the back." Ilza mothered her. "I'm sorry your spine hurts."

"Who wants to go across the Moon Bridge?" Claire interrupted. "Let's get a picture by the Peace Lantern!"

Claire kept the kids "at full stretch," exhausting them mentally and physically each day, for which the clergyman was especially grateful. Even Edgar learned to take a post-snack nap, albeit in Claire's lap, as she rocked and read him *The Giving Tree* or *Blueberries for Sal*.

"Looks like teacher has a new pet," Madison said. "Ssh," Claire admonished, gently taking his milk carton away so it wouldn't drop.

"Gesundheit!" she said when Edgar's sneeze woke him up. He sneezed again. "Gesundheit!" she repeated, to his snickers.

"Can you say 'excuse me'?" she said on his third sneeze. "'Cuse me," he said and sneezed again. "Mr. Sneezy Monster!" she said and tickled him to squeals.

Every day after the kids left, Claire and Madison would straighten the room and brainstorm about future activities. Madison suggested lacrosse or field hockey, both of which Claire found ridiculous. "How 'bout polo?" she joked. "Polo's a bit dangerous for children," Madison said, wiping crumbs from the table into her palm, missing the barb entirely.

"I was thinking more like kickball or maybe an obstacle course," Claire clarified. "Even swimming."

"That's a wonderful idea," Madison said. "We can use the pool at Burlingame. We have cross-club privileges."

"Why not the pool downstairs?" Claire asked. "We can play Marco Polo on rainy days."

Madison frowned and shook her head. "The indoor pool is still closed," she said. "Mold or asbestos or something. Duck-duck-goose is a fun indoor game, too."

Claire stayed so busy she'd practically forgotten about her cell phone in the coatroom. She had several messages from Martha, in escalating stages of playful orneriness mixed with accusations of abandonment. Claire called to apologize and make a date.

She also had dozens of missed calls, four or more a day, from a blocked number, most recently in the last hour. It was likely a telemarketer. If they ever caught her live, she'd politely ask them to take her off their list.

Chapter Eight

"What, is the Rolls in the shop?" Martha balked when Claire picked her up at the hospital in the Jess-chauffeured Lincoln. She had changed from her scrubs and wore makeup but still looked exhausted. "Jess, it's nice to meet you," she added. "Claire says wonderful things."

They'd planned a long-overdue gossipy lunch. Martha's love life was still stalled, but there was a promising prospect or two on the horizon. "I'm lowering expectations," she said. "Hovering just above prison. For now."

"I'll keep an eye out for eligible bachelors at the Union," Claire offered.

"Oh God, no." Martha cackled hoarsely. "I'm desperate, but I'm not *desperate*." "There are some surprisingly attractive young men...," Claire started.

"I like your new hair," Martha interrupted, sizing up Claire's sleek, shorter, blown-out style. "I almost didn't recognize you."

"Oh. Thanks. It was Fredo's idea," Claire said, smoothing down a side. "He's Nora's guy. I'm still getting used to it." "His name is Fredo? For real?" Martha asked. Claire nodded and said, "And he looks just like one."

"I feel underdressed," Martha said, looking around the tony Pacific Heights eatery.

"You look fine." Claire eyeballed the pricey menu and added, "My treat. Since I've been so incommunicado."

They chatted about a college friend who'd posted pictures of her newborn twins on Facebook. Martha called them "miracle babies" because of the extraordinary measures their friend had taken to conceive. "You'd be amazed what they can do these days," she said.

"Did you hear Dr. Kerr died?" Martha asked. "Her husband finally pulled the plug."

"Who?" asked Claire. "Our doctor," Martha said.

"Of course," Claire said, instantly guilty for having forgotten all about her. "That's terrible. Just awful. That's very sad."

"She would have wanted it that way," Martha said. "Of all people, she'd hate to waste away on a machine." "That's just awful," Claire repeated. "Very sad."

"The real housewives of San Francisco," Martha mused, side-eyeing the mostly female, archly elegant luncheon crowd. "Or the Stepford Wives? Live from the social pages. God, in my next life, I gotta come back rich and idle."

"How do you know they're idle?" Claire said, smile-nodding to a young wife she recognized from the club. "Don't be so quick to judge."

"Oh," Martha said, sizing up the young wife. "Okay."

"I'd introduce you, but I can't remember her name," said Claire. "You don't need to introduce me," Martha said, sitting up straighter.

"So is this what you do these days?" Martha asked, inspecting Claire's spring tweed St. John jacket. "Go out to lunch and shop and stuff?" "Not at all," Claire said. "I've hardly been out lately."

Claire talked about her Safe Harbor program, proud of the progress the children were making, especially Edgar, who was ever so slowly coming out of his shell. She lamented how the public schools didn't challenge them enough.

"They never have homework, so I assign them stuff," she said. "And they're just now discovering the joy of reading. Isn't that pitiful? I mean, what do they do in school all day?"

"Thank God for the Union," Claire went on. "They've been so generous to the kids. The Whitneys donated books and those flute recorders for our little band. And Mr. Stimson's dairy provides these flavored milks that haven't hit the market yet, although they're too sugary."

"Mighty keen," said Martha, stirring her Niçoise salad. "Mighty keen."

"The whole staff's gotten involved, too. It's really refreshing," Claire continued. "They treat these kids like royalty, and the club has never felt more alive."

"That's sweet," Martha said. "Between parties, I mean."

"The Union has a long history of charity in this town," Claire corrected her. "Their members created the library and symphony, most of the museums, and the club's founder built your hospital from scratch over a hundred years ago."

"So *that's* who to blame!" Martha squawked. "He's still killing me."

"I'm just saying, the club isn't what I expected," Claire said. "It's full of surprises. You know, Margaret Sanger was its first female member. You gotta admit that's pretty cool."

"Is that a Prismick?" Martha asked of the latte-colored purse hanging on Claire's chair. "*Quelle grande.*"

"Beats me," Claire said, ignoring the interruption. "Madison gave it to me."

"There's a four-month wait list," Martha interrupted again later, pointing to the bag. "For those who can."

"I didn't buy it," Claire said. "And I'll probably give it back to her."

Martha complained about her student debts, and Claire told Clancy's Lobster Night story, which wasn't as funny out of context. She admitted the rigors of Clay's new job had been "a temporary strain" on their relationship. "It'll settle down in a month or so," she said, "when he's done training." By the time the waiter cleared their picked-over plates, they'd run out of subjects.

Claire paid the bill and checked her watch. Madison had told her to take the afternoon off, but she was eager for an update from Edgar's social worker about his therapy session. She also wanted to check on his allergies, which were acting up with the change of seasons.

"I still need to see your apartment sometime," Claire said on the ride back to the hospital. "I might have a small dinner thing soon," Martha replied. "Count me in," said Claire. "But Clay's schedule is the wild card. He never has time to go out, it seems."

Martha looked at her. "You're joking," she said. "I thought that's all he did."

"What do you mean?" asked Claire.

Martha pulled a stack of magazines from her tote. She flipped through the new *San Francisco* to the "Scene" social section. Clay was on practically every page. At the Red Cross Gala, the Catalyst for a Cure Benefit, the MidWinter Gala, Zootopia.

"I thought they'd passed a law he has to bless every social event," Martha quipped. "I swear he goes to the opening of manhole covers."

"When...were these taken?" Claire asked.

He smiled at An Evening of Enchantment, the Guardsmen Sports Auction, the Art Inspiring Hope Gala. He wore a tuxedo or one of his many new bespoke suits and ties. He looked like a movie star. He was surrounded by people of all ages, all smiling, all familiar. Nora, Slade, and Madison had joined him at La Grande Fete at the Fine Arts Museum just two weeks before. The proud family.

"Why aren't you in the photos?" Martha asked. "Are you that camera shy?"

"I wasn't there," Claire said. "At any of them."

Martha flipped through the new *7x7* with more of the same.

"These?" she asked. "Nope," Claire said. "Not a one."

"Why didn't you go?" Martha asked. "Because I didn't know anything about them," Claire answered. "Because I wasn't invited."

"Oh," said Martha.

They rode in silence. Martha thumbed through the outlandish *Weekly World News.*

"Did you know Princess Diana and JFK Jr. live together on a remote island?" she asked, showing off the article. "They have two children. I bet they're beautiful."

"No," Claire said, turning back to the window and the traffic jam outside. "I didn't know anything about that either."

—m—

Clay didn't understand why she was upset.

"Those parties are work related," he told her that night. "They make me go."

"Who does?" Claire asked, watching him unknot his tie.

"The company's PR department," Clay said. "And Dad. Apparently, I'm supposed to be 'seen' a lot, since I just moved back. For business reasons, I guess."

"I just show up and smile for the cameras, shake a few hands, and jet," he added. "I hate those things, you know that." "Yes, I thought you did," Claire said. "I always assumed you were just working late."

"I have been," he said, unbuttoning his shirt. "I just told you; it's work related."

"So you change into a tuxedo and then change back before you come home?" she asked. Clay nodded. "I keep an extra tux at work," he said. "Nothing complicated about it.

"Do you want to go to these parties with me?" he asked from his bathroom sink. "I thought you hated those things, too. They're so phony."

"Well, I am your wife," Claire said. "Don't people expect me there? With our family?"

"No one's mentioned it." He shrugged and then turned. "Aw, do you feel left out?" "Shut up," Claire said. "Don't make fun of me."

"Fine," he said, padding to the bed. "I'll tell the PR gal to include you from now on. She'll assign you a personal shopper and a stylist to keep track of all your outfits so you never wear the same one twice, and then she'll send a makeup artist and a Botox specialist to..."

"Okay, okay!" Claire laughed, pulling him closer. "Forget it!"

"And then you'll be a fancy high-society lady in all the pretty pictures in the magazine, just like Madison," he went on, tickling her. "Is that what you want?"

"Not that!" she howled. "Anything but that!"

It had been too long since they'd made love. She hoped it would relieve Clay's stress, but he still woke up with nightmares, and she held and soothed him until he drifted back off to sleep.

—◊◊◊—

The next day, Nora's cryptic warnings finally hit home when Claire overheard the charming and gracious Colonel Crowe trying to blackball her from the club.

Claire tended to mind her own business, but the echo chamber of the club's interior light well made this practically impossible. The club's hyperactive heating system, coupled with San Francisco's bipolar weather, meant open windows, facing in. Vacuum cleaners, staff gossip in foreign languages, and guest room showers and toilets were politely ignored ambient noise.

Claire was accustomed to the long-term visitor one flight down, with his cigarette smoke and near-constant Stu Savage warnings filling her bedroom with peak oil, contagious cancer viruses, chem trails spewing poison, FEMA reeducation camps being built in Texas and Nevada, and her own imminent enslavement. *"Seven billion of us!"* he reminded her. *"Only a few of them! They can't win without our consent!"*

Damn straight, Stu. Claire smiled from her desk as she checked one of her favorite teaching blogs. She zeroed in on a report of an art project called "Peace Train," funded by a Midwest energy conglomerate. Literally a retired steam locomotive, traveling to parks in major cities, adding cars decorated by local children with the theme of world peace. Claire studied the guidelines, determined her kids would participate when the train came to San Francisco.

Then she heard Slade talking to Colonel Crowe. About her.

"We hoped special dispensation could be made for Claire," the normally dominant Slade seemed to plead. "Especially after what our family's been through."

"Claire is lovely and appealing with many promising qualities." The colonel's calm, resonant voice wafted in. *Good answer,* thought Claire. "But membership is out of the question, and you know why.

"We have few rules, but this is one," he added, "and exceptions are never granted. You know this."

By the time Claire peeked through her bathroom window and spied the Gentlemen's Lounge directly across the well, she knew the rule he meant. She'd long outgrown her sensitivity to being "illegitimate," but it stung to hear it discussed brazenly by mature adults. Especially these two. Claire felt small.

"The club welcomes those of humble origins. You and Nora are testament to that," the colonel continued. "But we don't know her origins at all."

"We've exhausted all avenues to identify the father," an atypically timid Slade said. "It's simply not possible." *Oh good God*, thought Claire.

"That many avenues?" The colonel *ts*ked. "You should be relieved your daughter-in-law didn't inherit her mother's morals." *Go fuck yourself,* Claire thought.

"You have yourself to blame for this awkward predicament," the colonel lectured. "Had you and Nora brought this issue to our attention earlier, we wouldn't find ourselves in this regrettable situation."

This doubly galled Claire, who'd never considered her life a "regrettable situation." Not as a displaced child, or the valedictorian of her high school class, or a cum laude scholarship student at Yale, where she'd also held down a thirty-hour-a-week job.

And how presumptuous, she thought, squinting at the silhouettes past the sheers across the well, to assume she and Clay wanted to join the club anyway. Clearly they didn't know them well.

"How will I explain this to Clay?" asked Slade, and the Colonel said, "The Clay I know will understand."

The Clay I know won't give a damn, thought Claire and went to shut the window, having heard more than enough.

"In the meantime, call off your attack wife," the colonel warned. "I appreciate Nora's maternal fervor, but I'm not the enemy here."

Claire stopped midshut at the mention of her mother-in-law and ally.

"She won't back off until you present her compromise to the whole committee," Slade warned back, with apology.

"It's the most outlandish proposal I've heard yet," said the colonel. "I'd be embarrassed to take it to them. It's ludicrous." "It's also very commonplace these days," Slade pressed.

"Has Claire even agreed to such a thing?" the colonel asked, and Slade said, "Given the alternative, I don't foresee a problem.

"You can also remind the committee," Slade added a slight arch, "of the project she started. And can stop. At any time..." "I'll take that under advisement," the colonel said dryly. "But they tend not to respond to threats."

Claire shrieked and jumped back from the window. Sting had alighted on the ledge, out of nowhere, with a loud flutter.

"Dammit!" Claire whispered—astonished the old, fat beast was mobile. "Shoo! Go away." She flicked her hand. It cocked its head and sat still.

Claire peeped around past the creature, to the Gentleman's Lounge. Colonel Crowe stood with parted sheers. Claire pulled back out of view. She heard him shut the window and waited a moment before looking again. The sheers were pulled, the silhouettes gone.

"Don't do that, Sting," she scolded, and the bird stared. Claire stared back to the point of embarrassment and unease and finally shut her window. She shooed it again through the glass—a futile gesture—and on its own timetable, Sting lifted away and disappeared.

Claire sat back at her laptop. As soon as Clay finished training, they'd find a new home and life of their own. She'd stay loyal to the in-laws and Safe Harbor kids, at least until school let out for summer. But she'd leave the club, with its perverse and provincial values, to stew in its backward pettiness.

When Ling knocked, she politely declined tea.

But she called down later and asked for dinner in her room.

Chapter Nine

The Masonic Lodge Philharmonic was more impressive than Claire had expected. They were preparing a special concert for the guests of the Union's upcoming Justice Ball weekend and had generously invited the kids to afternoon rehearsals. "Bring your flutes," Claire told them before heading across the square. "You might learn something."

The towering, multicolored mosaic in the front lobby caught their attention, and Claire had no answers about its dozens of mysterious symbols and solar-lunar images.

"Why is that man holding a star?" Rodney asked, and Angel asked, "Where's his face?" She pointed to the tall, blank figure in the middle clutching a large envelope.

"It's just Mason stuff," Claire explained. "It's not supposed to make sense to the rest of us. But it's very pretty, isn't it?"

"What's a Mason?" Condi asked. Claire wasn't really sure, so she said, "It's a club. Like the Union. But different."

Madison laughed. "It is not at all like the Union," she corrected. "How silly." She shook her head.

"We maintain a symbiotic relationship with the Masons," she told the perplexed kids. Claire stepped in and said, "Miss Madison means the clubs are friends and neighbors." "Yes, that's what I mean," Madison agreed. "The Masons are wonderfully supportive."

Claire didn't attempt to explain the all-seeing eye floating atop the mural. "It's always watching, so behave yourselves," she joked as they went inside. "Edgar, come blow your nose."

Thirty minutes of Chopin was the children's limit, and after the conductor led them in "This Old Man" on their own flutes, Claire ushered them back to the lobby to find a brutal rainstorm raging outside. A "late-winter squall," Madison called it, for which they were completely unprepared. "And I just got my hair done," she complained.

"I need to thank the manager," she abruptly remembered. "I'll meet you back at the club."

"Take your time," Claire said, amused by Madison's blatant lie. "We'll see you after the storm."

Claire huddled the kids together. "Buddy up!" she ordered before rushing into the deluge.

The club staff brought warm, plush towels and too-big terry robes to the drenched and screeching children quarantined in the vestibule. Claire was equally soaked, and they all pointed and shrieked for their most delightful bonding yet.

Ling took the children's wet clothes, and Claire herded the robe-shuffling troop to the foyer fire, making sure Edgar got a prominent spot up front.

"Who wants hot chocolate?" Madison asked, leading a staff member with a tray of paper cups. She was perfectly dry. The cups were marked with names, and she passed them around with cookies.

"Where did you come from?" Claire asked, baffled.

"The kitchen," Madison said, handing Edgar his cup. "I thought hot chocolate would hit the spot. It's milk-based. None of that instant stuff."

"How did you stay dry?" Claire asked, still toweling her hair. She also wondered, but didn't ask, how she'd limped back so quickly. Madison didn't hear the question, reaching over Condi to Anthony.

"Did someone give you a ride?" Claire pressed. "Yes, that's right," Madison said. "One of the Masons. I just had my hair done, you know."

He must have driven her to the back door, although that was still fast, Claire was thinking, when her cell phone rang in her purse. It echoed through the Grand Foyer.

"Sorry. I forgot," she said, retreating to the vestibule while the children snacked and huddled by the fire. It was her Unknown Caller. She answered.

"Hello. Is this Claire Willing?" a man asked, after an off-guard hesitation typical of telemarketers.

"I'm sorry," she politely interrupted. "This isn't a good time. In fact, if you would kindly remove my name—"

"Your landlady Mrs. Biddle gave me your cell number," the man said quickly. "I think I have your red box."

He apologized for having opened it, but he'd found her name inside and tracked down her now nonworking number at her now-empty loft. "I drove by Townsend and buzzed up, but no answer," he explained. "I didn't realize people lived in that neighborhood." He spoke rapidly, nervously. Claire was thrilled and cared only that her box had been found, but it seemed important for him to explain how he had located her.

"There's so little privacy on the Internet these days," he lamented.

He didn't entrust sending her box back to the freight company—which had accidentally dropped it off with his own shipment—having concluded they did "shoddy work." A final Google search had led to her old Santa Fe apartment, and Mrs. Biddle, and now here.

"Whew!" Claire said. "Thank you so much for all this effort. That box is very important to me. I thought I'd lost it for good."

"As far as I know, everything is still in it," he said, and Claire said, "Oh, I'm sure it is. It has no value, except to me."

"Do you live here in San Francisco? Are you in between homes?" he asked.

Claire laughed and said, "It must sound shady that I had a number and address and now I have neither. I'm new here. I don't have a permanent place yet. It's a little complicated."

"I see," he said. "I have your box here at work. I can drop it off on my way home."

"That is very kind, but you've done enough already," Claire insisted, uneasy about explaining her current living situation. "I can come to you right now, if that's convenient."

Claire found a Union Club pad and pen in the coatroom desk. She scribbled down the man's work address.

"Thank you again," she said. "I'm on my way."

—w—

She was a wet mess but didn't want to hold up her Good Samaritan on a Friday. She told Madison she had an errand and kissed Edgar on the head as they went up for naps.

Jess wasn't on duty, so she grabbed an umbrella from the coatroom, hopped a cab at the Fairmont, and gave the address. The driver kept the meter running while she got cash from a Union Square ATM. She would insist her box savior take a hundred-dollar reward for his troubles, no arguments.

She'd forgotten to ask the man's name, which was rude but not problematic since she was surely the only woman coming to retrieve a lost red box. They'd find each other.

"Sir, are you sure this is it?" she asked the driver a few minutes later on a busy street. She double-checked the address.

She stood in front of the San Francisco Museum of Modern Art with her umbrella and wondered if she'd written it down wrong. She looked around for office buildings and concluded the man must work for the museum. She went to the box office and bought a ticket, discounted this late in the day.

The four-story atrium lobby was peopled and buzzy. A tour group of uniformed students in their own after-school program passed by, and Claire made a mental note to bring her kids soon. A perfect field trip.

The elderly volunteer at the information desk was puzzled by Claire's scribbled note. "I've never seen our rooms numbered like this," the old woman said. She unfolded the brochure map and made a phone call and then circled a room on the third floor. "It must be this one," she told Claire, handing her the map. Claire climbed the central staircase.

The third floor was more sparse. Claire's map called it the "Emerging Artists" section. One of the galleries was curtained over with an "Installation in Progress" sign. It read "*Vicious Circles*: Coming Soon" and teased a blown-up image of an intricate connect-the-dot piece. Claire had seen a similar artistic style somewhere and realized her Good Samaritan must be a curator or installer setting up the exhibit, whose opening, according to the sign, was days away.

The security guard blocked her at the gallery entrance.

"It's not open yet, ma'am," he said politely.

"I'm meeting someone who works here," Claire said. She pointed to her map.

The guard cocked his head. "Next door," he told her.

The exhibit he sent her to was titled "Timeline" across its front wall in large block letters. Heavy drapes covered the entrance. Claire crept inside to blackness and silence, except for a low, droning hum. Her eyes slowly adjusted as she rounded a corner toward a glow.

Janet Leigh was silently stabbed to death in the shower, in extreme slow motion on a wall-sized screen. Two people sat on a bench in the middle of the room and watched. Claire got closer and glimpsed their faces. The art-goers paid her no notice. Neither had a box. She moved to the next room.

An angelic nun from a 1940s film filled the far wall, looking heavenward, fingering her rosary. Claire recognized the actress, a Liz Taylor lookalike, but couldn't place her. The room was more crowded, all eyes on the nun. Claire scanned the faces. There were two men, but neither seemed to expect her. There was a loud roar from the screen, and Claire spun to face the bloated, demonic Linda Blair cursing at her, superimposed next to the can't-remember-her-name nun. The art-goers drank in the paradox. Claire decided this exhibit was inappropriate for her kids and moved on.

A giant, transparent projector screen bisected the next room. A larger-than-life elephant lay on its side, seemingly paralyzed. The incessant hum was lower and more invasive. The room was almost empty. The elephant stared at her, moving its legs and blinking its enormous eyes and then was at rest again. Claire felt the projector's beam from behind the screen hit her face. It blinded her, and she repositioned herself.

"An animal is slow to realize it's been trapped...," said a dry voice from the screen.

Through the elephant, the silhouette of a man faced her. His hair was wild, his coat long. Claire moved closer to the elephant's peaceful, blinking eye and peered through to the other side. The silhouette stayed still.

"But once it does, it never stops trembling," warned the silhouette. Claire recognized the voice from the call, although his mood had changed. Perhaps she'd kept him waiting too long.

Claire walked around the screen and said, "Hello, I'm Claire. I came as fast as I could—" She stopped. The man was gaunt and shrunken. His frozen grin was missing prominent teeth. His caved face twitched.

He was extremely ill, or strung out, or a combination. He could have been in his twenties or forties. He looked very happy to see her.

He wore a black pirate patch over one eye, theatrically.

"You're not one of them. Not yet." He smiled. "I can tell." His remaining eye was glassy with joy or illness.

"Excuse me, sir, did you call about my box?" she asked quietly, although she saw it nowhere.

The feverish, wasting man looked vaguely familiar. Closer to twenties than forties. And needed help. Claire glanced back, emboldened by others in the far darkness of the room, absorbed in the art, but within reach. Any minute, she suspected, a roaming security guard would wander in, to be summoned if needed.

"Sir, are you okay?" she asked flatly. "Do you need a doctor?"

He tapped his eye patch. "You mean this?" he asked, now smirking, and shook his head. "I saw too much.

"See, they're going to kill you, Claire," he added. "When they're done with you. If you're lucky."

Claire had dealt with mentally disturbed people before. It was part of her training. But this person had targeted her and tracked her down and lured her to him.

"Why did you call me here?" she whispered. "What do you want?"

"You're our last hope," he continued, forthright. "Our only hope.

"Nobody will listen to me. Because I'm crazy, you know," he said, amused at himself. "But you're different. You're inside. People will believe you."

"The truth...about what?" Claire asked, feigning interest to keep him calm and talking until a guard came.

"The event, of course," he said. "The end of the world. You know it's coming soon."

"Is it?" she said, instantly regretting her humoring tone.

"I'm surprised they let you leave the club unchaperoned." The man humored her back and looked over her shoulder. "Or is Jess right behind you?"

He knew too much. She backed away. He stopped smiling.

"They'll turn on you," he said. "They're not your friends. They're going to kill you."

"No, they're not," Claire said, wondering why she argued. She backed away more.

"Don't be afraid of me," he pleaded. "They killed Dean. They'll kill you, too. When they're done with you.

"Find the day. The day of the event," he added urgently. "Warn the world. The holocaust is coming."

Claire turned to go. The man grabbed her arm with a red-stained hand. Claire flinched and then saw the bright stain was smeared paint.

"They'll never accept you," he said. "They're using you to kill others. I know. I've been there."

"Please let me go," she said, prying off his hand, which she threw back at him.

"It's too late for your children," he said, hunting her through the gallery. "But there's still time for the rest of the world."

"Help," Claire said softly at first, hurrying past Janet Leigh to the bright hallway beyond. "Help!" she said louder.

"The ninth protocol!" the man shouted as Claire ran down the stairs. "In the library! Read it! Stop it!" He yelled down into the atrium as she fled the lobby.

"You are not one of them!" he repeated. "You never will be! They are Satan's pilgrims!"

Claire found a security guard by the front door and said, "There's a disturbed man upstairs." "Yes, ma'am. We're aware of that," he told her.

She looked back up through the atrium. The crazed man was gone.

"We're taking care of it," the guard assured her. "He's scaring the visitors," she said. "And he needs help."

"Yes, ma'am. We're aware of that," he repeated.

Claire went outside. It was still raining and now rush hour. She opened her umbrella, dashed to the W Hotel, and grabbed a cab from their line.

—⚬⚬—

Madison was chatting with an old coot in the Grand Foyer when Claire returned.

"Hi, dear," Madison said. "Mr. Newhall suggested the children perform at the Justice Ball. A little concert or something. What do you think? Your umbrella's dripping."

"Where are the children?" Claire asked.

"Upstairs doing homework," Madison said. "Is something wrong?"

"No," Claire said. "Just making sure they're okay."

Madison laughed. "Of course they're okay," she said. "Why wouldn't they be?" She checked her watch and added, "I lost track of time."

The rain had tapered off, but Claire made the children huddle under umbrellas, close to her. She walked them across the park to the church door, where she handed them off to the clergyman. She gave each a hug and wished them a good weekend.

"You too, Miss Claire," said Edgar.

"Make sure he gets plenty of rest and liquids this weekend," Claire told the clergyman. "I think he's fighting off a cold."

She scanned the square and surrounding streets as she hurried back to the club, where Friday cocktail hour was in full pour.

Chapter Ten

Claire would have blown off the club's Casino Night that evening, but Clay, surprisingly, wanted to go. She searched her new wardrobe and settled on an embroidered Rag and Bone shift. Clay dazzled in his tuxedo. "Is that the home or office tux?" she teased.

"No tickling!" she squealed. "I just did my hair."

But the man from the museum still spooked her.

Which was silly, of course. He was mentally ill, clearly unhinged, but harmless. Had he meant to hurt her, he would have picked a less public trap than a museum.

Edie also wore a tuxedo to Casino Night, but she foxed it up with diamond chandelier earrings and rubies and emeralds on her fingers. "Red light! Green light!" she clucked at Claire, alternating bejeweled fists as they stood at the roulette wheel. "No more bets!" cried the croupier, normally the not-Dean waiter but tonight on double duty in a bright red vest.

Her stalker was also physically ill, medically sick. Likely on drugs, too. He was to be pitied, not feared.

"Claire, come sit next to me," Nora beckoned from the blackjack table. "It's the slowest way to lose."

"I'll save you from that treacherous woman," she whispered when Claire joined her, nodding toward Edie, who was already pawing other husbands. Nora hit and held at seventeen.

It had been easy to track her down, Claire realized. Anyone, sane or nuts, could have done it with Google. Clay's job announcement, their initial San Francisco address, even their old Santa Fe number, which would have led him to sweet, unsuspecting Mrs. Biddle and ultimately Claire's cell number.

"Set aside the fact—which I do—that she *annoys* me," Nora unloaded on Edie in Claire's ear. "Overlook the truth that she quite often makes my *skin crawl*..."

Had he threatened her, she'd have told her family and the police. She'd have reported him. But he hadn't threatened her. He'd warned her.

"But what I can't overlook," Nora continued, "is *that* behavior."

"Sorry, what?" Claire asked, having hit at eighteen and busted another hand.

"Leapfrogging to ever richer men, destroying families with nary a concern for the children, even her own." Nora slid a stack of chips over to Claire, already running low.

But he couldn't have Googled information about her missing box. That was something nobody knew about, or cared about.

"And no, she did not make a play for Slade, if that's what you're wondering," Nora went on, although Claire's mind was elsewhere. "She knows I'd kill her. Literally. With these." She waved both hands in the air and grinned. "And no jury in this city would convict me."

The only way someone who had tracked her, followed her, stalked her, and knew her addresses and numbers would know she was missing a box would be if he had stolen it himself. Either from the old apartment with its chronically broken front door, or from the moving van that sat out front, unlocked, while the movers loaded in. Why anyone would want such a thing, which held value only for her, made no sense. Then again, "making sense" was relative when applied to the deranged man who'd ranted nonsensically about the end of days and the coming holocaust.

"Sorry, what?" Claire asked, when Nora finally got her attention. "What did you say?"

Nora laughed at herself and said, "I'm just bitching about the members again."

"Oh yes," Claire said, and then she said, "If you don't like the members, why did you join in the first place?"

"I used to ask myself that all the time." Nora sighed. "Then one day I stopped asking."

Claire pondered if a madman motivated enough to track her down at her apartment could have also attacked her on that fuzzy, confused night when she lost her child. She immediately scolded herself and ordered her imagination to stop running wild. Her own unfettered mind had been the real stalker that night. In any event, the scrawny, shaky, one-eyed wraith she'd seen today hardly posed a physical threat to anyone but himself.

Across the Reading Room—the club's makeshift casino for the night—Slade flung dice around a cheering craps table. Clay looked over his shoulder and winked at Claire. She smiled and winked back. Her dealer reshuffled the deck.

But he hadn't only ranted about the end of the world. He hadn't just begged her to find the date and warn the world. That level of harmless insanity would be easy to dismiss.

He also knew about the children. Which meant he wasn't merely tracking her down online or to her old apartment. He'd been following her today. Watching when she left the club. With the children he claimed it was too late to save, whatever that meant. She decided a children's field trip to the art museum was a bad idea after all. Probably all field trips were.

"Good evening, Claire," said Colonel Crowe as he passed by, chipless, eschewing the gambling tables. "You look lovely tonight."

Madison was on his arm. "That Rag and Bone is you, Claire," she said, admiring her dress. Claire mustered a civil nod to the colonel and a "Thank you, Madison" and nothing more.

"Nora." The colonel tipped his head and went on. Nora turned to Claire and started to vent about "the new BFFs," then caught herself and zipped her lip. "Oh, don't get me started!" she said, amused. She was on a tear tonight.

But he also knew about Jess. Not just that she had a driver, a bodyguard around town. Anyone who cared enough to follow her would have known that.

"You okay, honey?" Clay asked Claire as she stood by the window. Clancy whooped nearby when his dinging slot machine cashed in. "You look a little pale," Clay added.

The crazed man at the museum knew Jess's name. He said he'd been here. When he grabbed her arm with his paint-stained hand.

"I'm fine," she said, stroking Clay's back. "The blackjack wiped me out."

Over his shoulder, Claire saw the connect-the-dot painting of the club. The named circles linking the members. The artwork Madison had described so wistfully. Painted by a former employee she'd called a "gifted, unsung genius," or something like that. One of Madison's odd, memorable phrases.

A member of the family, she'd called him, before he "went off the beam" with drugs.

"I think I'll turn in early," Claire said. "It's been a day. Do you mind?"

She didn't need to go to the library to flip through the club's photo album. She already knew.

Her stalker was Ethan. The one Madison called a "true paranoid." The one "who got away."

—⚌—

Claire and Clay went to his parents' for Sunday brunch and to see the new remodel. Madison joined.

It was a stunning Pacific Heights limestone Edwardian, along the "Gold Coast" strip, with clear views of the Bay. It sat directly down from Danielle Steel's singular mansion-—"A house," Madison sniffed, "as gaudy as her books."

"A house she *earned*," Nora clarified. "Those books don't write themselves." And then she added, "God bless that woman."

After the tour, they sat on the back terrace overlooking the Golden Gate Bridge. Nora had made the breakfast casserole and biscuits herself, since her staff went to church on Sundays. Slade mixed a pitcher of "Lonestar" Bloody Marys, heavy on Tabasco.

"Everything looks great, Mom," said Clay. "Yes, it's just incredible, Nora," agreed Claire, overwhelmed.

"It sure as hell should be," bellowed Slade in Sunday-casual jeans and a blue gingham shirt. "It cost double the estimate."

"Keeping me happy is a bargain at twice the price." Nora beamed and turned to Claire. "Aren't you hungry, dear?"

Madison debated with herself which Harry Winston jewels to borrow for the Justice Ball. Slade alerted Clay to a last-minute trip to New York that week. "Again?" Clay complained.

"Apparently you haven't closed the deal," Slade growled. "Your brother was a natural." Madison looked out across the Bay and said, "Touché."

Claire looked around the table. She'd deliberated all weekend and decided to tell.

"I met Ethan on Friday," she said. "Who?" said Clay. "*What?!*" said Nora.

She told them everything. The questions flew.

"Why didn't you take Jess?" Nora asked. "Why did you go meet a stranger by yourself? We've *discussed* this!"

"Who the hell is Ethan?" Clay demanded. "A former waiter at the club," Nora said. "After your time."

"He was Nora's pet project," Slade said, draining his Bloody. "Clearly not a successful one." "Oh shut up, Slade!" Nora said. "I tried my damnedest.

"He had such promise, such potential," she explained. "Claire, you should see his artwork. It's fascinating."

"I've seen it," Claire said. "I showed her," said Madison.

Nora nodded. "Yes, of course," she said. "In the Reading Room."

"I thought he'd cleaned up his act," Nora said. "Slade, you remember the specialists I brought in? For rehab?" Slade chuckled and said, "I remember the bill," and Nora said, "You never saw the bill, you moron."

"I thought there was hope." Nora shrugged. "But when he started stealing from the members..." "I've already told her this," said Madison, fidgety. "Well, I'm telling it again," Nora snapped.

"At least he's hanging out at museums," Nora mused. "And not in the gutter somewhere."

"And you think he stole your box off the moving van?" Nora abruptly asked. "What is wrong with him? What could he possibly be looking for?"

"I'm not sure he stole anything—" Claire started, but Slade interrupted her. "He's clearly a sick kid," he said. "A wacko extreme. I'm shocked he's still alive."

Claire had left out his cryptic rantings about Dean and his bizarre reference to "Satan's Pilgrims." She didn't see the value added.

"He does look very ill," Claire said, and Nora clutched her chest. "Don't tell me that. Oh, Ethan."

"He wears an eye patch," Claire added. "Why? What happened to his eye?" Nora asked.

"Probably just for show," Slade dismissed. "He was always desperate for attention."

"Poor Ethan," Nora said, meaning it.

"I'm sure we could find him again," said Claire. "If you want to help him."

"Why? What for?" Slade demanded. "It's the typical death spiral of so-called artists." Then he turned to Clay and said, "And a pitiful, wasted life."

Slade, clearly bored with the Ethan talk, grabbed the conversation in a Texan full nelson and steered it at Clay, who sat quietly. Apparently, it had been a bad week at the office, and Slade rode him full bore. "Dean-Lite," he called him, listing his shortcomings. "Not today," Nora fussed, spooning fruit salad. "It's Sunday."

"A sorry substitute," Slade continued, and Claire said, "That's enough, Slade."

There was a nearly imperceptible pause at the table, and Slade started to wind up again. "I mean it, Slade," Claire interrupted. "Zip it."

Slade and Clay turned to Claire. Nora looked down at her berries and said, "Tee-hee."

"It's okay, Claire," said Clay, and she said, "No, it's not." "Atta girl," said Nora, still smiling downward. Slade sat back in his chair, intrigued.

"Don't talk to him that way," Claire lectured him. "My husband is not a 'sorry substitute' for anybody. Including Dean."

"Dean, Dean, Dean," Madison muttered, putting her fork down too close to the edge. It fell to the floor. "Damn him." She bent down.

"I'll get it, Madison," Nora said quickly, reaching down, grabbing the fork. "I'll get you a new one."

"He's stupid," Madison said down to the table. "So stupid and so selfish."

Nora patted her hand. "Ssh. It's okay."

Madison yanked back. "Not really, Nora," she said. "Not really." She grabbed her crutch and leveraged up. The crutch slipped. Madison collapsed to the tile floor on her side, grimacing. Teamlike, everyone rushed to her.

"Are you okay?" Clay asked. "Oh, Madison, please be careful," said Nora. Slade and Clay helped her up by the elbows, as if trained. Claire stood back, useless.

Madison erupted. "Goddammit, no!" she cried, pushing them off, steadier. "How much longer will I have to do this?" she asked, looking from Slade to Nora. It almost seemed a plead. "How much longer?"

"Not much," Nora soothed. Madison ignored her, turned and limped through the French doors into the house. Claire's family looked at her apologetically in the silence.

Nora was the first to sit back down. "Dean's loss is still very raw around here," she said quietly. "With all of us, of course. But especially Madison."

"I'm sorry. I shouldn't have mentioned him," Claire said, taking her seat as well. "I should have known better." "No, Slade should have," Nora said, shaking her head.

Then she turned to Claire and said softly, "Madison was expecting their first child when all this...happened. It's been a double tragedy for her."

Claire deflated. "I had no idea," she said, shocked, scrolling back for any clue Madison might have given. She turned to Clay. "Did you?"

He nodded and shrugged and said, "I thought you knew."

After moments of awkward chatter, Claire folded her napkin and stood up. "I need to apologize."

"She'll be okay," said Clay, reaching over. Nora and Slade agreed. Claire gently pushed Clay's hand away and said, "I'll be right back."

"Madison?" she called as she walked toward the front of the mansion.

Madison's crutch was hooked over the bottom of the staircase banister.

Claire heard footsteps overhead, clacking closer to the stairs. She ducked back into the living room. The steps skipped quickly down the carpeted staircase. Claire peered in.

Madison stepped up to the entryway mirror. She checked her makeup, dabbed the corner of an eye, fluffed her hair with both hands. She kicked a leg backward and adjusted the strap of her heel, balancing on one foot. Moving from Claire's sight line, a slight pause before the click of the arm crutch. And then the hobbling limp back toward the terrace.

"I apologize for that little outburst." Madison glanced up as Claire rejoined the table. "Quite silly of me."

"Not at all," Claire said. "I was going to apologize myself."

Madison shook her head. "Don't," she said. "No reason to."

"There now," said a grinning Slade. "What was all the fuss about? I don't remember. Do you?" Claire looked around at her family. Nora shrugged and laughed. Clay cornered off another bite of casserole.

"Claire, could you pass the fruit, please?" Madison asked. "The kiwi is wonderfully tart."

"Yes, of course," Claire said. She smiled as she handed over the bowl.

Chapter Eleven

That night, while Clay slept, Claire took her laptop and sneaked downstairs to the Safe Harbor room. She hooked up the Internet cable from one of the children's computers.

Although she knew all the details, with updates, from Clay, she'd never seen the media coverage of Dean's assassination. Clay had made a pointed decision to avoid it, and Claire respected that. It had been a clear case of random violence, open-and-shut, and somewhat quickly forgotten, as Dean had yet to acquire national fame when he was gunned down.

The Googled stories were strikingly similar, as if written off a press release. Eyewitnesses described the same scene and lone gunman. Claire scrolled through blurbs from across the country.

Madison had hundreds of hits: The assassination made her an overnight celebrity. The comments on each page reflected empathy and admiration, feelings Claire had shared since their reunion a few weeks back. The crutch worked wonders for that. And even though Dean had faded, Madison stayed in the limelight, especially with the West Coast press. Claire wondered how many publicists she had.

Claire also wondered if they knew the crutch was a prop. Or had it been their idea?

One of the Madison hits, buried midway down the third search page, came from Stu Savage. He wasn't buying any of it.

Not the "lone gunman" from China, not the "senseless act of violence" from an unhinged lunatic. This was a carefully planned, targeted hit from the New World Order, JFK-style. Stu insisted "turncoat" Dean was about to spill the beans and had been preemptively "taken out" by the shadowy "superclass" group. Then again, Stu was similarly convinced they were controlling the world's population by poisoned water and contagious cancer with a preplanned global cataclysm on deck. He cried wolf nonstop three hours a day. He was entertainment.

And yet.

The top search hit, which Claire had pointedly ignored, was a YouTube video of the shooting itself. She'd known it existed but had never been curious to see her brother-in-law murdered live. According to the views counter, millions of others felt otherwise. Claire, perched on a child's chair, knees-to-chin, scrolled her cursor in circles. She finally landed, tapped "play."

A stationary camera framed the electrified ballroom. Hundreds of expectant supporters with their bobbled heads silhouetted against the bright stage and its patriotic banner: "Dean Willing: All Together Now!" They whooped and chanted. Some pumped fists or tooted plastic horns. Bruce Springsteen blared from tripod speakers.

A local female reporter, off camera, vamped with the anchorman, awaiting Dean's arrival. They discussed the blowout election returns, which hadn't surprised anyone, based on the city's voting history and the latest polls. They wryly noted the record female turnout, thanks to Dean's charismatic, matinee-idol appeal, not to mention his family's enormous fortune. They reluctantly reminded their viewers the congressman-elect was happily married. They applauded the loser's gracious concession speech at the St. Francis.

They mentioned the single camera feed in the Dean ballroom, provided by the tightly disciplined and message-controlling campaign. They questioned Dean's absence from the campaign trail over the last two days. The on-scene reporter shouted loudly to be heard above the excited, growing clamor.

To fill time, they cut to an interview earlier in the day with Madison, outside a polling station near Market Street. She wore bright yellow and shook hands with well-wishers, unencumbered by the crutch. She looked strained, tired, and was a little testy with the reporter.

"That's ridiculous," she responded to the charge her husband had arrogantly stopped campaigning at the very end. "Dean is out meeting with real people, hearing their concerns one-on-one, away from the cameras and photo ops. Dean knows what really matters." Madison shook another hand, patted a baby's head, signed an autograph.

They cut back to the ballroom feed. The crowd grew hotter.

The room erupted when Slade and Nora strode onstage, proudly beaming and waving. Nora wore navy with simple pearls; Slade was in one of his perfectly cut banker suits. He took the podium and basked for a moment before "hearing" a secret message from the crowd. He turned and pointed at Nora. The crowd erupted, while Nora blushed and shook her head. Slade whipped the cheering louder and stood back. Nora glared at him, covered her face and stepped to the podium, straining to reach the microphone.

Claire laughed from her little seat. Nora was red with embarrassment, struggling to mask it. She tapped the mike.

"What a surprise, Slade," Nora growled. "Just wait till I get you home...." The room roared, adoring her.

Nora was a natural.

"I'll never forget the love you've shown my boy," she said, not quite loud enough, but with sufficient sincerity to reach the back row. "You teach them right from wrong and pray they keep the courage of their convictions. Not yours. Theirs.

"And when they do, against all pressure..." Nora's voice warbled a bit, as it had on the few occasions Claire had seen her fight emotion. From the camera's distance, it was hard to tell if she brimmed with joy or sorrow. She paused a breath and leaned closer to the microphone. "This mother is so very proud," she rasped. "Do you know? Do you know?" Nora stopped, unable to continue. The crowd clapped and voiced its support.

Slade took Nora by the shoulders. She seemed instantly fragile, as he guided her from the microphone and stepped up to command it himself.

"Folks, what Nora means," he said, "is thank you for your tireless work on this campaign. It truly made all the difference." Nora smiled and nodded and looked offstage.

"But enough of the old guard," Slade thundered on. "It is my grand pleasure to present the next representative from this great district, our son, Congressman Dean Willing!"

The room lifted into the air. Hundreds of red, white, and blue balloons cascaded from overhead nets. Side cannons launched blizzards of silver confetti. Bruce Springsteen rocked anew from the speakers. Through the obscuring commotion, Madison in a pink tailored suit stepped confidently onto the stage, one hand *tick-tock*ing, the other leading Dean. The cheering pitched up to the edge of distortion.

The shot was loud, unmistakable. Dean crumpled forward instantly. Madison turned to his fall. As a wave of confusion briefly dampened the cheers, two more shots cut through the music. Madison collapsed, shielding her husband. Slade tackled Nora to the floor and covered her. The chaos escalated with a barrage of shots fired back into the crowd from security at the stage edge, half off camera, seemingly striking an unseen target. Chairs overturned as panic begat a crush.

The stampede was immediate, knocking the camera and tripod to the floor. A kick spiraled it to the side. Balloons and confetti continued to shower down over screams and rock music and the rush of silhouettes to the stage. The video ticked to the end, froze, offered a repeat.

Claire twirled the cursor in circles.

"What are you doing?" Clay asked from behind. Claire jumped and turned. He stood in his underwear at the door, bed-headed and scratching.

"Watching the Dean night," she said. "Why?" he asked through a yawn.

"Because I've never seen it," she said. He shrugged. "Me neither," he said. "Are you going to watch it all night?"

Claire closed and disconnected her laptop. "You've never been curious about it?" she asked. "About seeing my brother killed on live television?" Clay asked back. "I'll pass."

Claire went to the door and stopped.

"What?" Clay ribbed. "Which wheels are turning right now?"

Downstairs, the grandfather clock struck a three-quarter and went silent.

"Nothing," Claire said, kissing his forehead. "Let's go to bed. It's late."

—⚉—

The woman behind the desk at the main public library scrolled down her computer screen and said, "That book is checked out, ma'am. I'm happy to search our other branches, if you wish."

Claire smiled and said, "Could you, please? My local branch didn't have it either.

"A friend of mine," she added, "told me I could find it in the library, but he didn't say which one."

Jess idled outside in the Lincoln. Claire had come to return and renew books for the children. She told Jess she wouldn't be long.

The librarian furrowed and frowned. "That must be our only copy," she said, running her finger along the screen. She sucked an upper tooth. "*The Ninth Protocol*. Subject: conspiracy theories. We have many similar books on the shelves." Claire patted her stack and said, "Not anymore." The librarian peered through the lower half of her glasses and said, "I love a good conspiracy theory."

"They're fun, aren't they?" Claire smiled back. She peered around, unlikely to see anyone she knew, but checking all the same.

Ethan had begged her to find and read the book, after warning "They" were going to kill her when done with her—certainly the most intriguing book recommendation she'd ever gotten. From a drug-addicted, mentally ill, disgruntled former club employee who'd stolen from members to boot. She remembered a teacher in Lansing who'd been fired for drinking on her lunch hour and had lashed out with such outrageous lies against her coworkers it had taken six months of depositions to clear their names. Cast-outs often caused the most mischief.

But at least Ethan believed his own delusions, as ludicrous as they were.

"Do you know when it's due back?" Claire asked.

The woman double-checked and shook her head in disapproval. "Two years ago." She *tsk*ed. "I guess we should classify that as 'lost.'"

"I wonder why they didn't order a replacement," she mused, drumming her fingers. She fast clicked a matrix of keys. "That explains it. Out of print." She squinted and read, "Publisher: unknown. Probably self-published. Seems a very rare book." She looked up at Claire. "I'm afraid we're out of luck," she said.

"Can you tell me who checked it out last?" Claire asked. The woman said, "In this case, yes. It's so delinquent." Quick clicks. "Last name:

Simmons. Been inactive since. I can set up a notification alert, in case it's returned. But I wouldn't get my hopes up."

"No, that's okay. Thank you," Claire said, sliding eight books across the desk. The woman wanded the barcodes. "You've got quite a stack already," she said.

Claire loaded her tote. "Yes, I do," she groaned.

"Funny enough," said the woman, scanning her computer screen. "Simmons checked out these books, too. At least he saw fit to return them."

Jess dashed from the Lincoln to help her with the heavy bag. "I thought you were returning books!" he said, reaching out.

"I'm fine," she said, holding them close. "Thanks anyway."

—⁓—

The books were outlandish and repetitive. And highly addictive. She tore through them all the next morning, after Clay left on his two-day New York trip, taking breakfast and lunch in her room. Her first cram session since college.

They could have been Stu's talking points. It was the same nonsense he spouted daily—equally alarmist, but slightly more scholarly. The books, all old, had names like *America's Secret Establishment*, *The Shadows of Power*, *How the World Really Works*, and, winning the on-the-nose prize, *The New World Order*. The covers were starkly ominous, with occult images of pentagrams, skulls and bones, and the "all-seeing eye" pyramid lifted right off the dollar bill—and the Masonic mosaic across the square.

They dissected the Illuminati, Freemasons, Opus Dei, secret societies, Bilderbergers, the Council of Foreign Relations, the Trilateral Commission, a global cabal puppeteering world history for a nefarious, murky purpose. These "shadowy" groups—they liked that word—kept the world in constant turmoil through manufactured wars, depressed economies, staged assassinations, fabricated terrorism, false flag attacks, chaos and confusion ever on tap. "Everything you know is a lie," one book reminded at the end of every chapter. Stu shouted the same thing each day in between warnings of the coming "mass culling."

The villainous names were the typical laundry list: Rothschild, Rockefeller, Kissinger, Kennedy, Coolidge, Forbes, Whitney, Vanderbilt, and a few other names she remembered from the young heirs at Yale. James Flick, whose former bedroom she was in right now, figured prominently as one of San Francisco's original "titans." Stu added the Willings and other *nouveau riche* Silicon Valley billionaires to his enemies list for his radio show, a relatable touch, since they were the local low-hanging fruit among the "ruling class." Apparently, the New World Order welcomed new money as well.

Certainly Claire was aware of many of these conspiracy theories. The JFK assassination had been fodder for TV shows and movies, not to mention a congressional inquiry at the time, covered in all the history books. Ditto RFK, MLK, Princess Diana, JFK Jr., and others. Practically every famous untimely death had sinister, conspiratorial roots, if the Internet was to be believed. Some sites claimed JFK had been killed off by the CIA; Princess Diana by MI5. Even wilder ones claimed both "assassinations" were faked in elaborately staged productions. And, of course, everyone knew Sirhan Sirhan was under government mind control when he shot Robert Kennedy.

From the twentieth century world wars to AIDS to autism to 9/11 and the endless perma-wars that followed and continued, seemingly every catastrophic global event had been organized and controlled by an "unseen hand"—the default explanation for almost any tragic event. Famous talk show hosts and even outlier presidential candidates had openly pushed some of these fringe theories; cable networks had built their show business models around them. And Stu himself was surely cashing in from peddling paranoia and fear.

There was a knock on Claire's door as she reread a chapter. "Are you joining us today?" Madison called from the hall. "The kids are here." "Sorry, Madison," Claire said, hiding her book tote in the back of her closet. "I lost track of time."

The public fascination with this nonsense, Claire knew, was nothing new. Ancient folk tales always had beasts and monsters right outside the gates. But the oppressive fear felt more squarely, hotly in the zeitgeist these days. With more evidence to back it up. Was there any aspect of life that was getting better and not worse? Exponentially worse?

But the missing link in all the theories—which elaborately laid out the *who* and *what*—was the *why* and *how*. How could a relatively tiny group of elites subdue and control a world population of seven billion and growing? One of the older books—*None Dare Call It Conspiracy*, she thought it was, with the plain blue, worn linen cover—claimed, somewhat plausibly, that with overwhelming patience and Swiss watch precision over several decades, *centuries*, they had manipulated and trained the public to accept, even embrace, their subservient position. "Like the gradual domestication of dogs," the book with the all-seeing eye called it.

Stu often warned his listeners they'd been "numbered for slavery," each with a specific, predetermined role in the rapidly emerging New World Order. It was his rabid call to arms for an uprising, for revolution—even more than his crackpot conspiracy theories—that made Stu ridiculous, subversive, and somewhat heroic. "Join the resistance!" he shouted at the bottom of every hour. No wonder you couldn't turn him off, or take him seriously.

"Earth to Claire!" Madison called from across the kitchen as they iced freshly baked Sesame Street cookies with the kids. "Sorry, what?"

Claire said, looking up from her half-bald Grover. Madison pointed toward Caesar frosting Condi's face in Oscar green right next to her.

"Upstairs you two," she ordered, marching them toward the washroom.

The books ran off the rails on the *why* of the conspiracy. Some claimed the elites simply lusted for power, which Claire thought weak. They already had power; that's why they were the elites. Others linked the New World Order to the biblical prophecies of Revelations and Daniel, insisting these shadowy groups were suppressing the masses, preparing the global battlefield for the rise of the Antichrist and eventual Armageddon. Ethan must have latched on to this when he coined his colorful term "Satan's pilgrims" to describe the Union's members.

Like Stu, these books went a step too far, derailing their whole argument. The moment they dipped into the occult and end-time prophecies, they death spiraled into silliness. Which was too bad, Claire thought, because many of their claims made at least a modicum of sense. Like Anonymous, when they went overboard, they made fools of themselves and alienated the sane.

"Miss Claire?" Edgar looked up from her lap later, blinking. She was rocking him at story time and had gripped the book open. "Sorry, pal," she said, relaxing, wiping hair from his eye. Edgar slid the next page and kept reading his Magic Tree House book aloud. It was a story as fantastical and riveting as the one she'd been spinning in her head all day. But even Edgar had the common sense to know it was make believe.

Claire laughed at herself. Edgar scowled up at her again, looking for the joke. He smiled at her anyway. She was relieved his spring cold had run its course and he was happy again.

"Treats!" Madison called out, the milk-and-macaroon brigade right behind her. Edgar squirreled from Claire's lap to join the others. Madison did look steadier on her feet, Claire thought, and why not? The incident had been more than five months ago, and she herself claimed to be getting better every day. So what if she'd gone up and down the stairs at the Willings' without her crutch? Why had Claire immediately gone to cuckoo town?

"No, Edgar." Madison stopped him reaching for a milk carton. "That's Ilza's. Hers is the strawberry. Yours is the white chocolate. Right here."

"I don't want white chocolate," Edgar said. "Everybody likes chocolate," Madison told him. "And white chocolate is even more elegant. You drink it every day."

"He can have a different flavor," said Claire, arranging the cookies on the crafts table. "Edgar, do you want strawberry? Or peanut butter?"

"I thought orphans liked routine," Madison said, interrupting the milk service, holding them back. "I read that somewhere."

"They didn't mean milk, I'm sure," Claire said, hoping Madison would drop it. She didn't.

"Well, there's only one strawberry," Madison said to Claire directly, while the children watched and waited. "And Ilza drinks the strawberry. If Edgar wants a different flavor, he'll have to wait until tomorrow."

Claire thought it safer to ignore than confront Madison. "I'll get you one, Edgar," she said, reaching.

"No!" Madison snapped, pushing Claire's hand away. "We don't have extras! It's a very specific...Beggars can't be choosers, you know!" Madison grabbed Edgar's unwanted milk and limped quickly from the room.

Claire looked around at the silent children and said, "Miss Madison's having a bad day." Thankfully, Madison had a doctor's appointment the next day, so Claire did damage control through veiled self-esteem and empowerment exercises with the kids, topped off by an extra-long recess. Weary but satisfied with her solo duty, she herded the troop back across the park at the end of the day. The clergyman waited at the church door and scuttled them inside. "Be good!" Claire admonished them. "Be good!" Edgar shot back, waving hands from his ears.

"I will!" Claire promised.

"I'm glad he's finally feeling better," Claire said to the clergyman. "I think it was allergies, or a bug going around."

He stepped outside to her and closed the door. "I have to thank you, Claire," he said. "Edgar came to us in a cocoon of silence. I didn't think we'd ever reach him. I don't know how you did it, but I've never been so happy trying to shut a child up!"

Claire laughed and said, "He's a very special boy. He just needed a little extra encouragement." She turned to go.

"And we're grateful for the extra help," he added, almost embarrassed. "The city grants us a very limited budget for their health care. We do the best we can. It's extremely generous of your club to bridge the gap. And the kids actually said it was fun!"

Claire nodded. "You're very welcome," she said, heading off.

Then she stopped and turned back. "I'm sorry, what did you say? What was fun?"

She found Madison, back from her doctor's, straightening the easels in the Safe Harbor room.

"It was just a flu shot. What's the big deal?" Madison explained with a shrug. "I'm surprised you have an issue with this at all. Would you rather they get sick?"

"I'd rather you tell me before you take them to a doctor," Claire said.

"We didn't take them anywhere. Dr. Hopkins sent a couple nurses from the hospital. They gave them the shots downstairs. What's the harm in that?"

"When?" Claire asked. "Where was I?"

Madison leaned on her crutch and hipped her other fist. "Probably one of your excursions. I didn't realize I had to clear everything with you. I wasn't aware of this chain of command.

"Did you know," Madison went on, "these children have no medical records to speak of? Nobody knows which vaccines they've had or haven't had. It's all guesswork. Dogs at the pound get better treatment."

She wound tighter and kept going. "I was even going to ask the club's board to put them on our insurance plan, as dependents, so they could have real doctors and grow up healthy like other children. But I can't even do something as minor as *flu shots* without your constant attacking..."

"Madison, I wasn't attacking you."

"Is it possible that I will ever be able to do anything right?" Madison grabbed her stomach, collapsed onto the window seat, grimacing. Claire rushed to her.

"What's wrong?" she asked. "Are you okay?"

Madison nodded, bit her lip, massaged her waist.

"What happened at the doctor's?"

"Nothing!" Madison snapped. "Just routine tests. Just...nothing."

Madison breathed deeply and looked out the window toward the playground. She shook her head.

"Every month around this time, a reminder of what could have been," she said, straining to compose herself. "And what can never be." Claire eventually understood.

"Sometimes I feel so lonely," Madison continued, still looking out. "And useless. As a woman."

"Madison, no. Not at all." Claire held her hand.

"I'm a nuisance to Nora and Slade, although they have the decency to hide it. I'm the pesky reminder of everything that went horribly wrong, and the sooner I go away, the better."

"That's not true," Claire insisted. "They love you very much. And you're not useless. Look at these kids and how much we're helping them."

"But that's all I'll ever get," Madison said. "You get another chance to have one for yourself..." "And so will you," Claire assured her. "When the time is right." She stopped herself, since the "right time" implied a new husband, with Dean so recently gone.

Madison turned back from the window, sized up Claire's sincerity, and smiled.

"I'm so glad we're family," Madison said, hugging her neck with one arm. "Me too," Claire said, embracing her back.

"We really should plan a girls' night, just the two of us," Madison said, her arm linked through Claire's as they ambled toward the elevator. "Have you been to Studs in the Castro? It's a boy club." Claire said, "I have not."

"Oh, it's the best dancing in town," Madison said. "They think we're fabulous and buy us drinks. They'll worship us!"

Claire looked at her and said, "You want to go dancing?" Madison winked and said, "Getting there!" She lifted her crutch and, balanced on Claire's arm, did a gentle two-step. "I'm not dead, you know!" she said, laughing.

Dinner that night was a "stuff-your-own-taco" buffet, which Clancy thought fun, but Mr. Newhall didn't, ordering corned beef hash with poached eggs instead. Edie and Madison picked at spring greens and swapped war stories from the haute couture trenches where their Justice Ball gowns were still being "built," with two weeks to go. Madison had one fitting left and described the embroidered Swarovski crystals, while Edie cooed and purred.

"Vera suggested a goddess style, but I felt it inappropriate," said Madison. "And a bit twee." "Yes, that is a bit twee," agreed Edie.

They quizzed Claire, who didn't have a ball gown, hadn't planned on going.

"Of course you're going to the Justice Ball," Madison decreed. "Our children will be performing. And you live upstairs. It's a tad difficult to avoid."

"I'm not sure we'll be living here in two weeks," Claire responded. "But I'll come watch the children."

Madison inspected her. "I have a spare gown," she said. "I'll have it finished for you." Then she turned to Edie and said, "We're the same size, you know." "Enjoy it while you can," cackled rail-thin Edie. "It's a bitch to maintain."

After dinner, *Annie Hall* was screened in the Reading Room. "I need a good laugh, don't you?" Madison said, passing a red-and-white striped bag of popcorn. Claire kept one eye on Diane Keaton, the other on Ethan's artwork in the corner, his initials "ES" at the bottom.

She woke in bed at 3:42 a.m. from a shallow sleep.

She crept down the hall to the library. Caressed the wall, found the light switch. Woke Sting, who eyed her.

"Sorry, Sting," she said.

She climbed the rickety ladder to the second level, past the dictionaries and medical reference books in various languages, past the travel guides, to the flaking leather Union Club photo albums on the end. She slid one off the shelf, reached behind and grabbed the tiny, slim book with the faded red cover and the embossed "IX" on the cover, the Dewey decimal number written on the spine, the "San Francisco Public Library" stamped on the inside.

The book was typed, not printed. It was one of a kind. The title page said, *The Ninth Protocol*.

She flipped to the table of contents: "The Plan," "The Protocols," "The Crucible," "The Keep."

The book was forty-two pages long.

It triggered a piercing alarm when she took it over the library threshold. The alarm went silent when she retreated. "Sorry, Sting," she said again. The beast retucked its wings, watched her.

She was on her third reading, scribbling on a notepad from the librarian's desk, when Ling came in with the morning papers. The sun was rising.

"Good morning, Ling," she said, sliding the book under her. "I got up early today." Ling nodded. He put the *Chronicle*, the *Examiner*, and the *Times* on the ottoman. He straightened folders and papers on the desk. He emptied the oval, leather waste-paper baskets into his bag. Sting paid him no attention.

Ling swung the wall door and disappeared into the Gentlemen's Lounge. Claire lifted the tufted leather seat, slid *The Ninth Protocol* back against the frame, replaced the cushion. She sat and tested, felt nothing underneath.

"Have a good day," she told Ling as he swung back from the men's lounge with a tied bag. She clumped her written notes into her robe pocket, padded out the door.

She looked back at Sting watching her. It cocked its head.

She was waiting for Clay when he returned from New York that afternoon.

Chapter Twelve

"When you accepted this mission, did it self-destruct?" Clay made light, although weary from his cross-country flight and needing a shower. He stood by the library fireplace, watching his frantic wife molest the sofa.

"Ling must have put the book back," Claire said, feeling under both cushions.

"Where are you going?" Clay asked as she climbed the ladder and searched the second-tier shelves unsuccessfully. Mr. Stimson and Mr. Payson walked through on their way to the Gentlemen's Lounge. Claire abandoned the search for now.

"How's it hanging, Sting?" Clay asked the bird, who watched them both leave.

Fortunately, Claire had made copious notes. She spread the other library books across their bed. Clay humored her as he unpacked, undressed.

"It's a classic pyramid structure," she explained. "They reveal more secrets, *illuminate* you as you move up the hierarchy, until you reach the pinnacle." "Yes," Clay said, tossing socks in the hamper. "That was in the Tom Hanks movie. Or Nicolas Cage, right?"

"But you can only reach the pinnacle if—and this is the most important rule," Claire continued, squinting at her scribblings. "You come from a pure, genetically traceable bloodline. That's mandatory for the first son. Like royalty, he inherits all the power. And passes it down to his own."

"The heir and the spare," Clay said, sliding his Dopp kit back in the bathroom closet. Then he turned, stumped. "Power over what? These guys are royalty, you say?"

"They think they are," Claire said, encouraged by his curiosity. "But they're more like a cult. Seeking power over the whole world. That's 'the Plan.'"

"If you believe the books or websites…" she went on—and Clay interjected with "Which you shouldn't," but she steamrolled on—"then they control everything, and they're sorta genius about it. They even put out their own propaganda to inoculate the public against the awful truth. So that nobody believes it, nobody takes them seriously, until it's too late. I mean, right now you're laughing at me."

Clay fought a smile and shook his head and then, giving up, nodded.

"Like any cult, they identify and recruit the most promising candidates, usually the young and often against their knowledge," Claire continued. "With the right skill set and temperament to become part of the ruling class, the super class. You can be part of the New World Order and not even know it."

She followed an unclad Clay into his bathroom. "And the most ambitious work their way up the pyramid, performing specific tasks assigned to them," she reported. "Proving themselves and learning more horrible secrets along the way."

Clay stepped into his steaming shower. Claire leaned against the sink and talked above the spray.

"'The Protocols' are their organizational structure," she said. "Their 'New World' is broken into eight colonies, each tasked with an overarching mission, a specialty, a *protocol*. New York rigs the economy, making sure the rich get richer and the poor get destitute. With nothing in between.

"Where have we seen that happening?" Claire asked. "Everywhere!" Clay shouted on cue from the curtain and Claire shouted back, "Bingo!"

"London controls the press and disinformation," she went on, reading from her notes. "Moscow schedules wars and conflicts, Beijing undermines religion, wearing down people's belief in a higher power. And do you know what San Francisco is in charge of? Our mission?"

"Parking tickets?" Clay asked, ringing open the curtain, grabbing a towel.

"No," Claire said. "The World Game."

When Clay didn't get it, she elaborated. "Population control, Clay," she said. "Whittling down the masses to a manageable, controllable number. *Depopulation*."

"Oh, Claire," Clay said, stepping out. "You lost me on that last one. Are you serious about all this?"

"I know it sounds crazy," she said. "Until you stop and think about it." "No," he said, toweling his hair. "It sounds crazy *because* you stop and think about it."

He picked up one of the library books off the bed, inspected the skull-and-bones cover.

"Bonesmen? So I'm part of the conspiracy, too?" he said. "You realize now I'll have to kill you."

Claire grabbed the book and flipped through it. "Shall I read about your masturbatory initiation rituals?" she asked. Clay grabbed it back with mock horror. "No!" he shouted.

"See, this is where they jump the shark," he said. "I *know* that didn't happen, so it makes me doubt everything else they say. Even the stuff that sorta maybe makes sense."

"Well, if you guys weren't so secretive about everything," Claire said, poking his chest. "If you didn't hide it from your wives, maybe there wouldn't be so many crazy rumors out there." "I'll pass that along," Clay said, picking up the bedside phone.

After he hung up with room service, he looked at Claire, still brimming with information. "So is this what you do all day?" he asked. "Fester in conspiracy theories? Like a full-time job?"

"I *had* a full-time job," she shot back. "In Santa Fe. Don't forget that."

"So if this gang, this cabal, is so fucking brilliant," Clay said, sorting through papers from his briefcase, "then what's taking so long? This stuff's been around for decades. Centuries, probably." Before Claire could reply, Clay turned and said, "I'm sure you already have an answer for that." Claire nodded and said, "Yes, I do.

"They follow a preordained schedule, set to the Persian calendar, like the Ancient Mysteries," she said, and Clay said, "Of course they do."

"Controlled by a higher source of almost supernatural intelligence," she went on, ignoring his interruption. "The schedule moves slowly, precisely, but it's been quickening lately." "Quickening to what?" Clay asked.

"To the Ninth Protocol," Claire said, interrupted by a knock on the door.

Ling arrived with Clay's club sandwich with waffle fries and a root beer. "Claire, didn't you want to ask Ling something?" Clay said from the door. "What?" Claire said, on the spot. "Something you're missing?" Clay said, nodding toward the notes in her hand.

"Oh," Claire said, deciding against it. "I left something in the library, but it'll turn up, I'm sure. Thanks anyway, Ling."

Clay parked the tray on the bed, offered fries to Claire, who declined. She waited while he ate a few. He finally looked up at her and said, "The *what?*"

"The Ninth Protocol," she repeated calmly. "It's what everything is building up to."

Clay chewed quietly.

"The top-secret, cataclysmic, choreographed worldwide attack," Claire said evenly. "So apocalyptic that survivors clamor for order out of the chaos." She looked back down at her notes. "That chaos is called 'the Crucible.'"

"What kind of attack?" asked Clay. "The book doesn't say," Claire said. "Any doomsday scenario that would cause the collapse of civilization, I guess. But not a natural disaster. Man-made. Very intentional.

"And who steps in to soothe and provide?" she asked rhetorically. "With martial law to quell the terror they so meticulously created?"

"Is that a trick question?" Clay asked, smiling. "I can probably guess this one."

"And the masses are so grateful, they embrace their own slavery! Because at least they're *alive*! Or so they think..."

Claire thought she'd left something out and looked down at her notes. "Oh! Each of the eight colonies around the globe nominates a leader—someone very charismatic and, well, leader-like." She frowned and said, "A man, of course. The New World Order seems very chauvinistic. And during the chaos—the Crucible—these men will compete in some epic power struggle until one emerges as *the* leader. For everybody. For the whole planet."

"I'm king of the world!" Clay shouted from his *Titanic* mattress. Claire scanned her notes again to make sure she'd gotten it all. "Yeah. And then the evil new world goes on. The 'prison planet,' as Stu calls it. That's where the book ends."

Clay unfizzed his root beer and said, "I kinda like this plan."

"I don't think it's a joke," Claire said, perched childlike on the bed. "I mean, look around you—the world, the news, the life right outside these walls and down the hill. Everywhere you turn, everything's at a tipping point. You think it's all a coincidence?"

Clay scooted his tray, reclined on the bed in his robe. "And this cult has managed to brainwash its followers for unspeakable evil...for hundreds of years?" he asked. "Do they offer seminars?"

"Do you know what happens if they 'illuminate' you, reveal their plan, and then you refuse? Back out?" Claire said.

"I hope they kill you," said Clay. "That's what I would do."

Claire shook her head. "It's against the rules to kill their own members. They *disappear* you instead." "Yes, of course," Clay said, nodding.

"They fake your death, sometimes with these extremely elaborate schemes, and whisk you away to 'the Keep.' That book in the library had a sketch of an island somewhere. Where they live out their days in isolation."

"Like a Club Med for the rich and dead?" Clay asked, inspecting her. "They must let Elvis come and go, since people keep seeing him at the post office."

"Think of all the famous people who die mysteriously," Claire forged on, pacing. "Plane crashes, car wrecks, overdoses, assassinations. I mean, even Dean, if you really think about it..."

"Hold up there," said Clay, abruptly sharp, rising on the bed. "Foul."

"I mean it, Clay," and he said, "So do I, Claire. Stop it." He stood up, unsmiling.

"Have all the fun you want with this stupid stuff, but don't tie my family into it," he said. "I thought you were kidding around, but you sound nuts. And it's fucked up. My brother was shot dead on live television...."

"By whom?" Claire demanded. "Do you even know? A 'disturbed individual,' a 'Chinese immigrant.' That's it? That's all they reported!"

"Because that's all there is to it!" Clay said. "God, it's like you've caught a fever or something. Why are you bringing Dean's murder into this? You weren't even there!"

"Exactly!" Claire said. "Why weren't we?"

"Because I didn't like him!" Clay exploded, shocking them both. He took a breath, shrugged and said, "No conspiracy, just bad blood on my part. Going back, dunno, too far. Jealous brother stuff that I grew out of a little too late."

Postconfession, Clay sat back on the bed and scratched circles on the comforter. "Claire, where's all this paranoia coming from? What brought it on?"

Claire considered keeping it to herself, but then blurted, "Madison can walk. I saw her."

"Yes," Clay said, nodding downward. "Everybody knows that."

"What?" Claire asked. "You mean she's not..."

"Sh-she wasn't even hit. She...sprained her ankle in the fall," he stammered in frustration, as if reluctant to reveal the pitifulness of his sister-in-law. "She's been milking that stupid crutch for the sympathy vote ever since. Nobody's had the guts to call her on it, although Mom's getting close. Frankly, my parents don't know what to do with her."

"Good God," said Claire, although she had to admit the crutch was savvy. Even Martha, who knew Madison only from the social pages, had a soft spot for the crippled widow whose husband was cut down in his prime. Her strategy worked in a twisted public relations way.

Poor Madison, thought Claire. *So desperate to stay relevant in the city and in the family.*

"And you thought ...what?" Clay asked, softening. "Madison— loopy, out-of-touch Madison—helped fake her husband's assassination on live television so they could send him off to a private island somewhere?"

Claire considered the lunacy and said, "I...don't know what I thought."

"Were Mom and Dad in on it, too? Their own son?" Clay asked, fighting a grin. "Shut up, smart-ass," Claire said. "I said I don't know."

Clay tossed one of the conspiracy books on top of another. "We're supposed to be smarter than this, you know. Yale and all."

"Yes, I know," Claire said, tossing another book.

"Dad bought my way in," Clay said, inching closer with tickle hands, "but they tracked you down, way down in the swamps, because they must have thought you were pretty sharp."

"I am pretty sharp!" Claire protested, but Clay was on top of her, and she squealed with laughter until he stopped tickling and held her instead. "Your tinfoil hat is scratching me," he said, and she swatted him. "It's not my fault you have such an oddball family," she said.

He kissed her eyelid. "And you have an oddball imagination."

He held her face gently, inspecting her. "Do you want to move back?" he asked.

"Back...?" she said, startled. "To Santa Fe?"

Clay shrugged. "Is all this too much for you?" he added.

"What...would we do there?" she asked.

"What we were doing before."

"That wasn't much," she said with a laugh. She thought a moment and shook her head. "Because we can," he pressed. "We can leave tomorrow."

"No," she said. "We're not running away. We're just getting started here."

Clay traced his finger down her neck to her chest. "But we do need to move out of this club. Into our own place," he said. "Yes, please," Claire said.

He kissed down her neck. "Our own life. Less work. More fun." Claire nodded, submitting as he nibbled.

"We need to have a baby," he breathed into her ear.

Claire pulled back, looking into his eyes.

"For real?" she asked.

Clay pulled closer. "You ready to try again? Soon?"

Claire kissed his forehead, stroked his hair.

"Yes," she said. "Yes. Soon."

—॥॥—

The colonel surprised Claire by inviting her kids to Easter Brunch that Sunday.

"Everyone's been curious about them, and I thought they would enjoy the celebration," he told her one night after dinner. "That's very kind, Colonel," she said. His behind-her-back snubbing to Slade seemed remote and inconsequential now. After all, he hadn't taken pleasure in it; he was simply following club rules, as archaic as they were. Clay had nodded when she'd told him about it and said, "Old dog, new tricks."

Claire and Clay had agreed on their own rules, rendering the Union Club irrelevant. After Clay finished his current assignment—his first major solo presentation to the company's board—they'd quickly find an apartment and then look for a permanent home at their leisure. She'd miss the ironed sheets, changed daily. And the laundry and room service. Both minor trade-offs.

She'd get her teaching job. Or master's degree. Or even start her own charter school. The city could certainly use another. She'd stop nagging Clay, who was clearly under crushing pressure at the office. He still had frequent nightmares and night sweats, and she'd sometimes wake him just to calm and hold him closer. The last thing he needed was to come home to a punchy wife mired in too-much-time-on-her-hands paranoia.

She returned the books to the library with Jess's help. He was curious about them.

205

"They're alternate history books," she explained. "Well, conspiracy theory."

"Like that Mel Gibson movie? With Julia Roberts?" Jess asked.

"Something like that," said Claire. "But dumber."

Edgar's stubborn cold returned, so Claire took him to a pediatrician Martha recommended. The doctor suggested Children's Tylenol and Benadryl, which Claire had on hand. She paid cash for the visit, and Jess drove them by Baskin-Robbins for a chocolate chip clown cone.

The children wore their finest on Easter Sunday, courtesy of Madison's shopping spree. The club set up their traditional petting zoo in the Grand Foyer, roped off, the floor covered in hay. The children of younger members mingled easily with the darker, smartly dressed Safe Harbor crew, amid honking ducklings and spotted rabbits.

"It's good for them," Nora told Claire, pointing at the white-blond Embry boy cradling a baby goat for Ilza to pet. "This is the real world. The world as it should be." A duck escaped the makeshift pen, and Ling squat-chased it around the foyer to the children's squeals and laughter.

Jess wore a bucktooth bunny costume—mesh-eyed and grimy-furred from years of hugs—for the children's photos by the "Cotton Patch" picket gate. "Hold up!" Claire interrupted cameraman Allen, dashing to wipe Edgar's runny nose. His sudden sneeze spooked the rabbit from his arms, and Ling gave chase again to more squeals. "You want another rabbit?" she asked to Edgar's nods. "Yes, please," he said.

"You two look darling," said Edie from beneath her wildflower Easter bonnet. "Claire, get your picture taken with the little tyke." Clancy, in his bright madras jacket, agreed. Claire knelt with her arms around Edgar cradling his rabbit. "Smile!" she urged as Allen clicked away. He did.

"Thank you. Thank you for this day," said an emotional clergyman by the dripping swan ice sculpture. He was glowing from his spiked ambrosia punch in a clear glass teacup. "You're very welcome," said a charmed and amused Claire, blaming the liquor for his ebullience.

And then Madison pinged a glass from the staircase. "If you please!" she called out and summoned Claire up. "Me?" Claire asked in the spotlight, and Madison nodded with a wide smile, slapping her thigh with her free hand, as if commanding a dog to heel. The children lined up across the bottom step.

Madison thanked her "beloved sister-in-law" and "our wonderful guest" Claire for spearheading the Safe Harbor program. "Her idea, her brainchild, from the very beginning," Madison insisted, to applause. "It would not have happened without her." Claire smiled and resisted but eventually tipped her head to acknowledge the club's gratitude. Then Madison announced "an exciting new partnership, just approved by the club board, to ensure the continued welfare of our young charges." A "joint foster-ship," she called it, with a special trust endowed to fund the children's "enrichment until they turn eighteen."

The city's mayor stepped up to remind his fellow members it "takes a village," and the members answered with a fresh wave of applause. The kids smiled, and Ilza led the bows, basking in the attention.

Stompy gathered the children around the piano and led them in "Found a Peanut" before the front-lawn egg roll, which ended the day's celebration.

Claire walked the kids back to the church and hugged them all. She had a voice mail from Martha, reminding her of their upcoming double date, and numerous missed "unknown" calls, no longer unknown to her.

She deleted them all except one.

Chapter Thirteen

That week, Claire channeled the children's energies into the Peace Train project, which would "roll" through San Francisco in late spring on its cross-country tour. She registered on the website and noted its submission rules: water color on paper, to be laminated before submitting.

"Art is your voice, your message to the world," she told the kids, wandering the easels as they painted with quiet concentration. "And it lives long after you do."

She'd scolded herself for having taken Ethan seriously. At least he had the excuse of mental illness, drug addiction, and, if her hunch was right, delirium from a serious medical condition—all of which needed immediate treatment. Given the club's generosity to the children, she was surprised they'd abandoned an ex-employee with his own urgent problems. Unless, of course, he was also dangerous. He'd certainly seemed mercurial, bordering on schizophrenic, when they'd met at the museum.

He'd also told her it was too late to save her children, which was ridiculous; they were clearly protected and well cared for now, contentedly immersed in their art project. Ethan was, sadly, nuts. *Disturbed*, she corrected herself, admiring Condi's peaceful, hand-linking earth painting in blues and greens.

"That's lovely," she encouraged. "Add more people, if you want. You're good with people."

Unless Ethan had meant her own child, the one she'd miscarried. But he couldn't have known about that, or her initial pregnancy, unless he knew someone at the hospital, which was unlikely. Or was still in touch with someone from the club, one of the staff, which was more plausible. Thanks to Slade, everyone at the club knew she'd been pregnant; thanks to Madison, everyone knew she'd lost it.

"When's our snack?" whined Rodney in his spattered smock. "Not yet," said Claire, staring through parted sheers toward the rear parking lot. "Soon. Keep painting."

Down by the employee door, Stompy smoked and chatted up the not-Dean waiter, on his way to the Dumpster with a garbage bag. From a distance, the resemblance was even more striking. Up close, not so much. But from the second floor, or, say, the back of a ballroom, if he were dressed in a proper suit, he could almost pass for Dean's double....

Stop it, Claire told herself.

"Stop it!" Angel cried out, and Claire turned to Caesar dragging his brush across her pad.

"Caesar, no," Claire said, intervening. "That's Angel's. Paint your own." "Big baby," Caesar said, painting a swatch of red on Angel's arm.

"Yes, you're a big man, Caesar," Claire taunted him, taking his brush. "But we're not doing body art today." Caesar speared another brush from the water jar, dipped it in purple, and striped down Claire's nose.

"Okay. Yes, we are," she said, returning the favor in orange.

The paintbrush war engulfed the room and was louder, messier, and more fun than recess. Claire got ambushed by CJ and Anthony and turned to retaliate on Ilza and instead painted a thick pink streak down Colonel Crowe's navy tie. She jumped back.

"Oh God, I'm sorry," she said as the room hushed to silence. "It washes right out."

The colonel dismissed it, rubbing his tie with a handkerchief. "It's just cloth," he said. "And rather useless at that."

He looked around at the stiff children. "Sorry to startle you. I heard the commotion and couldn't resist," he said. "Am I intruding?"

"Not at all," Claire said, wiping her hands down her smock, sweeping back her hair. "You're always welcome to join us." She turned to the frozen faces. "Say 'Hello, Colonel.'"

The colonel tipped his head, wandered the easels.

"Edgar, would you tell Colonel Crowe about our art project?" Claire said.

He would not. Claire did.

"Peace Train, yes," the colonel mused in approval. "Sounds like a promising movement.

"May I see your interpretations of peace?" he asked the children. They looked to Claire for permission. She nodded, which they passed on to the colonel, nodding in unison.

"Those are lovely dolphins," he said to Ilza, "swimming in the peaceful ocean." Ilza, for once, was speechless. "Stars are indeed peaceful, aren't they?" he affirmed to Rodney's galaxy of constellations, patting the wary boy on the head.

The colonel stooped to investigate Edgar's triangle-roofed, chimney-spewing red house. Inside, by the fireplace, a stick mother read a book to her stick son. "Edgar, isn't it?" he asked. "Say 'Yes, sir,'" Claire gently prodded, and the rigid Edgar mustered a nod. "Is that your mother in the picture?" the colonel asked. He looked from the stick mother with flowers on her skirt up to Claire's floral dress and back again. He smiled and said, "Oh, I see. Yes. I get it."

"But to appreciate peace, one must first value war," the colonel said, continuing his inspection. "It is, after all, the favorite instrument of natural selection."

Oh boy, thought Claire. *Here we go.*

"War is a ruthless eliminator of the weak," he lectured on, "raising the level of courage, intelligence, skill, for all sides. It stimulates invention and creates the weapons that become crucial guardians of the peace. But most important, war undermines anarchism, creates discipline, and is the springboard of all civilization."

"Colonel." Claire shook her head. "I'm not sure this is the right place—"

"War was inevitable with unconquered lands in the balance," he went on, the children oddly attentive, following his movement. "But with everything now discovered, it's pointless. In a civilized, settled society, peace is actually the natural order of things."

The colonel surveyed the room. "And a truly lasting peace is soon possible," he finished, his voice cracking slightly. "If we keep working together, I think it's just around the corner."

"Let's hope so," Claire said, relieved but unsure where his topic would pivot next. Mercifully, the arrival of refreshments rescued her.

"Welcome, Colonel. What a surprise," Madison called out, directing Ling on the milk and cookie disbursement as the children politely waited for their personalized snack.

The colonel pulled Claire aside. "I must apologize," he said quietly. "For my inappropriate, disrespectful conversation you overheard a couple of weeks ago." Claire breathed in to gather a response, and the colonel added, "Clay had every right to confront me once you told him. He's your husband. And a man.

"I've worked for decades to make this club more inclusive," he continued. "I saw Slade and Nora's potential early on, twisted some arms on the membership committee, and the club is certainly the richer for it.

"I'm still twisting arms," he added, smiling, "And I hope to have good news soon. And then it will be up to you, of course, if you choose to honor us with your continued presence. I speak for many in my hope that you will. You've been quite a welcome jolt around here."

Claire stayed noncommittal. "I appreciate the club's hospitality," she said.

"Speaking of your father-in-law," the colonel went on, more hushed. "Slade is not only a self-made man, but a humble one as well. So you didn't hear this from me...." He went on to tell her about the college fund he'd quietly established for Claire's Safe Harbor kids.

"Full scholarship, wherever they go," the colonel said. "Like you, he wants to level the field."

"But you didn't hear it from me...," the colonel reminded her before goodbyes to the children. He declined when Condi offered to share her peppermint milk. "How very generous, but milk doesn't sit well with me these days," he said. "But growing children need all they can get."

—∿—

Claire tried, unsuccessfully, to get back in touch with Ethan.

His "unknown number" turned out to be a pay phone at the art museum, which she discovered when a perplexed visitor finally answered. She'd forgotten public phones still existed.

She wanted to reach him, she told herself, to offer counseling, rehab, medical treatment. To assure him the Union Club harbored no ill will and to extend a hand.

"Absolutely," Nora said when Claire brought it up during a Justice Ball tasting in the dining room. "If you can get Ethan back, total amnesty." She considered a porcini pastry appetizer and said, "We only want to help him. He knows he needs it."

She did not want to reach him, Claire convinced herself, to pick his brain about the nonsense he'd spouted or push him to elaborate on his delusional accusations. She wasn't looking for answers—about the club, Dean's assassination, the children he implied were in danger. His ridiculous warning "they" were going to kill her.

And it wasn't a sense of urgency, Claire persuaded herself, that made her lurk around the coatroom listening for her phone, or spend more time outside the club—in the park, at Grace Cathedral, around Nob Hill—where she could hold her cell, in case he called again.

He did, when Claire was on the elliptical at the Fairmont that week, listening to a *Fresh Air* podcast. He sounded even more unhinged.

"Ethan, please focus." She tried calming him. "You're not making sense." She paced the hallway outside the hotel's gym.

"The end is near," he stammered. "The date is set. It's in the club."

"Come back to the club," Claire said, stepping aside for a woman in sweats to pass. "We can talk it over. Let us help you."

His laughter was a childlike squeal.

"Their help is terminal," he said.

"Before they kill you, too—" he started up another warning, and Claire said, "Stop it, Ethan! Stop saying that."

"You think they won't?" he asked. "You think Colonel Crowe is your friend?"

"How do you know...?" Claire stammered and stopped. "Are you spying on me?"

Ethan repeated the warnings from the library book he'd hidden in the club. His voice was thin and broken with a hacking cough. "The world will listen to you," he insisted. "You are the last chance."

"Ethan, there's no date to warn the world about," Claire stressed. "No conspiracy. No New World Order. No one is trying to kill you or me or anyone. It's fiction.

"You're ill, Ethan. We can help you. Please let us.

"Ethan, are you there?" she asked, after a silence.

"If you believe that," he answered through a weary rattle, "then why did you answer?" And he was gone.

—w—

Hopeless, Claire decided. No wonder the club had given up on him.

An artistic, fertile imagination coupled with a chemical addiction latched around a mind-bending global conspiracy whose preposterousness made it an addiction all its own was certainly a recipe for the mess Ethan had become. Even Claire had come dangerously close to believing the fantasy in the books and the nonsense spewed daily by Stu. It was inevitable, she told herself, until you remembered how ridiculous it all was.

"Ethan saved my life," Jess told Claire that night after dinner, helping her tidy the Safe Harbor room. "So when he went back off the deep end, it was extra sad. But you can't help a bud who doesn't want it, you know? You just can't."

"The club sent Ethan to recruit you? And others?" Claire asked after hearing his tale. Jess nodded.

"Thank God they did. I'd still be homeless and in my own mess of trouble," he said, folding the easels. "I don't know how I fell that far, and you don't even wanna know the stuff I was getting into. The bottom of rock bottom. They straightened me out, no judgments. Got me off the smack, gave me a job, medical treatment, a place to live. Most important, gave me back my life."

215

"Nora ran the program for years," Jess went on answering Claire's questions, stacking the folded easels against the closet wall. "The 'Room at the Inn,' she called it. 'Saint Nora' we called her, until she made us stop. She's a class act. Doesn't like the spotlight.

"Ethan was her favorite, you could tell. Almost like a son," he said. "I guess he'd been a real mess when he came here, and she made him her pet project. So it hit her extra hard when he relapsed and started back with all that crazy stuff."

"You still talk to Ethan?" Claire asked. Jess shook his head. "Not since Halloween, or around then. That's when he started stealing things, for drugs I'm sure, and Nora gave up on him.

"She quit the whole program after last November. After Dean...you know," he said. "I reckon she needed a break from a lot of things. I can't imagine that kind of loss."

"How many of the staff came to the club that way?" Claire asked, standing on a chair to hang the children's still-damp watercolors to dry. "You mean 'off the streets'?" Jess asked with a grin, handing her the sheets, which she clipped to a makeshift clothesline.

Jess looked up, counting. "Lots. Doormen, waiters, even Stompy and his band. Hell, I met my wife in the kitchen.

"And people wonder why there aren't bums around Nob Hill, like the rest of the city," he said. "It's 'cause the Union cared enough to take 'em in.

"If it wasn't for the Union Club, I'd be dead by now," Jess insisted. "I know that much."

Claire straightened the books on the children's shelves. "How long have you been married?" she asked.

"Five years this June," he said.

"Any children?"

"Not yet." Jess grinned again and shook his head. "Still trying."

Claire nodded.

"Miss Claire," Jess said, "if we're done here, I might head down for a late dinner with my wife. That okay?"

"Of course," Claire said. "Thanks for your help."

And then she said, panicked, "Oh God. Dinner! Jess, what day is this?"

—⟋⟍—

Claire couldn't stop apologizing, but Martha was immune.

"There's this new invention called the telephone," she said, spewing a missile of smoke toward the cracked window. "It's the craziest thing. When it rings, you just...answer it!"

Martha sat at the small dining table in the living room of her cramped Tenderloin apartment. The table with flowers was set for four, candles extinguished, the kitchen a wreck from a complex meal never served. Her dress, hair, makeup—a rare effort these days—still immaculate.

"I didn't have it on me," Claire said. She clutched the vintage Amelus Bordeaux she'd grabbed from the Union's wine cellar. Useless now. She was almost two hours late.

"Right." Martha nodded. "I keep forgetting the weird rules up there. Your secret world."

"And Clay's out of town again," Claire said, ignoring her, "and, frankly, I've been so busy at the club. That's not an excuse. I'm very sorry. Where's your date?"

"He *did* call, at least," Martha said, stubbing her cigarette onto her plate. She went into the kitchen. "Last-minute hospital stuff. I've used that one before. It comes in handy." She ran the hot water, squirted soap into a crusted baking pan. "And I thought our first date went well. I've misjudged lots of things lately."

"But hey, at least I got lamb shank down," she said, pouring out her white wine. "And four stars from the neighbor's dog!"

"Let's go out for a drink," Claire offered. "Too late tonight," Martha said, flicking her hands, grabbing a towel. "I have an early call."

"Then dinner next week, anywhere. My treat."

"I can afford my own dinner," Martha said. "And I hate to drag you away from your club." Claire said, "Oh, Martha. Stop it! How many times can I say I'm sorry?"

"Never again is probably the best idea," Martha replied. "Like you said, at some point we all grow up a little."

"Yes, I'm rich, and you're not!" Claire erupted. "Really, who cares? I didn't go looking for it. Is that gonna wreck us forever?"

"You know, I used to wonder, before you moved here," Martha said, lighting another smoke, "why my hospital, which desperately needs research funds, turned down so many generous grants from fat cats in this town. All of whom, by the way, are apparently your fellow club members..."

"I'm not a member...," Claire said on cue, and Martha dismissed it, inhaling and tilting her head up.

"And then I heard rumblings," she went on, ribboning smoke toward the ceiling, "whispers, really, because no one knew quite what to make of it, that the Union Club had so many strings attached to its money, so much meddling and interference, and then last fall they targeted the Children's Hospital with a huge donation. Which the board turned down flat."

"What does this have to do with...?" Claire started, but Martha barreled on, scissoring the cigarette tightly.

"That was shocking, because, as you know, as you told me, your club's late, great leader—Flick, was his name?—founded the whole hospital. Donated the land, paid for the original building, was its first chairman of the board!

"Unfortunately," Martha continued, louder, "when his pesky essays on selective breeding and forced sterilizations of 'undesirables' surfaced, they took his name right off the building. If your beloved Mr. James Flick had his way, your 'children' wouldn't even be here!"

"Oh God, Martha, shut up!" Claire said, and she did. "All this anger and hate—insanity, really—because I missed one dinner?"

"I'm just making sure you know what kind, benevolent company you keep," Martha said. "And how far you've come since we met. I guess I shouldn't be surprised."

"When will you stop punishing me for your pathetic loneliness?" Claire said. "And just get a life?"

Martha leaned back in her chair, stared out the window.

"Soon," she said calmly. "My transfer came through."

"Congrats," Claire clipped. "Chicago is a wonderful town."

They'd sparred and fought many times before, but this was different. Claire knew neither would back down. After a pause to unwind and exhale, Martha said, "My coworkers are throwing a going-away party. Next weekend. If you're around."

"Okay," said Claire, and then remembered the Justice Ball, which she would have skipped, except the children would be performing, and she wasn't in the mood to cave to Martha, to let her win this one. "Well, no. Sorry. I have an event at the club."

"Yes," said Martha, flicking an ash. "Of course you do."

Chapter Fourteen

It wasn't the first time Martha had lashed out when she felt inferior. If anything, her latest outburst was an improvement over the passive-aggressive, underhanded digs that Claire usually swallowed and ignored.

But to insinuate—flat-out charge—that Claire was part of a eugenics operation, was a weird low, even for Martha. It made Claire angrier the more she thought about it, on the ride back in the Town Car, with Jess at the wheel.

That was Martha's real beef, of course. The Union Club, the Lincoln, the chauffeur. The new home they'd move into eventually, which, although Claire would insist be modest, would be grander than Martha's cramped one-bedroom Tenderloin apartment, especially if they wanted a child. She wouldn't apologize for that. Martha was simply jealous.

Claire thanked Jess and dropped by the Safe Harbor room to unclip the children's artwork. Carefully stacked the watercolor-warped paper, lining up the edges, in the protective portfolio. Slid the portfolio into the closet, behind the easels.

Martha was also bitter, which Claire realized had been simmering since college, when Claire betrayed their friendship by latching on to Clay. Martha had never forgiven her, which exacerbated her flare-ups and now bordered on rage. It was repellent. And to think she'd almost set Martha up with Clay's friend Bing. Martha just blew that chance. Soon she'd have a cat instead, and then more and more.

"*Where* are you again?" she asked Clay when he called that night. "I've never even heard of that town. Is it near Dallas?"

"In the middle of nowhere, near the panhandle," Clay said. "We're building something here."

"What kind of something in the middle of nowhere?" Claire asked.

"If I told you...," joked Clay. "Yes, I'm starting to think so," Claire sparred back. He seemed more confident and comfortable in his job these days. At times, he seemed to enjoy it.

"Miss you, love you," they said to each other. "Back tomorrow night," Clay reminded her as they hung up.

It was insane and insulting to suggest an essay by the club's founder advocating forced sterilization—if true, coming from the gossipy rumor mill of the hospital, likely peopled with other sad and lonely residents—was somehow incriminating against the club members today. It was more than a hundred years ago. How many unthinkable things were acceptable in the past? Even George Washington had slaves, hordes of them, and he was still on the dollar bill.

And Margaret Sanger's groundbreaking work for women's reproductive rights was only slightly tarnished by her advocacy of intelligent breeding, which Claire remembered her college professor soft-pedaling in lectures. Eugenics and euthanasia were simply hot topics of that era, and that Sanger was invited to be the Union's first female member was due, no doubt, to her many other historic accomplishments.

Claire looked at the alarm clock: 5:06 a.m. She'd only dozed through the night. Pointless to try to sleep now. She watched the sun rise and the Fairmont wake from her window seat.

Was Martha implying the Union Club still believed in eugenics? Or worse, acted on it? Including Claire? Martha couldn't think that of her best friend, even in her most 'round-the-bend moments. It was just an escalation of her needling, fueled further by the nonsense spouted from Stu Savage and his copycat conspiracy clones.

Claire shut her bathroom window to block him out while she toweled dry. She was sick of his gravelly voice and headache-inducing rants. All morning she'd endured his interview with an alleged doctor about the 3,000-percent increase in diabetes, cancers, autism, neurological disorders—all caused by the intentional poisoning of soil and depletion of vital minerals. Was it even legal to terrorize the public with such obvious lies?

She'd report Stu's inconsiderate downstairs fan who flaunted the club rules by smoking in his room, which wafted through the well and into open windows. He shouldn't be allowed to blast his radio this early in the morning either.

She brushed her teeth, added the barest of makeup. Recoiled at the mirror, and with her tweezers, surgically plucked a single gray hair. *Scram.*

And fuck Martha. Even if the club maintained the evil beliefs of its founder—whose bedroom suite she lived in, which was unsettling, although she'd be moving soon, to someplace new and modern and young—how would they even go about implementing them? Perhaps Martha envisioned a dark cabal of ingenious plotters, whereas Claire knew the club was mostly a gaggle of silly drunks. The world had little to fear with Edie and Clancy in charge of its imminent destruction, she thought with a cackle. How many sinister, history-altering deeds could Mr. Beasley log between naps and diaper changes?

Claire sat at her laptop, unable to concentrate on the day's teaching plan. Greece was in the news again, perennially on the verge of collapse. She'd teach the kids about Greece this afternoon. The Parthenon, Acropolis, Delphi. Ancient Greece, not the current mess. The kids would like the gods and monsters.

She ran down the back stairs. "Good morning, Stompy," she said, passing him on the second floor. "You're up early."

"Laying down some tracks while I got the inspiration," Stompy said, which Claire didn't grasp, although she guessed it was music related. He sounded unusually hoarse today. "Sore throat?" she asked. "Just a frog," he croaked back. "Stop smoking," she lectured him again, and, nodding, he held open the door at the bottom of the stairs.

And what did Martha mean by "strings attached" and "meddling" when the club offered research grants? Had she spiraled so low to suggest the Union tried to use her hospital for their supposed sterilization experiments? This was four-star lunacy, even for Martha at her nadir.

"Please don't get up." She waved down the staff as she waltzed into their dining alcove off the kitchen. "I'm not Lady Grantham." The joke fell flat with the non-PBS crowd, and Claire wondered why she'd tried it. She needed coffee. "May I take an apple?" she asked at the fruit basket on the sideboard.

She said "good morning" to Jess, who'd been trying, unsuccessfully, to have a child with his wife for the past five years. She said "good morning" to Ling, whose wife had died of cancer recently and who still stewed in silent anger at the world.

Claire looked across the quiet staff as they picked at scrambled eggs and bacon and sliced canned peaches. Two more carried their preplated breakfasts and squeezed into what seemed like assigned seats. She wondered how many the club had taken in "off the street." She wondered how many were married and childless, like Jess. Or how many others had died, like Ling's wife.

She wondered where weak, sickly Ethan, who'd recruited them all and had left only a few months ago, used to sit when he ate his preplated meals. She wondered when he'd morphed from the healthy, happy young man in the photo album into the skeletal, delusional mess he was now. What changed him?

"Thanks again," Claire said, shining her apple on her forearm. "Have a great day, everybody!"

She dashed down to Union Square to buy sheet music for the children's Justice Ball mini-concert. Flipped through categories in alphabetized bins and finally bought an anthology. Walked past a herd of disturbingly obese tourists outside the Sir Francis Drake. How could parents let their kids get so fat? It was child abuse, in its own way.

By lunchtime, which she wasn't hungry for, Claire felt sorry for Martha. She had pressures and anxieties Claire didn't have to worry about: an exhausting work schedule, student loans, monthly bills, a foul smoking addiction she couldn't shake. And a growing desperation to find a mate, at a stage in life when desperation developed a permanent, arm's-length stink. Fleeing to a new city would only briefly mask the symptoms.

Their slow-motion falling out was partially Claire's fault, she realized. She'd forgotten to tell Martha she was moving here, leaving her to read about it in the newspaper. What kind of friend did that? Martha had rushed to her side after her miscarriage. She'd recommended her own in-demand doctor and leapfrogged her to the front of the waiting list. In spite of her crippling schedule, she'd reached out to Claire and Clay for double dates, movies, concerts, for which Claire usually had an excuse, however legitimate. Claire had yet to invite Martha anywhere, to include her in her new San Francisco life.

And, of course, she'd completely forgotten about Martha's dinner party, which had been planned for weeks and wound up a pitiful disaster. That was inexcusably self-absorbed on Claire's part.

No wonder Martha felt abandoned, betrayed. And had taken it out on Claire.

She'd call Martha and apologize again. She'd go to her party and meet her coworkers and make amends, even if she had to take a break from the Justice Ball, which she refused to let consume her entire weekend at the expense of her oldest friendship. She'd keep her priorities straight. Hopefully Martha would forgive her.

"Are you sad, Miss Claire?" Edgar asked her that afternoon in the Safe Harbor room while the others were on the playground. She'd kept him inside, since it was misty out, which aggravated his lingering cough. They collaborated on a "Where's Waldo" jigsaw that inspired neither of them.

"Not at all," Claire said, startled by the question.

And then she said, "Yes, I am a little sad. Have you ever lost a friend?" Edgar nodded, and Claire remembered and said, "Yes, of course you have." She put down a puzzle piece and pulled him onto her lap, where she held him tightly.

"Someday, when you have a baby, will we still be friends?" Edgar asked.

She pulled back and looked at him. "Of course we will. You'll be friends with the baby, too. Like a big brother."

"But not a real brother," said Edgar. "Just a pretend one."

Claire was stymied, so she said, "Maybe...if I don't get you first." She poked under his ribs and he giggled. She dug in again, and he leapt off her lap. She chased him until they collapsed on the carpet in a pile of laughter.

Edgar's squealing protests morphed into a racking cough attack. He gasped for air and, hyperventilating, found it. Claire held him until his breathing normalized. She'd call the doctor for a new prescription. She'd check him for asthma.

"Ssh," she said, smoothing back his hair. "You're okay now." His forehead was hot and flushed from the chase. She shouldn't have pushed him so hard while he was still on the mend.

"Miss Claire?" Edgar said, tucking his feet under her crossed legs. "Please don't get me anymore."

"I won't, Edgar," she whispered, rocking on the floor. "No one's going to get you. I promise."

The white-coated staff brought the tray of refreshments. Claire grabbed cookies and Edgar's labeled milk, which they'd changed to plain.

"You don't have to wait for the others," she said, holding the straw to his lips. "Drink your milk. It's good for you."

Chapter Fifteen

Nora invited Claire to afternoon tea at Neiman Marcus, since the club was prepping for the big weekend. "You need to get out more often," Nora insisted. "A person can burn up in that place."

"Go, go," Madison encouraged. "Ling can help with the kids today. Can't you, Ling?"

Jess dropped them off. They first shopped the busy main floor, buying Tom Ford lipstick in two shades and handling the new Hayward alligator clutches in silvery pink and orange sherbet before taking the special elevator to the Rotunda restaurant at the top. "Good afternoon, Ms. Willing," the navy-suited maître d' said with a slight bow.

"Hello," they both replied and then chuckled at each other.

The oval restaurant was exquisite, ringed with proper ladies, and hushed. "I sit by the window," Nora said. "Unless you prefer the edge."

Claire peered over the central atrium banister down four floors to the cosmetic counters. She looked up to a stunning stained-glass dome and blinked off a wave of vertigo. "The window's fine," she said, righting herself.

They sat by the glass wall overlooking Union Square and spread strawberry butter on popovers while Sinatra sang "Three Coins in the Fountain." Nora ordered lightly for them both.

"Claire, are you happy?" she asked abruptly.

"Yes...," Claire said. "Yes, of course I'm happy."

"No, you're not."

Before Claire could protest, Nora mock frowned. "You seem worried all the time. I'm a worrier. I get it."

"Are you still scared for your safety?" she asked. Claire shook her head. "Good," Nora said. "You shouldn't be. I'm confident we have that under control now."

The waiter brought the tea case. Nora picked Lady Grey; Claire, black currant.

"I was miserable here at first, too," Nora continued, leaning closer over the kettle's steam. "Lonely as hell. Slade was always away, doing whatever it is they do for work. I felt like a war widow. But those sacrifices did pay off, eventually. Once you find your purpose here, your usefulness—and you will, trust me—everything will start to make sense."

"We're going to have a baby," Claire said. "I mean, we're going to try again."

"Oh God," said Nora, leaning back. "I didn't mean that purpose. That was fast."

The waiter brought scones and clotted cream and cucumber sandwiches.

"A baby," Nora mused, sucking a tooth. "Is Clay onboard with this?"

Obviously, thought Claire, but she phrased it more gently. "We made the decision together."

"Huh," said Nora, looking up at the lights that ringed the stained-glass dome.

"Are you sure?" she asked, snapping back. "What's the rush? You have so much on your plate right now."

"I have nothing on my plate," Claire said. "You know that."

"Well, you're busy with the kids in your program, which is a smashing success and a noble effort. And, of course, you'll be looking for a new home soon and moving and all that. My Realtor has a list as soon as—"

"Clay and I have discussed it," Claire gently interrupted. "We'll be pregnant soon."

"Huh," Nora repeated, and then she said, "What about adoption?"

Claire nestled her cup back in its saucer. "That's certainly an option...down the road," she said, scrolling for an appropriate response. "Although we'd planned on having our own first."

"You can do both, of course. I wish I had. In fact, I wish I'd *started* with adoption and *then* had my own. Because otherwise you just never get around to it, and then you regret it. And there are so many displaced children, at-risk youth, in need of a good home. Like the one you and Clay could give them."

Claire nodded into her plate, wondering what Nora was suggesting.

"Do you mean Edgar?" Claire asked. "Or the others?"

Nora said, "I hadn't thought in specifics." She crumbled a scone to dust. "I just thought adoption would appeal to you. Giving back, in a way."

"Yes."

"It's just a suggestion." Nora shrugged, hands in her lap. "Aren't you, of all people, open to raising another woman's child?" The question ended with a shrill tinge.

Claire nodded at the odd statement and gave up on a response.

Nora smiled and said, "I'm just thinking out loud." She pried open a tea sandwich and peered inside. "Sweet or savory, can't decide."

Across the Rotunda, by the elevator, a louder voice edged slightly above the conversational hum. In her periphery, Claire saw the maître d' hurry back toward his post.

Nora ticked off a list of personal "refurbishments"—final fittings, hair, makeup—dreaded but necessary before the weekend's events. This triggered a reminder about her luncheon for the visiting officers' wives. She'd forgotten the Bonn wife was vegan. "Such a pain," she grumbled. "Vegans shouldn't leave the house. Especially Germans." She grabbed a pen and a scrap of paper from her handbag and held her half-glasses to her eyes.

A fluster of motion from the front caught Claire's eye. She peered while Nora scribbled her to-do list. "I'll forget otherwise," Nora said, "and Frau Whatsherface will sit and stew. And waste away."

The maître d' was talking to a guest by the elevator, hemming him off from the restaurant. It didn't work. Claire looked closer. Ethan evaded the man and scanned the oval room. Unsteady, erratic. Even thinner, almost translucent. He'd given over to madness.

Nora tucked her note and glasses into her Chanel pocket. She sighed at her tea.

The maître d' looked flustered again. The restaurant's hum lowered. Claire pivoted away, toward the glass wall, and shrank in her chair.

"What's going on over there?" Nora asked, not bothering to squint so far. "There's a weird energy in here today."

"If you will not fight when you can win without bloodshed...," a surprisingly robust Ethan bellowed, considering his marked frailty. "If you will not fight when your victory is sure..."

Nora held her glasses back up and looked hard. "Who is that lunatic? Is Neiman's doing performance art now?"

"It's Ethan," Claire murmured, still shrinking, peeping back. "*What?!*" Nora cried, periscoping higher. "Impossible."

"You will ultimately fight with all the odds against you and only a precarious chance of survival...." Ethan continued making his way around the Rotunda, steadying himself on the banister. He looked corpselike, his good eye red and watery, his patch mercifully covering the other. His hands were still paint stained.

"He's been following me, calling me," Claire whispered, huddling closer. "That's outrageous," Nora said. "Totally inexcusable." She fished her cell from her bag and pushed a button. "Jess, Ethan has tracked us down in the restaurant. Yes, *that* Ethan. Thank you." She hung up and growled, "This is so embarrassing. Ye gods."

"Is he dangerous?" Claire asked.

Nora was taken aback and then said, "Only to himself, I think."

"But there may be a worse fate." Ethan drew closer, as the lady tea-goers watched him pass in a moment awkward but not flee-worthy. "You may have to fight when there is no hope of victory...."

The maître d' phoned from the front desk. Waiters in black vests and white aprons stood down, waiting for one of the others to intervene. Ethan targeted Claire and Nora, who looked away, ignoring him, mumbling to herself.

"Because it is better to perish than to live as slaves." He stopped inches from their table, racked and straining for breath. His skin was papery. There was so little left of him.

"Ethan, please," Claire soothed, patting the tablecloth.

"Yes, Ethan, you've made your point and gotten our attention," Nora said, looking up to challenge him. Her hand flew to her mouth. "Oh God! What has happened to you?" She bolted from her chair and reached out before stopping herself. She pulled back.

"Don't you remember?" He smiled through cracked teeth. "I'm your pet project. I wanted to see you one last time. And for you to see me."

"Ethan, we have to get you help," Nora urged, waving him closer. "To get you clean."

Ethan shrieked with laughter. "There's no cure for this," he said, presenting himself. "Stage four. There's no stage five."

"That can't be!" Nora insisted, shaking her head. "They promised!"

Claire looked from Ethan to a horrified Nora.

Two security guards appeared at the front. The maître d' whispered and pointed.

"Shame, Nora," Ethan said. "Taking your daughter-in-law down the same path. When you know where it leads."

The guards arrived. "Sir," one said. "Would you please come with us?" He gently cupped Ethan's elbow. The maître d' stood behind and nodded an awkward apology at Claire and Nora.

"God help you," Ethan said to Claire. "They'll never take you along."

"Take me where, Ethan?" Claire asked in earnest. "Who is 'they'?"

"Do you ever wonder, Nora?" Ethan said, ignoring her. "How they'll treat us in hell, you and me?" He held a steady gaze until the guard gave a slight tug. Not resisting, Ethan turned and went around the narrow passage bordering the Rotunda.

Nora touched the back of her neck with a trembling hand and stared down at her teaspoon.

"What just happened?" Claire asked. "What is wrong with him?"

"Dementia, addiction, take your pick," Nora said to her lap. "Heartbreaking."

Claire stood up. "Ethan, wait!" she called out.

"What?" Nora said, looking up. "Where are you going?"

Claire later had trouble recalling the sequence, as it happened nearly simultaneously. She caught up to the guards escorting Ethan. Up ahead, Jess emerged from the elevator and squared off at the front desk. Ethan screamed, "No!" and slipped from the guards' hold, dashing back toward Claire. She held out her hands and cried, "Stop!" Ethan pivoted toward the banister as she grabbed his arm. He leapt over the edge.

He dangled while she clutched his arm and begged him to grab hers. He was light and motionless, calm. The guards grabbed Claire to anchor her. There were screams, behind her— across, below—she couldn't tell. She heard Nora yelling to Jess.

"I'll take hell over the Keep," Ethan called up to her, limp. "Hold on, Ethan," she said through gritted teeth. "Please." Crowds formed on the cosmetics floor far below, then scattered.

"You'll never save yourself," he repeated to her quietly, privately, "but you can warn the world. If you care, find yourself in the vicious circles." "Yes, yes, I will," Claire said, her arm aching. "Please hold on." The guards pulled her backward, hoisting Ethan higher.

"They smile and smile, until they stop," he said, rising. "And then beware the ugly teeth...." "Please hurry," she called back to the guards. Jess grabbed her upper arms and hauled back farther.

Ethan smiled up. "It's your turn to pick a side," he said. "The torch is passed." He swung his free arm and hammered hers once with surprising force. Claire cried out, and her arm felt lighter. Ethan dropped away.

—⚏—

"No statement, and warn the media we'll press charges against trespassers," Slade directed Allen back at the club. "This is private property and a private affair." Outside the gate on the front sidewalk clustered local news cameras, having followed Nora in her retreat.

Claire sat in a wing chair by the foyer grandfather clock. Nora, inconsolable, paced by the dining room, while Clancy darted about in a calming effort.

Like everyone in the Rotunda restaurant, Claire and Nora had been detained and questioned by city detectives for more than two hours. *Yes,* they knew the "victim" and told the detectives how, when, and where. Nora freely chronicled their relationship from Ethan's recruitment off the streets to his rehabilitation and employment and finally to his recent estrangement, pausing to fight her own breakdown. "He won't have a next of kin," Nora assured them. "He had no one."

Claire admitted he'd been following her—*stalking*, although she avoided that word. She left out his theft of her personal belongings from the moving van. It seemed irrelevant now.

Only once, and briefly, had Claire permitted herself to glance over the banister. Ethan's body rested facedown, as if sleeping, on the white marble floor four stories below, marked off with yellow tape. The eye patch has loosed from his head in the impact and lay strewn aside. She was surprised a body so thin spilled that much blood. The store had been evacuated and sat silent.

"Ernie, thank God!" Nora had cried when a boss-looking man emerged on the top-floor crime scene. Nora introduced Claire to the chief of police, who was courteous and protective. "They can go," he ordered his minions, patting Nora gently. "I know where to find them."

Nora called Slade at the office, and Claire tracked down Clay in Nevada. "Holy shit!" he yelled before a barrage of questions that Claire interrupted. "I'm fine," she assured him. "Just shaken. But fine." She persuaded him not to cut his trip short. "There's really no point," she insisted. "One day won't make a difference. I'll see you tomorrow night."

"Love you," they both said.

Neiman's had snuck them out the employee entrance. Jess whisked them in silence to the Union, where the hushed cocktail crowd embraced them and caught televised updates from the Tap Room. The drama had been captured, from all angles, inside and out, on myriad cell phones. The news mercifully omitted the most graphic footage.

"You'd never recognize him," Nora said to Mrs. Hammond and Mrs. Crocker. "He's so wasted away. *Was*." Ling brought her a chardonnay, which she had trouble handling.

"Dude just freaked out," Jess explained to Allen across the way. "I'd never hurt Ethan. He just offed himself." Allen patted him on the back and said, "Don't blame yourself."

"Witnesses describe the unidentified man as frail and emotionally distraught," reported the anchorwoman from the TV above the bar. "It is unclear his relationship to local philanthropist Nora Willing or her unidentified guest, whom he accosted in the Neiman Marcus restaurant before jumping to his death. Details are still emerging about..."

"Would someone turn that damn thing off!" Slade shouted across the foyer. Stanwick, the bartender, hit the remote and poured more drinks. Waiters circulated trays to the jittery members.

Slade quieted the hall and requested a moment of silence in the memory of "our friend and family member, gone much, much too soon." Members bowed their heads, while a confused Mr. Stimson mouthed, "*Who?*" to his wife. Mrs. Stimson whispered in his ear, and Mr. Stimson nodded.

Colonel Crowe strode from the back of the club to Slade, conferred in the corner. Nora put down her wineglass and marched over. Without greeting, she pulled back her arm and slapped the colonel across the face. The club silenced.

"You promised he'd be okay!" she screamed at him. "You swore you wouldn't hurt him!"

Slade knew better than to calm her. Nora backed away, jabbing her finger at the colonel. "Liar," she hissed, her voice breaking. She revved up to attack again but abandoned it, shooed him away, and stalked across the stunned foyer to disappear beyond. Clancy followed after her. The colonel, unfazed, wandered with Slade and kept talking quietly.

"Thank you, Ling," Claire said, when he placed a glass of white wine on her side table. She saw a tear clinging to his eye, which he quickly wiped away. She watched him circulate the Reading Room, retrieving glasses. He paused by Ethan's painting, webbed with circles, and glanced back at Claire before moving into the Tap Room.

Edie and Bing and Mrs. Baker hovered around Claire. "Such a shock," and "I'm so sorry you had to go through this," and "Thank God you weren't hurt." Claire thanked them and excused herself. On her way upstairs, she passed the tables and chairs being readied for the ball.

The top hit on Google linked her to a site where she reserved a time slot and bought a ticket.

Chapter Sixteen

Claire went to the Will Call window, checked her watch, strolled into the San Francisco Museum of Modern Art on the dot.

She'd decided to follow Ethan's clues, at the risk of catching his paranoia, which she knew was infectious. It explained the zeitgeist popularity of Stu Savage, the plethora of conspiracy books and websites, the crowds at the museum for the exhibit, which required a reserved ticket.

He'd warned her about the Union Club in cryptic terms, she deduced, because he didn't know where she stood. After all, her father-in-law was club president, her husband had grown up there, and she lived in the founder's suite. And she had shunned and fled him the first time they met, in this very museum. She'd cried out for help.

But now she was back.

She'd slipped out of the club easily, as it was preoccupied with the Justice Ball, whose guests would arrive that afternoon. Staff scurried the halls, and delivery trucks backed into the parking lot as she darted out the service entrance. She'd grabbed a cab at the Fairmont.

"I slept fine, Clay. I'm just running errands before the weekend," she said into her shoulder-crooked cell, handing the driver a twenty. "Keep the change, thank you. No, not you, smart-ass. What time are you back tonight?"

The elevator line was long, so she climbed the black granite staircase to the "emerging artists" galleries on the third floor.

Ethan was a drug addict, she reminded herself. Or so the others had told her. And he was terminally ill, according to him. He might have been both. He was clearly delirious, spouting wild theories that were laughable until you investigated further and then realized they were possible, plausible, maybe probable. Until you thought about something else and came back, and they seemed ridiculous again. Until you started thinking about them anew.

"Ticket holders for the eleven twenty," a uniformed attendant called across the hallway, herding the crowd into a roped-off line. "Pardon me," Claire said, stepping on the man next to her. They were packed tight.

It was ridiculous—lunatic—to think Ethan had been recruited to the club under pretense of rehab and employment only to be infected with a form of cancer, as he'd implied. But Nora didn't find it lunatic; she must have thought it possible, taking out her rage on Colonel Crowe, as if he was to blame. But why would the colonel want to infect homeless people, or anyone, with disease? And how would he even do it?

God, listen to yourself, Claire thought as she shuffled toward the gallery entrance. Stencil-painted on the white wall, in red, screamed the exhibit title: "Vicious Circles: Conspiracy Art since 9/11." Below was an enigmatic description of the show. In keeping with the theme, the wall read, the artists were unnamed. There were no brochures nor audio tours. An employee scanned her ticket, and Claire rounded a dark partition into silent, spotlighted blackness.

The exhibit started its timeline—rather tastelessly, Claire thought—with children's period artwork, mostly in crayon and watercolors like her own kids did, although these depicted carnage and tragedy. Crayola twin buildings, airplanes, explosions, frowning stick people. Surely these or dozens similar had been all over cable news stories through the years, dramatizing the resilience and healing of that era's youth. Claire found it macabre, exploitative, tacky.

At the edge of the room by the door, a large white canvas. Two small circles dead center: Adam/Eve. *In the beginning...* No artist.

She migrated to the next room. So much for healing. Here were floor-to-ceiling photographs of war horror: bombed villages, dead children, beheadings, "collateral damage" in shocking, turn-away size and detail. It was a quiet room of confusion, despair, misery. Ethan must have taken a dim view of Claire if he expected her to "find herself" here.

By the door, another white canvas, more circles growing from the center, an expanding web of amorphous shape. A subtler, more sophisticated take on the version hanging in the Reading Room.

Room three was equally dark but increasingly congested, as guests lingered. Artistic interpretations of the Illuminati, Catholic church, NATO, Freemasons, the major news networks. The all-seeing eye, the low-hanging fruit of conspiracy art, peered out from its pyramid in various incarnations. There was chessboard and playing card imagery; Manhattan skylines engulfed in flame; Israeli flags the backdrop to trouble everywhere. A Satanic pentagram linked the United Nations to the Council of Foreign Relations to CNN to the Bilderbergers to, naturally, David Rockefeller. Lucifer hovered dead center, a common meme.

At the far end, a white canvas exploded in circles—taking shape, if you looked closely or stood at an angle, into the vague representation of a human face. Claire, like the others, tiptoed quietly in one direction and then another. Some whispered and exchanged guesses. One young woman leaned too far in and broke the light beam barrier, sounding a low beeping alarm. A gallery attendant waved her back, and the beep stopped. Claire studied up close, but not too close, to find the canvas background shellacked over with newsprint from the *Dallas Morning News*, 1963. The circles included "CIA," "Vietnam," "Cold War," "LBJ," "Richard Helms," "Malcolm Wallace." She weaved back through the crowded room, turned, took a step left. A pointillist John F. Kennedy made of tiny circles came sharply, magically into focus. Handsome, powerful, in his prime. Not the elderly man he'd be today, if he still roamed the earth. *If.*

Each room featured new circle-made faces. RFK (knitted together by "J. Edgar Hoover," "Meyer Lansky," "Jimmy Hoffa," "Sinatra," "Giancana"), Indira Ghandi, John Lennon, Talitha Getty, the artist gaining confidence and momentum—and anger—with each additional piece. Osama Bin Laden against a backdrop of magazine covers from around the world was riddled with gunshots that dripped yellow and pink. Princess Diana—young and radiant—bled red tears across stories of her death and faked death, her murder and faked murder. *Now a grandmother,* thought Claire. *Does she even know?*

The artist reflected the fury of the lies and chaos he depicted, even as he struggled to make sense of it. There was an enraged helplessness, a degenerative, whirling madness to it all.

It was Ethan's plea, his warning that the world was not what it seemed. It hit harder and spoke truer here—on canvas, in a quiet gallery that encouraged contemplation—than it did in person, when he just seemed crazy. Judging by the crowds, large swaths were curious and open-minded, at least to explore. *They're paying attention,* she thought.

Claire found herself in the final room.

It was the largest, most explosive canvas of the exhibit. A riot of circles intertwined, stretching off all edges. The darkest, densest clusters composed an eye here, an ear there, with dark, long curls framing the open, smiling face. Claire's passport photo, blown up to gallery wall size. Streaked and slashed with thick swabs of blood.

She threaded through the stumped, silhouetted crowd. Cocked heads, repositioned angles, wrong guesses tittered back and forth. Claire reached the canvas. It was papered over with her birth certificate, birthday cards, letters from her mother. Her turquoise charm necklace, her first earrings, two of her baby teeth affixed around her neck, on either side of her head, in the beaming openness of her mouth.

A quick scan of the hundreds of circles revealed names from the previous pieces, a progressive artwork narrative. The world led here, to her, in a chaotic, apocalyptic climax. It was the only labeled piece of the exhibit. It was titled *Last Chance*.

Toward the bottom corner swirled the Union Club members, linked, sometimes ensnared in multilinks, in a dense, beehive clump. A Yale circle sprang from several, including Slade, Dean, and Clay. Yale also begat Claire's circle, tethered in a dotted line, family-tree style, to her dead mother and empty father circle that contained only a question mark.

Claire was linked to Clay, and they begat nothing. Claire linked on her own to a large circle at the canvas edge, labeled "IX" in more alarmist red. From it sprang an urgent, slashing arrow, aimed at an emptiness on the canvas. Claire squinted and leaned in. Smoothed against the artwork in the bottom corner was a small, barely perceptible rectangle, rising slightly off the surface. Fully camouflaged and practically invisible, until the spotlight at the right angle cast the barest of shadow. Claire bent at the waist, tipped closer. Across the painted rectangle were scratched shapes, precisely etched with a sharp instrument.

"Excuse me," Claire apologized to the middle-aged man in tourist clothes next to her, as she sidled nearer the artwork. He nodded and stepped clear, a double take to Claire and back to the painting before folding into the crowd. She tapped the flashlight app on her cell and targeted the rectangle. The etched shapes were her initials.

"*If you care...,*" Ethan had challenged right before his death. She'd cared enough to be here. Ethan had made that the easy part.

A stone-faced museum guard in navy blazer with pocket badge queen-waved to get Claire's attention. He pointed at her phone's flashlight. Claire nodded an apology and tucked it back into her bag.

She stood upright and drank in her portrait while she fished around her purse. She found the metal emery board she'd recently bought to combat her nail biting. She ran her finger along its sharp, tool-like end.

Claire scanned the protective light beam shielding the art. It came from a source on each wall, a barrier inches from the paintings. Claire stared at her family circles: Slade, Nora, Clay, herself. She looked at the raised rectangle, clearly an envelope, addressed to her.

Without taking her hand from her bag, she tucked the emery board into a side pocket, its sharp edge sticking up, easy to find. She gently groped the bottom edges of her bag. She moved a pen, a compact, a crumpled Post-it note out of her way. The crowds around her thinned, recycled, refilled. Claire felt foil, ran her finger down it, flipped it around, punched her finger through two sections. She eyed the museum guard. When he looked away toward the newly arriving visitors, she slipped two squares of sugarless gum into her mouth.

The room settled back to silence as the fresh group took its positions at each piece. Claire maneuvered through the middle of the room, as the new clusters migrated toward the perimeter. At the door, by a frenetic piece linking Bill Clinton to a chemical company in China, she stopped and blended in, squeezing between a gorgeous black woman with beaded braids and the corner wall where the barrier light beam originated.

Claire softened the gum, rolled, flattened, balled it. She periscoped the hushed, reflective room. In one motion, while scrutinizing a demonic, steam-nosed Clinton, she stroked the corners of her mouth, lipped out the double wad of spearmint, palmed it, lowered her hand to her side, spread it puttylike across the light source.

The alarm started low and subtle, like a theater's intermission chime. A soft rhythmic tolling that, absent relief, grew steadier and louder. The crowds near Claire ignored it, but when it pitched to a whining beep, they looked around for its cause. Claire backed toward the center of the dark room.

The beeping got more insistent, and navy blazer guards crisscrossed in the adjacent gallery, seeking the illusive too-close-to-the-art offender. Tumult grew as the beeps morphed into a higher, steady stream, and the visitors began to trickle toward the exits. Claire reached into her bag, found the sharp end of the emery board, turned back to her portrait on the far wall.

The stone-faced guard stood sentry in his corner, while his colleagues fished for the alarm source. Claire pretended to study nearby pieces, keeping him in her periphery. The room was clearing out, and when she looked at the door and then back, the guard had left his corner and had entered the fray. About time.

Claire pulled the metal tool from her purse and walked toward her portrait. She held it like a scalpel. There was no one near. Her eye followed from the red arrow to the barely visible envelope. She tilted the emery blade, reached toward the canvas.

A fist clutched her upper arm. "Ma'am, we're evacuating the gallery," said the humorless guard above the now-piercing alarm.

"Oh, yes," Claire stammered. "Yes. Of course." She sheathed the blade with her palm and turned to him. "Is anything wrong?" she asked. The guard pointed up toward the siren. Claire nodded and stood still.

"Ma'am, we're evacuating the gallery," he repeated louder, above the wails.

"Yes. Yes, of course," Claire said again. She smoothed her skirt, sliding the emery down the waist band. She grabbed the bottom of her purse, hoisted it higher on her shoulder, upending it, spilling its contents on the gallery floor. They rolled in all directions.

"I'm so sorry!" she said, dropping to her knees. "Dammit!"

The guard considered and then unconsidered helping her. He looked back to his colleague in the next room, herding visitors toward the exit. "Ma'am," he said, and Claire, scavenging on her knees, grabbing her billfold and cell phone, fisting lipstick and nickels and a paper clip that defied pickup, said, "Yes, just a minute, please."

The overhead lights burst on throughout the gallery. Visitors, in various stages of panic, moved toward one door and then the other. A supervisor-sounding guard shouted out to Claire's stone-faced watcher. He called back to his boss and turned again to Claire. "I'm hurrying!" she assured him. They kept an eye on each other until he disappeared into the next room.

Claire sprang up. Braced one hand on her portrait. Unearthed a corner of the envelope with the emery tip. Carefully sliced along the edge, lengthwise, down the corner, across the bottom, all four sides. She gingerly fingered the back, peeled the envelope off, careful not to rip it. One glued patch clung on; Claire toggled a finger to pry it loose.

She slid the envelope into her bag just as the guard reentered the gallery. Claire hurried past and out the exit, weaving through the crowded halls and down the black granite stairs.

"There's something going on upstairs," she said to the guard by the museum's front door. "They're evacuating," she added, pointing back.

"Yes, ma'am, I know," he said, holding the door open for her. "Have a nice day."

Chapter Seventeen

*B*efore *I fled, I learned too much. And not enough...*

Claire sat in the taxi she'd snagged at the W. She'd planned to wait until she was back at the club, to steam the envelope open, to keep it intact. After all, it was part of Ethan's art. Once the cab turned on Howard and got stuck in construction traffic, she changed her mind. She ripped it across the top, unfolded a smudged, nearly illegible note on crinkled white paper. Ethan's penmanship was atrocious.

But based on the attack against me, this is what I believe....

Claire frowned. More vague riddles. Didn't he trust her yet? She'd just pulled off a brazen felony—likely on camera, she'd realized as she hurried from the museum, kicking herself for not wearing a hat and sunglasses—and set herself up, not merely for arrest, but for suspicion that she, like Ethan, had utterly lost her mind. Clay already feared she was on the edge, tinfoil hat and all. Enough decoding, deciphering. Ethan needed to cut her some slack.

Claire squinted.

The Protocols reside in the Oasis of Knowledge....

"Thank you, Allen," she said when he held open the front door. She was ill dressed in slacks, but the service entrance was too busy with deliveries, and the normal rules seemed suspended during the final preparations. One worker power-polished the Grand Foyer marble while three others rolled back the Heriz. Another dusted the chandeliers with a telescoping feather reach. The first floor was frantic and energized.

"Sounds great, Stompy," she said as he pattered "A Marvelous Party" in clipped, crisp British. "Very Noël Coward." He tipped his head from the piano in appreciation and launched into another frantic verse. She nodded at Ling, at another, and another, and ascended the Grand Staircase calmly.

Eight are in process, too late to stop...

She strolled down the quiet hallway to the library. The door was open.

But the Ninth, the Crucible, the date, is upon us.

Sting opened one dark eye.

"Don't start with me," warned Claire.

I know not where, but their Master resides in the east. And thus His wisdom resides in the east.

Master, wisdom. The end stages of Ethan's dementia. More nonsense riddles. Claire needed to salvage her day, go for a run, shower and prepare for the night's kickoff festivities. Clay would be coming home soon. Slade and Nora would want the visiting members from around the world to meet their daughter-in-law, clear-eyed and sane. Madison had kindly lent her not one, but two couture gowns: one for tonight and an even more majestic one for the main event Saturday. The children in their own new outfits would be singing in the Grand Foyer after the principal dinner. They still needed one more rehearsal. She didn't have time for this.

Claire looked around the library. Up to the painted constellation and the arrow pointing east.

Plainly hidden in view—the wisdom lies to the east....

"Not that plainly," Claire said aloud and then glanced around. Alone.

She looked up to the second-tier shelves, filled with antique books. She climbed the forbidden rolling ladder.

The *Encyclopedia Britannica, National Register of Historic Buildings, Strategies of Contact Bridge.* Wisdom, of sorts. But surely not what Ethan meant. She slid out the "D," "L," and "R" encyclopedias, holding the heavy volumes carefully, looking for clues tucked between. She ran her hand across the tops, shelf by shelf, cursing Ethan for his opaque shorthand.

Heels down below. Claire froze, holding "XYZ," and slowly pivoted her head. The club librarian straightened her desk, edged folders, thumbed through and clicked closed the green check-out card holder, stacked them all into the lower left drawer. She wiped crumbs off the surface, palmed them into the trash. Gave the library an end-of-day once-over—fortunately not upward, where Claire held her breath to keep the balcony from creaking an alert. Grabbed her tote bag from the chair back, knotted her salmon polka-dot silk scarf, and, with her custom sigh, heel-clacked from the room.

Claire looked back at the shelves. Hopeless. She checked her watch. The kids would be downstairs, needing supervision. The staff would be too busy to cover for her. She shimmied down the ladder.

Their Master resides in the east....

The Gentlemen's Lounge, in line with the ceiling's painted compass, also sat toward the east. According to the most feverish of the conspiracy books, "their Master" was Satan. Did Ethan literally think Lucifer lived behind the bookshelf door, where the old coots, titans, and red merries smoked cigars and voted on club hours, dress codes, squash tournament seedings?

"Have you seen Satan around here?" she asked Sting, fast asleep on its marble column perch. She could almost hear it snoring.

And to think she'd risked arrest—still a ripe possibility—for Ethan's dead-end clues, his fantasies. It would have seemed funny at a distance. But Claire wasn't at a distance. She'd bounce back to normal once she and Clay had a home, a life away from this suffocating place. This week. She wouldn't wait for something perfect, and it wouldn't need a yard for a survival garden, because in spite of Stu's daily brimstone, there was no imminent crisis, nothing to survive. Everything was in order. She went to the library door.

Eight are in process, too late to stop...

Claire turned back. Across the room, directly under the eastern arrow, if followed precisely down the curve of the wall: the three glass shelves against the antique atlas backdrop with the not-quite-accurate cartography and Old English and ancient Latin spellings. The eight glistening, clear Fabergé eggs sat on eight gilt perches. Claire looked down the empty hallway. Smoothly closed the silent mahogany double doors, clicked the knobs shut so she'd hear them turning from the outside.

She picked up the egg she'd handled before, on her first night. On the middle shelf, bejeweled with four gemstones. Held it up to the window; the foggy, overcast light was too dim to illuminate. Pivoted up to the ceiling spotlight targeting the shelves, rotated the egg to find the yellow "yolk" inside. She turned back, carefully thumbed the egg's latch across the middle, hinged it open.

The brilliant canary diamond, less harshly yellow without the egg's refracted light, was almond-sized and shaped, gripped by a platinum setting and ring. Speared through the ring was a tiny parchment scroll, which anchored and kept it from rattling inside. Claire lifted out the scroll and ring and replaced the egg on its perch. She looked around the library and caught Sting, still calm and dozing, peering at her with one purple eye.

Claire pulled the parchment, unrolled it.

Across the top it read, "IV." Below, in hand calligraphy, a short paragraph-length sentence, which, like the mantel's engraving, Claire knew to be ancient Latin from the "est" and "-tum" and "-ter," although she couldn't translate. At the bottom, in now-English: *London*.

She rescrolled, reringed, relatched. Reached for the first egg on the top shelf. Single-gem. Roman numeral I. Another Latin sentence. "-Unts," "-ants," and the word "media," an easy get. *New York*.

Across the shelf, in ascending order, the jewel count matching the numerals: *Bonn, Moscow, Beijing, Zurich, Johannesburg*. Each unique sentence in Latin. Claire picked up the last egg on the bottom shelf, riddled with gems. VIII: *San Francisco*.

Claire reloaded the egg, cradled it, stepped back from the glass shelves, counted.

The Ninth Protocol was missing. On the middle shelf, between eggs four and five—New York and Beijing—sat an empty gap where Ocean Atlantique, beaded with islands, spanned between continents. Claire scrutinized the glass shelf for telltale marks of where the AWOL egg had once sat; there were none. The ceiling spotlight hit the space precisely, removing any doubt that she was missing traces.

Claire flipped back in her memory. Had the ninth egg ever been there?

A familiar rustling behind her. Sting now fully awake and upright. It stared at the crystal egg she cradled.

"Carl Fabergé's secret collection of crystal eggs," Colonel Crowe said from behind. Claire spun, concealing the egg behind her back. He looked down at her pleasantly. "Unknown to the world," he lectured, nodding toward the glass shelves, still staring at her. "Quite intriguing, aren't they?"

"Quite," said Claire. She glanced over his shoulder to the still-closed library door. He must have slipped in through the lounge.

"They're from our sister club in Moscow."

"The Monolith." Claire nodded. "I've read about it. How generous of them."

"The set was a housewarming gift for James Flick when he built this place." The colonel tilted his head toward the middle shelf. "Plus one commissioned by Tsar Alexander III, too priceless for display."

"Someplace very safe, I'm sure."

The colonel lingered on the lower shelf. "One seems to be missing."

Claire held up the eighth egg, twirled it in the light. "Like you said, very intriguing," she said. She stooped to return the egg to its perch, then turned back to face the colonel.

"The president of the Monolith arrives today, soon," he said, glancing over to the mantel clock. "If you want to learn more..."

"Thank you, I just might," Claire said, smiling. "I have loads of questions."

The library doors flew open. Ilza burst in happily, proud to have found her target.

"Miss Claire! You're late for rehearsal! We're waiting!"

She beelined for Claire next to the marble column perch, arms out and open. Sting screeched, lifted, and attacked.

"Sting, NO!" Claire cried out. The beast's talons clutched the girl's scalp. Ilza screamed. Claire reached for the bird's breast. The colonel extended his forearm and the bird, fluttering, released Ilza's head and alighted on him, balancing with partial wings. Claire pulled Ilza away, checked her scalp, hugged her against her waist.

"You're okay," she soothed the shocked girl. "It didn't hurt you."

"You startled her," the colonel said, lowering his arm toward the perch. "She's harmless, but just a bit cranky at her age." Sting side-stepped off the colonel's forearm, back to its perch above the red velvet pillow. It flapped its wings once, as if to clean them, before folding them back to its side. It lifted one claw into its belly and settled back to stillness.

Claire ignored the colonel, gently ushered Ilza toward the library door. "You really need to get rid of that damn...," she scolded and then stopped and turned back. She stared at Sting, nesting calmly, protectively, above the red pillow.

"...bird."

Claire looked down at the plump pillow, up at the bird.

Sting stared back.

The colonel looked from Sting to Claire and held there.

"Come on, honey," she said, steering Ilza out. "We're late."

—∽—

She had to get out of here. With the children.

"Let's take the back stairs." She guided Ilza, unharmed, who'd recovered to babble proudly about her "bird attack."

There would be no greeting visitors for the Justice Ball weekend, no pageant or concert from her kids. She would whisk them back to the clergyman, with no explanation except that the Union Club's after-school program was permanently over, effective immediately.

Once the kids were safely back in the church's care—*not* in the club's stewardship—she'd sort out the rest. Ethan had led her to the book, the crazy book, which he'd stolen from the public library and hidden in the club—and which was now missing. In unemotional, measured terms, it laid out the protocols, the instruction manual, handed down through the centuries, like the Ancient Mysteries, that guided the shadowy New World Order as it coalesced to take over the planet. It couldn't be coincidence that the eggs linked the cities to specific missions, just like the list in the book.

Or that the club's founder James Flick installed them in a discreetly prominent place, *hiding in plain sight*, toward the east, where *wisdom lies*.

"Gang! Calm down!" she called out to the unsupervised kids, noisy and amuck in their playroom. "I need everyone to line up, please. Now!"

"Angel's in the john," said Rodney, launching a Nerf missile through the air. "Angel's in the *bathroom*," Claire corrected, intercepting it, waving him into line. "Hop to it, Rodney." She looked around. Edgar must have gone with Angel. He was a good buddy like that.

The wisdom passed down, like an owner's guide, through the generations. Each city, each colony, tasked with a specific mission on the road to apocalypse. San Francisco, for one, in charge of population control, also known as eugenics, AKA *depopulation*, at least according to the book, which thus far had nailed it with alarming accuracy. Impossible stuff—fairy tale fantasies, really—but the fact that the club believed in it, aspired to it, like a weird religion, justified her immediate exit. Her husband's too.

She'd go to a hotel—not the Fairmont or Mark Hopkins or the Huntington, too close. Probably the St. Francis or the one with the starry cabaret on the roof or maybe even the newer Intercontinental down on Howard. She'd call Clay on the way and promise to explain everything—as best she could—when he landed.

The two of them would lay it all out for his parents carefully. No wonder Nora felt so uncomfortable, even hostile, toward the club and its members. She was an outsider, nonilluminated, unable after all these years to put her finger on the source of her unease. "Fucking freaks," she'd called them that first night, keeping her distance. Little did she know.

Slade was a different situation. Unreadable. And newly elected club president. Impossible that he wouldn't know, that Colonel Crowe hadn't told him, of the Union's role in the New World Order's ultimate mission. After all, the colonel had recruited him, according to Nora. And mentored him. And eventually passed the torch. The "next generation."

She'd isolate Nora, convince her separately, or risk Slade's full-on Texan backlash. She'd worry about that later.

"Buddy up, everybody!" she called out. "We're going back to the church." "But we just got here," Condi said, echoing the others' confusion.

"There's too much going on here today," Claire said, counting heads. "The club's very busy getting ready for the grown-ups' party." The room whined in unison. "But we have to practice for the pageant," Ilza protested. "Miss Madison says practice makes perfect."

Claire noticed her hand trembling and lowered it to her side. The colonel was probably already in Slade's ear, having caught her red-handed, egg-handed in the library. Another one of their secret pow-wows, debating whether she belonged. She'd answer that herself.

Unless they were debating what to do with her now that she was onto their sinister secret.

"We can rehearse the pageant back at the church," Claire said, checking her purse for cash and Visa, ID and Clipper card.

If Ethan was to be believed—and he'd been unnervingly reliable so far—they'd attacked him when he uncovered the truth, causing him to flee, go mad, and ultimately kill himself. He also claimed they killed Dean, which had seemed preposterous at the time, like his other wild claims, but suddenly less so. Especially if Dean—like Ethan, like Claire—had been curious, been looking, and learned what they'd learned.

Maybe Ethan had warned him, too. And Dean had investigated on his own. Didn't Madison say they'd lived at the club, in the James Flick suite, in the days leading up to his election last November? Which were also, coincidentally, or not, the days leading to his assassination.

Angel returned from the bathroom, palms first. "I washed my hands!" she announced.

"Did you wait for Edgar?" Claire asked. Angel got in line with the others.

Unless they used those days—Colonel Crowe and Slade—to "illuminate" Dean on the eve of his certain election, as he started his rise to power. And Dean, like Claire, like any sane person, freaked out and wanted out. And they'd had no choice, as the book said, but to take him out of the picture. To kill him, or pretend to kill him, and send him to the Keep.

And bring in Clay. The "spare," as Slade grotesquely called him.

She had to get ahold of Clay before they did.

And then he'd calm her down, like he always did, and talk sense into her and explain everything. And take her by the hand, and point out how meaningless the eggs were, merely ornamental symbols of their sister clubs, like crests and seals, with their individual Latin mottos, like universities. They were just for decoration, for show. And—*see, silly?*—no ninth egg with the date of the world's destruction guarded by Sting in its pillow "nest." Although Clay would have to admit that would be a genius place to hide it. Cool, even.

After the weekend, after she'd met the visiting members from their sister clubs and found them as pleasant and harmless as the Union's own wacky gang, she'd realize how off-kilter she was. And once she'd settled back to normalcy, and stability, in a new home, then Nora would help her find a therapist, like she'd urged after the miscarriage. Mother-in-law knows best.

She counted seven heads, waiting. Angel stood on the end, buddyless.

"Angel, where's Edgar?" she asked. "Is he still in the bathroom?" Angel shook her head.

"Where is he?" Claire asked the room. "Where's Edgar?

"Did he come today?" she asked. "Is he home sick?

"Someone answer me!" she demanded. "Where is Edgar?"

"Didn't they tell you?" Ilza said.

"Tell me what?" Claire asked, and when no one answered, she kneeled and grabbed Ilza by the shoulders.

"Tell me *what?*"

Chapter Eighteen

"This is parent and guardian access only," Martha cautioned, rushing to keep up with Claire down the cloud-and-cartoon-muraled twelfth-floor corridor of the Children's Hospital. "I can only sneak you in for a few minutes."

"He doesn't have parents," said Claire, moving faster. "Which room?" she asked, eyes darting in each open door. She passed Dora the Explorer, Winnie-the-Pooh.

"Not this section." Martha waved her on, checking her iPad. "Keep going."

Claire had left the children in the Safe Harbor room, after Ilza told her Edgar had been in the hospital for three days. "Ling, please keep an eye on them," Claire had pleaded in the hallway. "I'll be back as soon as I can." She backtracked to the last time she'd seen Edgar. Monday. Or last Friday? It had been a frantic, unhinged week.

She'd run out the back, forgetting her phone, circled around to the coatroom, squirmed past Europeans and Asians, distinguished and stately, filtering in to the club's early-afternoon welcoming reception.

"Welcome back, dear friends!" Elegantly shriveled Mrs. Hammond grinned, shaking foreign hands. "I hope you had a nice flight," Mr. Newhall chimed in, slapping backs. "Might I offer you tea? Or a sherry?"

She'd unplugged her cell and darted across to the Fairmont's taxi stand.

"Can you please hurry?" she'd pushed the driver in Friday traffic. "Is there a faster route?" She'd called Martha on the way. Tracked her down in the staff lounge at her going-away party. "I need your help," Claire said without explaining. Martha still wore her sparkly tiara and Chicago Cubs jersey over her scrubs.

"Lateral sclerosis." Martha read the diagnosis from her iPad chart.

"What is that?" Claire demanded.

"A somewhat generic term for a sudden shutdown of the body," Martha answered, scrolling the file. "Very sudden in this case."

"Acute respiratory failure," she listed. "RSV, advanced viral pneumonia. It's a lengthy diagnosis."

They approached a double door in the hallway that read "CCU." Martha slipped a plastic card from around her neck.

"What causes it?" asked Claire.

"Idiopathic," Martha said. "No known cause." She tapped her card on the wall pad. The double doors opened automatically. The hallway was hushed, the walls white and cartoon free.

"How do you know him?" Martha asked.

I recruited him to the club, Claire thought. *I brought him in, young and healthy.* "He's a student of mine," she said. "And a friend."

"The last update, this morning, says room 1217," Martha said, scrolling her pad. She looked closer. "With a 'nonresuscitate' directive."

"Who gave that?" Claire asked, walking faster.

"His registered guardian," said Martha. "Slow down. We have to check in at the station." Claire didn't.

A weary nurse approached and paused at Claire, then saw Martha and went past to her. "Hold up a sec, Claire," Martha said, then spoke quietly, professionally to the nurse. Claire moved faster. 1211. 1213.

"She shouldn't be in here," the nurse murmured at a distance. "She really can't be in here."

"Claire, stop!" Martha called from behind, rubber soles dashing. "Please!"

Claire rounded the open door of 1217. Came back out immediately.

"Where did you move him?" she demanded of the nurse over Martha's shoulder.

"Claire, honey...," Martha said, waving back the nurse.

"Take me to him!"

"I can't, Claire."

"No!" said Claire. "*No!* Where *is* he?"

There were gravely ill children and their terrified parents throughout the quiet floor, and so Claire waited until she was outside, on the sidewalk, before she collapsed.

—◊◊—

Down in the Grand Foyer, Stompy, channeling his authentic self, played "All the Things You Are" at the fireside piano.

Clusters of visiting guests greeted, embraced Union members like long-ago friends. The all-hands-on-deck staff joined the white-coated waiters passing drinks and hors d'oeuvres. The crowd swelled as newcomers trickled in, waved, clasped hands, hugged, laughed. African royalty in traditional gowns and headdress flashed bright smiles at bowing Chinese and bespoke Continentals.

Slade reintroduced a rigidly cordial matron to a befuddled Mr. Stimson, and Clancy embraced a younger wife and showered her with flattery. She thrilled in their reunion, and her nearby husband, clearly unthreatened, tipped his head and continued his conversation with an unusually engaging Nora. He kept one eye on the high-wattage mayor who stalked the room for fresh prey.

Colonel Crowe listened and nodded in the corner at his apparent European counterpart/rival: smoother, svelter, rakish and authoritarian at the same time. The colonel shrank in his dashing, silvery presence, upstaged on his own turf.

During a brief lull in her round-robin greetings, Nora glanced up at Claire, as if she'd spotted her early on. She smiled and motioned her down. Claire smiled and tipped a be-right-there finger.

The children made the rounds—shyly at first, then more emboldened with Ilza's lead. They made fast friends and admirers among the eager and curious visitors, as Madison herded them toward the front door, where the clergyman waited to take them home for the night. He forced a smile, steely and professional. He'd break the grim news to them, gently and at the right moment, Claire surmised.

Stompy finished and stood to appreciative applause. He beamed and bowed, and elbows swinging, hotfooted toward the back stairs. The cocktail chatter continued music free.

"What are you doing hiding up here?" Edie cooed from behind. She was wearing an embroidered jacket over a black piano shawl skirt and had on fresh-from-the-lounge lipstick. "Aren't you joining in the festivities this weekend? Everyone's so excited to meet you."

"Oh yes." Claire turned and smiled. "I'm just going to change, and then I'll be right down."

Then she added, "I wouldn't miss it."

PHASE III

Chapter One

C laire closed and locked her bedroom door.

Went to her dressing room, where her luggage still sat open on the rack for its temporary stay. Two dresses under plastic that hadn't been there before hung nearby. Pinned to each was a handwritten note in Madison's elegant handwriting. "Friday" marked a storm-colored beaded princess dress with flared skirt, tasteful and deceptively simple. "Saturday" was a full-blown ball gown, sparkling platinum, intricately embroidered with the Swarovski crystals, haute. Claire wouldn't be here to wear that one, alas. She'd have been belle of the ball.

Claire debagged the night's semiformal dress, admiring its details. *Thanks, Madison.* She'd blend in with the others, no suspicions, no sudden moves.

She packed her bag lightly, leaving behind her San Francisco acquisitions and including only her Santa Fe favorites. The bag filled anyway, and she had to edit quickly, saying goodbye to a treasured but bulky serape sweater, a less-worn fringed skirt. She'd forget about them fast.

She clutched the ecru pamphlet she'd picked up in the coatroom: The Justice Ball weekend schedule. After "Welcome Cocktails" and once the club emptied out for the "Twilight Chamber Concert" at the Masonic Auditorium across the street, she'd make her move, starting and ending with the library. By the time they returned for late-night dancing and the buffet supper, she'd be long gone with the information she needed to expose to the world. She'd carefully weigh how to break that information, and to whom, or risk coming off as mad as Ethan had. She'd make smarter choices, pick a media giant—a Diane Sawyer or Katie Couric or even Barbara Walters, who'd likely crawl back from retirement for a scoop this hot. Hell, she'd crawl from the grave, if necessary. Because Claire wasn't a spiral-eyed whack job spouting drivel; she was a *whistleblower*, reporting from inside. And intensely credible. And the stakes could not be higher.

Unless media giants Sawyer and Couric and Walters were in on it, too.

Steady, Claire, she told herself. *Stay inside the lines.*

She checked her watch before slipping it off and heading to the bathtub. She had just enough time and needed to look fresh, not harried, not sketchy.

Her Visa and Amex would take her anywhere she wanted to go. Once she had the evidence she needed, she'd sneak out the back door with her rolling bag, to the Fairmont taxi stand—the doormen knew her, liked her—and straight to San Francisco International. Weekend red-eyes were unpopular; she'd get a seat somewhere east. She'd call Clay from the taxi and promise to explain everything tomorrow. They'd likely cross paths on her way.

Claire rinsed under the showerhead. She needed cash, in case they canceled her credit cards midair, stranding her when she landed. Surely they had that power, once they realized she was missing. She'd stop by an ATM, buy her ticket with cash. Less traceable, although more suspicious. She couldn't afford getting detained by the TSA, and she certainly couldn't explain anything, much less everything, to them.

Stay calm, Claire urged herself, toweling dry. *You'll figure it out.* She blew out her Fredo hair with a rolling brush, steadied her makeup hand.

Through the open window, Stu Savage weighed in from downstairs, as usual. Did the obsessed listener realize how on point Stu really was? He launched into his chronic rant, this time targeted at an on-air skeptic who challenged him about the fluoride-poisoned water exploding cancer and autism rates worldwide. Stu hammered away at the hapless caller, working himself into a furor that turned to screeches and then a hacking cough that stopped him cold.

"Goddammit!" Stompy shouted from below. Claire put down her eyeliner, went to the window, peered out and across.

Stompy sat on the windowsill in the downstairs guest room, streaming smoke into the well. He held a paper script and tapped his cigarette ashes outward. He shook his head.

"We gotta tape this shit *now*?" he complained. "I've been working since..." He listened to someone inside and nodded obediently. "Yeah okay," he said, taking a last drag. "Cue back fifteen seconds."

Stompy retreated, leaving the curtains open. Claire stood on her toes to peer down at a steeper angle. Stompy sat at a desk in front of a microphone and dials. He donned headphones and held his script. He nodded at the unseen engineer and launched back into the on-air tirade, expertly covering both roles. His mimicry ping-ponged with professional skill and ease.

Only a nut would take Stu Savage seriously, Claire had told herself from the beginning. "Perhaps that's the point," the colonel had mused one night at dinner. Stu Savage didn't exist; they'd had to invent him. And many more like him around the world.

Claire finished her hair and makeup, dressed in Madison's borrowed piece, placed her zipped rolling bag next to the door. Cracked it and listened. She checked her watch and went out into the hallway.

Staff bustled past her carrying trays, toward the wall-not-wall at the end, and disappeared beyond. Claire rounded the corner, looked down to the library. Its door was closed. She moved quickly, quietly. Listened against it, to silence. Turned the knob. Locked. Turned harder, to no avail. The colonel was onto her.

Claire retraced her steps, hurried down the back stairs at the end of the hall.

The Grand Foyer was thinned out, as the remaining stragglers migrated out the front door, on schedule. Claire waited by the stairs.

"There you are!"

Claire turned. "Hello, Madison." She looked effervescent in silver with pearls and crystal.

"The Christopher Kane is perfect on you. The color nails your timbre."

"Yes, Madison. Thanks for the loan."

Madison shooed it away. "Keep both. Just wait until tomorrow's Vera Wang. You'll look like a queen!"

And then Madison said, "I heard you ran off earlier." Claire said, "I went to the hospital." Madison's glow dimmed. She nodded.

"I can't discuss that right now," she said. "I can't even think about it. It's so horrible."

She clasped both of Claire's hands and said, "It all happened so fast. There were no warning signs. I didn't even know about it until yesterday."

"He's dead, Madison," Claire said.

Madison nodded again, quivering. "We mustn't blame ourselves. We had no idea his medical history before he came to us." And then she repeated, "It's just so horrible.

"Naturally, I told the church we'd handle all the final arrangements," she added. "But I really can't tackle that until after the weekend. I can't even think about it. It's so horrible."

"Yes," Claire said. "It is."

Madison took a step. Claire stood still.

"Aren't you coming to the concert?" Madison asked. "It's Chopin."

Claire shook her head. "I'm waiting for Clay," she said. "And I'm really not in the mood for Chopin."

Madison laughed. "That's funny," she said. "I've probably never been in the mood for Chopin."

She embraced Claire and said, "I'll see you after? You really do look lovely."

Madison turned back at the front door, seemingly conflicted, then smiled and went through it. Claire waited for Allen to close the door after the last stragglers. She clacked across the foyer, flustered.

"I'm so sorry, Allen," she stammered sheepishly. "I accidentally locked my bedroom." Allen smiled and said, "Are you sure?" Claire said, "Yes, it's stupid. I clicked the knob or something from the inside, I guess, and it locked me out. I was in such a hurry."

"I see. We can get you another key," Allen offered, and Claire said, "The staff's so busy. Can I just borrow yours?" Allen thought, and Claire fidgeted, and then he pulled a zookeeper key ring from his pocket. He thumbed through, inspected each one. "I should have a master for the guest rooms," he said, ticking through. "Somewhere."

Claire grabbed the ring. "I'm running late. I'll get it right back to you," she said. "Thank you so much."

She hurried back across the foyer, around the stairs, to the hallway. Several silvery men, including the colonel and his European rival, waited for the elevator. They held cocktails and chatted nothings, and other than the colonel, Claire didn't recognize any. She counted eight. The single black man stood out with his traditional African boubou in royal purple. He beamed widely and boomed laughter with another. Claire pivoted and retreated to the back stairs.

She raced to the third floor, holding the keys tight to keep them quiet. She picked through as she ascended, deciphering the abbreviated room labels: *coat, music, guest mstr, ktch, pool*. She flipped until she found *lib*, midring, grasping it. At the top landing, on the dim windowsill overlooking the interior light well, Sting, far from home base, clutched a gray matted rat in its talons. The bird kept its head down to its fresh kill but locked on to Claire with opaque, steady eyes. It sat still, monitoring her, as she crept past and out the stairwell door.

Off its perch, Claire thought, unfazed by the dead rodent, pausing at the hallway corner, peering around.

The library door stood wide open. Claire moved quickly, keys jangling. Halted when Ling appeared just inside, placing bowls of nuts onto the cocktail table. Claire clutched the keys, quieting them. Ling stopped and listened. Resumed his work.

The elevator dinged to her right.

Claire dashed down the short perpendicular hallway, toward the light well. She crouched beside the mahogany chest with granite top, hugging the wall so the lamps wouldn't out her shadow. She heard the elevator doors open, and the cordial conversation spilled into the hallway.

"No doubt the most lethal weapon on the planet today...," said one man with vibrating resonance in an accent Claire pegged as Russian. "And nothing in Europe can deflect it," said another, American. They lingered, in no rush.

"So sour that grape," chimed in a third—*sow*-er, German-esque— "since the US will be eliminated long before." It sounded like a taunt. "One learns quickly never to count her out," cautioned another in a crisp, almost elfin tone. Clearly British.

"Pardon me, is there an ashtray available?" a deep, silky voice purred. *Eeze zer?* Availa-*bull?* Another German? Swiss?

"We don't put them out," Colonel Crowe replied. "We don't encourage it." "Oh, I *zee*," the voice purred back. "Yes, I've *noteeced*." Swiss. The colonel's dashing rival. She heard the click of his lighter, smelled the pungent smoke an instant later. The cloud wafted into sight, just above her hiding spot.

"Ling," the colonel called out sharply, perturbed. "Would you please find the gentleman an ashtray?"

Ling came to the mahogany chest, opened the top drawer.

"I've never been a Ronaldinho convert myself," said the German, who had moved farther down the hall toward the library. "Younger, flashier, but less seasoned."

Ling shut the top drawer. Opened the next one.

"Plus Buffon learned his tricks in Berlin...," the Russian concurred.

Ling opened the bottom drawer, inches from Claire. She breathed in, held it. He paused, as if listening. She scrambled for an excuse, an explanation, came up empty, desperate. She heard Ling take something solid and clinking from the drawer, close it. Walk away.

"Which should have been in Cape Town," chuckled a *bossa* voice so rich and resonant and amiable, Claire pegged it as the African royalty.

"Thank you, Ling," the colonel said from down the hall, near the library. "Yes, thank you, Leeng," the smoking Swiss added.

Claire exhaled.

"Now, now," scolded the German, farther away. "Johannesburg gets the *final* World Cup. Surely that makes up for past slights." "Bittersweet, actually," responded the African, his booming voice retreating.

"Nonsense," the elfin Brit followed up. "The World Cup, or something similar, will resume in due time. That's already been decided."

"Gentlemen, I suggest we start," the colonel said from afar. "Feel free to bring your drinks inside." The voices drifted off, through the bookshelf door, Claire figured. "*Iz* smoking still illegal in *zis* town?" the Swiss asked. "And rightly so," answered the colonel. "After you."

Then silence.

Claire sat still, straining for sound. She crawled from her hiding place, peeked around the corner. The library sat open and empty. She tiptoed toward it. The flash of Ling's white coat inside, shutting the door.

She turned and glimpsed the framed architectural prints along the wall. The Union Club of San Francisco and its sister clubs in New York, London, Zurich. Its partners in Bonn, Beijing, Moscow, and Johannesburg. Each club, each city, represented in the Gentlemen's Lounge behind the bookshelf next to the Fabergé eggs. The colonel's peers, his top-level counterparts from around the globe, together, in private.

Claire hurried back to her bedroom, through the unlocked door, which she locked behind her. To her bathroom window, peering out to the illuminated sheers directly across the fogged-in well. She opened her window, listened and looked toward the two windows beyond, one cracked slightly. The sheers rustled, the silhouettes inside moved, settled, circulated, resettled.

The meeting began.

Claire thought.

Chapter Two

C laire leaned out the window.

She patted the wide ledge just below, stretching around the well, which was sporadically interrupted by fire escape ladders running up and down. Claire pushed her window fully open, hoisted herself onto the sill, kneed her legs up and around, scooted onto the ledge. Two stories below, the jewel-toned Tiffany dome fanned out to the edge.

Grabbing on to the window frame, Claire pulled herself to standing, close against the wall—the ledge adequately, if not comfortably, sized for maneuver. She scanned the other windows facing in. Some lit, some dark, sheers open or closed. If anyone saw her, she'd plead madness—truthfully, she thought, with a quicksilver smile. Claire edged, sidestepped around, toward the Gentlemen's Lounge window.

The heavy fog had wetted the cement and plaster. Claire stepped precisely. She tucked the key ring into her satin belt to free her hands for balance and leverage. She came to an escape ladder, squeezed underneath and past it, ignoring possible bad luck, and edged on. More confident, she skillfully conquered two corners and moved faster.

She arrived. Flat against the wall, she lowered, squatting near the cracked opening just above the sill. Listened, catalogued the voices, came up to speed. They'd moved past the World Cup chatter, on to "new business."

"I fear the sedentary lifestyle imposed on your Caucasian Rural Sector is out of balance," Zurich purred. "Lethargy can devolve into uselessness...."

"I don't disagree," said the colonel. "That's gotten a bit beyond us."

"We're also concerned with your sector's expanding chemical dependency," Bonn chimed in. "Both prescription and the more illicit sort."

"Yes, we're facing a public backlash here," said the other American voice, which Claire reasoned must represent New York. "We'd like to replace the domestic methamphetamine labs with foreign sources."

"We can supply," offered Beijing.

"On the other hand," London countered, "the Ethnic Urban Sector continues to benefit from chemical introduction. The most restive seem tamed by addiction and the related intersector diversions."

"Yes, but we have to maintain a viable workforce," Bonn resisted. "We have to pull back some."

The colonel huffed. "I hope we've been doing *something* right."

"Colonel, we are all heartened by your most recent report," London interjected. "I daresay we'd almost given up on you, with time so short and all."

"Yes, we're quite proud of our breakthrough," the colonel said. "The final stage required sustained testing with an adequate control group at the appropriate age level.

"Gentlemen, they don't literally grow on trees," he added, to laughter.

"Can you elaborate?" Zurich asked.

Claire strained to hear. She targeted the far window, cracked open. She waited for overlapping conversation, laughter—any distraction—to step past the near window, masked by the sheers. She crouched between the windows, near the open one, whose breeze-buffeted sheers offered a spotty glimpse inside. She listened. The colonel continued his presentation.

"We've known for years that the drug is effective in sterilizing adults, but as of today, we have successfully calibrated the exact safe maximum dosage for youth," he said. "If the autopsy confirms—and we'll know by tomorrow morning—then we can target broader sectors almost immediately."

"What's the delivery mechanism?" Bonn asked.

"Any liquid, really," the colonel answered. "We tested with milk, but juice, soda, water should provide similar outcomes."

"Corn, too?" asked Beijing. "I don't see why not," said the colonel.

"Very impressive," said New York, and London agreed.

"My only concern is your last experiment on your local population," said Zurich dryly. "The viral pandemic you unleashed."

"We've learned from our mistakes," the colonel countered. "That grew beyond our city, beyond our control. But that was decades ago."

"You mobilized a very public crisis," Zurich needled. "An international disaster, whose repercussions we still have to deal with. Why you chose the Homosexual Sector for that testing has always baffled me...."

"Which sector would you have preferred?" the colonel asked. "Might I remind you, we all agreed at the time."

"It has benefited my zone," Johannesburg offered brightly. "We've almost degraded our population to our target level...."

"And the whole world knows it!" Zurich snapped.

"That was *contagious*; this is *targeted*," the colonel snapped back. "And the targeted populations won't die off. They just won't reproduce, and they won't know why."

Zurich elaborated his skepticism. For once, the colonel lost his cool.

"Sir, we've completed our assignment on schedule, ahead of the Crucible," he lectured. "Have *you*?"

He flung open the window fully, yanked back the sheers, waving Zurich's cigarette smoke outward. He repeated with the other window, trapping Claire between the two. She hugged the wall, shrinking into herself.

"Gentlemen"—Moscow stepped up to make peace—"the Crucible is sure to bring unforeseen effects. We will adapt as needed."

London pivoted topics, to cool down the room. "Colonel, we should address your appeal. Your novice, the Prodigal, you call him?"

Slade had called Clay that, her first night at the club. So had Bing. His nickname. Claire leaned, listened.

"He's experienced the normal growing pains," Colonel Crowe explained, "but he's performed exceptionally, understands and accepts the task at hand, and is scheduled for advancement in the special election. His first major step into the public spotlight."

"We appreciate your cautious timetable," London piped in, "given your last failure."

"The younger generation is more resistant, a tougher nut to crack than we were," the colonel added, to knowing agreement. "We learned from our mistake last November. You can't spring this information at the last minute. We started much earlier this time."

"But his wife..." London seemed to struggle. "It's a very unique compromise you have proposed."

Claire leaned closer, stretching a leg to fend off a cramp.

"Her mother-in-law suggested it," the colonel said. "She's quite... energetic about the idea. And I have no objections."

"The Highest Source understands this family's value, empathizes with the loss they've endured," London continued. "But this young lady, I mean...has she agreed to this?"

Claire's contortions held her waist at a downward tip. The weighty key ring slid from its satin-belted grip. Claire's hand shot out, fumbling, jangling. The keys fell two stories, clattered onto a ruby panel of the Tiffany glass dome, slid several inches, stopped.

The room went silent. Claire stooped, contracted. Held her breath.

The colonel spoke from the window, looking out.

"Gentlemen, if we could continue tomorrow," he said, "we can still enjoy the second half of the concert. I'm confident we'll reach agreement on the remaining issues."

Claire heard the windows shut, the sheers redrawn.

She waited for silence and stillness, as the room emptied. She peered up, slipped past the windows, sidestepped to the nearest fire escape ladder, hurried down.

Claire hugged the ledge on the rim of the glass dome. Kicked off her heels, tested her weight with one foot. Stepped on, stepped off. Aiming for the metal dividers between glass panes, she spidered up toward the marooned key ring two-thirds toward the apex. Down below, through a translucent white pane, she spied the gauzy silhouettes of the Gentlemen's Lounge posse coursing the Grand Foyer toward the front door.

The unmistakable gait of Colonel Crowe caught her eye. He returned from the front door, stood in the center of the foyer, and summoned a staff member in a long white coat. The colonel gave orders, and the white-coat hustled toward the back. Colonel Crowe moved to the Grand Staircase, headed up. Claire scampered, reached out and snagged the key ring, retraced her climb backward, foot-feeling in reverse. She restrapped her heels on the ledge, saw-stepped back to an open window: Stompy's studio, now dark. She checked, lowered herself inside.

She passed the desk with his microphone, his headset, the dials and digital recording bay. She glanced down at the loose pages of script, of

"Stu Savage" rants and his equally irate "callers"—written, she knew, by someone else.

Stacked nearby were separate scripts for "SF Anonymous"—with typed reminders for a "British" dialect. Alter egos crying wolf, fanning flames of chaos, of disbelief, from all sides. Both professionally performed by Stompy, whose grimy brass ashtray needed emptying.

Claire went to the door, cracked, listened. White-coats hurried past, disappeared. Claire tiptoed to the back staircase. One flight down, through the kitchen to the parking lot, she'd be free. One flight up was the library and more white-coats and the colonel, all searching for her.

Claire went up.

By now she knew the sounds of the club as she would her own home: the differing cadence of floor creaks from guest rooms or hallways, running showers versus sinks, the particular whines of the swinging wall-doors leading backstairs. The third floor was empty, the rooms soundless. She took a clear shot to the library. Still locked.

Claire quickly found the key. She unlocked the door and peeked in. The room was empty. She went swiftly to Sting's vacant perch. She grabbed the talon-scarred velvet pillow, squeezed and kneaded it, then impulsively ripped it open at one of Sting's puncture points to an explosion of white down and nothing more.

She stepped back, puffed feathers away. Thought. Stepped up to the stone column, reached out to find marbleized wood. She grabbed the scrolled top and pulled, then braced her heel against the bottom and pulled again. It gave a fraction. She pulled and twisted, the lid jammed on its threading. Claire looked around. Grabbed the iron poker from the stand by the crackling fire. Pried its tonged end under the lid, at another point, and another. Gently added her weight to the leverage. The top popped free. She peered inside.

Glint caught her eye at the bottom. She reached down with one hand. Then both. Excavated a substantial ornate wooden box, gilded on all edges, latched across the middle. She thumbed the latch up; the lid held its grip, stuck from neglect. She ran her fingernail around the crack, pried it loose, popped it open.

Nesting inside, in billowed purple satin, rested the ninth Fabergé egg, perched sideways on its own stand. Claire gently unearthed and cradled it. Brilliant crystal like the others, but larger. Intricately bejeweled with nine precious stones nearly shrouding it, obscuring the contents inside. She held the egg carefully, tilted it open on its back hinge.

The egg was empty.

Claire tore through the rest of the gilded box, below the purple upholstery, to the wooden base. She searched the corners and the top and underneath.

She heard creaking floors downstairs. A cable car clanging outside. The guests would return soon, flooding the club for their late-night party. Claire started to repack the egg, to return the box, cover her tracks, preparing to flee with no more information than she started with. No date of the Crucible, of the destruction, to warn the world about. No whistle to blow at all.

She looked around at the explosion of feathers. Futile to clean up. She simply had to escape.

Claire glanced at the glass shelves of eggs. She'd take them all. Someone in the conspiracy world, an expert—and there were many real ones, unlike the phony Stu Savage AKA Stompy Jones—would make sense of them, piece the puzzle together. She grabbed the tote bag from the back of the librarian's chair. She'd load them carefully, adding the feathers for cushion.

But Ethan said the date was here, in the library. Like him, once she fled, there'd be no return.

Claire surveyed the shelves, the eight eggs. Stepped back.

The empty spot dead center, on the middle shelf. Brightly lit.

She looked up, at the spotlight in the ceiling, next to the "E" on the compass rose. The light illuminating the wisdom in the east. Hitting the opening on the center shelf.

Claire took the pedestal from the wooden box and set it in the spot. She gently perched the ninth egg, which glimmered in the light. She stepped away, looked, stepped up again to the side, out of the beam. Then she slowly turned the bejeweled egg on its stand. Stopped. Turned again, a fraction, picking a lock. Another fraction. The spotlight hit the center jewel. The egg came alive.

It exploded refracted bits of light, disco ball–like, from jewel to jewel and egg to egg, showering the antique atlas backdrop with a constellation of stars.

The biggest, brightest stars, colored by the jewels, hit specific letters squarely throughout the map. A pyramid of sorts, three rows, north to south and west to east. The top illuminated "I" of "Septentrio" sat by itself. Downward to "D" of "Mar Del Norte" followed by two letters after. The bottom row started with an "M" from "Mar Del Zur," offered another "M" of "America," technically the central one. "Tropicus Capricorni" gave up its "C" just south of the equator. A Latin quotation, inset in an ocean and ornately bordered, donated an "X" from its "Pax." Ten letters in all.

Claire stepped back, absorbed the whole. The ten letters formed a date, in code, in Roman numerals, or a combination of both. Month/day/year. The date that Ethan had warned about and had been unable to find. Hiding in plain sight.

She reached for her cell to take a picture. But it was down in the coatroom, of course. *Rules are rules.*

She grabbed a pad of paper, a blue pen, upending the perfect order of the librarian's desk. She re-created the pyramid, scribbling down the first tier, the second, the longer, more complicated third. Glancing up and back, perfecting her list, each letter in its proper place. She squinted at the final two letters.

A flash of movement reflected in the center egg. Claire spun.

Sting dove at her, talons raised. It screeched.

Chapter Three

It soared past Claire, targeted its prized egg on the middle shelf. Clutched it. Claire lashed out, knocking it free. It fell to the parquet floor just beyond the rug, cracking, shattering to a handful of large, jagged pieces.

Sting screeched again, flew up to the ceiling constellation, circled, turned, torpedoed. Targeted Claire, blocking her from the door. She shielded her face, swatted out. Resilient, Sting retreated up to regroup, screeched, spiraled back down. Claire grabbed the fireplace poker off the floor. Saberlike, she fended off the beast with its relentless, prime-of-life gusto.

Sting attacked again and then looped back up. Claire took advantage of the retreat to rush to the window by the shelves and unlocked, hefted it, and forced it open. Turned in time to strike the assaulting creature. It circled quickly, dove anew.

Claire held the poker crosswise, blocking Sting, nimbly fluttering midair inches from her face. It reached out its withered claws under the poker, grasping for Claire's throat. It flexed one talon, digging a rip down Claire's neck, drawing blood. Claire held it at bay, straining to push back against the bird's surprising strength. She stepped back, calculated, and in one pivoting motion, hurled the poker and attacking bird out the open window. Quickly pulled it down cockeyed, off its track.

Kneeling, Claire tried to jigsaw the egg back together, clacking bejeweled pieces unsuccessfully. A furious and shrieking Sting smashed against the window, fluttering mothlike, its panicked alarm sure to summon Colonel Crowe any second.

Claire looked back at the now-dead atlas backdrop, trying to re-create in her mind the final two Roman numerals. She strained, wavering. Outside, Sting struck the window, jolting her anew. Claire committed, grabbed the crumpled pad and pen, scribbled two letters. She ripped the sheet of paper, folded and tucked it under her belt. Raced from the library, shutting the door behind her.

She hurried down the back stairs, past the second floor, heard a wave of chattering Asian on the floor just below, then silence, as the stairway door opened and closed. Claire froze, a lingering presence in the stairwell beneath her. She saw a tall, elongating shadow ascending, heard a flat, steady clop of shoes.

Claire turned, dashed up a flight, down the second-floor hallway. She ruled out the Ladies Lounge; Colonel Crowe would check that first. She ran on, glanced back to the stairwell door opening, spilling light across the wall.

She rounded a corner, past guest rooms, trying doors, all locked. She briefly considered Stompy's recording studio, still unlocked from before, with its wide-open window that faced inward. But crawling back onto the ledge would be a final trap, she realized. She moved on, leaving the door open.

Claire ran ahead, her footfalls mercifully muffled by the Heriz runners. Instinctively, she reached down to quiet the jangling keys, which triggered a reminder. Thumbed through the ring as she hurried, located "music," its original name before she'd taken it over. She targeted the Safe Harbor room midway down the hall, darted inside, quietly closed and locked the door.

The windows overlooked and abutted the top of the Grand Dining Room wing, flush enough for an easy exit and escape to the outside, although still too high to jump to the ground. From the roof of the wing, she could wave and shout down to passersby in the park—there were usually pedestrians, even at night, and she scanned downward and located several strolling within hearing distance. They'd call for help.

A white van rolled up the narrow alley between the club and the park and turned in to the club's parking lot. A delivery of something, the driver her nearest lifeline.

She tried one window. Tried the other. Both stuck at six inches, window-guarded at her own orders, for the children's safety. A chair could smash through, with enough force. But the noise would give her away, reveal her to the colonel before she could get help from below.

Down the hall she heard a key click, a door creak. The colonel was looking. Methodically.

She scoured the room, desperate for a phone she knew it lacked. She hit a key on the children's iMac, waking it up. She opened Skype, bouncing its icon. Clay was still airborne, or too far away to help. Nora was with friend-or-foe Slade, too risky. Martha was at her going-away party, likely drunk, and would never comprehend the crisis in time.

Another click, creak. The colonel nearer.

She needed someone close, who knew the club and could get her out, whom she trusted. Someone the club had victimized, like Ethan, even if that someone didn't know it yet. He would, once she explained the horrible truth of it all. Claire ransacked her memory for the number she'd often called from her room when she needed a ride about town. When she needed a protector.

Claire dialed on the keypad. A phone rang loudly from the computer. She quickly lowered the volume to barely audible.

"Hello?" a man answered.

"*Jess!*" she stage-whispered.

"You have the wrong number," the man said.

"Please, you've got to help me," she barreled on. "I'm at the Union Club, on Nob Hill, the big brown mansion, and they're coming to get me. They're *right here...!*"

The screen flashed "disconnect."

Click. Creak. Closer.

Claire concentrated. Dialed again. A phone rang four times. A pause, and then a man's voice.

"This is Jess," he said properly, stilted. "Your call is very important to me. If you will leave your name and number after the beep, I will get back to you as soon as I can."

The automated "at the tone" message took over, louder, and Claire scrambled to pull the volume lower. The female voice listed all available options.

C'mon! urged Claire, wondering if her own outgoing message was this pokey and infuriating.

The messaged beeped.

"Jess, it's Claire," she said, close to the screen. "I'm at the club, up in the kids' room. I'm trapped! You've got to come get me. They're going to kill me, Jess! I've never needed you more. Please...!"

The click and creak arrived next door. Claire backed away from the computer.

She could charge when he opened the door, push past and make a tear for the Grand Staircase, down and out. Unless he'd brought reinforcements, staff to surround and subdue her. His own little army. They'd make sure the scribbled date she hid would never escape the club.

On the corner desk next to the blotter sat a mahogany organizer of club stationery. She grabbed a weighty ecru envelope and a Union Club pen from the green leather cup. Wrote *Dr. Martha Miller, San Francisco General Hospital* across the front. Pulled the crumpled sheet from under her belt and slipped it into the envelope. Claire paused and thought.

In the next room, the door closed, the search complete.

She slipped the sheet back out, retucked it under her belt. Then she grabbed a piece of matching Union Club letterhead, its interlocking burgundy letters top and center, and scribbled *Peace Train* diagonally in a bold, jarring hand. She folded it in thirds, then stuffed and licked the envelope and slid it into the corner mail slot, watching as it dropped down the glass chute, listened until it vanished in silence.

A key clicked into the door. Turned one way and then the other.

Still clutching the pen, Claire shot across the room to the toy chest, unearthed Ilza's pink squeeze flashlight, retreated to the supply closet, ducked inside, closed the door. Scrunched back behind the easels, she quietly unzipped the portfolio of watercolor paintings—ready for submission to the Peace Train. She squeezed the tiny flashlight on, picked the perfect painting, and raised her pen.

The room door creaked open. Steps entered, stealthy on the carpet. Claire finished scribbling, doused the light, held her breath. She strained to hear and calibrate.

The steps advanced, paused, resumed. Quietly went to the far side, lowered and locked a window. Then the other. Then silence. Claire waited.

A jolting barrage of "busy signal" beeps from the computer. Claire had forgotten to hang up. A series of keyboard clicks, and the beeps stopped. More clicks. More silence.

The doorknob to the supply closet turned. A full orbit of motion. Then it released.

There was a sigh, an exhale, from the middle of the room. More steps moving away, a click, a creak, another click. And then steady silence.

Claire waited, with shallow breaths. The silence held.

She waited, hearing activity on floors above and below. The club coming alive. It would fill up again soon. Claire slowly turned the knob, cracked the closet door, eyed the room up and down, listening. She unpretzeled herself, stood, and dashed out.

Ling stood waiting by the door.

"No!" Claire said. "Ling. Please."

He gently took her by the elbow and escorted her down the hall.

"You don't have to do this," she pleaded. "They're not your friends, Ling." He steered her toward the elevator, awaited its arrival. "If you only knew...," she added.

The doors opened to the vacant car. Ling guided her in. The two alone, descending.

"They killed your wife," Claire said. "She didn't die naturally. They were experimenting on her. They're experimenting on all of you. Testing chemicals. Toxic ones. Ethan knew it. Did you, Ling?"

He looked straight ahead. Claire backed against the wall, surveyed him from the side and behind. Her hand shot to her mouth.

"You shot Dean," she said.

He turned back to her, emotionless.

"I know it wasn't real. It was just pretend," she said quickly. "But still, they made you."

"Oh God, Ling, you don't have to obey them," she added as the car slowed. "You can leave, escape! They killed your wife! Why do you stay?"

The elevator opened onto the main floor. Ling steered her out to the empty Grand Foyer, stopped, listened to staff chatter from the back of the club. Pivoted her toward the front, checked his watch, released her.

"Go," he said.

Claire stood, confused. More staff descended from above, down the back stairs.

"*Go!*" Ling urged, pushing her forward.

The door to the vestibule stood open, unattended.

Ling turned, moved to the back stairs. He sounded an alarm in his native tongue as he climbed, diverting his colleagues up and away from her.

Claire raced across the deserted foyer, already prepped for the post-concert party. She passed the roaring fire, ran through the mahogany doors, by the empty coatroom, to the wrought-iron and glass vestibule door that led to the front steps. She turned the knob, grasped, turned harder, shook the door. It wouldn't budge.

She searched in vain for a turn latch and found a keyhole. She fumbled at her key ring, all sizes, labels cryptic. She tried three; the lock rejected each.

Outside, a clanging cable car whirred to a stop in front. Tourists clustered with cell phones, aiming for pictures. Claire banged on the door, waved frantically. Phones flashed, the cable car whirred on and disappeared.

Fingers trembling, Claire isolated another key. In the door's reflection, Sting gracefully rounded the Grand Staircase. Claire spun to see the tuck of its wings and then the fastest dive on the planet.

Chapter Four

S ting dug its talons into Claire's scalp, yanked her back into the foyer with supernatural strength.

She fell to the marble floor, shielding her face from the creature's relentless, darting obsession to gouge out her eyes. She struck back as Sting escalated its assault, crawled toward the round foyer table, now moved to the side near the fireplace. She swatted the beast away and struggled to reach the large chinoiserie vase exploding with lilies, roses, eucalyptus. She pushed, inching it to the edge, and it fell to the floor, shattering in pieces and spilling its insides.

She grabbed the biggest shard, wielding it carefully. Sting dived, and Claire slashed out, slicing it across the gullet. Stunned, the bird wheeled in the air, struck again, its beak open, wingspan extended. Claire grabbed it by the throat midair, clubbed it against the marble, smashing bones. Sting shrieked in rage, shot out a talon, dragging it down Claire's forearm. Claire swung and hurled the crippled beast into the open fire.

Partially aflame, Sting hopped from the fireplace freakishly, beating its smoldering wings against the floor as it wobbled in a circle. From above came sounds of staff. Claire ran toward the elevator bank as several descended the Grand Staircase. She heard others scrambling down the back, arriving soon. Trapped, Claire hit both elevator buttons.

The service elevator opened. Longer, industrial. Claire got in, jabbed a button until the doors closed. She scanned the panel, scrolling through her options. Her current floor was now peopled and hopeless; upstairs offered deeper entrapment. Her immediate hiding place was bound to reveal her soon. She scanned down to the "Pool" button. Pressed it. Again. It sat dead.

The staff squawking neared the elevator, shouting orders to one another in Asian tongue. Claire flipped the key ring, isolated the smallest, toylike key. Slipped it into the tiny lock at the panel bottom, turned it. Punched the "Pool" button. It lit up. The elevator hummed as it descended, the urgent clash of voices drifting up and away.

It stopped, settled solidly. The doors opened to a silent, dim passageway. Claire stepped out and felt her way along the painted brick wall. Sniffed a waft of gym-cleaning chemicals, cut with an antiseptic aroma familiar but unplaceable. She came upon a swinging door with a chicken-wire peep window. She peered in to find it empty, and she slowly pushed through it.

A small entryway angled around to the club's locker room. A white waiter's coat hung on a wall hook. As Claire checked the name tag, the coat fell from its hook. She held it up; it hit below her knees. A lab coat.

She wandered across the tiled floor, past the wood-framed sauna door, and cupped her face on the glass. The room was dark and deserted. The digital thermometer read 4 C. She went inside, shivering in the chill, and found a switch, flipping on the overhead orange bulb. Against the wooden walls, in place of benches, sat stacks of wide, industrial metal shelving, floor to ceiling. All empty.

Claire pushed through to the next room, listening for life, hearing none. The stinging smell of formaldehyde brought back freshman biology; she looked around a fully stocked, functional lab. Long, stone-topped research tables, centrifuges, PCs with rainbow-spiraling screen savers, rows of Corning beakers, test tubes, more lined on shelves, in cabinets behind glass.

She panned the room. On the wall behind, there was a large whiteboard—gridded, labeled, organized. Across the top, in one row, individual photographs of her beaming Safe Harbor children. On the hay-floored Grand Foyer, in Sunday dress, posing by the "Cotton Patch" gate with the adult-sized, grimy-furred Easter Bunny. Each child's column color-coded and catalogued with numbers and dashes, dates and miscellaneous notes trailing down the grid. One row kept track of "dosage."

The last column headed by Edgar holding a small white rabbit—protected, embraced by Claire. All smiles. His grid, numbered 362, was purple and busier than the others. Notes more crowded, dosages higher. Three-quarters down, written in large letters using a red marker, was "Failure." It was circled and underlined. Next to it was today's date.

A door slammed in a nearby room. Claire froze, listened. A faint, steady drip of water, a leaky faucet. She moved across the lab, toward the sound, to a door marked "Pool" in ancient, elaborate script. She slowly pushed it open and smelled biology class anew.

The room was expansive. It had a high ceiling, arched over with Guastavino tiles. The wraparound walls were intricate murals of mosaic—glittering with hills and trees and clouds. All familiar, she felt, from a long-ago dream.

The rectangular pool filled the room. It was bordered with blue striated tile, and it was empty and dry. It started shallow, dipping deeper. At the far end, an ornate fountain dripped. From the ceiling, on an extended arm, hung a large blossom of lights, a cluster of linked hexagons, each with dozens of bulbs, nonilluminated. Off to the side, a discarded gurney, padded and tight with white sheeting. The room walls lined with more gurneys, shelves, unplugged medical monitors, rolling IV drips.

In the center, under the lights, sat a white, rectangular porcelain table. It was bolted to an uneven platform, to accommodate the pool's rake. On the long table, filling less than half the space, lay a small figure under a sheet. Claire steadied herself lightly on the railing, descended into the pool, and approached the table. In the label window at the foot of the slab sat an index card marked "362." She reached up, flipped a switch, flooded blue-white halogen onto the little sheeted figure.

Claire grasped the top of the sheet.

"Claire, NO!"

Claire turned to Madison at the pool edge, looking down at her, still dressed in silver with pearls and crystals.

"You shouldn't be here," Madison scolded, and then softened as she descended the stairs in her metallic heels, without crutch or railing. "You're not quite ready." She smiled. "You know you're not."

Claire stared, still clutching the sheet.

"Why do this to yourself?" Madison *ts*ked, nearing with care. "Just remember how happy you made him."

She stepped closer.

"'Leave it better,' you always taught him. Remember? And he did. He taught us—well, those bright lab people—what the limit is. So they don't cross it again, you see?" She searched for the term and said, "The 'outlier,' I think they call it. Does that sound right? I've forgotten all my science." She chirped an awkward laugh and then corralled herself.

"He saved millions of children, you know," she continued, getting closer. "Children yet to be born. Because now we know the maximum dose for the results we need. You see? It's good for everyone, Claire. For *everyone.*"

Claire released the sheet.

"Oh, I'll miss him, too," Madison added, fighting emotion, as she reached Claire. "I loved that little boy. I didn't want it to be him. But it had to be *someone*, of course. If you think about it, it's really quite an honor. There's something sacrificial...well, almost biblical..."

Claire punched Madison across the cheek with a closed fist. Madison cried out, staggered backward and down, shocked. She stood, regrouped, faced Claire.

"It's o-okay," she stammered, nodding. "Yes, I'm okay."

Claire punched her again across the jaw. Madison stumbled, bleeding from the mouth. She recovered, stood tall.

"No, no. Stay put," she said, waving away the trouble with an embarrassed laugh. "I expected this. Really, I did." Claire followed her eyes and turned. Four clinic staff in long white coats stood at the far end, looking down.

"Claire, please," said Madison. "Let's make this pleasant, shall we? As pleasant as possible."

Claire ran.

To the edge of the pool on the shallow side, struggling to hoist herself.

"Gentle," Madison called out. "Very gentle, please." She dabbed blood from her lip, flicked it away.

Claire climbed on a gurney against the mosaic wall, reached up to the small frosted window near the top, secured by prison bars. She reached through the bars, unlatched, pushed the window open on its chained hinge. From her ground-level view, she spied familiar Fairmont doormen across the way, welcoming guests.

"Help!" she called out from a gap in the shrubbery. "Hello! Please!"

One of the doormen turned, listening.

"Over here!" Claire screamed, banging on the bars. "Help me!"

A clinician grabbed her leg. She back-kicked him, cracking his nose. He recoiled against the others.

"Claire, stop this!" Madison ordered, ascending the pool stairs. "Good God."

Claire moved down the gurney, climbed to a higher shelf. It reached a larger, stained-glass octagonal window, inset with the club's quadrant crest. She felt around its edge, unpinned its corners, spinning it on its pivot hinge. She balanced on the bottom frame, vaulted up and into the doorlike opening.

"No, no, no!" Madison cried, running at her. "Stop it right there!"

Claire looked across. A dark SUV pulled up to the Fairmont, blocking her view. "Here! Over here!" she screamed again. Her torso out the basement window, she clawed at the shrubs, the grass, the soil. Madison grabbed the hem of her flared princess skirt. Beads popped loose, showered down.

"This is ridiculous, Claire," Madison said, straining. "And embarrassing." They both strained; the skirt sounded a warning before ripping at the seam. Claire reached back, yanked, finished the job. Madison fell back into the basement with a fist of silk.

"Really, Claire?" Her voice faded away. "Christopher Kane? *Couture?*"

Claire sprang to her feet, raced to the verdigris iron fence swirling with dragons and sea monsters, too tall to scale. She banged the iron, screamed, waved at the Fairmont guests arriving under the porte cochere across the street. They stared back—then down and away and at one another awkwardly—then turned and funneled inside.

The clinic staff pulled through the window, clawed the ground, each helping the next out.

Claire ran.

To the rear parking lot, full tonight, past the white delivery van backed up to the service door, threading dozens of cars stack-parked, edging around tight bumpers. She escaped through the gate, across the narrow alley at the club's edge, into Huntington Park, past the dancing children's fountain. Targeted a crowd of well-dressed pedestrians migrating toward her, silhouetted against the Masonic Auditorium.

"Help!" Claire cried out, waving at them. "Hello!"

"Claire?" Edie called from the cluster, her cigarette glowing from its wand. "Is that you?" She emerged into the light, grinning through her concern.

"My goodness, Claire!" Clancy added, assisting an older woman up the brick pathway. "What has happened to you?"

"Are you okay?" Bing asked. "Stop, Claire!"

The crowd spread out into a wall, moving toward her. Claire pivoted, tore across the park, past the playground, heading toward Grace Cathedral.

At Taylor Street, a car horn beeped with hesitation and then with insistence.

"Claire!"

She turned to the shiny black Lincoln, rolling slowly, the driver's window open.

"Jess!" she called out, running to it, waving. He stopped. She ran around the front, jumped in.

"What happened to your neck?" he demanded. "And arm?"

"Go!" she begged. "Just go! I'll explain."

He did. She did.

"Sting did that to you?" he said. "What the hell? Why?"

She explained more as he drove on, huddled toward him over the armrest.

Jess sat silent. Claire unloaded the rest. She told him everything.

Jess exhaled, circling Union Square. "Claire, honey, no. I've been there six years, never seen anything like that," he said with emphasis and patience.

"Have you been down to the pool?" she asked.

Jess thought and shook his head. "Never had a reason to. It's closed."

"No, it's very much open!" Claire insisted. She elaborated.

He listened, puzzled, as he turned down Market Street, stopped at a light. "None of this makes sense," he said.

"That's because they haven't *illuminated* you," Claire explained in sharp breaths, struggling not to hyperventilate. "It only makes sense to those at the very top. I don't think Nora knows. I don't think she even knows what happened to Dean. Madison's definitely in on it, because she's so close to the colonel."

"Yes," Jess said, driving up Jones, roaming in circles, heading nowhere. "Okay."

"Experimenting on children?" he added, glancing at her with a tinge of pity. "Really, Claire?"

"They killed Edgar!" she cried out, trembling. "Took his body back to the club, to the basement. They're going to...to..."

"Ssh," Jess said, patting her leg. "Okay. Okay."

Claire focused, collected herself. "They experimented on adults first," Claire insisted, leaning forward. "The staff. Your food, your medicine. They've been testing eugenics drugs, to set maximum doses." Jess's confusion deepened.

"For population control," she clarified.

Jess nodded. "I see," he said.

"Ling knows it's true," Claire added. "He knows they killed his wife with a lethal dose. That's why he helped me escape."

"He did?" Jess asked.

Claire nodded.

"Huh," Jess said, mulling it over.

"How many years have you and your wife been trying to have children?" she asked him. "Did you ever think of that? Did you ever wonder *why*?"

Jess looked at her, looked back at the road. "Huh," he said. "Yeah. Some."

"I know it sounds crazy," she added, to soften the blow. "I thought so, too, until I really looked into it and connected the dots.

"It drove Ethan insane," she went on. "He helped them recruit all of you. He thought he was doing you a favor, saving your life. And when he found out their bigger plan, and that he was part of it, he snapped. It killed him, faster than the disease could."

"Yes." Jess nodded. "He surely snapped."

And then he said, "What disease?" "Whatever it was," she said. "Cancer or whatever side effects from the sterilization drugs. God, it's horrible. He lost an eye, too. Did you know that?"

He shook his head. "Damn," he said. "Poor Ethan."

Claire's hand shot to her own eye. "Oh God! Sting!" she cried out, remembering the beast's gouging obsession. "Ethan said he saw too much." Jess kept focused on traffic.

A police car merged onto Taylor, ahead of them.

"I don't care what happens to me. I'm telling the cops everything," she said, inspecting herself in the visor mirror. She smoothed her hair, checked her scratches. "I do look deranged, don't I?"

"Your dress is torn," said Jess, slowing, as the police car moved ahead. "You look a little beat-up." Claire laughed, surprising herself, and said, "I do, don't I? I'll explain that to them, too. Just follow the police car."

"Claire honey, we need to get you bandaged up first," he said. "That looks ugly."

"Police first," she insisted. "Or to the station over the hill. On Vallejo, I think."

Jess nodded.

Claire closed the visor and laughed again, because she was free. She thought she might cry, which made her laugh more.

"Thank you again, Jess," she said to her savior. "Thank God for you."

She pointed ahead. "Look, the cop's pulling over," she said. "Pull up beside him."

Jess weaved around the police car, sped up Taylor.

"You just passed him," Claire said, looking back and then forward again. Jess kept his eyes on the road. "Should I go to the station instead?" Claire asked, and then nodded her own answer. "You're right. One of the higher-ups. The boss."

Jess accelerated up Nob Hill. Claire reached for her seat belt harness. She fumbled with the latch and leaned in to focus until it clicked. Jess peeled a sudden right into a building's underground driveway. Claire grabbed the armrest for balance.

"Is this a police station?" she asked, peering out at the narrow white lane snaking deeper into the building. "Is it?" she repeated, scanning the closed-in walls.

Jess stopped the car, turned it off.

Claire looked around the near-empty underground parking garage. The elevator sign pointed up: "Masonic Auditorium."

"Why did you...?" she started and then turned back to Jess. He stared at her.

She didn't bother with her seat belt, with the door.

"No, Jess," she pleaded. "No, Jess."

"I'm so sorry, Claire," he said, reaching for her neck.

—⟶—

The happy cling-clang had whirred overhead and passed into the distance. The mine-shaft tunnel lanterns streamed along the ceiling, one after another. The gurney wheels squeaked and rattled, occasionally jerked. The white-coats on both sides guided efficiently, professionally. One smiled down at her, patted her arm. She smiled back, tried to return the gesture, but was strapped down.

The incline, rickety turn, swinging doors, a distant drip. Guastavino tile arched high above, more white-coats scurrying, chirping orders back and forth in Far East tongues. They wore surgical masks. A waft of biology chemicals came and went, its undernotes lingering. A click, a lowering, her head rolled sideways to glimpse the mosaic murals across the way. Workers swarmed, unstrapped, a gentle lifting onto a waiting bed lower still. She looked up again, the arched tiles even higher above.

A clip, a tear, the remnants of her dress removed, destroyed. *Sorry, Madison.*

Antiseptic swabbing, a chill, a covering, warmer now. Legs raised, positioned, awkward, but not uncomfortable.

She looked over at the separate operating theater across the busy pool, a distinctly particular procedure on a small brown body on a slab. Four masked workers in blue scrubs huddled, hunched, consumed with their project—concentrating, excavating. On the brown child's wrist, hanging off the side, a toy watch, the blue cartoon arms wide open, still keeping time.

A delicate hand repositioned her head, fitted a clear rubber mask. She breathed in and out and heard it.

Inside, Claire screamed and screamed.

Chapter Five

The bed was firm and soft, the head almost imperceptibly elevated. The pillowcase smelled bleach clean.

Soft voices, rhythmic beeping, professional hands. Safety.

Piercing halogen lights high overhead. A horizontal red stripe bisecting the white wall. Emergency room, perhaps recovery. A private room soon, with a window.

Claire slept.

———

Asian chatter. Temperature check, blood pressure.

"Good morning." The nurse smiled. "How are you feeling?"

"Good, thank you," she mumbled. "What time do we go?" Her throat was dry.

The nurse laughed, shrugged. Called to the side.

"There's bleeding," she said.

"Bleeding?" Claire asked, alarmed.

"Just a bit," the nurse said. "We'll change the sheets."

She plumped a clear drip bag hanging nearby. Adjusted a spigot on the plastic tube.

"Ssh," the nurse said. "Sleep, dear."

Claire did.

—⁓—

"Hey, princess," said Clay on the edge of the bed. He stroked her face, smiling.

"The baby," she said, her voice raspy. He was hazy in her sleep vision.

"Yes," he said, nodding.

She struggled to lift herself up, but a spasm set her back.

"My neck," she said. Clay nodded, his hand on her shoulder.

"I should have watched you more carefully," he apologized. "You're safe now, princess."

Claire felt a familiar discomfort and vaguely recalled her positioning into stirrups.

"The baby," she said, resisting sleep. "How's the baby?"

"The baby's fine." He beamed down at her. "Didn't they tell you?"

She exhaled. "It is?" she asked.

Clay nodded again. "More than fine," he said. "All systems go." Hence the stirrups, the lingering tinge of violation, all for the good.

The red numbers on the beeping machine read 14:23. The colon was blinking. She tried to decode the military time, gave up. Afternoon sometime. On some day.

She relaxed into her pillow. "When can we go home?" she said.

"Soon," he said. "Sleep. Just relax. We're all fine."

She closed her eyes. The baby was fine. She knew.

She could feel the life inside her.

—⁓—

She'd dreamed it all.

Not the fall in their apartment; that was real. She knew she needed carpet on the slat stairs. Especially wet from the bath, which she had been. She moved carpet to the top of her to-do list.

The intruder? A scary possibility. She'd find out when she woke and got answers. Either way, the building needed to fix the downstairs door, or they'd break their lease and move. The ad promised a "secure entryway." Top priority, above the carpet. No, both were important.

But the rest of it—the underground pool/chamber of horrors, the demonic Sting (funny how her subconscious projected such gusto onto the creature), the sinister cabal at the Union Club—a vivid, twisted nightmare that delighted more than disturbed her because it was over. Dreams, she recalled from junior year psychology, lasted only split seconds, no matter how eternal they seemed.

Everyone at the club had been friendly and harmless. Wacky, even. How odd to envision them so villainous and two-faced. She'd accept Madison's lunch invitation the next time offered.

Most important, her baby, their baby, still healthy, still growing.

She wanted to cry with relief. Not here, in front of the nurses.

That meant Edgar was a dream, too. That felt off. He seemed the most real. Such was the nature of it. At least his death wasn't real either. She wondered what black recess of her mind created that beautifully innocent boy with such an ungodly tragic life. Not to mention the gruesome autopsy, which freaked her even now. Dissected on a slab by a clinking arsenal of scalpels.

Claire shuddered.

Maybe she needed more therapy. She liked the Safe Harbor idea, though, which must have been festering deep in her brain. She added it to her list, a future project.

A nurse undressed her, sponge bathed her in half-sleep, which was embarrassing, although she submitted. She kept her eyes closed and giggled when the nurse used a cold rag with even colder soap on her stomach.

"Tickles," Claire murmured, feeling the slick gel spread out.

"Almost done," the nurse said.

Nora and Slade would drop by soon, she knew. They'd probably already come while she was sleeping. She felt bad for ruining their night at the deYoung event. She hadn't wanted to go anyway. She'd return the dress to Madison, unworn, still in plastic.

"Would she like her pajamas?" the nurse asked as she dozed.

"I think so," Clay answered. "I'll run up and get them."

"I can do it," the nurse insisted. "You stay here."

It was refreshingly cool, and she was tucked in against any chill, by kind, attentive professionals. She was likely in the Willing Wing, although she frowned on special treatment. From a distant room, echoing through an air shaft, came familiar piano melodies that lulled her. Live entertainment: another perk of the VIP floor, she reasoned. Her beautiful husband at her side, gently palming her hand, waiting to take her home. To their home. Their baby safe and protected inside her.

She felt a tear in the corner of her eye. Clay's finger tenderly wiped it away.

The clock blinked 16:47.

She slept. Martha would drop by soon. They were still best friends.

—ᴍ—

She awoke with a start. Restless and fidgety, but less groggy. A good sign.

"Hey, babe," Clay said, close again, smoothing hair from her forehead. "You okay?"

She nodded, hoisting herself slightly.

She looked down at her white satin pajamas, bright and freshly pressed.

"How long have I been out?" she asked, croaky.

Clay held a straw from a blue plastic cup to her lips. She sipped water, bathed her throat.

"Long enough," he said. "You were tossing."

"Crazy dreams," she told him, and laughed once. "You have no idea."

"You're okay now," Clay said. "Everything's okay."

He leaned in to kiss her forehead. Colonel Crowe stood behind him, over his shoulder. He wore a tuxedo.

"Oh. Hello," she said. It was kind of him to come. Odd, unnecessary, but kind.

"How are you, Claire?" the colonel asked.

She struggled to sit up straighter, wiped her eyes.

The room was cavernous.

"Am I...still in recovery?" she asked.

Clay looked back to the colonel, who smiled and nodded.

"Yes," said Clay. "Yes, you are," added the colonel. "And doing nicely."

She rubbed her eyes, awakening their focus.

A red horizontal stripe bisected the white wall behind the colonel, a small-windowed door flush and blended in. She looked to one side and then the other. All the walls were white, pockmarked with faint dark splotches. The floors made of bleached wood, glossy and scuffed. She looked up to the bright inset spotlights in the ceiling high above. To the glass-walled observation deck just beneath, peopled with Asians in long white coats, some scurrying, some observing.

She drank in the converted squash court. Her bed dead center, just off the service lines. The beeping machine skipped and sped up.

305

"Oh my God," Claire said.

Clay smiled and said, "Ssh. You're okay."

"You're going to kill me," she thought, and must have said.

"Why would we do that?" the colonel asked warmly. "But we can't have you wander about in the state you were in." He turned to Clay. "See, this is what we meant by 'too much, too soon,'" he instructed.

"Although you could have picked a better weekend for your meltdown," added Slade, emerging from behind her bed with a chuckle. He, too, wore a tuxedo—single-breasted, notch lapel.

"Unfortunate timing, yes," said the colonel. "But everything that rises must converge."

"You look well," Slade told her. "Calm and rested."

Claire clawed at the bed's arms for leverage. Clay gingerly restrained her.

Clay, back from Nevada. From Texas. Overseeing the reeducation camps, still under construction, soon to be filled.

"You're one of them," she hissed at him, in front of his father and the colonel. "They illuminated you."

"We don't use that term," said the colonel. "We educated him."

"*Brainwashed*!" said Claire.

"Honey, no," Clay soothed her. "They didn't need to. Wait till you hear what it's all about. It's beautiful; trust me...."

"Dean said no. You said yes. Oh God, Clay! *Say no, Clay*!"

The beeping quickened.

The colonel stepped up. "Over time, you'll understand," he said. "You're a clever girl. You know it's pointless to fight evolution. Cruel, even. This is just the natural progression of things...."

Ethan was right. *The Ninth Protocol* was right. Even Stu/Stompy, as ridiculous as he tried to sound, was right all along. Inoculating the public, like the book warned, so that nobody sane would believe him.

Yet here it stood in front of her. Three generations of the New World Order. All handsome.

Forgive me, Edgar! I brought you to these monsters!

Edgar, who likely lay on a shelf in the repurposed, refrigerated sauna-morgue. His remnants, at least. Congealing.

Claire convulsed.

A nurse checked the EKG station next to the bed. "Try not to excite her, please," she told the men before stepping back.

Claire looked down and over—hooked to an IV from her elbow, sensors across her chest and wrist, connected to the beeping machine and monitor. The clock blinked 20:12.

And her baby still dead, as it had been for months. Lucky child.

"You killed our baby," she said to Clay.

He shook his head in protest. "No, Claire, I did not," he stressed. "Never."

"I mishandled that one," admitted the colonel. "And the proper term is 'terminate.' Jess made quite a mess of it, but the buck stops with me. To your credit, it was more challenging than we'd anticipated.

"We like you, but we know so little about you," he explained earnestly. "And we do have to follow the rules, like them or not. So we needed a little breathing room to figure out our strategy. For your benefit. Do you see?"

"But we worked it out, honey," Clay said. "We're all set now. We're good."

"The colonel pulled the right strings," Slade added. "We're forever in his debt."

"Not at all," the colonel demurred. "She's certainly earned membership. If she accepts..."

To join their cult. As wife of their future leader, whom they'd methodically groomed to take over the colony, and perhaps the world, once they'd destroyed and rebuilt it. To reign over it.

Satan's pilgrim.

Claire looked at them, wild.

"Oh God," she said, pushing back from her husband. "The Antichrist."

Clay recoiled. The colonel frowned and shook his head. "We don't use that term," he said. "We don't traffic in myth.

"But with Clay's ambition, coupled with our guidance, there's no limit to his rise," the colonel went on. "Especially with someone so attractive by his side. A real partner. You're a natural, Claire. The world will adore you. We're going to need that."

"See, princess," Clay said, sidling closer, "I said I wouldn't do this without you. That was my deal from the beginning."

Wake up again, she told herself, *and all this will be gone.*

"I'm not one of you," she said. "Never."

"Don't say that, honey. Not until you've heard it all."

"Plus it's a bit late for that," the colonel added. "After all the help you've given us. Don't you think?"

A face pressed up against the door window, a knock. "Did you want this?" Madison breezed in, carrying the platinum bejeweled ball gown in tissue, under plastic. "Hello, dear," she said to Claire. She wore her own couture gown, in gold, and extra makeup, especially around her mouth—swollen, bruised, unmaskable. With opera gloves, she hung the dress on the IV stand, next to the plastic drip.

Through the air vent came faint children's singing, accompanied by piano.

"The kids are entertaining the guests," Madison said proudly. "They look splendid."

"They sound splendid," Slade encouraged. Upstairs, they sang "This Old Man." Ilza was the loudest.

"Who's looking after them?" Claire asked. "Stompy," said Madison. "Okay," Claire said.

"The guests were very excited to meet them," Slade added. "They're quite the celebrities this weekend."

Claire moved to rip the IV from her arm. Clay restrained her.

"No, honey, no," he said. The nurse agreed, securing the tape. Another nurse stood ready, if needed.

"I will *never* bring a child into this sick world of yours!" Claire said.

"You'll never have to," the colonel said, stepping up. "Not your own, at least."

Claire stared, silent.

"You haven't told her yet?" Madison asked, fidgety. She checked the time on her diamond Chopard. "It's getting late."

The colonel nodded at the nurse, who clicked on the monitor over the beeping machine.

"I trust you will appreciate your sister-in-law's generosity," he said, caressing Madison's back. She bit her lip and looked away.

An ultrasound repeated its recorded sonographic imaging. A grainy black-and-white Doppler radar across a womb. Dead center, color-highlighted, floated five tiny, irregular dots.

"That image is about an hour old," said the colonel. "The miracle of life is an awful thing to behold, in the truest sense of the word."

Transfixed, Claire's hand shot to her belly. "What...have you done?" she asked.

"Embryo transfer," said the colonel. "So simple and nontraumatic, you wouldn't have known. I saw no need to tell you, but I defer to your husband on family planning matters."

Clay, excited, clutched her hand. "We did it, princess," he said. "We're going to have a baby, just like you wanted."

"No," Claire said. "No..."

"Madison's been donating for the past few months," the colonel explained. "And then Clay did his part. Separately, of course."

"And they're yours," Madison added, brightening. "All yours." She turned to the sonogram, her face falling a bit. "Already growing..."

"We only need one," the colonel explained. "The strongest, of course. And male."

"It's the only way, honey," Clay continued. "Just for the heir. And then we can have as many as we want. You and me."

"We want to keep you, Claire," Slade leaned in, *sotto voce*. "In the family. We *do* love you...."

Claire stared at them, at the sonogram, unable to speak. Or think.

"No one is forcing you," the colonel said. "If you refuse, well, then you've limited our options substantially. But we're prepared for any eventuality."

"No, we're not," Clay interjected. "I'm not." He leaned closer to Claire. "I need you, Claire," he whispered in her ear. "We're a team. Over time, soon, all this will make sense."

She pushed him away with both hands.

"Why...did you marry me in the first place?" she asked.

"I didn't know the rules!" he insisted.

"And it didn't matter then," Slade added. "He was second son. Now he's first."

"The metrics have changed," said the colonel calmly.

Claire erupted. "No!" she heard herself scream. "*NO!*"

"Could you people have fucked this up any worse?" Nora demanded, storming through the court door, slamming it behind. She was professionally coiffed and wore a dazzling copper gown with diamond pavé necklace. She pointed at Claire with her porosus crocodile clutch.

"Amateur hour the whole way!" she yelled at the others. "From your clumsy first act to this pathetic curtain call. Look at this girl! She's terrified!"

"Nora, please," Slade said, but she'd have none of it.

"If you'd let me break it to her earlier, we could have avoided this debacle," she said, winding up.

She looked around the squash court, at the hospital bed and medical equipment, and cackled. "Unseen hand, my ass. No wonder this club is the laughingstock of the whole organization."

"Calm yourself, Nora," the colonel cautioned.

"Oh, shut the fuck up, old man!" she shot back, whirling. "We all know you wanted to get rid of her." She paused to pivot to Claire and said, "He did, you know. He wanted to kill you straightaway. Don't let him tell you otherwise. That was *his* solution. I hired Jess away from him, just to be safe."

She turned back to the colonel. "I'm wildly immune to your lies," she told him. "Under your medals, you've got all the honor of a white-trash street thug."

The colonel slapped her hard across the face. She staggered but didn't flinch. "Careful, Nora," he warned, past his threshold. Slade and Clay said nothing.

Nora regrouped, unfazed.

"What are you gonna do? Kill me?" she taunted, nose to nose with him. "Good God, *Colonel*. After all I've been through, do you really think I'd care?"

She returned to Claire.

"I fought so hard for you," she pleaded, up close. "Won't you meet us halfway? Of all people, can't you raise another woman's child?" On the monitor, an embryo floated left, right.

"To stay...in this family?" Claire said. "Nora, you killed your own son."

Nora reared up. "Shut your mouth! Dean's fine. He's just..."

"At the Keep," said Claire.

The others looked to the colonel, who thought for an instant and then nodded.

"To wait out your apocalypse," Claire went on. "And your Armageddon."

The colonel froze. "Our...what?" he asked, zeroing in.

"The Crucible," Claire added. "The Ninth Protocol. Or are you going to deny that, too?"

Clay, puzzled, turned to the colonel. "What's she talking about?"

"Quiet," the colonel ordered him. "You're not there yet."

The colonel thought. "This is a first," he said finally, approaching the bed in a rare quandary. "I respect you, Claire. The best and the brightest. You've illuminated yourself.

"But you're out of sync," he added, restoring his poker face. "You've learned the ends before the means. There's the rub.

"A little knowledge is such a perilous thing," he lectured her. "Especially from your unreliable sources. Clay, what's the very first thing we taught you?"

"'He who knows the Secret does not speak...,'" Clay quoted automatically.

"'He who speaks does not know the Secret,'" the colonel finished. "At least not all of it." He glanced around at the others and made a decision. "I guess we have no choice."

He pulled a metal folding chair next to the bed, scatted Clay away. He leaned in closer, sharing a secret.

"Deep down, isn't this what you've always wanted, your whole life?" he asked Claire, probing. "For the world to change? For the better?"

"Not...not like this," she said.

"With all change, there is loss," he continued with an understanding nod. "But in this case, there's such tremendous gain, for all humanity. A lasting peace. Harmony. Every child a wanted child, with love, a purpose. A world in balance—forever. It's going to happen soon, with or without you...."

Claire scanned the bed with its too-high railings trapping her, the room surrounded, the observation deck with its professional onlookers ready for any trouble, the door past which dozens of workers, myriad guests—a *mob*—lay in wait.

They smile and smile, until they stop, Ethan had warned. *And then beware the ugly teeth....*

No exit. *Huis clos,* from freshman French.

Claire thought.

She'd be no use to the world, to anyone, if they killed her.

Claire focused.

The beeping machine quickened. The nurse approached, concerned.

Colonel Crowe studied Claire. He motioned the clinician to disconnect the IV drip. "We won't need sedation," he said. "I think she'll be very open to what I have to say."

He turned to Claire. "Isn't that right?" he asked. "Aren't you weary of struggling? So very weary?"

The nurse withdrew the needle, applied a bandage. Unhooked the sensors from Claire's wrist and chest, clicked off the monitor. The beeping stopped.

"You can walk out the door, if you so choose," the colonel said. "We won't kill you. Eventually you'll take care of that yourself.

"A little knowledge," he repeated, "can be such a maddening thing. You've tasted a bit of that, no?"

Claire stared, silent.

"And you can join Dean and the others, if you wish," the colonel offered, with a shallow shrug. "Technically, that option shouldn't be available to you, but the board has made special dispensation. In gratitude for your services already rendered.

"But such a selfish waste of your talents, don't you think?" he chided. "You're too valuable to languish at the Keep. There's a new world coming, Claire. Stay and help us build it, why not? The way you think it should be...

"Not to mention, you owe us," he added evenly. "We identified your potential early on, gave you an education, opportunities. To have you on deck, at the ready if we needed you. And now we do. It's only fair to give back, don't you think?"

"Please, honey," Clay urged. "Stay."

"Claire, won't you have us?" Nora pleaded. "We'd love to have you."

Claire looked around at the madness that filled the room. The monstrous evil that had infected them all—intelligent, educated, thoughtful—individually, on its own schedule.

Pretend now, she told herself. *Escape later.*

Claire relaxed, slightly, against the bed cushion.

"There now," the colonel said. "Shall I paint a picture, the whole picture? And then you can decide which path to take."

Claire sat still. The colonel beckoned to Clay.

"Come closer," he said. "This will be new to you, too." Clay perched on the edge.

The colonel turned to the nurses. "Ladies, would you excuse us?" he asked. They nodded, collected their files and personals as he continued.

He looked to Slade, Nora, Madison. "I'll meet you upstairs, after her decision."

"I brought her dress and makeup," Madison indicated. "Just in case."

"The guests are eager to meet you," Slade encouraged, squeezing Claire's foot. "They came all this way."

"Tonight's the big night," Madison reminded her. "The one we've all been waiting for."

"We shall see," said the colonel. "We shall see."

Nora knelt, in her gown, on the squash court floor. "I want to stay," she said. "I want to hear it all again.

"I *need* to," she added.

"Me too," said Madison. Slade nodded and stood behind Nora, hands on her shoulders.

The Willing family gathered.

"Very well," said the colonel, turning back to Claire. He took a breath.

"Relax and drink it in," he began. "It's not the end. Quite the opposite. It's a sublime beginning. And then you decide. Both of you together. You decide..."

The nurses slipped through the door, gently closed it. Peered back one last time through the window. Carried on their way.

Upstairs, the singing went on and on.

November 27

"Jack! Stay where I can see you, please!"

Good luck with that, she thought, hurrying to keep up. After nearly two hours, starting with the locomotive and working his way back, he hadn't slowed down a joule. Fortunately, it'd be dark soon. Other parents had already started their exodus, with spotty results. The unseasonably mild weather further thwarted their roundup. It had been the first year she could remember not needing a wrap of any kind for the Macy's Thanksgiving Day parade a few days before.

Maybe global warming had its perks, after all.

She couldn't recall the last time she'd been to Strawberry Fields. She'd scarcely been to Central Park at all since moving to Hoboken last spring, with its serviceable, utilitarian parks and playgrounds. She missed the big city's grandeur, the sense of community, the unique, special exhibits, like this one. She missed the zoo.

She didn't miss the Manhattan rents. No longer an option.

"Sit tight till I catch up, Jack!" she called out. He'd migrated to the London car toward the rear, red and double-decked, like their buses. But this one was blended over, tastefully, with children's artwork. Jack hopped inside and ran back and forth, taking turns honking the horn with children he'd met and would never see again once they trekked back across the Hudson to Siberia.

Indianapolis apparently wasn't important enough to merit a car in the exhibit. Certainly it ranked below Paris, Chicago, even Atlanta. But also Nashville, St. Louis, Tulsa? It crushed her to think about leaving New York altogether, but if the offer came, she'd have no choice. Unemployment had dried up in July, her savings were quickly evaporating, and Christmas was only a few weeks off. Damn those ads that turned Jack onto the new Wii. Some of the games were so violent. And expensive.

Hopefully the public schools were better in flyover country. Safer. Metal-detector-free. And maybe, over time, with luck, she could afford a private school, at least for his last few years, the important ones. College, absent a scholarship, seemed magical thinking at this point.

Her ex would balk at taking Jack out of state, but—*fuck him.* Considering how delinquent his payments, she knew the judge would side with her. She needed the job. They had to eat.

Leaving New York didn't mean failure. It wasn't suitable for kids anyway. And Zabar's was overrated. No, it wasn't.

She didn't have the offer yet, she reminded herself. It might never come. The others hadn't. And then what?

How did we get here? she wondered, and then forced her mind elsewhere, as she'd trained herself, to avert sudden panic.

A mother snapped at her son inside the Sydney car. A youngish pair of conflicting parents quarreled—screamed, really—by the pagoda-*esque* Tokyo. Didn't people used to hide their anger, their rage, at least in public, in front of the kids? She strained to remember what that was like. Had the city always been a powder keg?

The irony of such fury at a peace exhibit would have seemed comical to her once. But not today, not this year.

She breathed deeply. It really was a clever exhibit, and impressive, stretching the length of the field with its rainbow of colors and festive shapes. Joyous and playful and moving. She was glad she'd seen it on the news and carved out time before it moved out this week. Jack loved trains. And it was free.

Where was Jack?

"Jack?" she called out, scanning the cars. "Jack?" She moved quickly, scanning, searching the windows.

Clang, clang, clang! And his unmistakable laughter.

She exhaled, relieved. He'd found the caboose, naturally. Everyone's favorite.

A Technicolor cable car. Psychedelic almost. Perfectly San Francisco.

"We gotta go soon, Boo," she told him, climbing inside. He looked adorable by the bell, wearing it out. She aimed her cell phone camera. Perfect for their Christmas card. "Look to Mommy, Jack! Smile!" He did. She clicked. "Now give the bell a rest, please!" she pleaded.

The children's artwork covered the walls, too. And the ceiling. She ran her finger along pastel doves and Magic-Marker peace signs. Purple puppies and same-sex stick couples. Each laminated and appliquéd, a permanent part of the traveling exhibit. Up close, she was even more impressed by the effort. And the sunny childlike optimism gave her an unexpected lift.

She took more pictures. The walls, the ceiling.

"Come on, Jack. It's getting late," she said, to predictable protest.

She herded him toward the back door.

"Hold up a sec, Boo," she said.

On the back wall, near a top corner—quilted amid watercolor dolphins and a crayon galaxy of stars, next to a triangle-roofed home with mother and child at story time by a roaring fire—sat a three-tiered pyramid of letters and symbols, scribbled in pen. A frantic arrow demanded attention.

She stood on tiptoe, squinted.

"I Day" read the top two tiers.

The third a string of Roman numerals, starting with "MCC." A calendar year, she realized, puzzling them out, embarrassed a San Francisco school child knew them better than she did.

But it wasn't a child's handwriting. More like a sloppy adult's. One of the parents. One of the Bay Area helicopters. She squinted again. It looked frantic, panicked. Non-peaceful.

It held her.

"Mommy," Jack whined, mentally prepped for the next adventure, from the back deck.

"Coming, honey," she said, aiming her phone.

She took a picture. And another.

"Can we go ice skating?" Jack asked. "Under the Christmas tree?"

"Now?" she said, taking his hand. Admission. Rentals. She did the math.

"Next time, Boo," she said, leading him around the Imagine disc—rose-strewn, as always. "Next time."

—∞—

"Yes, all the way to the top, please," she said, lowering the backseat window. "Take your time." She flicked her lighter, inhaled.

"Sorry, ma'am, no smoking," the Paki-sounding cabbie said, tapping the sign. "De law."

"The window's down!" she countered, streaming out. "I'll add it to the tip."

Jeezus, she thought. Fucking Nazis everywhere. She'd quit in the New Year. Again.

They passed familiar streets and shops and sights heading up. She missed her old city, even the perennial fog and gloom, especially after Chicago's brutal summer. She looked forward to the Midwest winter, if it ever came. She was tempted to stop at Lotta's for her favorite sticky bun, but she was already late. She'd grab one after lunch.

And maybe she'd take the afternoon off, to visit her old haunts, including a bar or two. She'd shock David and the gang at Hidden Vine. She hadn't seen them since her going-away party. They'd ask about the men in Chicago, naturally. There was little to report. Surely that would pick up as her residency wound down, freeing up her time. One could dream.

Nobody would miss her at the pediatrics conference. After the initial check-in, nobody cared. She'd catch up on everything tomorrow and the next day. Including a follow-up with the hospital's head administrator, who'd sought her out that morning, weirdly, about an upcoming fellowship opening. She was surprised he knew her name, much less her résumé. She leaned back in her seat, wondering how that had come about, and exhaled straight ahead.

"Miss, please!" the driver complained at the expanding cloud. "Will mess up car!"

"Sorry. Sorry!" she said, tossing her cigarette out. "My bad." She foraged through her Coach bag, found her sugarless gum, punched out a square and then a second.

The e-mail, out of the blue, had surprised and secretly delighted her. Innocuously written, but clearly a feeler for détente. Although they hadn't spoken in months—and even then it had been abrupt, angry, and confusing, absent a proper goodbye—she'd kept up with her, virtually, in the online social pages she still scanned, out of nostalgia and a certain homesickness. And raw nosiness.

She looked great in the magazines. Clearly grown into her role and her element. They were a beautiful couple, as always. The newest stars of the city. And, as of a few weeks ago, the talk of the nation. Youth + beauty + the political machine = a special election and fast-tracked career. Zoom.

And then the surprise invitation—engraved, on pink and blue extra-heavy card stock, addressed with hand calligraphy—had shocked her on two counts: that it existed, and that she got one.

She needed another cigarette. Would this be awkward and uncomfortable, or an up-front pressure release and then steady smoothness? She had so many questions, most of which she'd decided, in advance, to keep to herself. Especially the first one that popped to mind, after the initial e-mail. She'd counted and recounted and puzzled, amazed at her friend's resilience and sheer stubbornness, once she'd set her mind to something.

They were both stubborn with each other. They were getting too old for that. High time to mellow.

"Miss?" the driver asked in the mirror. The cab had stopped. "Yes, thank you!" she answered, wadding bills. She tissued her gum.

The towering Christmas tree dominated the park. She scanned the playground, the benches, the creepy dancing-child fountain. Why were they meeting way up here...?

"Martha!"

She turned. "Hey you!" She waved and yelled back at the bench. "Sorry I'm late." She hustled, elbows swinging.

"There's this new invention called the telephone!"

"Eat me!" she shouted. "The stupid conference ran over. Stand up, bitch!"

Claire did. It was a struggle.

She looked gorgeous.

"Omigod, stick a fork in you," cried Martha. "This is so beautiful!"

Were it not for her globe-sized stomach, no one would have known. Damn her. Perfect even in late pregnancy.

Martha rubbed her belly, flung her arms around her.

"Twins?" she said. "Really?"

Claire nodded, sparkling. "His and hers."

"Names! Gimme names."

"We're still sorting that out," said Claire. "Clay has his favorites, I have mine.

"I'll win," she added with a grin. "The fuck you will," approved Martha.

"Martha, I miss you so much," a beaming Claire said sincerely. She wore velvet and cashmere in Yuletide shades and maternity shapes. Her complexion was glowing, not the least bit splotchy.

"You have the ovaries of a guppy," Martha blurted out, breaking her self-imposed embargo. "That was weirdly fast. As in, 'barely medically possible' fast."

"Why wait?" Claire said. "It's been very smooth so far." Then she puffed her cheeks and sighed. "But I'm ready to get these damn critters out."

Martha laughed. Claire folded their arms together. They strolled.

"I hate to miss the baby shower," Martha said. "Please thank Madison again for including me. It sounds überextravagant. Her invite was thick enough to chop vegetables on."

"She's been planning it for months. I wish she wouldn't make such a fuss, but"—Claire paused and shrugged—"it seems to be extremely important to her."

They talked about Martha's stillborn Chicago relationships, Claire's new Pacific Heights home—under renovation, behind schedule, over budget. "Hopefully we'll be in before the babies come. Fingers crossed."

Claire described the strange, exciting saga of the campaign and election night. "Right there in the Fairmont." She pointed. "That was something. It was madness."

"When are you moving to DC?" Martha asked.

"Oh, I'm not," said Claire, pooh-poohing the notion. "Clay's going to commute. He's renting in Georgetown. He's at 'freshman orientation' right now with the other newbies."

"Do I have to show him more respect now?" Martha grumbled. Claire scrunched her nose and said, "I don't."

Martha dangled the morning's unexpected fellowship offer from the hospital's new Willing Institute of Pediatric Studies. "Flattering and out of left field," she called it, eyeing Claire.

"That sounds like a terrific opportunity," said Claire, feigning surprise. "I know they have big plans for that place."

"And you had nothing to do with their preemptive strike?"

Claire pursed a smile, looked ahead.

"Did you think I'd let Chicago keep you forever?" she asked.

They strolled more, away from the tree and the park.

"Did you know a dude named Bing at school?" Claire asked abruptly. "A year ahead of us, I think."

"*Bing?*" Martha shook her head. "No. Why?"

Claire played it off. "Nice guy. Good guy. Friend of Clay's. Decent-looking."

Martha groaned.

"*Very* successful," Claire added. "Very eligible."

"Gay?" Martha asked. "Pedophile? Eunuch?"

"Not that I know of," said Claire. "Just hasn't found the right mate. Yet."

"Now look, bitch—" Martha started, and Claire stopped and turned. "No, *you* look, bitch," she cut her off. They both laughed. It died down quickly.

"I want to apologize," Claire said earnestly. Martha shook her head, and Claire insisted. "No, I mean it."

She unloaded her mea culpa. The blown-off parties and dinners, the unreturned calls. The passive-aggressive catfights and impulsive, deeply regretted attacks. The months of neglect bordering on abandonment. It was sincere. And what Martha needed to hear and returned in kind.

Martha rubbed her friend's shoulders. "We were both...in flux," she said. "We've been there before. We'll be there again. And we've always survived."

"We have, haven't we?" said Claire.

Martha nodded. "And always will."

"Just don't pull any of that shit on me again," Martha added with a double hack.

"And you," Claire said, poking her chest, "need to quit smoking. It's time."

"Blah. Yes." They locked arms again, continued down the sidewalk.

Martha grappled and then said, "But I gotta ask: What was that freaky letter you sent to me at the hospital?"

Claire looked ahead. "Letter?"

"They forwarded it to me in Chicago," Martha continued. "Postmarked in April sometime. On your club's letterhead. It said 'Peace Train,' in your handwriting. Just that."

"'Peace Train'?" Claire ransacked, ping-ponged her mouth.

Martha nodded. "Just that. In sloppy scrawl. Were you smashed or something?"

"I don't know," Claire said, confused. "I hope not."

Then she added, "But, honestly, my mind was in a funny place there for a while. Around that time, I think..." She looked at Martha and shrugged.

"Your mind *lives* in a funny place, freaker!" Martha said, and then inspected her. "But look at you now. I've never seen you so...centered. Mature. You're like a different person."

Claire nodded, exhaled. "Sooner or later, we all grow up," she said, and then turned with a smile. "Thank goodness."

"Should we grab that cab?" Martha signaled. "Does Sociale still have a big lunch crowd? Can we get in?"

Claire stopped walking. "Why don't we just go here?" she asked.

Martha looked up.

"The Union Club?"

"Why not?" Claire said. "They've really upped their game. They have a delicious Niçoise now."

"Oh," said Martha.

"It's light. Although I'll probably get the cheeseburger."

"Yes."

"Plus it's right here," Claire said. "I'm sure you're in a hurry."

"I'm not in a hurry."

"Even better. We can hang out after lunch."

Claire started up the stairs. Martha stood still.

"Is that Asian dude still skulking around?" she asked.

"Ling? No...," Claire said with the barest inhale. "Ling's not there anymore."

"What about the damn bird?" Martha asked.

"Sting? Yes." Claire laughed. "He's definitely a survivor. Don't ask me how."

Martha followed a few steps. Stopped again. Looked up at the windows, shrouded with sheers.

"I hadn't planned on...I mean, do I need my passport?" she asked. "A letter of recommendation?"

"Shut up! You're a brilliant young doctor. That's fascinating. They'll love you."

Martha self-inspected. "I'm not dressed right," she said. "I'm a little Ann Taylor today."

"You look fine," Claire insisted. "I'm the mess."

Not true. Then or ever.

Martha hesitated.

"What is it?" Claire asked from the front porch.

"Nothing. It's just...I've never been inside before."

Claire mock pouted. Came down to Martha.

"I remember the first time I walked in here," she said, tucking arms again. "You made fun of me that day, remember? How nervous I was?"

She led Martha up the stairs. "But it's just a building."

Allen opened the glass and wrought-iron vestibule door. Greeted them both.

A clanging from the street. Martha turned to the cable car at the light, tourists clustered to the side, aiming cell phones. A little girl on the end waved.

"Martha?" Claire called from the vestibule.

Martha smiled at the little girl, fanned a half wave back.

Then she turned and walked through the door.

Acknowledgments

First, I must thank my parents, to whom I dedicated my debut novel *S'wanee*. Henceforth, they'll hold court in the Acknowledgments Hall of Fame, where they belong. Ditto my sister Debra, who is equally perplexed by and supportive of what I write.

Sincere thanks to the following friends and family for eyeballing previous drafts and offering valuable insights: Bo and Kathryn Lasater, Ted Simpson, Mary Unsworth, Jacqueline Mazarella, and Owen Moogan. Much gratitude to Ryan Rayston, Jennifer Howard, and Henri Kessler for their bolstering of the story in its infancy.

Special thanks to Pat O'Meara, Suzanne Fawcus, Devan Hidalgo, Terri Grimes, Patty Turrisi, Marely Cheo-Bove, and Holly Bingham for being early supporters and champions of my work. I hope someday to meet them all.

To Mr. Craig Baumgartner, who gave me a glimpse inside.

To Dave Glass for chronicling San Francisco over the decades through his camera. I was lucky to discover his astounding photographs and suggest you do, too.

To my copyeditor Penina Lopez, for making sense of it all.

To my cover designer Chad Zimmerman, for his artistry and wonderfully skewed eye.

To my team—Charlie Ferraro, Dallas Sonnier, and Will Rowbotham—who should take this ball and run with it.

And most of all to my book agent Helen Breitwieser, whose steady hand turned my occasional boil down to a simmer. She pushed this novel over the finish line.

About the Author

Don winston grew up in Nashville and graduated from Princeton University.

He currently lives in Los Angeles. His first novel *S'wanee: A Paranoid Thriller* hit #3 in Kindle Suspense Fiction. *The Union Club* is his second novel.

www.donwinston.com

ALSO BY DON WINSTON:

The Top Five Kindle Suspense Thriller

S'WANEE
A PARANOID THRILLER

A spellbinding campus. A new family of friends.
A semester of death.

High school senior Cody's prayers are answered when he's recruited on scholarship to the college of his dreams: a stunning and prestigious school tucked high in the Tennessee hills.

But the dream turns living nightmare when his classmates start to die off mysteriously. Is it Cody's imagination, or are his friends' tragic deaths a sinister legacy handed down through the generations? And is he next on the roll call?

A coming-of-age, paranoid thriller in the vein of Ira Levin, *S'wanee* weaves psychological suspense with dark humor in its brutal descent to a shocking climax.

S'wanee. Where old traditions die hard.

ENROLL NOW.

A first look at Don Winston's upcoming paranoid thriller...

The Gristmill Playhouse

A Nightmare in Three Acts

Betty Rose Milenski dreams of Broadway. Talented, ambitious, and obsessed, she was the biggest fish in college. But New York is a harsh wake-up. Unemployed and ignored, she faces a career as cocktail waitress instead of on the stage. And the clock is ticking.

She jumps at an internship at the country's most famous summer stock playhouse, in spite of its bizarre, all-controlling reputation. There, she joins a family of eccentric and endearing fellow actors and bonafide stars, lorded over by the benevolent dictator Rex Terrell. With nonstop shows to sold-out crowds—tucked away in a charming, Americana village—the Gristmill Playhouse is every actor's summer dream.

But when a fellow intern mysteriously quits and warns her to flee, Betty Rose struggles to separate truth from make-believe even as she rises toward stardom. Is her growing terror and dementia a form of self-sabotage, or is the Gristmill grooming her for a final curtain call?

The Gristmill Playhouse. There's no business like it.

Marian Maples, Broadway Legend, Dies at 88.

By PAUL YARDLEY
Published: June 12

Marian Maples, the irascible, brassy four-time Tony Award winner and stage, film, and television actress for more than six decades died Tuesday night in Manhattan. She was 88.

She died onstage at the Booth Theatre, during a performance of the revival of *A Little Night Music*, according to her longtime agent, Wes Ward.

A prolific performer in regional theatre, on tour and in summer stock, Ms. Maples appeared in more than three dozen Broadway shows throughout her career, including her final stage role, for which she was nominated for Best Supporting Actress in a Musical at last June's Tony Awards.

Equally accomplished in comedies and dramas, she began her career as standby for Ethan Merman in the 1950 musical *Call Me Madam* before moving on to starring roles in *Bus Stop*, *Sail Away*, *Company*, and many more.

Ms. Maples went to Hollywood sporadically in the 1950s and '60s and appeared in a handful of B-movies, including *The Violent People* with Charlton Heston and *Who Killed Teddy Bear?* with Sal Mineo. She also did a two-year stint on the daytime drama *The Edge of Night* in the mid 1980s as well as numerous guest spots on primetime programs, for which she garnered four Emmy nominations and two awards.

But it was in the Broadway theatre where Maples made her mark, with star turns in musicals by Rodgers and Hammerstein, Cole Porter, and most indelibly, Stephen Sondheim, who famously called her his "salty muse."

A workhorse till the end, Maples encapsulated her career seven years ago in a one-woman show entitled *Look Who's Here*, for which she won her final Tony for Best Special Theatrical Event. The *Boston Herald* called the retrospective "Not just a witty catalogue, but a deeply moving fast-forward through a life filled equally with love, loss, joy and regret."

In addition to her talent, Maple was known for her tart take on the vicissitudes of a mercurial industry, about which she could be equally sanguine. "It's like the old prostitute once said,'" she quipped in an NPR interview last November: "'It's not the work. It's the stairs.'"

An invitation-only memorial is scheduled for Friday at the Shubert Theatre. On Thursday night, Broadway theaters will dim their marquee lights for one minute in honor of the late actress.

ACT ONE

Chapter One

"He just called, stuck in traffic," the girl said, poking in with her cordless headset. Roughly her age, stringy hair yanked back in a band. "He's on his way."

"Thank you." Betty Rose smiled back from her straight-back chair, hands in lap.

"Can I get you coffee or tea or something else?"

"Water's fine, thank you."

"Sparkling or flat?" the assistant asked. She was too young to have such dark circles.

"Flat, please."

"Chilled or room temperature?"

"Oh." Betty Rose thought and said, "Either. I'm easy."

The girl seemed relieved and pulled out again, tapping her ear piece, answering another call with a "Siren Talent" sighed into her mike.

Poor girl, thought Betty Rose. *Run ragged here.*

Her chair felt awkward, which she blamed on nerves, but after a few repositions and shuffles, she realized it was almost imperceptibly diminutive, shorter to the ground. The modern slab desk loomed taller in front of her, as did its chair with a monogrammed "WW" back pillow. Betty Rose smiled; she'd read about this old trick. And then a fresh pang of nerves at the realization these people knew what they were doing.

It was common, she knew, for agents—the crafty ones—to stage dominance over anyone across the desk, especially actors. Each did it in their own way. The lower rent ones, she'd learned over the past few months, were the most heavy handed and obnoxious: hours-long waits in cramped rooms choked with other desperate actors, snippy receptionists, dismissive, hostile responses to the responses from their grilling. Agents who ran their offices out of musty apartment buildings were the worst. Mostly failed actors themselves, exacting revenge on new dreamers.

And Betty Rose endured it all, even from the lowest rent, because without an agent, any agent, she wasn't going anywhere. She couldn't even start.

But Siren Talent Agency was high rent and bicoastal—both here in prime midtown and new offices out in Beverly Hills in the same building, she'd learned, as Ron Howard's production company and Gersh. Siren was on the rise, gaining on the Big Three. She could never have gotten a meeting here on her own.

So when a Siren agent summoned her, even with a half day's notice, Betty Rose scrambled to cover her waitress shift—easy enough, as Friday's tourist arrivals were a tip cash cow—dropped fifty for a blowout at the Tribeca Drybar, and arrived twenty minutes early, cooling her heels in the lobby, so the June humidity wouldn't frizz. The assistant had sounded urgent on the phone— "Wes needs to see you this week, tomorrow,"—so maybe, just maybe, Siren needed an actress just like her for an audition soon, this week, today.

Here, the lobby was spacious and calm, almost soothing. The office energy was frantic but orderly, as agents closed deals on Broadway star turns, national tours, the occasional guest spot, both in New York and L.A. Everyone on the floor was pitching clients, fielding offers, booking jobs.

Here, they offered visitors—even non-client, out-of-work actors— four choices of water.

Betty Rose sat up straighter. Katharine Hepburn, she'd read in the Garson Kanin book, had four-inch platform shoes custom built for her meetings with Louis B. Mayer, and insisted on standing so she would tower over her MGM boss. Betty Rose needed Hepburn's moxie.

She lifted up to pull and smooth her floral charmeuse skirt taut. She'd chosen her outfit with care; artistic, but classy. Betty Rose knew her "type" from the three-week casting workshop she'd found in a *Backstage* ad. "Great look, great read," had said the former casting director of *All My Children* after Betty Rose's cold read. "All-American Girl Next Door. I wish I'd found you when I worked on the show." And a delighted Betty Rose had said, "Thank you!" and thought her $295 decently spent.

She studied Meisner Technique twice weekly at City Center, with its repetitions, activities, intentions, and breakthroughs. She climbed the creaking, uneven stairs up to Eighth Avenue Studios for jazz dance on Monday/Wednesday/Friday (in Studio C, eyeing, with hope and envy, the spirited Broadway replacement dancers rehearsing in B), and was saving up to train with the voice guru/legend who taught Rachel York and Cheyenne Jackson and Elaine Paige and, until a rumored falling out, Audra McDonald from his fabled apartment at the Apthorp. Maybe Betty Rose could take her spot, if she passed her audition and made the waiting list. The guru's name on her resumé would, she knew, open magic doors. For the time being, she did her vocal warmups every morning in her kitchenette, with the windows shut and the exhaust fan on, so as not to bother the neighbors who loudly stayed up late and likely slept late.

She read *Backstage* daily with its tips on dressing for auditions and finding the spiritual core of her characters and the moment before "zero"—useful and silly in equal measure, she thought, knowing the difference between obscurity and superstardom was a quantum leap of intangibles and sheer guts.

She'd learned the difference between "theater" and "theatre."

She'd spent dearly for her new headshots—trendy photographer/ makeup/retouching/reprinting—and opted for clean line framing over full-bleed for a more classic look. She stapled them to bright white, heavy stock paper on which she'd laser printed her acting resume at the FedEx Office, crisp and clean. She leaned over to straighten it perfectly on the glass desk, so he couldn't miss it.

On the long, stainless table under the mounted television sat a proud row of photographs in silver, brass, and leather frames: the same flamboyant, pudgy man beaming with the archly buff and plucked Nick Adams on the *Mathilda* red carpet; an openmouthed guffaw with Stephanie Block at Sardi's; at Joe Allen's with Idina Menzel, mock-wrestling away her fresh Tony; genuflecting before a seated and bemused Rosemary Harris at the Russian Tea Room. At the table's edge sat a little sock monkey wearing a *Urinetown* sweater, next to a company-autographed *Playbill* cover of *Forever Plaid*.

Gay, she thought, with some relief. She could dial back the sex appeal, her shakier hand, and focus on her fabulousness. The Gays loved fabulous, and it loved them back. So did she.

Betty Rose inspected her reflection in the window overlooking the Avenue of the Americas—it was just gloomy enough outside to double as a mirror. She swiveled and posed and grimaced; nobody looked fabulous, let alone movie star, with a fluorescent key light.

The New York actor's learning curve was steep, but she'd scaled it quickly, handily since arriving in January. At the bottom of the agent scale was the Bruce Leonard type, who charged actors up front, and whom Betty Rose had enough sense to flee. Up several notches was the Dulcina Eisner ilk, a reputable veteran with clients on Broadway and off. She ran her boutique agency from a West Village brownstone basement and held open singing calls the first Tuesday night of each month. Betty Rose had waited her turn with a dozen other incarnations of herself, listening awkwardly to those ahead of her, and when called, unleashed the final sixteen bars of "Johnny One-Note" to showcase both her belt and high notes in front of Ms. Eisner's desk. The agent, elegant but weary, thanked her for not singing anything from *Wicked* and regretted she already had three of her "type" in her stable. "But you're got a strong high C," she encouraged. "I wish you all the best."

Siren was top tier: They worked in teams, coddling each treasured client for stage, television, and film, both coasts. Even a hip pocket arrangement, just their logo on her resumé, would catapult her to the next level. She knew, of course, whose back they were scratching, which ironically burdened her with more pressure, not less.

The voice arrived first.

It materialized abruptly, she gathered, from the elevator and grew louder, sonar-like, as it moved from the lobby and through the hall, toward her. It barked, harried and playful, as it traded goodnatured barbs with an unheard opponent over its Bluetooth. It multitasked orders at its assistant as it exploded into its office. Betty Rose smoothed her lips and her skirt once more.

"...relax, Joyce, this isn't my first rodeo. If he doesn't trust me by now, why'd he ask in the first place? Look, I'll call him after tonight's show. Of course I know the number...he changed it again? *Lauren, do you have the new number?*" the agent spat, rounding the desk as he pocketed his phone, and then murmured, "Sorry I'm late-ish..." He wore a solid navy suit with candy stripe shirt and pink-and-white polka dot bow tie and a heavy watch. Fortyish, he had round tortoise shell glasses and wild, flaming hair that almost matched the orange silk spritzing from his breast pocket. He was a jolly, classy confection. He stood over his desk, Joker-like, surveying the battlefield.

"The memorial at the Booth went long," he said without looking up, and before Betty Rose could answer, he added, "and then I had to say 'hi' and 'hello' and 'thank you' to that whole cabal clusterfuck. And then traffic and all. Tourists. From Iowa, I'm sure."

"That's quite all right," Betty Rose said, "I was just..."

"Marian would have liked it, I think," he pondered. "The Battle-Axe Brigade turned out—Lansbury, Stritch, *Chee-tah*—although, really, what else do they have to do? Marian swore she'd outlive them, but *c'est la guerre*. Sondheim. Woody and his daughter-wife. Bernadette sang 'Send in the Clowns.' God, what a vision." He studied his computer screen. Scrolled up and down.

"Marian Maples?" Betty Rose asked. "Her memorial?"

"I mean, dying on stage," he *tsk*ed with a laugh. "*Quelle drama!* She would howl at the cliché of it all, but it was rather inevitable. She was rarely anywhere else. At least she'd finished 'Liaisons.' *Lauren, where's the Big Guy's new number?*"

"On your call sheet, Wes!" Lauren shouted back from her assistant's perch.

"Do you mean Marian Maples?" Betty Rose repeated, inserting herself.

"My client, yes. Know her?"

"I know *of* her. She's a legend. I saw the lights dimmed on Broadway last night. For her."

"Oh, I missed that," Wes said, still scanning his computer. "How was it? *Where on my call sheet, Lauren?*"

"It was very moving. The whole district was dark and silent for a full minute, right at eight." *District*. Like a pro. An insider.

"At the very top!" Lauren called back, and Wes, squinting, said, "Bingo. *Thank you!*" He plopped down in his chair and looked over at

Betty Rose and said, "What?" even though she hadn't said anything. And then he added, solemn, "You know, we'll never see another like Marian again."

"I know," Betty Rose said, hushed, sympathizing.

"This new crop, I mean, *bleh...*" he spat, shrugging in boredom. "They want it easy. As Uta Hagen said, 'They have no disciplines.' No offense."

"Not at all," said Betty Rose. "I agree."

"Lauren, who is this skinny wisp of a thing in my office?" the agent asked abruptly and then picked her headshot off his desk.

"Julian's girlfriend! Yes!" he eureka'd, clasping his hands. "His college sweetheart!"

"That's me," Betty Rose said with a laugh and then made a point: "But he's older."

"Oh, he talks about you constantly. My *actress* girlfriend. Oh, he's a big fan."

"He'd better be," she said, winking and wondering if she were being too chummy.

"We love him here. People still talk about his set for *Salome* at the Houseman last fall. He worked magic in that sardine can."

"Yes, I've seen photos..."

"His career, in the past year..."—he clap-zoomed his hand straight up—"...like a rocket! Is he still doing the *Cloud Nine* reunion at Minetta Lane?"

"Oh yes," Betty Rose said with pride. "He's finishing the model at our apartment. It looks..."

"And I hear he's up for *Streetcar* at the Acorn, for Daniel Sullivan! How you make that set look fresh and new, on that stage, I'll never know..."

Betty Rose nodded blankly, unaware. Julian didn't count his unhatched chickens. "The doors are flying open for him...," she said.

"You got that Kate Middleton thing going," the agent interrupted, comparing her live to her headshot. "You get that before?"

"Yes, I have," she said, happy to pull focus.

"Waitey Katey they call her."

"Ha. Yes."

"There's always a demand for that fresh kind of look."

"I hope so. Yes. That's good," she stammered. *Turn up the fabulous,* she scolded herself. *Chill, he likes you.*

"Betty Rose. Excellent name. Got some Laura Bell Bundy going on there. Know her?"

"I know *of* her. I think she's..."

"The original Sister Christian in the workshop of *Rock of Ages*. Did you know that?"

"I didn't."

"Why'd you add 'Rose'? To the 'Betty'?"

"It's what I've always been called," she said. "Both together."

"'Betty' alone is a bit old fashioned. A little *Mad Men*."

"Yes," Betty Rose said. "It sounds lonesome by itself."

"Rose is very *Golden Girls*," he added. "Love it. You're a sight for sore eyes."

She laughed. He laughed. She leaned closer, folded her hands on his glass desk.

"*Ack,* what is this?!" he squealed, squinting at her headshot. "Betty Rose *Milenski*?" He scrunched his nose.

"Yes," said Betty Rose.

"Have you picked a stage name?"

"I would never change my last name," she said simply.

The agent laughed and looked upward. "Well, you *will*. And I'd suggest sooner. Today. That Polish thing won't work."

Betty Rose sat still.

Wes the agent clasped and Simon Legree'd his hands. "Bernie Telsey would love you," he said. "He's a grizzled ol' bore, but he casts almost everything. He'd put you in regional first. Maybe bus-and-truck. Probably *Mamma Mia*."

"That's excellent," Betty Rose said, relieved to pivot off her last name. "I'd love to meet him." She leaned in, coconspirators.

"Look at these roles!" he said, excited, studying her resumé. "Laurie, yes yes, of course. And Julie and Nellie. And both Marias—German and West Side. Good, good." He looked up. "No Marian?"

"I did Marian," Betty Rose corrected, straining forward, pointing.

"Yes, I see it. All the standards. And Sandy, of course. Wow. Emily?" He lowered the resumé, impressed. "*Our Town*? How versatile."

"Yes, that was the most rewarding because it was a straight drama and a good reach," said Betty Rose, thrilling at his appreciation.

"*'Does anyone ever realize life while they live it...every, every minute?'*" he quoted, swiftly moved to emotion. "We don't, do we? We don't."

"*Saints and poets maybe...*," she finished for him, commiserating. "That's such a beautiful line."

"And then she croaked, right?" he said, bursting in shrill laughter. "Such a long fucking play."

They discussed Douglas Carter Beane's new musical and the upcoming season at McCarter Theatre and dished on the latest cat fight between Kristen and Idina—manufactured and mined for publicity, they agreed. Wes primed her about the new projects that would start casting in the fall and dangled an invitation for her and Julian to visit his country home in Woodstock over the summer.

The agent fawned. Betty Rose blushed. And basked.

They bonded. Betty Rose felt fabulous.

"Now I'm going to give you some advice, Betty Rose. Maybe the most important you've ever gotten. Are you listening, Waitey Katy?"

"Yes, Wes," she said, coquettish.

"Do something else with your life."

"Oh."

"Give this up. Right now."

She sat back in her chair, holding a tight smile. Wes got serious, leaned closer.

"I've been an agent for fourteen years," he said, centered. "And it's just not going to happen for you, my dear."

"I see," Betty Rose heard herself say.

Her throat tight, she looked around for the water—sparkling or flat—that the turncoat assistant had failed to bring.

"You're unusually lovely and apparently talented and clearly intelligent," the agent went on, "and it's a waste to go down this dead-end path. Marry Julian and have babies and develop a skill set, and then come back and thank me in twenty years for this moment."

"Yes," Betty Rose said, and then said, "No. No thank you."

"Northwestern is a good school," Wes said. "You'll get a real job."

"I'm a theatre major. With honors," she managed to say.

"But this resumé is bullshit," he accused, waving it.

Betty Rose reddened. "No sir," she corrected. "It's all true."

"It's college. And Beech Grove, whatever the fuck that is..."

"It's a...school..."

"A *high* school. Goody. It's amateur. It's worthless."

"Oh," she said. She felt sweat in her scalp. It would frizz her hair.

"You haven't a single professional credit to your name. At your age!"

"I'm only twenty-four," she said, instantly wishing she'd shaved off three.

"At twenty-four, Julie Andrews had three Broadway hits and a Tony nomination. Bebe Neuwirth was wowing in *A Chorus Line*. Betty Buckley was already starring in..."

"I...had to take a little time off," Betty Rose interrupted.

"Nobody nobody nobody cares," Wes said, tapping his watch. "Tick tock!"

They sat. Wes sighed and fidgeted.

He bolted from his chair, paced by the window.

"Jay Binder takes chances," he said. "And he still owes me for Kelli O'Hara. He's holding Equity calls this week for Roundabout."

Betty Rose shrank.

"What?" Wes challenged. "You too good for an open casting call?"

"I...can't go to an Equity audition," she said.

"Behind in dues?" Wes frowned and reached for his wallet. "Good grief, I'll spot you, just go straight to their office on Forty-sixth and settle up..."

"I don't have my Equity card," she said quietly. "I'm not in the union. Yet." She felt a trickle down her lower back. It would stain her blouse.

Wes sat. Glanced back at her resumé, tossed it to the floor, buried his ginger mop in his hands.

"Worse than amateur," he said. "A dilettante."

"No," Betty Rose protested, but the agent cut her off.

"Betty Rose, I've seen thousands of wannabes flit into town, all with the same dream of landing on Broadway..." he explained.

"It's my only dream," said Betty Rose. "Ever."

"...and one thing is constant," he went on. "Those who have what it takes, that motor, prove it immediately. We're talking the point-zero-zero-one percent. They live, sleep, breathe the business, obsessed. They don't just want it. They will not, cannot live without it. The other pros sense that obsession, give 'em a shot, feed 'em to the wolves. And ignore the rest. Like they're ignoring you."

"But they haven't seen me," Betty Rose insisted. "Or heard me."

"Only five percent of Equity members make a living wage from acting, and of that five percent, almost all are poor," Wes continued, his frustration rising. "And here you sit, not even in the union. Do you realize how Herculean, how practically impossible the task before you is? Wake, up Betty Rose! I am begging you—*begging you*—don't start down this road!"

"But it's too late, you see," she said, trying not to hear him. "I've already started."

Now he was angry. "Do you know why Hepburn never had children? If her child were sick, and she had a show, she said she'd smother her child rather than miss a performance! Could you do that? That's why I got out of that game. I'd sell my mother but not kill a child!"

Betty Rose recoiled. "I doubt she meant that literally..."

"And that's why you'll never win this game!" the agent erupted. "You're not 'fresh,' you're not 'undiscovered,' you're not 'misunderstood.' You're just not cut out for it!"

Betty Rose stood up, refusing tears.

"I'm very sorry about your client," she said politely. "And I'm sorry to have bothered you. Good afternoon."

"Betty Rose, wait!" He stopped her just in time. "Close the door." She did. He sat back down. She stood still.

"I apologize," he said. "It's been a tough week, losing Marian. I shouldn't take it out on you. Julian is very important to us here, and I'd do anything I can to help you. But without your union card, my hands are tied."

She knew he was right.

"What can I do?" she asked, an open plead to a new, fabulous friend.

Wes sighed, spun his chair toward the window, thought. It had started to rain. He sucked his cheek and moments passed and he spun back to the wall, past signed posters of *Aida* and *Grey Gardens* and a vintage *Oh! Calcutta!*

He focused on a framed and faded photograph of a red and white barn with a large water wheel behind an ancient elm. It stood apart.

He winced.

"No, I can't," he muttered. "I really can't."

Wes pivoted a glance at Betty Rose, unflagging by the door. Back to the barn. Tapped his tooth, exhaled.

"Well, maybe...," he continued to himself. "God help me. Dear God help me. Maybe there is something..."

Chapter Two

Surprisingly, Julian didn't like the agent's idea.

"Summer stock?" he asked. "Does that still exist?"

Betty Rose had raced downtown on the R to their apartment on Mulberry, stopping in Duane Reade for a cheap umbrella to protect her blowout. It frizzed anyway.

"It's not just any summer stock," she said, palming argan oil down the lengths. "The Gristmill Playhouse is the most famous in the country. It's a renowned training ground."

"Oh, is that what he told you?" Julian asked. He was in his typical work uniform: white wifebeater, grey sweats, barefoot. He darted around his maquette in the dining alcove, obsessively tweaking the dollhouse set model against bright green grass and cloud-spotted blue sky. Betty Rose thought it looked dreamy.

Julian didn't like her account of their meeting. He thought the agent sounded "abusive." He was irresistibly protective.

Betty Rose defended him—he was just trying to help her get her Equity card, the crucial first milestone. Union membership rules were impossibly Catch-22: you couldn't work without one, and you couldn't get one until you worked. *Backstage* devoted whole issues to this nightmarish obstacle that vexed most new actors. But the union also had a Byzantine point system and ephemeral loopholes and short cuts desperate actors were always looking to exploit. The agent potentially had one.

"Yeah, I've heard of the Gristmill," Julian said, squatting for a head-on angle. "It's in that Pennsylvania artist's colony-tourist-trap-hippie village. Between the candle makers and glass blowers and fudge shops."

"Do you know how many theatre legends got their start there?" Betty Rose instructed, clearing cups and plates and coffee press from the tile kitchen counter. "Not just actors, but musicians, directors, even set designers."

"Wow, he did the hard sell," Julian said with a chuckle. "Did he mention its reputation as a weird, all-controlling commune? The word 'cult' pops up a lot..."

Betty Rose clicked the countertop ironing board open. "That's 'cause actors are freaks!" she said. "Especially in a group. But they're my peeps, babe. With the Gristmill on my resumé, earning points, people will take me seriously. No one has yet."

"An apprenticeship? AKA 'free work.' Formerly known as 'slave labor,'" Julian pressed. "Why do they need someone now? Hasn't their season started already?"

Betty Rose tested the iron, put it to work on a black skirt. "Wes knows the director. He's going to ask a favor. He got his start there, too."

"A lot of good it did him," said Julian.

"I'm behind, Julian—two years!" Betty Rose said, her voice pitching up. "Even Monica has an agent and a manager and a touring gig with *Bring it On.*"—Monica, her eager, half-talent classmate who'd stolen the show at Northwestern's New York showcase only because Betty Rose had missed it.

"Hey, I know directors," Julian said. "And I meet new ones all the time. I can ask a favor, too."

"It's not the same," said Betty Rose, ironing harder. "You're my boyfriend. There has to be a sense of discovery, word of mouth. That's how you made it."

Julian looked around at the cramped apartment. "I made it? When?" he said, laughing. "Is this all there is?"

"You paid your dues," she went on. "And it paid off. Now it's my turn."

Julian turned to her. "It's just...you're green, BR. Naïve. I don't want them to take advantage of you, that's all."

"Well, I gotta find my way, like everyone else." She stopped ironing. "What's wrong? You really don't want me to go?"

"Not there. Not the Gristmill Playhouse. It has a weird rap, BR."

She rolled her eyes. "It's three hours away, you'll come visit, I'll be back right after Labor Day..." She grabbed the iron as it scorched her skirt, burning her hand.

"Dammit, what am I talking about?" she said. "They haven't even said yes. I set myself up every time. Even the smallest thing, free work, such a mine field! What am I doing?"

Julian held her hand under the cold water. Gently patted it dry. Held her, still trembling.

"Hey, what is this?" he chided. "Where's the tigress I knew?"

"I don't know," she said. "I'm just frightened. All the time."

He kissed her forehead.

"You've had a hell year, BR. It would have crushed anybody else. I'm not just in love with you. I'm pretty much in awe."

"At least I have one fan," she laughed, wiping an eye.

He kissed her mouth. Her neck.

"Are you seducing a young, needy actress?" she asked with a smile. "God, you're all the same."

His hand moved down.

"I can't be late to work," she protested. "They'll write me up."

On the counter, her cell phone buzzed. She jumped, grabbed it.

"That terror's kinda hot," said Julian, unrelenting.

She checked the screen. Her acting class scene partner. Ignore.

"We have time," Julian told her, lower. "Take the express."

"Nice try, jackass," she said as she succumbed. "They're all local."

—‍ɯ‍—

Rain and near-lateness notwithstanding, Betty Rose kept to her afternoon ritual of getting off at Forty-second Street—her favorite street—and walking five blocks through Times Square in the pre-Broadway crush.

She maneuvered the rubberneck throngs along Broadway Beach, darted west on Forty-fourth to the less-congested and inspirational Shubert Alley, heralding *Newsies* and *Book of Mormon* and *Chicago*-Now-With-Billy Ray Cyrus. She weaved back and passed the pigeon-hatted George M. Cohan sentry over Duffy Square, targeted the blood red TKTS staircase and pealed off again on Forty-seventh toward the Hotel Edison bar.

The Rum House was typically sparse until pre-theatre, then hectic for an hour, and quiet again after curtain. During the first act lull before the intermission mini-rush Betty Rose served Brooklyn Lagers to a polite, ticketless couple from the hotel and kept checking her waiter's apron pocket for cell phone vibration.

"Excuse me, miss," said the tourist woman with midwest apology. "We ordered the Dark and Stormy."

"Yes, you did," said Betty Rose, checking her pad. "Be right back." She dabbed sweat off her forehead with a cocktail napkin.

"Who stole my beers?" howled the other waitress from the bar. "God, you're a hot mess tonight. You poach my table and now this?"

"I'm sorry, Erin," said Betty Rose. "Hot mess is right."

Like Danny the bartender and Claudine-at-the-piano, Erin had worked at the bar so long, she could anticipate its every move. Goodnatured and jaded—and defiantly sour—Erin was, for a not-yet-made-it-actress, the impossible age of thirty-three. She was still striking and poised and instinctively stood in third position, waiting for stage directions that would never come. The Rum House now suited her; she'd never leave, thought Betty Rose, who'd been there an unexpected four months.

"How was your meeting?" Erin asked, and Betty Rose said, "It was nice, thanks."

"They gonna hip pocket you?" Erin pressed, and Betty Rose said, "I hope so."

She'd learned not to share much with crepe-hanger Erin, lest she abandon all hope herself.

Danny, mid-fifties, smiled and separated fresh egg whites for a Pisco Sour. "They'd be lucky to have you," he said. He'd been handsome once, thought Betty Rose. A young leading man. A potential star.

Claudine had worked there the longest. Over-dyed and made-up and in gauzy black whose slimming effects had long-diminished returns, she finished her set with a torch-songy "Matchmaker" and fished the singles and pocket change from her tip jar and lumbered grandly out the back. She'd sit out her break, Betty Rose knew, in the hotel lobby, playing Sudoku on her phone and telling Eighties Broadway tales to any visitor who cared.

"How long will the singer be gone?" asked the timid midwestern wife when Betty Rose brought the corrected cocktail. "She's a bit loud, don't you think?"

Betty Rose winked in commiseration. "She does bang a bit," she said to the tourist. *Probably from Iowa,* Wes the agent would say.

Wes, who'd promised to call the Gristmill and then call Betty Rose and had clearly forgotten to do both. Typical agent. Unless they'd rejected her outright and he was protecting her from a double dose of bad news on the same day.

She busied herself at the bar in case the lobby manager poked in. Erin asked her to cover her Saturday shift so she could go to Southampton with her new "boyfriend." There was always a new one. "I'll be back before the Sunday night rush," Erin promised.

"Do you know anything about the Gristmill Playhouse?" Betty Rose asked.

Erin took the chewed-up stirrer from her mouth. "My God, the New Hope Freak Show?" she said. An acting classmate of hers had gone a few summers back and had fled soon after. "And I mean *fled*," she added. "The stuff that goes on there..."

"Like what?" asked Betty Rose.

"My friend wouldn't tell me everything, I think she was scared or something, but it's like a concentration camp. They work them to death, especially the newbies. I'm surprised Equity doesn't crack down."

Erin's friend sounded lazy, which was common. She "had no disciplines," as Uta Hagen would say.

"Plus they're so secretive, so underground," Erin added. "They must, like, recruit their own members, like Hogwarts. Have you ever seen them post a casting in *Backstage*?"

Betty Rose hadn't. The Paper Mill Playhouse, the Long Wharf, the Goodspeed Opera House, yes, all the time. Not the Gristmill. Then again, the vocal guru she longed for didn't advertise either. He didn't need to.

"Tons of stars come out of there," Danny piped in, muddling mint. "Every so often, another pops. Sutton Fraser's just the latest."

Broadway's long-standing "it" girl, on the cusp of queendom. Last year's Tony winner for *Anything Goes,* after three consecutive nominations.

"Overrated," sniffed Erin. With her tray and apron.

"If they ever offer you a gig," Danny encouraged, "I'd grab it. I'd grab everything."

Older-wiser Danny was at the acceptance stage of his non-career where he wished the best for those just starting out. Erin would get there, thought Betty Rose, once she worked through her own bitterness. It crept up fast, she feared, catching herself in the bar mirror.

Betty Rose covered Erin's tables while she went to smoke outside under a scaffolding. The rain lingered.

There'd be no call, no offer. There never was. Which was just as well, since Julian was so against her going. He'd stayed loyal to her after graduating a year ahead and moving to New York to start his career while she finished out her degree. And then her unexpected return to Indiana, much longer than either had expected, had caused a barely perceptible but bound-to-happen strain, in spite of his caring and understanding and insistence otherwise. She shouldn't risk another separation so soon on a whim dangled by an agent who turned his nose up at her Polish name.

Christine Baranski, anyone? she thought. *Jane Krakowski?*

She'd find other opportunities in town, with a flurry of castings for fall and winter shows and tours, roles she'd win on her own, or with Julian's help, which she'd be a fool not to accept. After all, he had a head start and was her biggest fan.

But Wes the agent had no reason to feign his professional and personal interest. He seemed genuinely invested in her career, her newfound champion. That's how careers took off. He said he believed in her and promised to help. She'd win him 'round on her name.

There was no call that night. Nor Saturday, Saturday night, nor Sunday.

The Rum House was always bedlam after the Sunday matinees, starting with *The Boyfriend* revival at the Friedman across the street. The young cast had pegged it as their go-to spot from the beginning, celebrating nightly since previews, through opening night, and now in their second month, still giddy with their fresh hit. Their weekend started Sunday at five-thirty, and they tipped big and knew her name, and she'd take pictures for them, as a group or with visiting friends and family, proud parents who'd come to their kids' Broadway debut and couldn't stop beaming. The gang was always loud and Betty Rose's age, or younger.

She was at the bar, loading her tray with daiquiris and skinny margaritas when her apron pocket vibrated a steady purr.

"Where you going?" Erin demanded, sun-kissed from her Hampton weekend. "Now?"

"Hello?" Betty Rose said into her phone, huddled under the outside scaffolding, avoiding drips from the late afternoon shower. "Hello?"

She nodded and nodded. "Yes. Absolutely."

She scribbled instructions on her pad, her phone tucked against her shoulder.

She said "thank you" many times. She dabbed her eye.

Betty Rose stood in the rain, watching the twilight river of taxis and the crush of summer tourists, trying to catch her breath.